8

D1491572

A
TRAITOR'S
HEART

A TRAITOR'S HEART

BEN CREED

WELBECK

First published in 2022 by Welbeck Fiction Limited, an imprint
of Welbeck Publishing Group based in London and Sydney.
www.welbeckpublishing.com

A CIP catalogue record for this book is available from the British Library

HB ISBN: 978-1-80279-193-8
XTPB ISBN: 978-1-80279-194-5
E ISBN: 978-1-78739-628-9

Printed and b   (UK) Ltd., Croydon, C .0 4YY

'Everyone sees what you appear to be, few experience
what you really are.'
Niccolò Machiavelli, *The Prince*

'Thus men forgot that all deities reside in the
human breast.'
William Blake, *The Marriage of Heaven and Hell*

Prelude

April 12, 1945

So this, thought Oberst Franz Halder, is what Death looks like.

The girl was about twelve years old. She had freckles, strawberry-blonde pigtails and an intelligent, sharp-eyed look. Instead of a black cape, she was dressed in the uniform of the *Bund Deutscher Mädel*, the girls' answer to the Hitler Youth. Instead of a scythe, she was holding out a woven basket containing about thirty polished brass cylinders, each five centimetres long. Each containing a glass vial filled with cyanide.

'*Entschuldigen Sie bitte, mein Herr*. Would you care for one of these?'

Halder waved her away and carried on loitering at the back of the hall. He smoothed the sleeves of his Luftwaffe uniform and kept his eyes peeled for the baron.

Around him, a few hundred candles sputtered. A dozen third-tier Nazis shuffled out of the drizzle and into the draughty Beethoven Salle, the smaller concert venue being used after the Berlin Philharmonic had been bombed out of its home. They were trying not to look hungry, trying to show they didn't care as Germany collapsed about them. Most of all, trying very hard not to think about the moment, any day now, when the Red Army would parade down Unter den Linden while staring at their wives and daughters.

The cold, damp air was beginning to warm with the scent of French perfume, the last dregs that Berlin's high society matrons could coax out of a bottle. In the half-light, a few Waffen-SS and Wehrmacht officers queued to pay homage to Albert Speer, the Third Reich's Minister for Armaments and War Production.

Somewhere, Halder knew, the Gestapo would still be watching.

He glanced at his smudged programme. The final aria of Wagner's opera *Götterdämmerung* – Brünnhilde's last great moment before riding into her beloved's funeral pyre – would open the concert. The playing order had been devised by Speer himself. Halder watched the minister preen before his obsequious guests.

A mournful oboe, tuning the orchestra up for the Wagner, hushed the audience.

There was still no sign of the baron. Halder took his seat and waited for the interval with gnawing impatience. He scratched at the patch of red skin at the base of his neck.

After a minute, a man with a duelling scar, hooded eyes and morose expression sat down beside him.

'Ah ha! You made it, Baron von Möllendorf. I was beginning to worry.'

'I shall miss Wagner,' said the baron, skipping a greeting. 'The master of the leitmotif. Those mystical layers of musical expression that mutually enhance each one's meaning and combine to magnify their power . . .'

His voice cracked.

'Are you all right, Baron?' Halder asked.

'Pardon me. I have not eaten for a while.'

'Not many have. To business then. Best be quick before the Lancasters come. You have it?'

Von Möllendorf nodded.

'Here,' he said, handing Halder a soft leather briefcase. 'Your people were most helpful. We completed the task.'

Silence. The soloist, blessed with the physique of a dramatic soprano and the sardonic expression of a cabaret singer, padded onstage to applause. *Götterdämmerung*. The Twilight of the Gods. The burning of Valhalla.

'My dear Oberst Halder, what a pleasure,' said a voice behind him.

Halder turned and looked straight into the genial face of Reichminister Speer.

'A meeting of minds,' said Speer. 'One of our greatest nuclear physicists deep in conference with Hitler's most trusted adjutant. I am glad you have found each other.'

The minister leaned forward.

'Good luck, gentlemen,' he whispered.

The conductor lifted his baton. *Götterdämmerung* began . . .

After the concert, as Halder headed for the exit, the little girl from the *Bund Deutscher Mädel* barred his way again. This time she took one of the shining brass cylinders out of the basket and held it up to him, as if it were a delicious bonbon from Fassbender & Rausch.

'They have asked us to offer them to everyone. In case a swift and honourable end is required, Herr Oberst,' she said.

'Do you know what Goethe said?' he asked her. '"Death will come anyway, whether you are afraid of it or not."'

Oberst Halder sighed and muttered a single word under his breath. His unique battle cry:

'*Neubrandenburg.*'

He stretched out a hand towards the cylinder.

One never knew . . .

ACT 1
GOLD

1

The corpse had the room to itself. A luxury in Leningrad, where such bourgeois pretensions could attract jealous attention from your neighbours, even accusations of a counter-revolutionary sensibility. The kind of whisper that might elicit a midnight visit from the organs of the state. Luckily for this comrade, thought Major Oleg Nikitin, his brains are already splattered on the wall. Which at least meant that the victim – one Comrade Samosud – was, unlike the rest of the city's one million citizens, beyond the reach of the MGB, the Ministry for State Security.

Even in such a small, mud-caked room crammed full of men perspiring into their uniforms, Major Nikitin did not pass unnoticed. His missing eye – the empty socket encircled by a scaly lava of scars – made sure of that.

Four of those MGB officers in long coats and large caps rimmed with blue bands poked into every grimy corner and examined every surface. They peered at the locks, the window, the exposed light bulb, the gas hob that didn't work because the gas supply didn't work either, at the filthy bucket, at the dust under the sagging bed, and in particular at the dark stain on one wall, new but dried.

Looking on were two officers from the *militsiya*, ordinary street-level police. They were present on the orders of their superior officer but were reluctant to do anything that might get them noticed. Mute witnesses to something or nothing – whatever the MGB best required them to see. Nikitin understood their predicament. He had, after all, once been an MGB officer doing the intimidating.

The men from state security tramped an irritable orbit around the room's centrepiece, which was a slumped body that had been tied to a wooden chair. In the right side of the dead man's head was a neat hole. Beneath it, a second one.

'Comrade Major Nikitin? Oleg, is that you?'

Nikitin ignored the speaker, pulled his own cap lower and shouldered his way to an empty patch of wall in order to regard the corpse from another angle. In the early winter dusk, up here on the fourth floor of this handsome but neglected building, the watery street lamps were no help. And the flickering light bulb was already grating on his nerves.

The corpse wore a grey shirt and a dark-blue padded jacket, both of them open and hanging loose on its stout frame. On the bottom half was a pair of olive-green army-issue trousers and one brown slipper – he couldn't see the other. The dead man looked like he had been in good condition. His pectoral muscles were well defined, the outline of his thighs and calves were visible.

'Oleg?'

Fuck your mother.

Passing unrecognised had been wishful thinking. If his military uniform hadn't made him stand out, the scar tissue that swarmed all over his face always did the trick. It was hard to keep a low profile with a face like his. But, as his bad luck would have it, one of the MGB officers was a comrade of long standing.

'It is you. What do you think you are doing here?'

Nikitin glowered at the speaker. Rumyantsev – an MGB major. Ambitious but not overly blessed with brains. A few months ago, in another life, they had been on civil terms.

'How nice to see you again, Volodya,' said Nikitin. He gestured at the body. 'Looks interesting. What is your conclusion?'

Rumyantsev looked around and barked at his men – who had paused in their endeavours and swivelled their ears towards this conversation – to mind their own business and keep searching for evidence. He turned back to Nikitin.

'I am surprised, Oleg,' he said in a low voice. 'Surprised to see you alive. Alive and in this room, in the uniform of GRU military intelligence, asking me questions. I have heard all sorts of things about you. Should I shoot you now to save time and file my report later?'

Nikitin bared his stained teeth.

'Inadvisable, Volodya. Defence Minister General Pletnev commands me now and he is a man with a long memory. If you want a couple of tanks and an infantry detachment up your arse, of course, then go ahead. And there are other members of the Politburo with a keen interest in my brains remaining inside my head.'

Rumyantsev adjusted his blue cap.

A chill draft blew through a gap where a window should have been. Like last year, the northern winter had come early. Leningrad was already blanketed in snow, which hid some parts of the Sennaya Market area that were improved by invisibility. But the snow could do little to spruce up the area's more basic accommodation: hovels that had been endlessly subdivided, some partitioned by little more than curtains, or a combination of mud-spattered towels and dirty laundry. This one was a notch up. Samosud, whoever he turned out to be, had had no roommates, though there was precious little to adorn his room other than the bed and the useless hob.

'General Pletnev, eh? The Hero of the Seelow Heights. You do have some impressive friends,' said Rumyantsev. 'I'm curious, how did you get here so fast? Was it them?' He nodded at the cops. 'Still got informers in the militia? Letting you know about a mysterious murder?'

That window must have been broken recently, thought Nikitin. No one would have left it with the temperature dropping like it was. Even a couple of pieces of cardboard or plywood and some mud would have been preferable to the late-October wind. And there were shards of glass on the ground that no one had swept up.

Shards of glass on the inside of the room.

'Is he like the other one?' asked Nikitin, pointing at the dead body.

For a split second, Rumyantsev looked furious.

'The other one?'

Yes, I know about the other one . . .

'Well, it has been a pleasure, Major Rumyantsev,' Nikitin said. He marched towards the door.

'Wait!' snapped Rumyantsev.

The two ordinary militia officers didn't move but the MGB agents felt for their pistols.

'In the name of Soviet revolutionary justice, I . . .'

'If you utter the next words, Volodya, they will be your last,' roared Nikitin, whose pistol had materialised from nowhere and was now pointing at Rumyantsev. 'You blue-hats may have power over the life and death of every Soviet citizen, but that power stops with officers of the military's Main Investigative Directorate, where you have power over nothing – not the colour of my piss or the smell of my shit – and if you reach another inch for that Nagant then I shall make you the second corpse in this room and I'll be sure to send Comrade Beria himself a card of condolence.'

Rumyantsev kept still but his gaze never faltered.

'You're dead anyway, Oleg,' he said. 'They say Beria wants you dangling on a hook. With your feet tapping along to "Dark is the Night". Today or another day. He'll get you.'

Nikitin saluted with his pistol, backed out of the room and began to walk down the stairs.

'*In the dark night, I know that you, my love, are sleeping,*' he sang as he went. '*And are furtively wiping a tear by the cradle . . .*'

The lyrics of the song – much loved by Leningraders as part of the soundtrack to Leonid Lukov's wartime film *Two Soldiers* – made him think of Kristina, his wife.

*

Nikitin waited and watched from across the square, cupping his cigarette – a Polish import he didn't much like – in his palm. The MGB officers left, bickering about the next Zenit–CSKA match as they got into their black car.

Moments later the two militia officers appeared, carrying the corpse on a stretcher and struggling with the dead weight. The top half of the body was covered with a coat, while a pair of worker's boots dangled either side of the wooden poles. With each jolt, the left boot gave one of the officers a vengeful kick to the groin. The officers slid their cargo onto the back of a truck: a wartime ZIS with an outsize wooden crate screwed to its fuselage.

People – housewives shopping for supplies, workers who had been let off shift early – were stopping and staring. That was unusual. The Soviet citizen was not meant to come face to face with crime, let alone take an interest in it. But the crowd kept forming until the militia yelled at it to disperse.

The ZIS trundled off and order was restored. Nikitin gave a loud whistle. Spotting him, the militia officers hurried over.

Without a word, one of them felt in his pocket and handed over its contents. A rolled-up piece of paper, about six centimetres long.

'Just as you said, Comrade Major,' said the young militia officer. He was frightened and eager to please. 'At the back of the throat.'

Nikitin smiled.

'Well done. Anyone else still up there?'

'No, Comrade Major.'

'Very well. Give my regards to Captain Lipukhin,' he said. 'Obviously you will now forget about this or . . .'

The two men reddened, nodded, and fled.

Nikitin watched the passage of people to and fro across Sennaya Square for a few minutes before he ventured from his doorway and ascended the creaking wooden staircase back up to the deceased's apartment. He had to move fast.

The stain on the wall was at the same height as the victim's head. He had been shot while trussed to the chair. Nikitin soon found two neat holes amid the red stain on the wall – Rumyantsev and his MGB agents had removed the bullets. Small-calibre pistol rounds.

But he was looking for something else, and within five minutes of groping under cupboards and flicking away spiders and cockroaches, he'd found it. A slightly uneven floorboard under the bed. He lifted the board and his fingers closed on the cold of metal.

A gold medallion, just like the other one. With the same unique stamp.

That made two of them. Two men murdered in the same way, both with scraps of paper in their mouths. Both in possession of the same medallion.

Over the past year, Major Oleg Nikitin had seen friends cross the street to avoid him. Allies had turned to enemies. But his new masters – the GRU – were equally distrustful of him. Even contemptuous. And, for a reason he could not yet understand, impatient.

Nikitin was by training and temperament an interrogator, not an investigator. Now he had more evidence, yet still little idea of how to interpret it.

But – several thousand kilometres away from Leningrad, in the wastelands of the Siberian north – there was one man who could help him.

Provided he was still alive.

2

'Thoughts of love, of home, of women's bodies, a foolish belief in justice . . . None of that will get you through this. You have to find something to hate.'

The old lag who had given Revol Rossel this piece of wisdom on his very first day in Igarka had long since had his throat slit.

The stupid zek hadn't even taken his own advice . . .

Rossel had, though. To the letter.

Something to hate.

Right now, fuck your mother, it was the piece of gravel that had found its way into the toe of his left boot.

The former senior lieutenant in the People's Militia and the five other tethered men strained like a team of carthorses as they tried to move an enormous barrel full of rocks and rubble through the Siberian snow, one painful footstep after another. Three prisoners in front of the barrel, which was shaped like a giant cotton reel, doing the pulling. Three behind. Their eyes ached, their frozen nose hairs pricked them like miniature icicles, their breath broke into a million crystals as soon as it left their mouths. Moving this primitive steamroller, with each pass they flattened the ground another metre for the sleepers and rails that would be laid down from Igarka to Salekhard.

All 1,300 kilometres of it.

Life in a Corrective Labour Camp, under the jurisdiction of the GULAG, or Main Camps Directorate, stripped away the layers of a human being. Left you with almost nothing. As if some mischievous Slavic god was rubbing away at a tiny point on your skull with sandpaper to see what they might discover there. Usually, it was hunger. Because hunger slowly became all that you were.

'Let us say a prayer together,' said Babayan, the thick-bearded priest with messianic, pale-blue eyes, heaving at the barrel to Rossel's right.

'Not another prayer – give us all a fucking break, you Armenian halfwit,' shouted someone.

To his left – shuffling, stick-thin and pale as the permafrost – was Alexander Vustin. A singer, a baritone soloist in Stalingrad's main opera house, a precocious composer of some repute, and now, like many other "politicals" in the camps, an Enemy of the People.

It had been ten long months since Rossel had disappeared into the GULAG system. Two en route to the far north by rail, road and barge. Eight at this colony, so new and remote it was known only as 105th Kilometre, its distance from Igarka. In that time, he had talked about music with Vustin more than he had with anyone in his life. Of the Russians, Shostakovich was good but Prokofiev superior, Vustin proclaimed. Rachmaninov was sometimes kitsch, sometimes great, mostly pleasant. Stravinsky was the genius. Khachaturian could kiss Vustin's arse and anyone else's arse. Rossel was inclined to agree.

'Until Prokofiev lost his nerve and started worrying about what the Party thought of his music,' Vustin had said, shivering so much he could barely find his mouth with his roll-up, 'then he was *dermo*, complete crap, like those simpletons who founded the Russian Association of Proletarian Musicians. Nothing but pompous cantatas for the masses – bombast that signified nothing . . .'

Their conversations had helped to keep Rossel sane. Vustin had not been so lucky. As a boy, Vustin's mother and father had been burned alive in the Nazi bombardment of Stalingrad. Now, as his moods changed, his brittle eyes roamed everywhere, trying not to meet your gaze. Any loud noise would shock the boy. He would throw up his hands to his ears and begin to sing random operatic arias – the Italians, like Verdi or Puccini – as a poetic coping mechanism. Only Rossel's voice would settle him, make him listen, let him see the world again. He could draw Vustin back from the brink of madness into the shared reverie of their musical discourse.

Under their feet was a layer of sand over a layer of ballast, over more sand, over a layer of logs and brushwood. And somewhere in the mix, a layer or two of bones. You either continued laying the line or became part of it. Come the summer, the whole mess would almost certainly sink into the thick, soul-sucking Turukhansky mud.

The haulers, enmeshed in rope, had marginally the worst of it. It was not much fun for the men pushing the barrel behind them, either. Such was its size – almost two metres in diameter – neither group could see the other. They were, however, united in misery. Daily brothers in a bleak despair. Not far away, another group toiled: chopping wood, hauling steel rails. And then another. And another.

Rossel's team staggered as the barrel slipped on the iron-hard ground, dragging them to the left. His knees buckled. The big toe of his left foot ground into the little stone.

Fuck . . .

'Back!'

A guard fifty metres away, one foot on a tree stump, yelled and waved his arm. 'That way, bastards – follow the line, fuck your mother . . .'

The men grunted in unison and bit their lips as they hauled the barrel back on course.

But nothing could stop Babayan praying.

'*Gospodi, Isusye Khristye, syne Bozhii, pomilui menya greshnago* . . . Lord Jesus Christ, Son of God, have mercy on me a sinner . . .'

'Your God had better compensate us for this shit one day soon,' muttered a man from the other side of the barrel. 'Or, as long as he offers me a place by his fire, I'll sin all the Devil likes.'

Babayan spat on the ground, the brown froth turning to ice.

'The Lord already rewards us,' said the Armenian. 'Only yesterday I had a vision of Our Lady of Kazan walking down the track towards us. The good lady and two others. Shadows in the snow, like my mother once saw upon the slopes of Mount Ararat, resting place of the Ark of Noah.'

Babayan's chest rattled. The old priest fell silent for a few paces.

'Little girls, little boys,' said the disgruntled zek. '*Babushki, dyedushki*, cows, pigs, chickens – makes no odds, I'll stick my dick in them all. Anything for a place by that fire.'

This far north, high above the Arctic Circle, there were many ways the human spirit could be broken. One was the first moment of real cold. Not just the arrival of snow and frost but the first day it reached minus twenty-five, minus thirty. The realisation that descended upon all the prisoners that it was only going to get colder and darker. It hit them all hard: the politicals sentenced under Article 58; the *Vory*, the Thieves – and their deadly rivals, the *Suki*, or Bitches; and Hitler's orphaned warriors, the clutch of German POWs who had never been sent home.

All of them.

Once the ice crawled into your bones there was no hope of a thaw.

This year, the moment had long since passed. Already, in the first week of November, everyone in the camp was sick with something. Bones ached, chests wheezed, teeth rattled, fingers rotted.

Then, sometime in February, came the unshakeable conviction that winter would never end. Without fail, that was a day for someone to step beyond the wire into the forbidden zone. Become target practice for the guards. The other side of your last breath, some zeks reasoned, had to be a warmer place than here.

'So two other figures followed the Blessed Lady,' Babayan resumed. 'She was as plain to see as you or me but the others were mere spectres. Still, I recognised them – the last Tsar himself, Nicholas, and his poor child, the boy Alexei. God has raised these martyrs to his kingdom. His mercy is infinite.'

As the wind and snow swirled, whiteness danced all around them. Rossel kept his eyes fixed ahead of him on the dirty trail that curved into the taiga. Here was a world of nothing. And they were at its centre.

In another, distant life, he had been a student of the violin at the Leningrad Conservatoire. Despite teenage years wasted in a state orphanage, despite the stigma of his parents' political mortification, he'd still had the talent to force his way in. Enough to dazzle his professors, to excel in his exams, to prompt predictions of an exceptional career.

But he'd been a loose-lipped young man who liked to joke and tell stories.

Too quick with smart remarks. Too candid.

In the Soviet Union, candour could be a fatal flaw.

He had paid for that.

Not just me.

What would Mussorgsky have made of these brittle, jangling flurries? he wondered. How would that great composer have scored this void?

Igarka was a place that made the concept of infinity seem close to hand. Tangible. That of mercy, impossibly remote.

*

Another hour gone, another hour spent listening to the incessant chatter of your own teeth. But Igarka's hourglass was illusory. Sand slipped to the bottom, yes, but it never emptied. And just like the grains in the glass there was no possibility of escape.

To the left and the right, Rossel knew, was thick Siberian forest, though there was a wasteland of fifty or sixty metres,

19

cleared by other prisoners, before you got to the treeline. The railway was due to head west, though no one in 105th Kilometre believed it would ever be completed. Great chunks of it had already sunk into the mire in the summers or simply shattered in the winters. North – maybe two hundred kilometres away, they reckoned – was the edge of Russia and the shore of the Kara Sea. At their backs was the Yenisei River, which if you followed it south would eventually take you to Krasnoyarsk or on to Mongolia.

But to the zeks of 105th Kilometre, these were meaningless, abstract points of context. All they knew was that the railway track stopped about fifty metres behind them and until they had prepared the way it would go no further. And if they stopped moving their human steamroller, the four guards watching them with rifles at the ready would shoot them where they stood.

Gospodi, Isusye Khristye, syne Bozhii . . .

Babayan's daily prayers, Rossel understood, would not be answered. Perhaps the Armenian sensed that, too. For in Igarka, it was the Devil who was omnipotent and omnipresent – in the shape of a guard, an informer, a Thief; in the chill in your bones and the dead weight of hopelessness you felt pressing down on your soul as soon as you opened your eyes each morning.

Rossel stumbled.

Fuck your mother . . .

And sometimes just a stone in your shoe.

Even a slight incline meant trouble. After you'd hauled the steamroller for a couple of kilometres, another centimetre or two felt like you were climbing Mount Elbrus. An upward slope made Rossel's muscles scream; a downward one put all their lives in the hands of the men behind the barrel, heaving back on the wet wooden beams that were fixed like a yoke to its rudimentary axle. And crushing a foot meant not being able to walk back to the camp – a death sentence. No zek would waste one drop of their own precious strength on carrying an injured worker.

At least it had stopped snowing.

Some days it was better not to talk. On other days, talking was what got you through it. Today, Rossel, decided, he would indulge Babayan's babblings.

'What do you see when you look beyond the forest, Revol?' said Babayan. He was certain the old priest wanted to save his soul.

Rossel grimaced as the steamroller veered to the left.

'I see Leningrad. The trams bursting through Theatre Square,' he answered. 'The twinkling chandeliers of the Glazunov Hall in the conservatoire, when I was a student there.'

The barrel let out a banshee wail as it creaked and groaned across the packed ice and snow.

'I see the Anichkov Bridge, and a young fool declaiming the poetry of Mayakovsky through a loudhailer. "Behold what quiet settles on the world. Night wraps the sky in tribute from the stars. In hours like these, one rises to address. The ages, history, and all creation . . ."'

A boy who should have known better.

'Ah, Mayakovsky,' said a man further along the row with a deep sigh. 'Now there was a real *muzhik* – a lover, a drinker, a madman. They say the thought of suicide was like a cancer in him. At first, a whisper. In his last days, a never-ending scream.'

21

Rossel didn't know the speaker but the accent was Baltic. A Lithuanian, perhaps. There were plenty of Balts rotting in the string of camps along the line, all the way to Yermakovo.

Inside his head, Rossel swore. He shouldn't have mentioned being a student at the conservatoire. It was a mistake to reveal anything. Every tiny morsel of someone's soul might be something for the Thieves back at camp to bite into.

If they ever found out that he had been an officer of the Leningrad militia . . .

They would tear him to pieces.

'What else, Revol?' urged Babayan.

'Just pull this fucking thing . . .'

For the next hour they struggled in silence, reserving all strength for their labour. *Shock work is the path to liberation!* declared a ragged banner nailed to the side of the main barracks back in the camp. The camp commander would point to it every time someone was pulled out of roll call, beaten by the guards and sent to the isolating cells.

The sun, which had made only the most reluctant appearance that day, soon retreated again. That meant it was about three o'clock. In another hour, perhaps less, it would be time to return.

'How many years?' said Babayan.

'What?'

Rossel was only half-listening. They had only a few minutes of rest every hour – some zeks had quotas measured in kilograms of coal or fallen logs. Theirs was measured in metres. A tiny shortfall meant less bread, a smaller measure of soup – lukewarm water with a scrap of fish skin in it. He kept his eyes on the treeline.

'How many years is your sentence?' repeated the priest.
Rossel shrugged.

Babayan frowned. 'Everyone counts every day of their
sentence. Everyone knows how long they have served and
how long they have left.'

'Not me. I am here for as long as one man wants me to
be here.'

'Comrade Stalin?'

Rossel found this worth a smile. He shook his head.

The priest grunted. 'I hear it all the time. "If only the
great Stalin knew about this place," the new lads say, "he
would put a stop to it. If only Stalin knew . . ."'

Rossel sighed and forced his shoulders forward in the
yoke.

You have to find something to hate.

Even before arriving in Igarka, even before being sent
out on the long march to the furthest outposts of this
GULAG cluster, long before he and his fellow prisoners
had hauled every tool with them and been forced to build
their own barracks, he had found something to hate.
Someone, at least.

Major Oleg Nikitin.

At first, a whisper . . .

Sometimes, the detective knew, what was true of suicide
could also be true of murder.

3

Up ahead, the distant watchtowers and searchlights of the camp bled a line of light into the darkness. Like phantoms, the column of zeks floated towards it.

Rossel shivered and pulled his ragged scarf tighter around his head. The cold was so intense now it was burning his exposed skin. Raw wind whipped the snow into flurries that stung his face. His gut was growling. Everyone was thinking about one thing. Bread. Except Babayan, whose head was filled with God and the royal family. And Vustin, whose young mind was, as ever, a tangle of musical notes.

'*Gospodi, Isusye Khristye, syne . . .*' chanted the priest.

'Shut it, you dirty Armenian piece of shit. Unless that God of yours is a baker,' shouted a prisoner behind them in the column.

'*Gospodi, Isusye . . .*'

A young guard had drifted closer to the main phalanx of prisoners without them noticing.

'God is dead, Armenian pig,' said the guard. 'Christ is in the sewer. Not another word out of your filthy mouth.'

Do as he says, Rossel thought. He is a zealot, too, every bit as much as you, Babayan. I can tell. I remember them well from my days in the League of the Militant Godless.

'I shall pray for your soul, young man, which shall come to His mercy . . .'

That was a bad . . .

The guard closed the distance to Babayan with unexpected speed and smashed the butt of his rifle into the priest's head. Babayan reeled. He fell into the arms of one of his fellow prisoners, who cursed and pushed him away. He managed to keep on his feet but was no longer walking.

'Don't stop for him,' muttered another zek. 'Don't help the stupid piece of shit. I want to eat.'

'The struggle against religion is the struggle for socialism,' shouted the guard.

It was a slogan Rossel knew well. It was etched on his brain from the endless assemblies of the League of Militant Godless that he had attended as a youth. He had been determined to outdo his comrades in atheist fervour; desperate to wish away God's prying eyes and God's judgment; and – most of all, concerning the fate of his mother and father – to wish away his own judgment, too.

They heard the bolt being drawn back on his rifle. The full stop at the end of Babayan's next sentence would be a bullet from a Tokarev SVT-40.

'Excuse me, comrade. May I interject?'

Rossel felt a twist in his gut. It was Vustin's high-pitched warble. Brought up by his grandfather, a rich landowner – now a hated *kulak* in the eyes of the Soviet state – the boy's naivety was such that even in Igarka he made no attempt to disguise his education and upbringing.

'Who do you think are you, Comrade Interject? The fucking tsar himself?'

The guard shoved his face spit-close to Vustin's. He raised the tip of his rifle and fired into the air.

Vustin blinked twice, put his hand over his ears, and began to sing. A touch of Tchaikovsky. An aria from *The Queen of Spades*.

Now the guard aimed the rifle straight at Vustin.

'Stop singing, *mudak*, or so help me I'll . . .'

But Vustin couldn't stop.

'"*Here come our warriors, our little soldiers, Aren't they smart? Stand aside, there, stand aside! . . .*"'

The guard shoved the rifle into the side of Vustin's head.

'You won't stop, then I'll stop you.'

'"*The foe is wicked, be on your guard! . . . Flee or sur-render! Hurrah! Hurrah! . . .*"'

The Tokarev jammed on the first shot, which enraged the guard even more. He ripped out the magazine and yanked at the bolt.

Rossel's throat tightened. He stepped out of line. They were only fifty metres from the fence. The other guards were yelling now, hurrying towards the commotion. A searchlight from one of the watchtowers, drawn by the shot, had picked them out.

'Comrade, please, wait!'

Rossel's voice was muffled. It sounded impotent in the howling wind, the snow and the dark. He raised his hands in surrender and opened his mouth to implore the guard to show mercy.

'The boy is unwell, he does not understand. I can some-times reason with h—'

The second bullet hit Vustin in the forehead. He went down without another sound.

*

The dead man's tongue lolled out of the side of his mouth.

'It looks, for all the world,' came Babayan's ethereal voice from behind Rossel, 'like the serpent that made its home in Eden.'

A red-faced lieutenant, panting after the exertion of running through the drifts, snapped at the guard who had killed Vustin. 'Idiot! More forms for me to fill in three times over. One less prisoner to push the barrel. You're not fit to guard the shithouse, Dernov.'

Another guard kicked Babayan in the ribs as he knelt over the dead Vustin and ordered him to head for the gates. The Armenian groaned and held his side. Blood was still trickling down his face.

'You can drag him back the rest of the way, blockhead. You,' the guard pointed to Rossel, 'you help him. The rest of you bastards – back to camp, quick.'

Then both he and the lieutenant ran to catch up with the labour brigade, cursing in unison as they went.

Rossel looked down at Vustin. His eyes were open, his expression serene. The hole was neat. In the glare of the camp lights, he could just make out a dark halo spreading around the young composer's head.

Angry at the dressing down he had received, rather than the murder he had just committed, Dernov's face was flushed.

'What are you waiting for?' he shouted.

They took an arm each and began to drag Vustin towards the camp.

'A martyr,' Rossel heard Babayan mutter under his breath. 'The boy has the look of the little tsarevich, Alexei. And the aura of a slaughtered saint . . .'

*

As Rossel and Babayan arrived back in camp, the rest of the brigade was already lined up in the main parade ground. They broke ranks when the composer's corpse was deposited on the snow and the guards made no effort to stop them. In the camp, clothes were priceless.

A fight soon broke out over Vustin's coat.

'What do you want, Rossel?' said Denikin, a professor of Marxist literature from Kursk, as he bent over Vustin's body. 'His socks? His pants?'

Marx's manifesto, Rossel remembered, said Communism could be distilled to a single sentence: the abolition of private property. The professor must have missed that lecture.

As the prisoners tore open Vustin's jacket, a piece of paper flew out. Then another, and another, fluttering and floating over the roll call area, over the camp's inner fence, up among the snowflakes in the searchlight beams and onward into the night. Rossel chased one down and caught it. He looked at it and ran back to the squabbling prisoners, booting them out of the way and joining the mêlée, ignoring the elbows to his face and blows to his ribs. He ripped the coat out of the hands of a burly Ukrainian who thought he had triumphed. Then he reached inside and his rag-covered hands brought out more paper, which he jammed into his own pockets. Rossel looked around but the guards were still too busy watching and laughing at the fight for Vustin's clothes.

Soon the corpse was naked.

He flung the coat at Denikin. 'Here,' he said. 'I think Marx would want you to have it.'

Then Rossel stepped aside and stood still as he watched more of the papers drift over the fence and disappear into the darkness.

They, at least, were free.

Babayan approached, touching Rossel's arm.

'All of a sudden, you seem at peace, my friend,' said the Armenian. 'What was written on Vustin's papers?'

Rossel turned to face the old priest.

'A miracle of sorts, Babayan,' he said. 'One greater than anything in your holy books.'

4

A detachment of German PoWs had come out to the far extremity of the railway work to cart out and lay the sleepers. They were a pitiful sight – hunched, weak, friendless, bullied. They must know how the world regarded them and their fellow countrymen, thought Rossel. And yet, no longer the Wehrmacht's gleaming legionaries, they still looked bemused at how far they had fallen.

It was not the first time the PoWs had been called upon to assist with the railway's construction. They had set to work with only rudimentary directions, measuring the distance between sleepers with lengths of rod and a certain choreography. At rest time they huddled together.

All except one, who leaned on a sloping tree stump a couple of dozen metres away from his *Kameraden*.

Holding up a smoke, Rossel approached. He kept an eye on the guards but they took no notice.

The Fritz was watching him sidelong. Rossel realised that every German in the camp had to make judgments on every Russian, instant assessments of whether they represented danger or indifference.

'Walter,' said the German, extending his hand.

Rossel took it.

'Rossel,' he replied.

Walter frowned. 'Rossel? *Sind Sie Deutscher?'*

Rossel shook his head. 'Russian. But descended from the Volga Germans. *Povolzhskiye nyemtsy.* Volga, Volga. Immigrants. Long time ago – eighteenth century, I think.' He made a looping gesture to indicate the passage of time. Walter seemed to understand. 'My father,' Rossel added. 'Papa. Communist. Bolshevik. Didn't talk about much his ancestors.'

Walter talked on in German, a babble that might have been a commentary on Communism, immigration or the weather. The Fritz took one last heavy drag on the wad of *makhorka* – the roughest of rough tobacco, which Rossel had lent him – and handed it back.

'*Wunderbar. Vielen Dank!'*

The German PoWs numbered around thirty. They had spent seven years in the Soviet Union and found themselves in an Arctic labour camp that didn't even have a proper name. Neither guards nor Russian prisoners mixed with them enough for them to learn more than a few words of Russian. In the eyes of the more rabid camp commanders, fraternization could mean a few more years on the end of your sentence.

But what did that matter to him, he thought, a man who hadn't even been told how long his own sentence was?

Rossel was tempted to get Walter to teach him a few obscenities in German. Just to confuse the guards. But Walter looked a little on the cultured side.

'You like music, Walter? Beethoven, Brahms, Schumann?'

Walter nodded.

'Brahms, *da* . . .' The German hummed the last bars of a Brahms lullaby. '"*Morgen früh, wenn Gott will, wirst du wieder geweckt.*" My mother used to sing . . . to me sing it.'

'"Tomorrow morning, if God wills, you will wake once again."' Rossel repeated the line in Russian. He smiled. 'Some days in Igarka I have wished God might will the exact opposite . . . I was a musician,' Rossel said, pointing to himself.

'*Musiker?*' Walter approved. 'Mozart, Beethoven, Wagner.' He asked a question Rossel didn't understand but the word 'instrument' was the same in both languages. Rossel mimed playing a violin. Then held up his left hand, pushing down with his right on the glove and rags entwined around it to reveal the absence of two fingers.

'NKVD did this. Or MGB, as they're called now,' he said.

Walter thought about it and winced.

'*Physiker*,' he said, tapping his chest. '*Raketen*.' He made the obligatory whooshing sound and pointed at the sky. Then he pointed out a few more of his fellow POWs.

'*Physiker, Chemiker, Physiker*,' he said. '*Ein Kernphysiker*,' he added, jabbing a hand at the tallest, most drooping POW: a man in his late fifties with a long scar across his cheek and a glazed expression in his eyes. The latter had been beaten senseless by the guards shortly after arriving at the main camp in Igarka. Life 105 kilometres further west had not improved his health. He was now no more than a simpleton. But he was a favourite of the Thieves, who made a pet of him at their nightly card games in the camp forge, feeding him scraps and calling him *Tsar Suka*, King Bitch. What the criminals liked, Rossel thought, was how far they sensed the man had fallen. His features were aristocratic but his hunched shoulders, wary eyes and cowering demeanour now gave him the bearing of the humblest servant. His fellow countrymen tried to protect him but they didn't have the will or the numbers to fend off the Thieves.

'Not soldiers?'

Walter shook his head.

'Nein – ich meine, ja . . . in den letzten Kriegstagen.'

A whistle blew. Rossel nodded at Walter, who bowed.

Ten years ago the Germans had conquered most of Europe. Now they were grateful for a free puff on a cigarette.

*

It took some dark stars to align for a night like this.

Such nights came when the labour gangs had left a prisoner or two for dead. Not that the other zeks cared much now for lost comrades. But, for a few – once they had chewed on mouldy black bread and drunk rank broth – the emptiness that was left inside was filled with the anger of impotence.

They came when the craziest Thieves from antagonistic clans got off shift at the same time. A challenge to play cards. Insults. Challenge accepted. High stakes – including other men's clothes, tobacco and lives. Such nights came when the stench of one hundred men crammed into one barrack hut mingled with the bittersweet tang of *samogon*: homebrew brewed from pilfered yeast, sugar and leftover grain or potato skin, or diluted industrial alcohol. Mix it all up in the cauldron of the barracks, add a dash of brutal struggle against a ruthless enemy, and you conjured up chaos.

There were two big barracks like these. In one ruled the old-school *Vory*, the Thieves, the ones who adhered to the vow never to cooperate with the authorities. In the other ruled the *Suki*, the Bitches – criminals who saw power and opportunity in working, even at arm's length, with the State.

War had broken out between them, war that was vicious and unending.

In both barracks survived the politicals – cowering intellectuals who had written the wrong book or staged the wrong play, or academics, like Denikin, who had proposed the wrong theory. Banished to the coldest corners, wondering if their lives were spinning with the dice at the game of craps taking place in the centre of the wooden building, where there were flickers of light and warmth. To be a political was to live your life as prey. To survive, a man needed to be vigilant. The remotest points of the Soviet justice system, GULAG satellites such as 105th Kilometre were the most lawless places on Earth.

But that didn't mean there weren't rules. And in Igarka, a Thief called Kuba was the one who made them. As a would-be rival was finding out.

Sobol was in a bad way.

On his bunk not far from the centre of the hut, sweating, writhing, clutching his stomach, the thickset thief had repeatedly soiled himself.

'Fuck you, Sobol, it smells like Death's arsehole in here,' said a pug-faced man with a tattoo of Lenin on his neck.

Sobol groaned. He was oblivious to the curses and kicks of the prisoners in the bunks around him, which doubled in vigour with each bout of retching and every involuntary bowel motion. From time to time he would scream out garbled phrases. Once, he cried out for his mother, earning raucous mockery from the barracks at large.

Further down the barracks, the tattooist Oblonsky set out his tools. A needle, fashioned from a piece of metal wire that had been heated until it split, threaded through an empty fountain pen. The ink was made from ash or the soot of burnt tyre rubber, mixed with urine. Some camp tattooists claimed to use alcohol to sterilize the mixture, but in 105th Kilometre there was not a drop of alcohol that went undrunk.

'Poisoned,' said Oblonsky, gesturing at Sobol. 'Kuba's orders. Sobol let his guard down.'

Rossel undid the laces of his camp-issue smock.

'*Poganka?*'

Oblonsky nodded.

'Back in the summer,' said the tattooist, squinting at his handiwork, 'somebody picked and hoarded a load of it and slipped a sample into our friend's ration.'

Russia was a nation of forest foragers. The Death Cap mushroom claimed the lives of a few unwary souls each year. It was known to be an agonising way to go.

'He was making a play for Kuba's throne. Normally Kuba gets Medvedev, the Bear, to sort that stuff out. This time he was more . . . subtle.' He nodded at the shitting, shrieking wreck a few bunks away. 'If you can call it that.'

Oblonsky inspected the progress of his handiwork to date – the outline of a large seabird on Rossel's chest – and grunted. 'The other wing today, or most of it. Whatever you can bear. If Ilya Repin had painted on a canvas that squirmed like you do, his daubs would have taken him a lot longer. That's what I tell all my customers.'

The tattooist set to work, puncturing Rossel's skin repeatedly with quick jabs, moving millimetre by millimetre.

Rossel set a piece of old tyre between his teeth and kept as still as he could.

The first buildings of this penal labour camp had been hewn out of timber from the vast northern forests four or five years previously. Intended as just another staging post on a project that consumed prisoners in their hundreds, it had swelled almost to the size of a central camp – the hubs from which expendable workers were sent out to colonise the wastelands above the Arctic Circle.

A speck of grit in the snow to which other specks had clung, and stuck, Rossel thought.

A stocky Georgian with a broken nose appeared at Oblonsky's shoulder. He pointed at the bird on Rossel's chest.

'Hey, you. Albatross. Get ready,' he said. 'Tomorrow night, Kuba wants to hear another one of your stories. Better make it a good one, too. He's not been in the best of moods lately.'

5

In your dreams you could escape. You could walk past the Sphinxes that guarded the Fontanka's elaborate Egyptian bridge. Visit the Hermitage and fall in love with your favourite painting all over again. Stand outside the Kirov Opera, float through its walls and . . . just listen.

But then morning dropped like a guillotine. And you woke up back in 105th Kilometre.

Outside, a luckless Mongolian conscript was sent out to amble around the barracks and hammer two pots together. The perimeter lights were turned on. It was five o'clock.

Inside the barracks the glow from the lights, even amplified by the snow, was muted by the thickening patina of ice on the windows. Every muscle aching from his labours by day and constant shivering at night, Rossel stared up at the misshapen icicles hanging from the rafters. He coughed. The rasping in his chest was something else to worry about. In the camps, if another prisoner didn't steal up behind you and slit your throat, Death – typhus, tuberculosis – hid inside you, waiting.

Some zeks rose immediately. It was the only way to warm up: to get moving, to go rooting for scraps of cloth or anything going spare that might be bartered. Or it might be your turn to take out what Babayan, in a rare attempt at humour, called 'Satan's chalices' – the big pisspots.

With an effort, Rossel got as far as sitting up. He had only one blanket but before winter had arrived he'd had the foresight to stitch pieces of rag into it. Even pieces of cardboard, or scraps of tyre. Anything that might trap and warm some air. In the bigger camps, especially the transit hubs, zeks would bargain anything that wasn't nailed down. In 105th Kilometre, there was nothing spare to bargain. Every scrap was precious.

Take a man's blanket and you took his life.

Stiff and sore, Rossel slipped his own blanket from his torso, felt for his bowl and makeshift fork inside the bag of kindling and sawdust that he'd constructed as a pillow, and slid down from his bunk. Oblonsky was snoring like a bear. He followed a group of three or four zeks out of the barracks, intending to head straight for the canteen.

Over to his left, he saw Babayan, head bowed and making the sign of the cross several times, facing the barracks and crouched over the spot where Vustin's body had been discarded and stripped. As usual, the Armenian was saying a prayer.

'Let those who fear the Lord say his love endures forever . . .'

Babayan heard Rossel's boot crunching in the snow and looked up.

'Vustin was like Venerable Isaac, the hermit of the caves,' he said. 'An innocent, a Fool-in-Christ, as we say.'

He resumed his chanting.

'The Lord is with me, I will not be afraid. What can any man do to me?'

Rossel cast an eye around, partly because it was wise to watch your own back but also because the number of things the powerful could do to the weak out here were limitless.

'Will you not pray for him with me, Rossel?' said Babayan.

Rossel shook his head.

'As I have told you, I was once a member of the League of the Militant Godless,' he said.

Babayan frowned. 'The enemies of Christ,' he said.

Rossel nodded.

'They left their mark. I'm no believer.'

The old priest looked forlorn.

'You're wrong my friend. Our new saint, our great martyr, our Holy Vustin told me he'd never met someone who looked so like he was carrying a great sin inside him.'

'A great sin?'

Babayan smiled.

'That's why the boy liked you, Rossel. All martyrs aspire to carry the Lord's cross. He was jealous of your soul's burden.'

*

A spatter of watery buckwheat gruel did little to stop the ache in his gut. Rossel, eager to find a moment of solitude, rushed it down, stashed his slice of black bread inside his jacket for later, skirted the main parade ground and sat on a log behind the infirmary, by the camp's eastern perimeter fence.

He pulled out the papers he had recovered from Vustin's coat and unfurled them with icy fingers. They were rectangular and yellowing. The typed lettering was beginning to fade but there was no mistaking the nature of the documents.

STATEMENT

'In the interests of Soviet justice and of suppressing all threat of an outbreak of counterrevolutionary activity in the northern administration of correctional labour camps, Bureau XXVI of the regional Ministry for State Security orders the shooting of ARTYOM KERZHAKOV the sentence to be carried out without delay.'

Each document was dated, the earliest from around July 1949 and the latest only three weeks ago, and the names on each were scribbled in block capitals. The signatures were hard to read but Rossel thought he could make out a Major Kirillov. It was a name he had not encountered in 105th Kilometre, or in any of the transit camps through which he had passed, many of which would certainly have been subject to the oversight of the Ministry for State Security, the MGB.

The empty spaces were all filled in by hand. It was a roll call of the dead.

Abramov. Akunin. Alexeev. Astilin. Bogdanov. Braginsky. Vertukhin . . .

Rossel leafed through them. The documents were brief and banal. He tried to picture the faces of the condemned, wondering if they had ever seen these papers, the bureaucratic imprint of their fate.

Vorilov. Vrasensky. Dolgorukhov. Dmitriyev . . .

He counted to the end. Twenty-four in all.

On the reverse of each was line after line of musical staves, ruled by a meticulous hand.

Time and key signatures, constellations of notes grouped in quavers and semiquavers. A composition of unrivalled ambition. Something only a composer of the calibre of Stravinsky, or Prokofiev, or Shostakovich would even have thought of attempting.

It is so precisely written, he thought, printed music looks amateurish by comparison. Either exposure to the cold or a poor-quality ink, the brittleness of the paper, or a combination of the three, had caused the notes to fade. But if held up to the Siberian sky it was all still legible.

There was one that had survived well. The hand was firmer, the notes rounder, even more confident. Rossel tried to follow both melody and harmony in his head but the fugue soon twisted into an impregnable complexity and he could only follow in outline.

It was the only one with a title:

Fugue 13: The Song of Lost Souls.

Most of Vustin's fugues would challenge the technique of the most virtuoso pianist, even in a country full of them. But Fugue 13 was simpler, more lyrical, more heartfelt.

Folding the papers, Rossel tucked them into his jacket. He sat for a few minutes more, until the commotion of roll call.

'Fall in, link arms. If you make so much as a step to the left or the right it will be considered an attempt to escape and the guards will shoot to kill without warning . . .'

If Babayan was right and Vustin was a saint, then the martyred boy had left behind a hymn for all the ages.

6

Captain Verblinksy – pale, thin, pompous and number three in the hierarchy of the camp administration – came to the end of his morning address and raised his head.

The prisoners, almost two hundred of them, were silent, standing in four blocks according to their barracks, contemplating the day before them.

Real cold – minus thirty degrees and worse – came in spells. One had arrived overnight. They had all felt it in their bunks. Rossel glanced along the line of his brigade. The weak would already be feeling weaker. But falling behind on the quota meant smaller rations. Faltering in the fulfilment of your duties meant curses and kicks, being spat on by your comrades.

It was customary for those who had not made it through the night to be dragged out to attend roll call. It made identification of the dead that much easier. But the deceased, whether they had given in to hunger or cold or fallen prey to the attentions of the Thieves, usually had one thing going for them – they were in one piece.

This morning, next to three complete corpses, there was something else.

A severed head.

The captain pointed to it.

'Who the fuck is that? And where is the rest of him?'

An answer was not forthcoming. Verblinsky, eyes wide in outrage, scanned the faces of the punishment brigades but learned little.

A shout came from one of the watchtowers. A guard was pointing at something. Two things, in fact. Two snow-dusted objects: one at the far end of the main parade ground, next to the gates, the other over to the right.

'You,' said Captain Verblinsky, pointing at two zeks. 'And you. Go.'

The two prisoners at the end of the line went to investigate. By the time they were halfway across the parade ground, another guard was pointing in a third direction. Arriving at their first destination, the men bent over to inspect. One recoiled and began to gag. The other, unperturbed, perhaps even relishing his task, picked it up. Then they progressed to the next point, a further fifty metres or so away.

They completed their compass-point tour of the parade ground and returned to Captain Verblinsky, dumping two legs and a torso on the ground before him. The gesture reminded Rossel of newsreel he had once seen. The Victory Parade in Moscow in the summer of 1945. Stalin's armies hurling the standards of the Wehrmacht, Luftwaffe, Kriegsmarine and Waffen-SS at the feet of their great leader.

Poor Sobol.

His agonies had ended in the night.

Captain Verblinsky gulped.

A huge man, a Thief, began to chant through sharpened teeth. It was Medvedev, Kuba's second in command. Known as the Bear, a play on his name.

'In this camp, Kuba, leader of the true Thieves, the Thieves-in-law, rules over every breath taken,' he said. 'North, south, east and west, between the rising and the setting of the sun. *Suki*, this will be your fate too . . .'

The captain glared at him. Not sure how to proceed. Then he ordered the two men who had fetched Sobol's constituent body parts to fall in.

'Band!' Verblinsky shouted. 'Begin!'

The motley prison band struck up 'The Internationale' and Rossel watched the first labour brigade peel off from the far end and shuffle towards the gates, heading to the wastelands. A clear sky was clouding over. His stomach was already growling.

> *Vstavai, proklyatyem zakleimyoniy*
> *Vyes' mir, golodnykh i rabov . . .*

> Arise, you who have been branded with a curse
> A world of the starving and enslaved . . .

The words echoed round his head as Rossel shoved broken hands into his armpits, not for the first time cursing the absence of two fingers on his left and the badly functioning fingers on his right. Playing in the camp band did not spare you from outdoor duties, but it trimmed time spent doing them. And it spared you from joining the vanguard of shock workers who laid the railway tracks.

Two guards, young, surly and suffering in the cold, were summoned to remove the four quarters of the unfortunate Sobol on a stretcher. They scooped up the convict's remains but had not got ten metres before one stumbled, spilling their gruesome load. One of the prisoners started to snigger. Sobol's head had landed under his mangled backside, while his legs pointed in opposite directions.

A moustachioed Chechen in front of Rossel pointed.

'He made my life miserable. Now that bastard can lick his own fucking arse.'

The man next to him collapsed in laughter. Everyone joined in, even the guards. Grinning, the two young guards tried to pick Sobol up again. No luck. This time his head bounced twice and rolled towards a big Ukrainian who picked it up and, dropping into a crouch, made as if he was about to boot it over the perimeter fence.

'Hey, boys, look at me, I'm Lev Yashin,' he said. Yashin was Dynamo Moscow's new young goalkeeper.

Hovering over them, Captain Verblinsky cast loud aspersions on their parentage.

The band wheezed its way to the chorus. In the first weeks of 105th Kilometre's existence, full-throated singing had been obligatory. But it had not been a long-lived tradition. Now only a few politicals made a mocking effort to join in.

> *Eto yest' nash poslednii*
> *I reshitel'ny boi*
>
> This is our final
> And decisive battle . . .

A juddering sound came from above. All eyes looked skyward and the laughter died away.

The source was impossible to pinpoint at first but it grew louder until it filled the air. The band was silenced, the labour brigades stilled.

Rossel had only seen a helicopter once before. They were barely used by the Red Army during the war and his only sighting after that had been at an airfield south of Leningrad, not long after he'd been sworn into the militia. He supposed some of the zeks were seeing one for the very first time.

The prisoners gazed towards the clouds, watching the path of the squat, dark-green beetle as it swooped, chattering, towards the ground, zeroing in on a landing spot beyond the camp fence. But the guards pounded a few heads with their rifle butts and the zeks resumed their reluctant marches.

The route taken by Rossel's brigade out to the railway tracks had brought them to within a hundred metres of the helicopter's landing point, close to the camp commandant's living quarters and the MGB barracks. Here, they were beyond the fence and the outer patrol zone.

The helicopter's rotors were still. The whine of its engine had faded.

A small door just behind the rear left wheel was flung open.

A muffled figure emerged from the helicopter's belly, and then another. Now two more. A delegation of uniforms from the camp administration ran up to greet them and the new arrivals pulled down the thick collars of their coats.

Rossel knew the face straightaway. He stopped marching.

The guard alongside him broke step with a curse and hefted the butt of his rifle. Rossel moved his feet again but kept staring at the cluster of figures around the squat fuselage.

Someone to hate.

Major Oleg Nikitin, the MGB officer who had exiled him in this frozen wasteland, was shaking hands with the commandant.

A fifth person emerged from the helicopter. Smaller than the rest. Nikitin turned to welcome them into the group.

As the commandant spoke and gesticulated, the fifth figure looked around to survey the surroundings. The coat they were wearing was too thin for the harsh northern winter.

The brigade marched on but one by one all heads swung towards the new arrival. As though the line were a carnivore that had just picked up a scent.

A woman.

A shout behind them. The brigade halted and a guard, stumbling in thick, badly fitting boots, caught up.

'Prisoner 457, come forward!'

For a moment, he did not understand. It had been so long since anyone in officialdom had addressed him, Rossel had almost forgotten his number.

'You,' said the guard. 'Follow me.'

7

As if he was fanning out a deck of cards before dealing them, Major Nikitin swept a hand over the wooden table, making a sound like sandpaper. The major placed two Manila files on one side of the desk and three packs of cigarettes on the other.

Rossel, slumped in a chair that had uneven legs, looked around this inner sanctum within the main administration building. A couple of logs burned in a small brick fireplace. The flue wasn't up to much and the room, all wood, festooned with red banners – *Forward to Communism, To Freedom with a Clear Conscience* – was smoky and rank. But it was also something almost unimaginable. Hot. As the fire warmed his skin, he felt as privileged as a guest at Leningrad's Hotel Astoria.

Nikitin glanced down at the files. Then back at Rossel.

'You don't look so good, comrade.'

Rossel raised his left hand.

'I apologise,' he said. 'Since you had me sent here, I have not been able to devote as much time to my health as I would wish. The task has been made more difficult, of course, because several years ago an MGB interrogator crushed my hands and removed some of my fingers. As you will doubtless recall, Comrade Major.'

Nikitin sat back.

'And yet, when we last met we parted as –' the major paused – 'I might even say friends.'

Rossel began to shiver and was overtaken by a coughing fit. He wanted to spit in the major's face. If he closed his eyes for a second, he could picture the pleasure of setting about Nikitin's scarred features with a length of pipe. Gouging out his one good eye. Condemning him to darkness. Obliterating that sneer.

Instead, he wiped his mouth.

'You're in a military uniform? Not MGB?'

Nikitin gave a nod.

'Still the detective, I see,' he said. 'A transfer. To the Main Investigative Directorate. GRU. Military intelligence.'

'Comrade Malenkov came through for you, then? Offered you protection?'

It had been a year since Rossel and Nikitin had stood in the moonlit snow on the shores of Lake Ladoga, MGB troops pointing submachine guns at their chests, half a platoon of Soviet special forces pointing automatic rifles at their backs. A few feet away, as if oblivious to the stand-off, two pretenders to the Kremlin's throne, Georgy Malenkov and Lavrentiy Beria, took a moment to decide that a stalemate suited them both. And then retreated. But only to fight another day.

Nikitin had made a fateful choice of his own. He had deserted Beria's side. Not many crossed Beria and lived. Yet here he was.

'He arranged it, yes,' said Nikitin with a scowl. 'They hate me, though. In the GRU, I mean. They think I'm Beria's cuckoo, sitting in General Pletnev's nest.'

'Pletnev? The Hero of the Heights?'

General Pletnev was famed as the officer whose troops had smashed through the last German forces defending Berlin. The Battle of the Seelow Heights. A man who had turned disaster into triumph.

'General Pletnev is defence minister now, Revol,' said Nikitin. 'Stalin moved Marshal Zhukov to the provinces. Early retirement. For the good of his health, if you get me.'

'What had he done?'

'Riding on a white horse at the front of the Victory Parade for the Great Patriotic War? Thousands cheering, people throwing their hats in the air? Stealing the limelight from Stalin like that? A foolish error. Pletnev is smarter. He doesn't like parades. And even if they'd made him ride in one he'd have the good sense to turn up on a donkey, right at the back.'

Rossel pointed at the cigarettes. 'For me? How kind.' Without waiting for a reply he reached out and took all three packs.

The major ruffled his own hair, hard. Flakes of skin flew into the air among the thin blue trails of smoke.

'When I left the MGB, Malenkov and Pletnev had a price for their protection. All the dirt I had on Beria, please. Who was he fucking? How many girls? Any of them underage? Every last smear of shit on his shoes.'

Rossel lit the cigarette. In the camps, at his lowly level in the hierarchy, the best you got was *makhorka* – and even that rough tobacco was cut with dust, dead insects, hair, Christ knew what else. Smoked in newspaper. This was in a different league – actual *papirosi*! *Festivalniye*. A folkloric dancing couple with rosy cheeks adorned the pack. The girl reminded him a little of his missing sister, Galya.

Wherever she is, he thought for what must have been the hundredth time since arriving in Igarka, at least she's not here.

He preferred *Elbrus* but . . .

Rossel sat back and drew in the smoke. He exhaled.

'My father used to say that a warm fire and a good cigarette was as close to Heaven as any man needed to get.'

'One of Beria's girls was my daughter, in case you've forgotten,' muttered Nikitin.

Rossel had not forgotten. Lavrentiy Beria, who had survived and then prospered as head of the Soviet secret police, was still one of Stalin's closest allies. He was also, as Rossel and Nikitin had found out, a monstrous and sadistic sexual predator, among many other vices. Not a good enemy for either of them to have acquired.

'About that, I am truly sorry,' said Rossel.

Nikitin stood and went over to the fire.

Rossel took advantage of the pause to pull another *papirosa* from the pack. He lit it with the first and stashed the pack inside his smock, along with the other two.

Nikitin watched him do it with the familiar grimace that made the patch of scar tissue flow across his cheek. He looked down at his olive-green uniform and touched his epaulettes.

Rossel watched him pace between the desk and the fire. Nikitin was a survivor. As a former MGB interrogator, he was also an expert in human weakness and pain. But he didn't have the guile for Party politics.

They had not seen each other for almost a year. Rossel was surprised to learn that the major was still alive. Not many left the Ministry for State Security of their own volition. Nonetheless, Nikitin seemed to have wound up under the protection of General Pletnev, and the general had succeeded in fending off Beria.

Rossel stared out through the tiny window. Soon he would be back out there, facing his own challenges in a world where the Thieves and Bitches waged constant war with each other, pausing only to victimise the politicals. The prospect weighed on him. A few moments of respite had made him feel only more fatigued.

The *Festivalniye* tasted of everything he had been missing.

He drew too much smoke into his lungs and began to cough again, then recovered.

'Article 58 of the Penal Code, they said at my trial, or what passed for a trial,' said Rossel. 'Charges brought by none other than Oleg Yurievich Nikitin, Major, Ministry for State Security.' He mimicked the judge's high-pitched zealotry. 'Revol Rossel is charged as an Enemy of the People.'

He sat up in his chair.

'As you say, we parted as friends. And yet you are the reason I am here. Now you want something.'

'I hid you in plain sight, Revol,' said Nikitin. 'After we drew attention to Beria's connection to the illicit importation of jewellery and his other extracurricular activities – and believe me, his rivals were very interested in what we discovered – you were a marked man. Until now, no one came here to look for you, did they? Beria had put a price on your head. I figured the camps were the safest place to hide you. The last place he'd look other than under the minister's own bed. Would you rather be alive here or dead somewhere else?'

Rossel shrugged.

'That's a question every man here asks himself every single day. The answer he gives mostly depends on the weather, or how long ago he took his last beating from the guards or the Thieves.'

The two of them fell silent. Staring at the face of a man he had once considered an unlikely ally, Rossel looked for any flicker of regret or remorse. But that was the advantage of a face disfigured by an incendiary bomb and a soul that had withered a little with each tortured victim. Nikitin didn't give much away.

Rossel sighed. He was already tired of this game. He pointed at the two Manila files.

'So tell me then, why are you here?'

The major ran the flat of his hand across the tabletop again. Then he picked up the first file.

'Why else would I need you? Someone has been murdered.'

*

It took two more cigarettes for Nikitin to go through everything.

Two bodies in Leningrad, found in the past couple of weeks. Both men. Both showing signs of being beaten and tortured, possibly during an interrogation.

'Whoever did it left them sitting in a chair, with two bullet holes around the right temple,' said Nikitin.

He pushed the two files a couple of centimetres in Rossel's direction.

'The first was a welder by the name of Katz. His body was found on a bench in the wooded area of the Alexandrovsky

Garden, between the statue of the Bronze Horseman and St Isaac's Square. The other was called Samosud. A printer and bookbinder. His corpse was found in his own apartment. In Sennaya Square. But each man had two neat holes in the same place.'

At the mention of familiar Leningrad haunts, Rossel felt the pangs of homesickness.

'During the blockade, I once walked past six corpses as I was strolling down Nevsky Prospect during my regular afternoon constitutional,' Nikitin carried on. 'You'd think Leningraders would be used to dead bodies. But the city is already filled with rumours. They've given a name to the killer – "Koshchei, is here, Koshchei walks among us."'

Rossel sat a little more forward in his chair.

'Koshchei the Immortal? After the monster in the folk tale?'

Nikitin nodded. 'Sorcerer, not monster. Or a bit of both. Newspaper editors have been rebuked for giving the story credence, but not before the stories had been published. Militia officers have been disciplined. Leningrad Party officials have been ordered to get a grip on these foolish rumours. But the name has stuck.'

Rossel thought about this. The folk tale was known to every Russian child. Rimsky-Korsakov had based an opera on it. Koshchei was the villain of Stravinsky's ballet *The Firebird*. He killed for pleasure, abducted the lovers of heroes, and concealed his soul inside animals or objects to protect it, thus keeping himself immortal. Or hidden in an egg, or a needle. Or a needle inside an egg. Rossel's faulty memory of the folk tale had not stopped him from improvising when telling the story to a crowd of Thieves in his barracks. He made no apology. Storytelling had kept him alive – the Thieves adored a good tale.

With a stubby finger, Nikitin nudged the two folders another half centimetre towards Rossel.

'Here's a new twist on the folk tale,' he said. 'Both dead bodies had their tongues cut out and rolled-up pieces of paper placed inside their mouths.'

Rossel stared at Nikitin. Taking revenge on the man he had considered an ally had occupied his thoughts for months. Developing an interest in a couple of murders in Leningrad was the last thing he cared about.

'What was on the pieces of paper?' Rossel asked.

'Katz was left for anyone to discover him, in a place where dozens of people lived or passed by every day,' said Nikitin, ignoring the question. 'But no one saw how he got there or who killed him. No one heard anything – and trust me when I say that the victims would not have endured some of their torments in silence. Samosud was killed in his own apartment. But, likewise, his neighbours heard nothing. The first corpse was found by an old gossip who for her own reasons thought it must have been the work of Koshchei. She told her friend who told her friend and now, well. They say the MGB department that monitors phone calls is astounded by how many people are whispering the name.'

A knock at the door broke the silence.

'Telegram for you, Comrade Major,' said a guard. 'A request for you to call the Yenisei Railway Camp Administration.'

As Nikitin followed the man out of the door, Rossel stared down at the files. But did not open them.

8

On his return several minutes later, the major placed a chipped tin mug next to Rossel.

'Tea?'

Some interrogators would sit still. Say nothing. Wait for their victim to fill the vacuum with incriminating talk. If they were not forthcoming, the interrogator would do his paperwork for a few hours and then leave, making way for the next inquisitor. The victim was given no respite. And so on, for hours. Days with the stubborn ones. They called it the Conveyor Belt.

That had never been Nikitin's style. He had always dealt in fists, boots and clubs. And, occasionally, in sharpened steel. Instant results. Rossel glanced down at his own left hand.

But, today, he had offered him sweet tea.

'Do you know what zeks mean when they talk of the *myaso*?' said Nikitin.

Rossel nodded.

'When someone plans an escape, they go in two or threes,' he said. 'Say two men plan the escape. They invite a third. He's the *myaso*. The meat, the walking larder. He only gets as far as the point where other two decide that they're feeling hungry. The *myaso* gets a chance to sleep by the fire – "rest and warmth, comrade, you've earned it, our turn to take watch." So the fool goes to sleep by the fire. And ends up on it.'

The corners of Nikitin's mouth turned upwards.

'Your old friend Sergeant Grachev has escaped from a camp at Vorkuta. He's taken a young boy called Yenin with him, a political. A student.'

Grachev was a name Rossel had not heard for a while. He would have been happy to keep it that way. A sergeant at Rossel's old police station in Leningrad, Grachev was as crooked as they came – a belligerent barrel of a man who never stopped talking about his exploits in the Great Patriotic War. The Fritzes he had killed, the minefields he had strolled through to get to all the *Frauen* and *Fräuleins* he had violated. The vengeance he had wreaked on the German nation in the name of Mother Russia. More than once, Rossel had encountered Grachev regaling junior officers with these war stories, holding them in thrall, a moment of calm amid the habitual chaos of the police station – a sooty, gloomy mansion on Vosstaniya Street that had once belonged to a merchant. Grachev was a thug with grey teeth and a penchant for spending too much time with any woman in the cells who took his fancy. He had a contempt for authority, a contempt he upgraded to loathing when it came to Rossel, who he regarded as moralistic. And for years, nobody had ever known much more about Grachev than that.

But a man like that made enemies. One of those enemies had found out that Grachev had, as a young man, been on the wrong side in the Civil War. A few well-placed whispers later and Major Nikitin and a detachment of MGB troops had arrested the entire police station, Rossel included. Guilt by association – it was all the MGB needed to put any Soviet citizen on a cattle truck to nowhere.

Some of the militia officers had been released. Many were not. Grachev was given a ten-year term to play his part in that area of the Soviet economy run by the Main Camps Directorate.

Nikitin moved over to the fire, picked up the spike that served as a poker and gave the grate a prod. In spite of himself, Rossel shuffled to the edge of his chair to share the warmth.

Why now? Grachev was many things but not a fool. The chances of surviving an escape attempt like that were either none or slim. It was not something the sergeant would have attempted unless . . .

Two bodies in Leningrad . . .

Grachev escapes.

And now Major Oleg Nikitin travels however many thousands of kilometres just to bring me the news . . .

Nikitin pointed to the tin mug.

'Why not drink some of that tea? And then you could take a little look at those files. If you want any more answers, detective.'

*

Samosud had a long, thin face with hooded eyes and big ears.

The details on him were scarce. Avraam Samosud. Born in Moscow in July 1907. Citizenship: Russian. Ethnicity: Jewish. Discharged from the army in 1947, by which time he had made it to sergeant. Wounded in action twice. The file listed several family members, including his parents.

All were marked as having died in 1941. As Jews, that pointed to one thing – Einsatzgruppen, the Nazi mobile death squads who had followed the Blitzkrieg into western Russia.

Rossel placed the file back on the desk and opened the other document.

Katz. Born in March 1912, in Novosibirsk. A thick black moustache and a high brow. A mournful, pessimistic face. Like the pictures of the exiled Trotsky. The kind of man, Rossel thought, that might greet the bullet that killed him with a 'What took you so long?'

His recorded citizenship and ethnicity were the same as Samosud. The file listed commendations for his participation in agitprop theatre and other forms of cultural enlightenment for his fellow troops. He had also served in a mechanised unit. Katz had fought in Stalingrad, where he had been wounded. Discharged in 1946. His parents' names were listed with no record of any death date. From Siberia, his family would have been well behind the lines.

'There are theories,' said Major Nikitin. 'One, it was an opportunist escape. Grachev saw his moment and grasped it.'

Rossel shook his head.

'That would be rash and suicidal. Grachev is neither. What camp was he in? What were his duties?'

'The main Vorkuta camp. Not one of the colonies but unpleasant enough. In his first week he got into a fight and beat one of Thieves up so badly they spent three weeks in the infirmary. Mostly he was a loner, according to the commandant there. They gave him loner's jobs. Cleaning the place, digging ditches. Some spells in the coal mines. Open pits. But he was surviving.'

Rossel leaned forward.

'That means he was watching and waiting,' said Rossel.

Nikitin smiled. Then nodded.

'Evidently,' said Nikitin. 'And then perhaps he heard of the fate of his former army comrades . . .'

'Excuse me?'

'Ah yes,' said Nikitin. 'You read the files but missed the most interesting part. Look again.'

Rossel fumbled for another cigarette with one hand as he reopened the files with the other.

Katz and Samosud both served in the Red Army. No surprise – most able-bodied men had been called up.

The 8th Guards Army.

The army that Grachev had fought in, as he never tired of reminding people. Because the 8th had made it right across Europe and all the way to Berlin.

Nikitin turned away from the fire and looked straight into Rossel's eyes.

'You see? And not only the 8th but, when the militia dug a little deeper, the same division, the same regiment,' he said. 'So I made it my business to find out where the sergeant had been fulfilling his debt to Soviet society. It took a while but I got there, and I sent some of my new associates to chat to Grachev while I came here to find you.'

Rossel closed the files. 'But now he has disappeared into the forest,' he said.

'Yes.'

Rossel sat back.

'My days as a detective are over, Major. You ended them when you had me sent here.'

Nikitin glanced down at his own jacket and toyed with a button.

'If you help me, Rossel, I can get you out of here. For good.'

Rossel stood.

'I'd like to go back to the barracks now, Major.'

Nikitin shook his head in disappointment and took out a photograph from his wallet.

He placed it on the table between them.

The face in the picture was younger and thinner than the one Rossel knew but was unmistakable.

Vassya.

Rossel picked up the photograph.

'Is she well?'

Nikitin stared at him.

'Why not ask her yourself, detective?'

*

The whole process – Nikitin's swaggering departure, Vassya's reluctant entrance, Rossel's bitter disbelief – was agony. Rossel responded to the appearance of his former lover in the only way he could think of. By pulling out another of Nikitin's cigarettes.

Five minutes or more passed in silence. To his surprise, Vassya broke first, filling the void with words of confession.

'After you were taken, Revol, I tried to find out where you were,' she said. 'I joined the parents and sons and daughters outside The Crosses who throw tins and loaves at the windows with messages tied to them to get word, even a single word, of what has happened to their loved ones.

I even walked past the Bolshoi Dom once in case Nikitin would come out and I could plead with him. Honestly, I flew Polikarpovs into the night sky and the Fascists' flak during the war and I never sweated as much as I did on that day. All for nothing. For six weeks, nothing – no rumours, no contacts. You had disappeared. So, I packed a bag and waited for my own visit from the Chekists. And then I did something very foolish.'

'Which was?'

'I began to hope.'

She sighed.

'Not for you. For myself. Began to hope I had been forgotten.'

After the war, Vassya had resented nothing more than the insult of being forgotten. She had been a Night Witch – one of a group of women pilots who flew mission after mission over German lines in ponderous biplanes, cutting their engines to conceal their presence and position. Gliding at reckless altitude, they dropped bombs from the darkness onto the heads of their enemies.

When peacetime came, they were ordered out of the cockpit and out of the air force.

But she was right. There were times when it was better to be forgotten.

'Six weeks went by,' she said. 'I began to breathe a little easier. Then a certain Captain Karpov of the Ministry for State Security calls at the communal apartment and leaves a message with one of the neighbours. Everyone had pity and fear in their eyes. Everyone wanted to say how sorry they were. No one dared. The message was that I had to go to the Bolshoi Dom.'

For a Leningrad citizen, a summons to the city's MGB headquarters was never good news.

'Captain Karpov has a desk and an office and looks at me as if he cannot wait to kill me himself. He has your file on his desk. He asks questions about us, about you: how long we have known each other, the usual. And after all of fifteen minutes of this he instructs me to go home and pack some essentials and "prepare myself for a long journey." So I prepare myself.'

Vassya reached up and ran a hand through her hair.

'Next morning I come back and Captain Karpov isn't there. I ask for him, and another MGB officer looks over from his desk and says that Captain Karpov was arrested the previous evening and would not be coming back. He advised me to go home and await further communication, with a glimmer of a smile that told me I was the luckiest citizen in the entire Union of Soviet Socialist Republics. So, I did.'

Rossel tapped his right hand on his chest.

'Remember the bird carved on the mantelpiece at Vosstaniya Street station that I used to offer up superstitious entreaties to? These days, I have it inked on my chest. But your story explains why it hasn't brought me any luck. You, Tatiana Ivanovna Vasilyeva, have used up everybody else's.'

Vassya glanced down at the table and did not reply. Once, she would have smiled at that.

Rossel wanted to shout, to accuse her of betrayal. But even in bed, after their lovemaking, they had for the most part stared at each other without speaking. With someone new, you watched what you said in case you ever had to justify it, or repudiate it, at some unknown point in the future. That was instinctive. You loved Stalin, you loved the Party, you loved the Revolution and everything it meant, and that was enough. Apart from the sex, for the most part all they had shared were caresses, kisses, looks and silence.

What does she really owe me?

Perhaps they had not felt for each other as he had thought.

Here and now, part of him despised her. Full-cheeked, full-breasted, sullen, dark, withdrawn.

Just swap places with me for two days, bitch. I'll wait here by the fire.

'I'm sensing you didn't come all this way just to study the architectural magnificence of the GULAG system,' Rossel said.

He looked for a reaction but neither her eyes nor her mouth or anything else revealed the slightest thought. Her voice was dry and matter-of-fact.

'In the air force, if you were a real survivor, you never counted your sorties,' she said. 'You'd go up, drop your bombs, hope that you had killed some Nazis and land again. And the next day the same. And the next . . . In a dogfight, every piece of you has to be focused on today. It's the part that's thinking about tomorrow that ensures you never make it back again. As I said, I had begun to hope. Hope only for myself. That was a foolish mistake. I have a good job now, a very good job – a senior engineer on the new underground system. I'd like to go back to it.'

'And Nikitin has said that will happen if I come back with you?'

Vassya nodded.

'He understands you, Revol. Like I do. He can force you to come back with him. Of course he can. But he knows that won't help him. Because you'll only play along, pretend to play detective but hold back on the insights he really needs. The little things only you notice. He needs you to volunteer. Ready and willing to help. And I am what he thinks will make you do that.'

In the camp's crude but inventive barter economy the remaining *papirosi* would have been gold, but Rossel fumbled inside his jacket with shaking fingers, desperate for a distraction. He dared not look at her any longer. He picked matches off the desk but the bloody things wouldn't keep still and he hurled the half-burned ends onto the floor, hoping they might set fire to the place.

Two deep drags later and he had composed himself. He took a last look at the fire. He would have to make up a story to explain his absence from the labour brigade. But he knew the other zeks would be more interested in a lengthy description of what it felt like to be sat next to a hearth for an hour. If they discovered that he'd sat next to a woman, an actual woman, for a few minutes, they'd go insane.

He glanced through the window again. Already twilight. It must have been more than an hour.

The door opened and Nikitin came back in.

Rossel looked up at Vassya and the major gave them both a bright smile.

'Can I go and get my supper now, Major Nikitin?' he said. 'We might have potatoes tonight. It's a real feast when we do. I find them the perfect accompaniment to the maggots that wriggle in the bread.'

Nikitin's smile vanished.

'In the morning I go to Vorkuta to investigate Grachev's escape,' said the major. 'In a day or so I will be back. When I land, you will give me your answer. If it's no, then you stay here for the next thirty years and I'll make no further attempts to help . . .'

But Rossel was already through the door, pushing past the surprised guard, and out into the cold.

He had trusted the major once before. He wouldn't make that mistake again.

9

Oblonsky's voice was so low Rossel could barely hear it. But he strained his ears – the tattooist was a normally a cheerful man and it took something serious to put him on edge.

'There's a new prisoner here, Revol. A *svodnik*, a pimp. And a bit more.'

He tapped his needle on Rossel's skin without penetrating it.

'A Leningrader. He's been saying things about you.'

Rossel stiffened.

'Not to the Thieves, not yet,' muttered Oblonsky. 'Just sounding us out down here, around the edges.'

'What kind of things?' said Rossel in an undertone. But he knew.

Oblonsky tapped away, not raising his head, concentrating on his subject's flesh.

'That you're a gundog. A militia officer.'

Tap, tap, tap.

'Is it true?'

Rossel pointed at his own chest,

'That line is not quite inked correctly. See there, where the beak of the albatross is.'

Oblonsky dabbed at Rossel's skin, wiping away blood. He scrutinised his handiwork but Rossel knew he wanted more information.

'Listen to yourself, Pasha,' Rossel said. 'Me, a gundog. Here, in Igarka. How does that make any sense? Who is this pimp, anyway?'

'On the other side of the barracks, three bunks down, top bunk. His name is Grishin. He arrived a few days ago. He's trying not to look at us now, but he is.'

Rossel took Grishin in. Not tall but broad-shouldered. A broken nose and a sly, card-sharp's face.

Oblonsky resumed digging under Rossel's skin.

'True or not, if he tells the Thieves – if he tells Kuba and Medvedev. People noticed you were gone today. The wrong sort of people. First, a helicopter arrives, and then you're pulled out of the railway brigade. You're being talked about, Comrade Albatross.'

This time Rossel couldn't help it. A dip of the head, a flutter of the shoulders. To anyone not paying much attention, it was nothing more than the usual flinching when a needle bit too close to bone.

But Oblonsky knew better.

'I hope I get to finish this stupid fucking bird, that's all I'm saying, comrade,' whispered the tattooist, 'otherwise it will be a sorry waste of all my best ash and piss.'

*

Next morning the temperature was thirty below but the sky was clear. Rossel listened to the clatter of the helicopter rising into the air as Nikitin headed towards Vorkutlag, the centre of the GULAG's regional cluster. If he could have found a way of summoning the forces of the earth and skies and bending them in a certain direction, he would have brought the machine down.

He was surprised by the strength of his longing for Nikitin's death.

*

A day hauling the barrel could grind the spirit but Rossel was glad to be clear of the camp. It got him well away from Vassya, for one thing. She must have been confined to the commandant's quarters. He bent his head into a stiff breeze as the brigade tramped out once more into a sombre morning and towards the furthest point of the line, eyes fixed on the ground. Silent. Babayan crossing himself as usual. Each man left alone with his own torment.

By afternoon, the sun's fleeting appearance was masked by thick, low cloud. The huge barrel skidded this way and that. The old priest blasphemed when his ropes got tangled round his neck but the cold took his voice away. Behind them, the Germans swore and squabbled as they tried to get iron stakes in the solid ground to break up whatever lumps and humps the human steamroller had failed to flatten.

The sun disappeared in a hurry and the prisoners fell silent when the guards saw how little progress they had made and cursed them for idle bourgeois bastards who would soon taste Soviet justice. Someone cursed them back, saying the taste of Soviet justice would be better than the taste of the pigswill they got to eat. Each of them, calculating how meagre that evening's ration would be, despaired. Every next step seemed impossible until you took it. Then, somehow, you managed to take one more.

It was a day like any other.

10

No one was watching as Rossel sucked the dregs from his plate and slipped a sharpened utensil, a knife, up his sleeve. He dragged his legs over the bench and headed for the door. Close behind the pimp Grishin.

Rossel had expected Grishin to bear left and head to the barracks but instead he walked straight on. On their right was a row of smaller huts – stores and scrap metal, workshops, fuel cans, tools and machinery that were useless until the ground thawed for a few weeks in what passed for summer. The greenhouses of 105th Kilometre stood at the other end of the camp, slumped in their constituent parts, waiting for someone to care enough to rebuild them.

Grishin walked with the stride of a man not yet reduced to the demands of corrective labour. Someone who was already playing with favours. A man like that, Rossel understood, would have fought more than one fight already during his transportation to Igarka.

He had to be wary.

But the newcomer didn't know the layout of the camp. He would not yet have appreciated the possibilities afforded by the narrow gap between the generator hut and the kiln.

Now was the time.

Rossel picked up his stride, ran through the snow to cover the few metres between them and grabbed Grishin by the collar of his jacket. He shoved him into the gap between the two buildings, blocked at the far end by the roof of the kiln which, derelict, had slumped to the ground. Grishin – straining, wriggling – wheeled his whole arm in surprise. But froze at the feel of sharp, jagged metal at his throat.

Eye to eye, the two of them lurched further out of sight in a vicious embrace.

Even if the thrum of the generator would drown out his screams, it would still have to be quick. Rossel, baring his teeth, placed his right hand over his left for the killing stroke.

Then Grishin lashed out. A big fist slammed into Rossel's stomach. The blow bent him double but one of his flailing hands caught Grishin by the collar.

As the pimp tried to force his way back out to open ground, Rossel kicked, catching his shin. Grishin lost balance and sprawled against the side of the generator hut. Rossel, despite the shooting pain in his abdomen, tackled him.

The two of them went down in the snow.

Grishin was the stronger but not nimble enough. Rossel pinned Grishin's upper arms with his knees. He raised his knife.

Grishin writhed, clutching at Rossel's clothes.

Freed a hand.

Raised a forearm to ward off the blow.

Something fluttered between the pimp's fingers. Sheets of paper, torn from Rossel's coat pocket in the struggle.

'Please, no, I beg you,' shouted Grishin, his face contorted with terror. 'I fucking beg you, I won't say anything, Gundog – I wasn't going to . . .'

Grishin struggled some more under Rossel's legs. But then went still.

Holding the knife with one hand, Rossel eased the papers from Grishin's fingers with the other. He stared down at them.

Vustin's compositional hand was immaculate. His clefs, his sharps, flats, rests, bar lines, semiquavers, the dots of his staccato and the sweep of his slurs . . .

These were his scriptures. His psalms.

More pages fluttered and flew away – some pinned against the wall of the storeroom, some vanishing into the shadows.

Rossel rose to his feet.

In the war, yes. But not now. This was different.

On the other side of this he would become somebody else.

Grishin backed away, hands raised.

'I won't let you down,' he said. 'I won't say anything. I promise – not a word. I'll bite my tongue and clench my lips together, tight as a virgin on her first fuck. I won't say anything, Gundog, I promise.'

Grishin walked towards the huts, repeating his vows. Rossel knew they were worthless.

The promise of a criminal was, after all, exactly that.

*

At night, the limits of Soviet authority were demarcated by the lights of the perimeter fence and the watchtowers. In the darkness between, inside the huts and in the shadows they cast, the Thieves and Bitches reigned.

In the gloom of his barracks, Rossel stared up at the ceiling, fighting his exhaustion, trying to stay awake, listening for the approach of Grishin or someone the pimp might have bribed – a 'louse', a lesser thief – to slit his throat. Yet the less rest he got, the worse the following day's hard labour would be.

The *Suki*, the Bitches, ruled the Eastern Barracks. They were willing to work – if it suited them. Since they were rewarded for working with rations and even weapons to use against their rivals, it often did.

The *Suki* also dominated the Northern Barracks but the few veterans of the Great Patriotic War within its walls were disinclined to be as servile as the intellectual weaklings who made up the bulk of the political prisoners. Those who had fought at Stalingrad, at Kursk, at Warsaw, at Berlin, were familiar with violence. The violence within the Northern Barracks had cost seven lives in the past two months alone.

Whether in the dark or the light, the German POWs cowered in Barracks Four, the Southern, never venturing beyond their hut except for labour duties, food and the obligatory scrub and ineffectual delousing once a fortnight. Only then moving together in numbers. Like the musk deer that roamed the taiga at night, ever watchful for the wolves. Some were battle-hardened and able to fight back. But many had only been thrown into the front line at the end of the war when the regular soldiers were either dead or wounded. Fighting was alien to them.

Rossel's bunk was in the Western Barracks. This was where the old-fashioned Thieves, the long-established crime clans, ruled the roost – purists who would rather break an arm than lift a finger for the state. In most camps they were a dwindling force. In 105th Kilometre, rallied into psychopathic fury by Kuba and Medvedev, they were as of old.

At the top were the men of ingrained criminality who lived by the sacred Thieves' Law:

Help other Thieves. Have nothing to do with the authorities. Keep your pledges to other Thieves or pay the price.

Rules and hierarchies stretching back decades. A Thief-within-the-law was to be feared and respected. Never crossed.

Night was a favourite time for the Thieves to settle individual scores with any politicals who had dared display defiance. They prowled the barrack hut, their movements covered by the snores, sobs and growling stomachs of eighty men.

Usually, Rossel did his utmost to put all thoughts of food out of his head. After a night spent dreaming of *syrniki* and *solyanka*, some inmates had been known to step across the perimeter wire in the morning. Preferring death to an almost empty plate.

Tonight, though, he indulged himself. Better to think of that than Grishin. Finally, even though his reveries were filled with *pelmeni* and *pirozhki* and other miracles, he drifted off . . .

*

A hand on his shoulder.

Three men – a *shpana*: a high-ranking Thief-within-the-law, and two henchman – were shaking him awake.

As they filed out of the door, the senior Thief clapped him on the back.

'To the casino, Comrade Albatross,' the Thief said. 'Time for *shobla yobla*.'

Time for the Rabble.

*

After midnight, the *Suki* slipped past the beams of the watchtower searchlights to the factory, while the Thieves and their acolytes sidled into the forge. As they reached it, Rossel crossed into a world of heat and noise. The *shobla yobla* was in full session.

At two tables, a couple of dozen Thieves played cards. They hardly looked up. If his past as a lieutenant in the Leningrad militia was laid bare, Rossel knew their indifference would not last long.

A twist of fear in his gut.

He began to cough again.

In the far corner of the room stood the grinning figure of Grishin.

11

In the centre of the forge, perched on a stool on top of a rickety platform, sat the Emperor of 105th Kilometre. Very short, almost a dwarf, he was a dark-skinned Dargin from the north Caucasus. His swarthiness and love of rum were the reasons he had acquired his nickname: Kuba, after the Caribbean island.

Next to him stood Medvedev, better known as the Bear. It wasn't just a play on his name. The Bear was former weightlifter from Crimea, a giant of a man, adorned from head to foot with tattoos. His bald head and face were completely covered in them, and it was almost impossible to spot even a small patch of white skin. When he grinned, which was often, he bared his pointed yellow teeth, which had been filed into fangs.

At their feet sat their pet creature. Tsar Suka. The hunched, hollowed-eyed, scar-faced German whom Walter had pointed out to Rossel. Among the Thieves, he was indulged, even adored. They were Russians, after all, and so took great pride in keeping a pedigree Aryan as their house mongrel, even one well past his prime.

Rossel was shoved to the near left-hand corner of the room, not far from the door and not close enough to the warmth of the forge. His head was still a blizzard of tiredness and dread. Try as he might, he could not rally his senses.

In this Thieves' court, Kuba and Medvedev, applauded by their imbecile court jester, were infamous for the intricate cruelty of their sentences.

At the tables other Thieves were bickering, pushing and shoving, scratching heads or licking lips as they considered where to place their stakes. The game was *shtoss*, Rossel thought – fast and furious, a magnet for sharps who could count cards or palm them.

Unless they got caught. And if they did, a knife would settle it.

Rossel spotted Misha the Axe in the melee of gamblers – laughing, threatening. '*Pora spat', polnoch, skoro zapoyut petukhi.* Time to go to bed, it's midnight, soon the cocks will be crowing,' shouted Misha in Thieves' slang. 'But I'll ring your neck like a fucking chicken, my good friends, if I find the Ace of Spades hiding in your shoe.'

The rules of *shtoss* were simple enough. The thirteen cards of a single suit were spread out in two rows. Gamblers placed their stakes – coins, buttons, lumps of wax – on whichever card they fancied. Presiding over a separate deck, cards face down, was the dealer.

The top two cards of the deck were turned over. The first was the winning card, the second was the loser. If you'd picked the winner – the matching number or face – you'd doubled your stake. If you'd picked the loser, you kissed your money goodbye.

Rossel saw Kuba whisper into Medvedev's ear and the giant nodded.

'Last round, ladies,' he said.

The clamour intensified. Those on a losing streak wagered everything they had left; those who had kept an eye on what had been discarded and what was still in the deck made fevered calculations.

One last shot!

If Grishin had told them of his past in the militia, Rossel thought, that was all he had.

*

Silence fell upon on the forge.

Kuba clambered down from the stool and stood next to Medvedev. The difference in height between them was so great they looked like a bear and her cub. But it was very clear who was in charge.

Kuba's voice dropped into a plaintive, childlike call. 'Comrade Bobkov, Comrade Bobkov . . . Come out, come out, wherever you are.'

The sweating Bobkov was a political prisoner who had been an entertainer, a comic actor who had strayed from Marxist–Leninist norms. Short and formerly plump, now no longer so, he was shoved into the centre of the room.

'Prosecutor?' demanded Kuba.

A spindly crook with a protruding jaw and a low hairline, standing not too far from Rossel, stepped forward.

'Alexeyev,' he mumbled through his gums.

'Eh? What's that, Arsewipe? Aweks . . . Ayek . . .'

As the crowd hooted and clapped at Kuba's gurning mimicry, the toothless Alexeyev stood still and impotent.

'All right, all right, calm down,' said Kuba, affecting magnanimity but delighted with his court's reaction. 'Speak, Alexeyev.'

'I saw him talking to one of the guards,' said Alexeyev, pointing to Bobkov. 'To a Chekist, not one of the army conscripts. On the far side of the parade ground, behind the coal store.'

The general merriment was instantly replaced by disappointed groans. So what? Informants in a camp were a fact of life. They were treated with contempt but mostly tolerated.

There must be something worse than . . .

'And then Vanya goes into solitary when the guards find his stash of moonshine. They gave him a good battering with their truncheons, too.'

The groans turned to growling. It gathered strength. Bobkov began to tremble.

Kuba raised a hand to quell the Thieves. Rossel watched them lean forward, impatient for the verdict.

Kuba rubbed his hair, short and rough as a ploughed field, and wrinkled his nose.

'They tell me you were a comedian, Comrade Bobkov?' said Kuba.

The defendant nodded.

Kuba raised his hands, palms upturned, and glanced around the room.

'Then make us laugh and we will let you live.'

Bobkov stood still. Lost for words. Petrified.

Medvedev flexed his muscles, which rendered the entertainer even more mute, until a couple of blows round the face brought him out of his trance.

'Right, right, make you chuckle, of course. Young Ivan is . . . Young Ivan is . . .' Bobkov found his voice. He began to gabble at high speed, '. . . in mathematics class and the teacher asks him, "If coal costs one hundred roubles a tonne and your father orders five hundred roubles worth of coal, how much does he get?" Young Ivan replies, "Three and a half tonnes," and the teacher slaps him around the ears, calls him an imbecile. "That is completely wrong!" says the teacher . . .'

Bobkov tried a cheeky grin but didn't pull it off. His voice went into punchline mode. '"I know," says young Ivan. "But my dad says that's what happens at his factory every fucking week, what are you going to do?"'

Bobkov waited for laughter. None came.

Sweat streaming down his brow, he kept digging. He started on a joke about a Soviet expedition of Egyptologists who needed Beria to extract a confession from a mummy to determine its age, but before he got halfway through Medvedev yawned and the comic faltered.

Hell, Rossel thought, is a comedian in a silent room.

Now Bobkov segued into a story about a servant at Stalin's dacha who was fooled by an older, wilier colleague into hoarding the contents of the generalissimo's daily chamber pots in a cupboard 'as if they were pure gold'. Until one day the secret stash of Stalin's shit is discovered.

A couple of titters. Sensing he might be onto a winner, Bobkov raced on.

'Unwilling to declare that Stalin's precious turds were just shit, the political officers are forced to admit that the servant is now the richest man in the Soviet Union.'

Bobkov hesitated. Then he rolled his hand into a fist and raised it upward to signify he was delivering the coup de grâce.

'But to their relief,' he added, 'they realise they are now able to declare him a bourgeois capitalist pig and have him arrested as a hoarder . . .'

Total silence.

Kuba prodded Medvedev. The giant-sized Bobkov up and hit him in the face with an axe handle. The comedian dropped to the floor.

Alexeyev, the prosecutor, bent down and slit Bobkov's throat. As the blood began to flow, Tsar Suka jumped to his feet and began to hum manically – a fragment of a piece of music that Rossel thought he recognised but couldn't quite place. The room collapsed into laughter.

At last, Bobkov was a hit.

*

'Comrade Albatross, we've always liked your stories. But tonight, I'd prefer a song.'

Kuba resumed his elevated position on his stool and pointed at Rossel. A Thief grabbed Rossel's arms and pulled his gloves and rags away.

Tsar Suka stared at Rossel's broken hands, mesmerised. He pointed at Bobkov's body. Kuba grinned, then stepped down from the stool, leaned over and ruffled Bobkov's hair. A couple of the Thieves got to their feet; but no further, uncertain how to proceed.

'His Highness, our noble Tsar, is pointing out that funny bones here has got some fingers he now doesn't need,' said

Kuba. 'A competition, then. If our friend the Albatross does well, he leaves here with some useful spare parts. But if he does badly, we cut off his *khui* and give it to Bobkov. If Hell's everything I'm hoping it's going to be, a spare prick might come in handy.'

Amid general cackling a battered, broken violin was shoved into Rossel's arms. Despite himself he stared at it. The bridge was smashed and the strings ran ragged from the pegs to the tail. Other than his own, which he had left behind in Leningrad and since the war had only ever tucked under his chin to breathe in the memory of playing, it was the first fiddle Rossel had touched in more than a decade. He felt the urge to press it to his lips.

'No, not a fiddle . . .' The instrument was snatched away by Medvedev. 'How about a guitar? Hey, ladies, imagine – Stumpy here playing the guitar!'

The Thieves roared.

Rossel glanced across at the door to the forge. No one was guarding it. If he could get close enough . . .

Another part of his brain said that if you tuned the guitar the right way, all you needed was a thumb and a finger.

What songs did the Thieves like? Rossel thought back to the snatches of Thief life that had reached his ears as a street-level policeman. Glimpses into that world from rare informants.

No, there was no inspiration there.

But then he had it. A song he'd picked up in the transit camp where he had waited for a month before his dispatch northwards.

The story of Kolka the Pickpocket. An all-time criminal favourite.

'A guitar? All right then, Kuba,' Rossel said. 'Get me a guitar and I'll play you something' – he pointed at Tsar Suka – 'even our Tsar can sing along to.'

Kuba nodded. A Thief was sent. After a minute, he returned with another battered instrument with a piece of rough rope as a sling.

It only took one of the remaining two fingers on his left hand to produce four approximate bar chords; and the scarred, broken but still-attached fingers of his right to thrash the thinning strings.

Rossel slipped his right arm through the sling and let the instrument settle under the crook of his arm. He had another ten seconds to finish working out the harmony in his head before plunging in.

In Moldavanka they're busy playing music.
With drunken revelry resounding all around . . .

*

As Rossel played, some of the Thieves beat their fists on the table to the rhythm.

Kolka the Pickpocket was (according to the song) a slave sent to work on the White Sea Canal project, who had turned from the criminal life and embraced the right-eousness of the Soviet ideal. Such was the strength of his new conviction, he had even turned his back on a rescue attempt by a clan leader – and had earned himself a death sentence in the process.

Tell them, Masha, that he don't thieve no longer.
He's cast it off, that criminal life, for labour . . .

Rossel fumbled his way from one chord to the next, striking discordant notes, slipping and sliding one-fingered along the fretboard in his quest for the right harmonies.

As he did so, he moved a little further towards the edge of the circle, closer to the door.

He's understood that now he is far stronger

He had to sing like a Thief, with grit in his throat and a snarl in his voice.

That this canal has been his bloody saviour . . .

Thanks to the simple harmony, Rossel settled into the cycle of the chords. He raised his eyes from the instrument and stared back at the front row of gaunt, hungry faces. He'd have to win them over with bravura and some erratic tuning.

He took another stride towards the far edge of the circle.

The song's final verse told of the *pakhan,* the clan boss, giving the order for Kolka the Pickpocket to be taught his lesson. There would be no happily ever after for Kolka, not even after embracing Communist virtues of corrective labour. In the Soviet Union, it was hard to escape your past. Perhaps that's why the criminals loved the song. They saw themselves in it.

Another step.

And another.

One more . . .

But then, shaking his head, Medvedev stepped in front of him and showed his sharpened yellow fangs.

Rossel retreated to the centre of the room. He hurled his knuckles into the final chord and kept his arm aloft as the sound died away.

Instead of the raucous glee that greeted renditions of the song in communal kitchens up and down the Soviet Union, in the forge of a corrective labour camp in northern Siberia it resulted in only silence. Everyone looked to Kuba for his reaction.

But it was Tsar Suka, his ageing court jester, who broke the spell.

Brutally twanging on the battered violin and humming a tune – a falling scale that eventually got too low for his voice – the German circled Rossel.

Heart pounding, understanding that his life depended on the whims of a capricious halfwit and a sadistic dwarf, Rossel was still dimly aware that the melody was prodding a memory in him.

Tsar Suka started again, lips open but yellow teeth clenched, getting louder and slower as the scale descended.

Kuba and Medvedev watched their pet Aryan with glee.

'What's that?' asked Kuba.

The German broke off, bowing his head like a mischievous child, showing his thinning hair.

Not an orthodox scale, the intervals were wrong. And there was that skip to the rhythm at the start . . .

'What's that?' repeated the head Thief, more loudly.

Where had I heard it? Yes, of course . . .

'Wagner,' said Rossel. 'A favourite of Hitler and the Nazis. His operas were based on Nordic myths. Great stories, Kuba, you would like them – heroes and dragons and dwar—'

Rossel stopped himself. Medvedev bared his teeth again.

'Dwarves?' said Kuba.

Rossel nodded.

A couple of Thieves sniggered.

Kuba stepped towards him and pulled out a big knife.

'You're a tall man, Comrade Albatross. Handsome, too. At least, you would be with a few more meals inside you. First man I ever killed looked a little like you. I was sitting next to him on a tram in Moscow. A young girl in a red beret, maybe five or six years old, was staring at us both. The little princess glanced at me, then back at the tall glass of water. Then she smiled . . .'

'That's when he knew,' said Medvedev.

Kuba nodded.

'"Mummy, look, there's a funny little man sitting over there, a dwarf" – that's what the little bitch was thinking.'

Kuba used the tip of his knife to prise out some dirt from underneath one of his fingernails. 'So, when he gets off the tram I follow the giraffe into the park. Sneak up behind him. And make him a present of a nice a ruby necklace – slit his throat.'

Rossel's eyes were fixed on the tip of the knife. But his voice sounded calm.

'In the opera,' he said, 'a dwarf called Alberich forges a ring of stolen gold that gives the bearer the power to rule the world. Gods, heroes, villains, all fight over it. But the ring is cursed and everyone who takes possession of it dies, one after the other. Until the rule of the gods ends and the time of men begins. Something from that is, I think, what our friend Tsar Suka was singing.'

Kuba's eyes moved around the room, gauging the mood of his Thieves. In the warmth and heavy smoke, the death of Bobkov, the song of Kolka the Pickpocket, talk of stolen gold, the drawing of the knife . . . all that had hypnotised them. Something caught Kuba's eye. He walked towards the forge before reaching for a small object on a worktable, testing its temperature with quick fingers before deciding it was safe to handle. He picked it up, flattened his hand and slipped the brass washer on his stubby finger.

Kuba had found a ring. Putting his knife away, he threaded his way back to his throne and sat back down.

'They say Stalin sometimes calls himself Koba, after a Georgian king. Me, I think Uncle Joe wants to give himself airs and graces. So, first he mispronounces my name. Then steals it. A ring. A crown. A state. A camp. They always belong to the man who has the balls to reach out and take them.'

Kuba smiled at Rossel. It began as sunshine but ended as ice.

'Grishin here says you used to be a gundog, a militia lieutenant. That's a real shame because I always liked both your singing and your stories.'

Rossel went for the door but was too slow. A thicket of hands, two of them Medvedev's, seized him.

Someone kicked him hard in the back of the knees, dropping him to the floor.

Kuba pointed to Grishin and threw him his knife. 'Start with his prick.'

He then gestured to the dead comedian. 'If Comrade Bobkov here doesn't want it we can feed it to one of the guard dogs.'

The pimp grinned and stepped towards Rossel.

I knew I should have killed you when I had the chance . . .

Rossel closed his eyes.

He tried to retch and could taste bile but, pressed hard into the damp boards by the Thieves, the puke only clogged up his throat. An image of his mother and father, proud Communists until the Party devoured them, rose in his mind. And another – Sofia, a woman he had once loved; her face in quiet repose, turning to him, softly smiling.

He braced his body for the first cut of the knife. Tried to blank his mind.

A pounding at the door to the forge. Then it was smashed open.

He felt the weight lift from his chest and limbs – a short-lived respite as a heavy boot then thumped into his head, followed by a knee thudding into his sternum. A semi-automatic rifle went off close to his ear, deafening him.

Then camp guards were hauling him out into the snow by his hair and the collar of his jacket.

Above the clamour, a familiar voice, berating everyone for their anti-Soviet tendencies and cursing them all for bastards, threatening to have them all slaughtered. Major Nikitin.

And another sound. That of Tsar Suka's rambling, Wagnerian leitmotif.

The camp's fool grinned and shook as he sang his song to the starry Siberian sky.

12

Rossel had been in the air only five times. Days after the Siege of Leningrad had been lifted, he twice went on out-and-back transport missions to pick up rations for the forces defending the city – a Yak-6 so rickety that the Fascists didn't even bother to shoot at it.

The only other time had been a night-time flight in a Polikarpov biplane piloted by Tatiana 'Vassya' Vasilyeva, with Nikitin as the other passenger.

The major, he remembered, had thrown up.

As the rotors of the Mi-4 began to turn, the helicopter spurted dark-grey smoke from the twin exhaust pipes that protruded like stunted horns from its nose. Rossel glanced at Nikitin, who was watching the blades spin with a look of admiration on his face.

Vassya stood to one side, well wrapped up against the cold. As the blades turned even faster, kicking up snow, she lowered her head.

Nikitin clapped him on the back.

'It's only to Salekhard, and then we're on the ground again. After that, a regular plane to Moscow, and another to Leningrad.'

Leningrad.

Just hearing the word spoken out loud made Rossel feel giddy.

The major wrenched open the large hatch at the side of the Mil Mi-4 and levered himself in. Rossel turned to bid farewell to the fences, barbed wire and watchtowers of 105th Kilometre, and to the buildings and people within. Just as he was turning back, he caught sight of the day's labour gangs setting off. Two were heading in the direction of the railway line.

He could just make out the stooped figure of Babayan at the front of the first. At this distance, the old priest looked like he was leading a line of forlorn pilgrims out towards the saints to whom he prayed. Our Lady of Kazan, Blessed Nicholas II, Alexei the Tsarevich, and the newly canonised Vustin.

All his shadows in the snow.

As the dead boy's comrades fell in behind the ghosts who'd marched before them, a fragment of Vustin's gulag hymn came to Rossel. He longed to feel a bow in his hands. Pianissimo, he thought, that's how I'd play it. Almost unbearably gently.

And slow. So slow.

*

Wearing really warm clothes – socks, boots, a thick coat and padded gloves – for the first time in months was enough to distract Rossel from the Mi-4's fumes and noise. The pilots sat above the cabin, the only people with a view. All the passengers were bathed in a harsh red light.

The one thing he could not ignore was sitting opposite him, collar up and fur hat pulled down. Rossel tried to catch Vassya's eye, to read her expression, but she would not turn towards him. Eventually he gave up. He found himself staring all around the cabin, at straps and cables, at the ladder that led up to the cockpit, at metal plates bolted to the floor – all in an effort to ignore her. But occasionally his eyes betrayed him and his stomach churned not only with the fumes but also with his emotions.

It took a while before he realised that Nikitin was trying to shout something at him. Rossel caught only snatches – how Grachev had definitely escaped with another prisoner, a much younger man. 'Probably the *myaso*,' yelled Nikitin. 'But our men closed in on him too fast. They got separated – or, more likely, Grachev left the boy to be caught, while he disappeared.'

The constant roar of the engines was giving Rossel a headache. Vassya was still a statue. Nikitin started to laugh.

'Apparently Grachev kept on boasting to the boy about some tart called Odette. How he was going back to Leningrad to find her.'

That didn't sound like Grachev, thought Rossel. A woman waiting for him by the fire? Not ever likely.

And one called Odette?

Under them the floor shuddered. Nikitin threw out an arm; grabbed Rossel's shoulder to steady himself. Vassya fought for balance. They hovered for a moment more.

Then, at last, they landed at Salekhard.

*

Onwards, further south.

The engines of the rusty Douglas, a wartime present from the Americans, were thrumming.

A hand on his shoulder. Rossel's eyes blinked open.

'I need you to look at something,' said Nikitin.

Rossel had drifted off in pitch darkness. Now the sun, its soft rays rippling along the aircraft's wing, had deepened into red.

'I thought I'd let you rest. But now, here's some homework.'

The major handed him a small piece of paper that had been written on in Roman script. A concise and deliberate hand had been at work. The paper was wide and thin – perhaps fifteen centimetres across, but only three or four in height – and curled at the edges, as if it had been rolled up and then smoothed out. Rossel took it. It was good quality, a little rough. The ink was jet black.

His hand shuddered to the rhythm of the engines and he struggled to decipher the script. As a student at the Leningrad Conservatoire he had been curious enough to translate occasional chunks of operatic libretti. But his Italian was never more than basic.

> O dolce notte, o sante
> Ore notturne e quete
> Ch'i disïosi amanti accompagnate

'I have had it translated,' said Nikitin.

He pulled out a small notebook from within his jacket.

'That means . . . "Oh gentle darkness, oh sacred and sweet nocturnal hours that attend fevered lovers . . ." Or something like that.'

94

Rossel turned it over. There was nothing on the back except a small patch where the ink had bled through.

'When we found this little ditty,' the major added, 'it had been rolled up and placed in the mouth of a man who had been tortured with pliers, had cigarette burns all over his body, and then finished off with two bullets to the brain.'

Oh gentle darkness, oh sacred and sweet nocturnal hours that attend fevered lovers . . .

As Rossel repeated the phrase out loud, he glanced across at Vassya. She was sleeping.

He sat straighter.

'After or before?'

'After or before what?'

'Did they place the paper in the victim's mouth after or before they killed them?'

Nikitin shrugged.

'After, I think. Does it matter?'

Rossel turned and stared down out of the window at thin blue line that twisted and turned through a grey patchwork of city blocks and the outlines of canals. The Neva River.

He was home.

It is a miracle.

He turned back to face the major.

'To me, no,' he said. 'To our murderer, possibly.'

'In what way?'

Rossel thought for a moment, then sat back in his seat and shrugged.

'Inserting it before killing is an act of inflicting a final humiliation upon the victim. Inserting it after – well, that's sending a message to whoever finds the body. A message to you . . .'

He stared down at the piece of paper in his hand before glancing back up at Nikitin.

'. . . a message to us.'

ACT 2
VALKYRIE

13

Nikitin's black, bug-like GAZ Pobeda drove out of the military airfield on the southern edge of Leningrad and set off to the opposite side of the city. The front and rear lights of cars, trucks and trolleybuses flared in the early morning half-light. Although it was nothing like as cold as the far north, Leningrad was a port city and the winters got under your skin. Snow lay piled up in the gutters while the wet roads gleamed and hissed under the tyres of the hesitant, irritable traffic.

At Moscow Square they turned east, rolling past Lenin striking a dramatic pose – when did he not? – and along Prospect Slavy. *Slava Gorodu-Geroyu! Glory to the Hero City!* proclaimed a huge red banner stretched above the road. Up the ramp, onto the bridge and they were over the dark waters of the Neva, the river flanked by warehouses. Beyond those, new residential buildings were being constructed for the heroes of the Hero City. But like the Siberian railway he had left behind, Leningrad's heroic status was built on bones.

The road bent north and in another twenty minutes they were already as far as the Piskaryovsky area. Nikitin turned off the main road and nosed his way down a series of side streets until he brought them to a halt in front of an impressive greystone apartment block – the kind that was usually reserved for Party officials.

The major took some keys from his coat pocket and handed them to Rossel.

'I still have the odd friend among the blue-hats,' he said.

'This belongs to a member of the MGB?' said Rossel. 'That seems unlikely.'

'Of course not. But I heard it had just become vacant and will only be reallocated in a couple of weeks. It will do for now. Be grateful, comrade – the knowledge and the keys cost me a couple of bottles of Armenian cognac.'

Rossel looked down at the keys.

'Who used to live here?' he said.

'Drugov, Ivan Vitalyevich Drugov. Big Party man. Proud Bolshevik, all the way to his bootstraps. Also the director of the Museum of the Defence of Leningrad. Or rather, former director. He was arrested days ago. Now, I suspect, he's lying on the floor of a cell in the Bolshoi Dom, face down in his own shit.'

Leningrad's citizens were proud of its status as Hero City. But not everyone in Moscow was so enamoured. Particularly Comrade Stalin.

'The place is probably riddled with microphones,' said Nikitin. 'Don't even talk in your sleep. Shout out an old girlfriend's name – Rosa, I love you – and, chances are, next morning at the factory where she works, Rosa doesn't make it in.'

'What did Comrade Drugov do?'

'Section 1A of the idiot's guide to the Penal Code – guilty of understatement.'

'Understatement?'

'The role of Stalin in the defence of Leningrad was insufficiently emphasised in his overall exhibition.'

They looked at each other. Compared to the sacrifices made by close to a million dead soldiers and civilians – not to mention those who somehow survived the starvation, disease and bombardment – Stalin's role had not been significant.

That said, he had made his presence felt. Not least through the offices of Oleg Nikitin, who before the Great Patriotic War had – in his capacity as an interrogator with the People's Commissariat for Internal Affairs, the precursor to the MGB – ended Rossel's promising career as a violinist by separating a couple of fingers from the hand to which they belonged.

Nikitin shook his head. 'Someone is always listening,' he muttered. 'Whatever it is, whether I'm here or not, don't say it. If you get sent back, even I won't be able to get you out again.'

Rossel held up his left hand.

'It's nice to hear you're thinking about my well-being, as always. Especially considering how we first met.'

*

"It was a time when only the dead smiled, happy in their peace."

A line Vustin often repeated from Anna Akhmatova, a Leningrad poet whom the boy revered, came back to Rossel. She was someone else Moscow wasn't keen on: the Party marking Akhmatova out as an artist "in whom fornication and prayer are mingled", her poetry "distant from the people." The last accusation alone was enough to condemn her. But, so far, she had not been arrested.

Vustin, he remembered, would sing fragments of the unpublished poem, trying it out in a major and then a minor key. He had heard the poet read from it in person at a secret recital in Leningrad and instantly memorised them. 'I have based an entire cycle of twenty-four preludes and fugues on her work,' he had once told Rossel as they toiled together in the Igarka snows.

At the time, Rossel had presumed this was another of his fanciful notions.

He placed a hand on the remnant of the music in his pocket. He had been wrong about that.

Dead bodies were waiting for him. Come the next morning, he and Nikitin would review the facts of the case – the method of assassination, the inscriptions on the scrolls of paper inserted into the mouths, the identities of the victims. What linked them? And what had they done to deserve such a baroque demise?

But that was tomorrow.

Rossel yawned.

He went to the window of Comrade Drugov's apartment and drew back the curtain an inch with his crooked left forefinger.

His neighbours, it turned out, were the glorious dead. He could see little besides the pinprick lights of passing vehicles, but out there, behind a screen of young trees, was the Piskaryovskoye Memorial Cemetery. Almost six hundred thousand of those who had perished in the Leningrad siege lay at peace in 180 mass pits. Half the city was there – an army of soldiers, policemen, firemen, nurses, teachers, students, grandparents, mothers, fathers, children . . . For a moment, Rossel felt as if all it might take was one blast of the horn on Judgment Day for them to march en masse towards him.

He was tired, but sleep felt a long way off. He turned around and surveyed his new home. It was, when compared to the conditions of 105th Kilometre, palatial.

But there are ghosts here, too . . .

They stared back at him from silver frames, arranged on top of a Steinway piano. Ivan Drugov and his family. In his position at the Museum of the Defence of Leningrad, Drugov was – or had been until recently – in charge of a large complex near the river, just to the east of the Field of Mars and only a short distance from Rossel's old militia station. The museum featured gas masks and ration cards, photographs of heroic resistance, burnt-out Nazi tanks. It had opened shortly after the end of the war. What would happen now that its director was in chains, he could not tell.

In the main photograph on the piano – surrounded by his wife, young son and daughters – Drugov was dark and thin-faced, with sharp, penetrating eyes. An academic who had done very well for himself, he had about him the purposeful air of a confident Soviet bureaucrat; of someone whose life had taken a turn for the better after the revolution. Now, it seemed, Fate had taken it in a different direction – the most likely destination for the Drugovs would be a cattle train like the one that had taken Rossel to Siberia, months earlier. And then a GULAG facility.

Next to the picture of the Drugov family was one of the older daughter, a girl of perhaps seventeen, holding a violin in one hand and the certificate of her graduation from

Special Music School No 5 in the other. She was pretty, with long dark hair tied in a pigtail and a serious expression – one that suggested intellectual curiosity.

Everything was just as it must have been moments before the family had heard that knock on the door. A half-completed jigsaw of the Battleship Potemkin was lying on a glass coffee table; a book, Gogol's *Dead Souls,* was open and face-down, balancing on the arm of red velvet chaise longue. A copy of *Sovetskaya Zhenshchina* magazine with a picture of the actress Lyubov Orlova on the cover lay on a leather footstool, next to a hand-crocheted white cushion that had tumbled to the floor. On a dining table in the corner of the room, cutlery and plates has been set for five people. On the stove in the kitchen was a congealing pan of *solyanka,* a sour beef stew.

Nikitin had, it seemed, brought him back from the dead only to make him captain of a ghost ship.

The main bedroom was small but comfortable, with a matching oak dresser, chair and bed. On the dresser were more framed family photographs – the Drugovs laughing and smiling on a beach in a Black Sea resort; the boy in front of the Winter Palace in a white shirt and flowing red necktie, the uniform of the Young Pioneers; and the girl, looking less serious this time, stroking a large black cat. There was something about her, in the intensity of her gaze, that reminded him of his sister, Galya. Even though she had been missing for half his life.

Where was the cat?

The thought struck him that, somewhere in the city, an MGB man was coming through the door of his own apartment holding out a new pet. A gift for his excited children.

On the bed was a dark jacket and trousers, chosen by someone who had been told Rossel was tall, and a white shirt, chosen by someone who had been told he was enormous.

Something else, too. A pistol. An ageing Nagant with a cut-down barrel that hinted at past use as an assassination weapon. He assumed it had come from Nikitin and he was disgusted. But he'd rather have it than be unarmed.

Beneath the bed was a scuffed pair of shoes. At least they fitted.

Every night for almost a year, Rossel had slept in his bunk in one camp or another, dreaming of a bed like the one that belonged to the Drugovs. He yawned again, the desire to sleep finally building, and pulled off his grubby coat. As he moved towards the bed, he caught the eye of the Drugovs in another family photograph: father in uniform, fish-scaled with medals, and everyone else in their best clothes. Staring at him, sombre, judgmental and mute.

Rossel went around the room, turning every photograph down on its face, before collapsing onto the bed.

As he closed his eyes, he thought of the message the murderer had left on the body.

'Oh gentle darkness, oh sacred and sweet nocturnal hours . . .'

Koshchei, he suspected, would probably like this place.

14

Rossel had slept until midday – hours of uninterrupted, dreamless sleep for the first time since his arrest – before Nikitin had turned up and started banging on the door. Somehow, it had only made him feel even more exhausted.

'We haven't got much time, comrade. But you look like you need feeding up. I was going to take you to a state-run canteen near the Mining University,' said Nikitin. 'I figured, after the fine dining options available in our glorious corrective labour camp system, even their shitty meat patties would taste like the caviar they serve to the Party bigwigs at the Hotel Astoria. But then I remembered this Georgian place.'

They left Nikitin's car on Kronverkskiy Prospect and walked north, leaving the Peter and Paul Fortress and the Neva River behind them.

This part of the city was just out of his old territory as a militia officer. Like most Leningraders, he had been here dozens of times. After Igarka, returning felt like putting on an old suit. Leningrad could present a face as cold and impersonal as a diamond. Its heart beat in its alleyways, around corners, in secret places you had to know about . . . But, if you knew where to go, you would be seduced. Its outside, however, was prim, respectable.

Whereas the GULAG locked you in, Leningrad shut you out. Unless you were in the know.

Down a side street or three, and Nikitin led them into a courtyard full of well-polished cars. Above an ordinary wooden door was a line of swirling characters: Georgian script, which Rossel couldn't read.

'I know Tamara, the woman who runs this place,' said Nikitin, levering open the door. 'You don't look like one of her regulars and you'll probably scare the other diners but she owes me a favour. Levon, her husband, was a stubborn man. Too stubborn. See that?' He pointed at the letters, stencilled in bright red paint above the door. '*Shemome-chama*, it says. Roughly translates as "still eating even when you're full". Which I'm confident you'll be doing shortly, Comrade Rossel.'

The staircase was rickety with a listing steel banister. Nothing hinted at the presence of a restaurant until the second floor, where there were more red Georgian letters on the wall.

'I used to eat here with my wife, sometimes the rest of the family.'

Nikitin's face coloured slightly. The major, Rossel thought, was not by nature one of life's romantic souls. But he was devoted to his wife and children.

'Even my mother would concede defeat when it came to Tamara's cooking,' said Nikitin, resuming his composure. He knocked on the door.

'During the siege, after a year of nothing in their bellies, the neighbours would paint over the sign. They couldn't stand walking past it any more. Levon would paint it back again. They'd paint over, he'd paint it back. Once they take your name, he told Tamara, there's nothing left to take.'

'A man of principle. I like your story,' said Rossel. 'In the camps, men of principle are thin on the ground.'

You'd fit in there well, you *mudak,* he thought.

'And then one day a neighbour broke in and slit his throat,' said the major.

Nikitin's grimace seemed to suggest that Levon's fate was a suitable end for any man stupid enough to stand up for a principle that was not to be found in the works of Marx, Lenin or Stalin.

The door half opened. Tamara was small and plump. She had a grin that suggested it didn't come easily but it materialised for Nikitin. Heat, steam and the aroma of spices rushed out into the cold air and made Rossel's head spin.

'I was still an MGB officer then. So, I found out who the killer was and took him into the Bolshoi Dom,' added Nikitin over his shoulder as the door opened the rest of the way and they walked into a room draped in red velvet. 'Sadly, he expired before he was able to answer all of my questions. Tamara assures me that no one has complained about the sign since.'

*

After months of guarding a mouthful of rotten fish in a bowl of warm water from the skeleton in the next bunk, Shemomechama dazzled.

In comparison to his labour camp, even a proletarian *stolovaya* would have seemed opulent. But *this* establishment – its unexpected majesty; its glittering clientele, all suits and gowns; and its tall thin glasses filled with *Sovetskoye Sham-panskoye* . . .

The restaurant, stuffed full of the elite and their syco-phants, seemed to extend for a hundred metres in every direc-tion. Rossel wasn't sure he could even see the far walls; there was too much food, too much intrigue, too much privilege in the way. He hoped he still had a flea or two, and that the fleas would transfer themselves to others present. And multiply.

Some of the other diners had had the same thought. They were staring at him, a skeleton in a new suit. And, to judge by the looks he was getting, they were contemplating having him thrown out.

But the uniform of the man guiding him to a banquette in the far corner was enough to make even Party members think twice. Military, but with something extra, something unfamiliar. That and the scarred face, boxer's shoulders and Tokarev pistol at his waist.

Tamara fussed around them, placing a bowl of flatbreads on the table and filling two glasses to the brim with Georgian wine. The table was partially hidden by a wooden screen.

'*Lobio* – a big bowl. *Kupati*, I never leave without trying your wondrous spicy *kupati*, Tamara.'

Rossel stopped listening to Nikitin's recitation of Geor-gian culinary splendours and reached for the bread, the two remaining fingers of his left hand closing on their target. He brought it to his nose, brushed it against his lips. The first bite was indescribable. Rossel tore into the remain-der, gnawing at it, turning his head away from the room in embarrassment, but unable to stop.

'You look like the monk who just left the monastery and wandered into a *bardak*,' said Nikitin, laughing.

Rossel gulped down the last morsel and recovered some semblance of self-control.

Nikitin wasn't looking. Instead, he was unscrewing the base of one of two candle-style bulbs attached to the wall. The light went out as he removed the whole fitting. Putting a finger to his lips, the major peered inside. He pulled out a small metal cylinder attached to a wire. A blade appeared in one hand and Nikitin cut the wire, pocketing the cylinder. He repeated the process with the other fitting but found nothing. He met Rossel's gaze.

'Microphones,' he said. 'Every table, broadcasting all their petty intrigues and casual misdemeanours – backhanders, fiddling the quotas, siphoning off factory stores for the black market. Affairs. Jumping the queue for a car or a fridge.'

'Are these customers particularly dumb?' asked Rossel.

'There's always one really stupid one,' said Nikitin, 'boasting to a lover or thanking a business partner for something they got *po blatu.*' *Blat* was the word for getting your hands on something through connections. A Thieves' word, it had infiltrated everyday Soviet life.

Nikitin raised his glass.

'And after half a bottle of vodka everyone else catches up.'

*

Tamara reappeared, laden with steaming dishes.

Rossel peered around the screen and stared at the nearby tables, marvelling at the casual way in which the clientele were consuming the finest caviar, the most succulent smoked fish, the most expensive champagne.

'I was a dead man walking,' said Nikitin.

Rossel looked back at the major, who was using a flat-bread to scoop up a thick, creamy sauce. There was a pause as he manoeuvered it into his jaws.

'Like I told you in the camp,' Nikitin added, still chewing, 'Beria's extra-curricular activities had not gone unnoticed. Especially the girls. Especially the younger ones.'

Rossel leaned forward and lowered his voice.

'Perhaps that's why the minister used to give them flowers afterwards. So he found it easier to live with himself.'

Nikitin shrugged. 'Fuck your mother, this stew is good.'

He dug deeper into the sauce with one hand, fumbling for a napkin with the other.

'After our last little adventure, I was the toast of the entire Politburo,' the major mumbled between mouthfuls.

'Last little adventure' was an understatement. Beria's predilection for girls, some of them very young, was only one of the minister's secrets that Rossel had investigated as a militia officer. Secrets that when uncovered might have been fatal to almost anyone else.

But Beria was indestructible. And vengeful.

'Malenkov's people loved me,' continued Nikitin. 'So did Kaganovich's. And Molotov's. But they were like women – all over me one minute, giving me the cold shoulder the next. From what I hear, right now it's civil war in the Politburo. No one knows who's in favour and who's out in the cold, whose coat is hanging on a rusty nail. Something's even brewing against Beria. Every delegation that came to see me was brandishing a new list of his possible victims. Knives are being sharpened for that bastard. Not before time.'

As Nikitin talked on, Rossel closed his eyes and inhaled. The smell of the spices, the walnut sauce, the melting cheese . . . he thought he might be delirious. The scent of the Georgian wine alone was enough to intoxicate him. Nikitin was piling into it.

'For a month I was the most important person in Minister Malenkov's entire universe. My farts smelled like roses. Then . . .'

'Then?' said Rossel, opening his eyes.

'The job I was promised as Malenkov's personal bodyguard turned out to be a job as a nightwatchman at Hospital 37 down in Kupchino. Kupchino, fuck your mother. I was a sitting duck. Have some *lobio*, it's delicious.'

The major spooned some of the bean stew into Rossel's bowl.

Rossel watched, mesmerised, as Tamara arrived with more dishes and lowered a skewer of lamb onto his plate. Trails of fat glistened amid the nut-brown meat. He had never seen peppers in so many colours, or smelled so many fragrances. There was more meat on that one skewer than a zek would get in three months in Igarka.

He grabbed the skewer.

Nikitin sucked at his fingers.

'One night a couple of Black Ravens roll up at the hospital and half a dozen blue-hats get out.' He smiled. 'Not easy to hide a handsome face like this –' he jabbed a greasy thumb at the scarred side of his face – 'I had to wrap my head in bandages, tape a drip to my arm and climb into a bed in the Burns Unit. In the morning I got out of there. But now I had no job and it was only a matter of time before they hunted me down.'

Yet another course arrived. Nikitin was right about the food, especially the *kupati*.

Wondrous . . .

But the major pushed the plates to the side of the table. 'Enough of eating,' he said. 'Let's talk about murder.'

*

Nikitin stood up and repositioned the screen so their table was almost entirely invisible to the rest of the room.

'Do you remember a film called *The Mandrake*? Before the war – thirty-seven or thirty-eight?'

Rossel nodded.

'A Boris Tarkovsky film. Everyone went to see it,' he said. Tarkovsky was a commanding actor with legions of female admirers. But a supposedly whimsical comedy a few years back had not done his reputation any favours. And, if the rumours were true, vodka had left its mark.

'You're right, everyone did,' said Nikitin. 'They say Stalin himself loved it – perhaps even more than *Volga-Volga*. And it appears that our killer, Koshchei the Immortal, is a fan, too.'

He held the chicken wing between his hands and picked the bits of skin off it with his teeth. He dropped the bones onto a plate and washed his hands in a finger bowl.

'*The Mandrake* – that's where the words in the victims' mouths are from,' the major continued, raising a glistening finger. 'Not our Soviet film. The play by Machiavelli, on which the film was based. That's why they're in Italian.'

'How did you work that out?'

'I asked a woman in the Defence Ministry who was a liaison officer with the Communists in Italy for a few months after the war. Nina recognised it straightaway.

After the film did so well, the New Moscow publishing house brought out an updated version of the play and asked Tarkovsky to write the foreword. Nina swoons over Boris. Buys everything he touches. So . . .'

'If it's no great mystery, then why do you need me?' said Rossel. 'It sounds like the Main Intelligence Department, or whatever you call yourselves . . .'

'Directorate.'

'. . . has it covered. Thanks for the dinner, but . . .'

The two men glared at each other and for a moment, angry though he was, Rossel could remember what it was like to have those dark, half-hooded eyes fixed on you.

But this isn't a cell. I'm not at your mercy now.

Nikitin picked up a napkin and gave his hands and mouth a thorough wipe. He reached into his leather case and took out a set of photographs, pushed some of the empty plates to one side and spread them on the table.

There were six in all. Two featured seated men: both with two neat shots to the right temple, though the other side would be less neat. The next pair of images were close-ups of the jaws of the deceased. Their tongues had been cut out and a rolled-up piece of paper had been inserted part-way into each man's throat. The final photographs were of the strips of paper, unfurled so the writing could be read.

'Two men with their tongues cut out. But each sings a silent song,' said Rossel.

Nikitin nodded.

'Like I told you in the labour camp, we know for certain that both were in the same platoon as Sergeant Grachev, who broke out of his camp. And listen to what the lines in Italian mean . . .'

'I don't get it,' Rossel broke in. 'You don't bring a zek back from those frozen wastelands to help you investigate. Not when you can whistle and have a dozen GRU officers at your command, plus all the Machiavelli scholars in the Soviet Union. You don't need me, so why—'

Nikitin slammed a fist down on the table hard enough to make the cutlery jump.

The major breathed in and out, calming himself.

'You remember I have a wife, a son? And a daughter, Rossel?' he said.

Rossel looked back at him.

'Well, right now I have one person, the Defence Minister, standing between *them* and the cells and interrogators of the Bolshoi Dom. General Pletnev is an impatient man. War heroes are being killed. He wants results in this case, and fast. I have Beria's hand on one shoulder and Pletnev's on the other.'

Nikitin the family man. Isn't that sweet?

'I need your help,' Nikitin said, looking like it hurt to prise the words out of his mouth. 'But I can offer you something in return. I can ensure you never have to go back to Igarka.'

There was a distraction across the restaurant, at the entrance. Unseen by them a militia officer, a youngster, followed Tamara's finger until he spotted Rossel's table and came hurrying over.

'I need an investigator: a proper one, a gundog, someone like you who won't let go,' said Nikitin. 'You did it last time, Rossel. When the only way out was to find the killer, you found the killer. I'm ex-MGB, I'm tainted within the GRU. My new brother officers are going to watch me drown and not lift a finger to help me.'

The young policeman came round the screen and threw an ungainly salute.

'Major Nikitin? I was told I would find you here.'

'Yes.'

He moved closer.

'There's been another one.'

15

All along Kamennoostrovsky Avenue was a line of banners, either flowing from the tops of the lampposts or draped down the fronts of the buildings facing the street. Stalin was the most prominent person to be shown, but he was accompanied by the senior members of his Kremlin court – Beria, Malenkov, Khrushchev, Kaganovich, Voroshilov, Bulganin, Pletnev . . . Beneath them all came the slogans and proclamations: *Leningrad's Rebirth – a new future for the children of the Hero City; All-Soviet Party Congress November 1952; Long Live Our Victorious Nation!; Long Live our Dear Stalin!*

Rossel, Nikitin and the young militia officer halted at the gardens that lay before the neoclassical pillars guarding the entrance to Lenfilm. Along with Mosfilm, it was one of the Soviet Union's major film studios.

A stray dog, sheltering from the wind that was whipping the snow into flurries all along the avenue, had pulled an old boot under a bush and was licking at it. Rossel reached into his pocket. Without Nikitin seeing, he had wrapped some *kupati* inside a napkin and taken it from the restaurant.

Rossel tossed the sausage onto the ground and the animal pounced on it. He reached down and patted its head.

'This way, Rossel,' said Nikitin.

The three men strode up to the grand portico of the studio. Nikitin took off his fur hat as he fumbled for his ID to show to the policeman guarding the door.

'Welcome to the land of make-believe,' he said to Rossel, extending an arm to allow him in.

Rossel looked over his shoulder at the parade of Party leaders and slogans. *All Hail the Triumph of Communism and the Freedom of the Peoples of the World* . . .

'I thought I was already living in it,' he said.

*

Two huge stage lights magnified the dead man's shadow against a white backdrop, creating the impression they were in the presence of a sleeping giant.

The corpse was about thirty years old, his long hair already flecked with grey. A big man, he was propped up in the middle of a medieval-style set on huge golden throne: itself a stage prop for yet another film of Ivan the Terrible's life, this time a musical.

His head lolled backwards, the mouth open. Two bullet holes were clearly visible in the right temple.

A militia captain saw Nikitin and saluted smartly. The major nodded back.

'Has the MGB been here?' he said.

'Not yet, Comrade Major.'

'Good. You did well in sending young Titov here. There will be compensation.'

'Thank you, Comrade Major. But *they* won't be long, they have . . .'

The captain stopped and swallowed. It was wiser not to comment on the activities of the MGB.

Nikitin patted him on the shoulder.

'Then we'd better get a move on.'

This was a cramped corner of the Lenfilm studios. The throne left little room for anything else. Rossel kept still, his shoulder blades pressing into what felt like a flimsy plasterboard screen, while a militia photographer bustled round the corpse. Two other policemen, looking bored, stood to one side, occasionally peering down the twisting corridor that had brought them here. He didn't recognise any of them, including the captain, and was relieved about that. On the other side of the throne, wedged between the stage lights, was smaller and older man – dressed in worker's overalls, fidgeting and looking pale: a props man, who had discovered the body.

The militia captain's thin ginger moustache did not suit him well, though it did distract a little from his bulging eyes and permanent air of anxiety. At least he was doing his job: making notes, ordering the photographer to take certain shots, going over the facts. The Lenfilm props man had found the body not long after filming and other technical work had finished for the day. He had stayed on to fix a problem they'd been having with Ivan's crown – the glue on the costume jewellery kept drying out in the lights and every time the actor moved his head an emerald or a ruby dropped off. Then he had remembered the old props for a long-forgotten film about some tsar or other and come looking for them in the maze of storerooms and mini studios.

'And encountered this jolly scene,' concluded the captain, still flipping through his notebook.

'Do we know who this is?' said Nikitin, poking the corpse with a finger. 'He's a fat bastard – must weigh a hundred kilos.'

The captain nodded. 'The props man, Comrade Petrov here, knew him. Says he has a girlfriend, a bit-part actress who is working on the film. We'll pull his work file from the administrative office but I'm sure his colleague will tell you more.'

'Akimov.' Props man Petrov found his voice. 'Vyacheslav Semyonovich Akimov. Usually an electrician and general odd-jobs man.'

Rossel took out a *papirosa* and lit it.

'Usually?' he said.

He heard Nikitin grunt in satisfaction as he asked the question. A crime scene, Rossel realised, was something the major had known he would not be able to resist.

Petrov grimaced, revealing a top row of crooked teeth. 'They gave him a part in the Ivan the Terrible musical drama. Some sort of nobleman. The actor was ill and they're on a tight schedule. A non-speaking part. All he had to do was march about in fancy clothes and mime one line of a song – and three of the words were *Ivan, Ivan, Ivan* – and then get executed by the tsar. It's that scene they do in every film and play about Ivan. The bit about Boyar Fyodorov. You know – where Ivan has Fyodorov dressed in his own robes before he has him done in. But Akimov was awful. Seventeen takes and he still hadn't done it right. The director was going crazy.'

Rossel moved closer to the corpse and looked into Akimov's wide, staring eyes.

'Looks like take eighteen isn't going too well, either,' he said.

'King for a day,' said the captain. 'Poor bastard, not even that.'

Rossel and Nikitin peered into Akimov's mouth.

'There it is,' said Nikitin. He inserted a finger into the dead man's jaw and flicked at the cheek, as if afraid the victim might wake up and bite. At the fourth or fifth attempt, he got what he was after: a tiny roll of paper with words on it.

Nikitin pocketed it.

'The tongue's intact,' said Rossel, straightening. 'Not cut out like the first two.'

'Maybe the killer ran out of time. Heard our man Petrov coming,' Nikitin said.

Rossel took a draw on his cigarette.

'Comrade Petrov,' he said, 'one more thing. Was Comrade Akimov here in the army during the Great Patriotic War?'

Petrov nodded. 'He signed up from the start, made it all the way through. He was proud of it. Wore his medals on Army and Navy Day.'

'All the way to Berlin, correct? With the 8th Guards?'

'Yes.' Petrov looked surprised. 'Did you know him?'

Rossel shook his head.

The two junior militia officers stirred into life like they knew trouble was coming.

'Comrade captain,' one said. 'It's the blue-hats.' MGB officers wore distinctive blue-trimmed caps. 'They're coming.'

Nikitin turned to Rossel.

'Time to go,' he said.

16

Nikitin swore at his car as the ignition rattled and died. On the fourth attempt the engine came to life and they set off, heading north, weaving through the streets until Nikitin turned the steering wheel to the right and came to a halt in a quiet courtyard.

'Koshchei the Immortal,' Nikitin said. 'No one sees him kill, no one sees him come or go, no one sees him dump the bodies of his victims. Leningrad talks of nothing else. Even stranger, the stories are in the papers.'

Rossel looked at him in surprise.

'The papers?'

As far as the Soviet press was concerned, crime did not exist.

'Not any more,' said Nikitin. 'But it was, and for almost a week.'

No wonder Koshchei has everybody's attention.

'As a child,' Rossel said, 'my grandmother would tell me the old tales of Koshchei. How he would hide his heart inside a box, or an egg, or a bird.' He tapped his chest. 'Back then, I sometimes used to wonder if he was hiding inside me.'

The major fumbled in his pocket and pulled out the scrap of paper.

O dolce notte, o sante
ore notturne e quete,
ch'i disïosi amanti accompagnate . . .

'Mean anything to you?'

The hand was precise, each letter the same size as the one before it.

'*O dolce notte* – Oh sweet night – and then something about peaceful nights,' said Rossel.

Nikitin grunted. 'I thought you said you knew Italian?'

'Any classically trained musician knows a little. Though perhaps not enough to translate poetic messages left in the mouths of murder victims.'

'What else can you make out?'

'I don't know – something about lovers.'

'Not much love on display for Comrade Akimov,' said Nikitin.

'What do you know about Machiavelli?' asked Rossel.

Nikitin thought for a moment.

'Not much. He wrote the handbook for plotters and schemers. *The Prince.* You won't find it in the House of Books, but there must be more than a few members of the Central Committee who like to stay up late at night thumbing its pages.'

Survival at the very top of the Party must take more cunning and more emotional energy than I will ever possess, thought Rossel.

'Have you still got the translated copies of the other two?' he asked.

Nikitin reached into his coat and pulled out two pieces of paper. Rossel took them and read:

That ignorance is bliss is widely known;
How bless'd the imbecile is with head of bone!
He thirsts not after gold, nor aches for pow'r,
Believes what he is told, hour after hour.

The second had a similar feel. Trickery, and a certain smugness.

How gentle is deception
When carried to fruition as intended.
For it defies perception.

'How did you get your hands on them?' said Rossel.

'I have kept up my contacts in the militia,' Nikitin replied. 'Every other officer is informing for someone. MGB agents took the scrolls from the first two crime scenes – but not before the militia had photographed them.'

They sat for a few moments in silence.

An educated killer. One who appeared to have a grudge against a very particular group of war veterans. And who enjoyed taunting the authorities and investigating officers with enigmatic references to deception.

'I could spend ten years going back through the records at my old militia station and I still wouldn't pull out anything that would link a man to a crime like this,' said Rossel. 'For a start, the killer's actions seem deranged – and yet his handwriting is very controlled and precise.'

Nikitin started the car again.

'I remember Tarkovsky in the film of *The Mandrake*,' he said. 'He was Callimaco. A slimy toad who kept trying to shag some old bastard's wife. I had no idea it was based on a Machiavelli play, though. Who did?'

Rossel sat back in his seat and closed his eyes.

When he opened them again Nikitin was almost smiling.

'That's what I need to see more of, Gundog,' the major said. 'You, thinking hard. Being a detective.'

17

Akimov lay pale and naked on the slab: the white flesh of his stomach and chest covered with cigarette burns and plier marks; a hole in the middle of his right thigh. Rossel looked away and reached for the tobacco inside his coat pocket. His years as a militia officer had done little to improve his appetite for the still numbing sight of a man who only yesterday had lived and breathed as he did. Now just an inert object lying on an autopsy table.

Besides, most corpses were straightforward cases. Drunken knife fights; crimes of passion; the winter cold claiming another person 'without a defined place of residence'; the loser of a dispute among the Thieves. Most of Leningrad's ordinary dead did not call for much detective work. And it was not worth asking about those who fell prey to the attentions of the MGB. Those inquiries had already been made, the conclusions already drawn.

In his previous career as an officer in the militia, only one set of victims – a quintet of dead bodies left lying in the snow – had called for a prolonged investigation. The victims had been left as bait. Rossel had taken it.

And look where it got me.

'Comrade Senior Lieutenant Rossel, I was hoping I might bump into you again. You look . . .'

Dr Maxim Bondar took a step back.

'Well, I'll be honest, only a touch better than poor Comrade Akimov over there. You need to find a wife quickly, comrade. A nice fat Ukrainian girl who will fill your stomach with *kotletki* and *borshch* and *salo*.'

Dr Bondar was balding, middle-aged, and as thin as his own scalpel. The pathologist's guttural accent gave away his Kievan origins. It was rumoured that Dr Bondar was able to put his access to reliable refrigeration to unintended but lucrative uses. One rumour in particular said that he was considered a good man to store black-market beluga for those who could get it but didn't want to take the risk of storing it on their own premises. The nickname *Ikra*, or Maksim Caviar, had stuck. He didn't seem to mind.

'Not the *salo* you get here – that's dog fat, or horse if you're lucky. You want the real stuff. And a soup cooked by a real Kievan temptress who will put in plenty of marrow bone and then ladle in the cream.'

Dr Bondar's morgue was within The Crosses: a prison Rossel had been in several times as a militia officer and once as an inmate. The latter stay, albeit brief, had not been pleasant. The regime in The Crosses was notorious.

The morgue was concrete almost from floor to ceiling, save for a few white tiles that were clinging on like barnacles. A black hose was coiled in a corner and it was wet underfoot.

Akimov had been moved here during the night from the Lenfilm studios. Now that they got to look at him in detail, they could see that his final moments had not been pleasant ones.

Rossel blew out some smoke.

'It's not currently "lieutenant", Maksim,' said Rossel. 'Comrade will have to do. But it's good to see you.'

'Not lieutenant? I don't . . .'

The pathologist stopped himself. He pursed his lips; looked from Rossel to Nikitin, and back again.

'You have been away, Comrade Rossel?' he said. 'To take a little air, perhaps, or the waters of Mineralnye Vody?'

'That's it, Maksim, exactly right. Lots and lots of bracing fresh air.'

Rossel gestured to Nikitin.

'This is Major Nikitin of the GRU. He's in charge.'

Dr Bondar gave Nikitin a look.

'In charge? Right, I see. It's just that . . .'

'Yes?' said Nikitin.

The pathologist cleared his throat. His eyes darted between his two visitors, hoping for sympathy from at least one of them.

'The MGB have also taken a strong interest in my recent cases. May I assume you are coordinating with them?'

'You can assume what you like, comrade,' barked Nikitin. 'These murders also lie within the provenance of military intelligence. Defence Minister General Pletnev strongly suspects that such depravities could only be the work of enemy agents or their Fifth Columnist allies. Isn't it obvious to you that no Soviet citizen could have committed such terrible crimes without the help of outside collaborators? And this man was a decorated veteran of the glorious Red Army. His fate shames us all.'

Dr Bondar pulled a handkerchief out of his coat pocket, blew his nose, and stood to attention.

'Obvious, yes, Comrade Major. I would be honoured to help General Pletnev in any way I can, no matter how small. As would any citizen who knows the glorious story of The Hero of the Heights. To storm those Fascist positions on the Seelow Heights when all seemed lost was an act of extraordinary bravery. Those who were there say it changed the course of history . . .'

As he walked around the body, Dr Bondar talked on – growing more and more effusive in his praise of the general. Much in the manner, Rossel thought, of a man who is talking to a couple of investigating officers while his mortuary fridges are filled with caviar.

*

Dr Bondar extended a hand towards the body as if introducing it to dinner guests. He was ten minutes into his examination.

'Fairly clearly, our man Akimov has been tortured and then killed with two pistol shots to the head. Let's assume that this is the work of a single killer. The tongue was probably cut after death.'

'Why do you say that?' asked Nikitin.

'Well, this is a big, powerful man and doing so while he was alive would not have been easy.'

'Pair of forceps,' said the major. 'Grab a hold of the bourgeois piece of shit, squeeze the cheeks and there you—'

Rossel cleared his throat.

'You must have such fond memories of the Bolshoi Dom, Comrade Major,' he said.

'To be certain,' said Dr Bondar, 'one would have to find the rest of the tongue.'

Rossel nodded. 'Please, continue.'

'Both shots to the temple were fired at point-blank range with a Mauser C96,' said the pathologist.

'A Mauser – a German pistol?' said Rossel.

'Initially, yes. But these days it is a mass-produced weapon that has been used in numerous countries for decades. The weapon could well be of foreign origin, but that does not tell one much about the citizenship of the assassin. It was fitted with a silencer. It fires 7.63 by 25 millimetre bullets – the basis for our own Tokarev 7.62 millimetre rounds, as it happens.'

'How do you know it was a Mauser? Did the militia or the MGB find anything else apart from the bullets?' said Rossel.

Dr Bondar strutted over to a metal cabinet, opened the door and pulled out a large pistol with a long barrel and a bulbous grip. With its large box magazine in front of the trigger, it looked almost too big for a holster.

'This was stuck down Comrade Akimov's trousers,' he said.

Nikitin's face darkened.

'This bastard Koshchei is taking the piss out of us,' he said.

'Leaves the gun but takes the tongue,' said Dr Bondar.

Rossel took a step towards the body. 'Do you know when this one was killed, Maksim?'

'Estimated time of death for this one I have at a little more than twenty-four hours ago. So, given that it is only eight a.m. now, that would be early in the morning yesterday. That is based on both the significant continued degree of rigor, which can indicate that the corpse was moved after death, and loss of temperature of the body.'

Dr Bondar picked up a thermometer as if to emphasise his point. Rossel didn't like to think too hard about where the pathologist had last put it.

Nikitin tapped a finger on the back of a chair with impatience.

'Listen, Comrade Caviar, we haven't got all day. Are the injuries to Akimov here the same as those on the other two? Katz and Samosud? Or not?'

The pathologist coloured a little. Then shook his head.

'Not quite. All three suffered silenced pistol shots to the head. All three were tortured with a knife. But Comrade Akimov here also had a leg wound. Caused by a round fired from long range, which entered his thigh at an angle, made a mess of the femur and ended up embedded in the kneecap, and *that* will have stung. A 7.62 by 54 millimetre round, which indicates a Mosin–Nagant 1891/30. Which, as I'm sure you know, is a sniper's rifle.'

Rossel thought back to the last time he'd seen a Mosin–Nagant fired in anger. It had been by a Russian sniper who had lain for days in a half-dried slick of mud as he picked off Wehrmacht soldiers in the retreat that marked the end of the Volkhov Front, a breakout campaign to lift the Siege of Leningrad. June 1942. A failure. A slaughter. But the sniper had done his best to even up the score.

'A sniper likes a distance kill,' said Rossel. 'This is different. Eye to eye, in their faces.'

'And why not the same wound on the others?' said Nikitin.

Rossel shrugged. 'Akimov needed slowing down?'

Nikitin began to button up his coat.

'Anything else for us, Comrade Dr Bondar?'

The pathologist shook his head and picked up a small saw.

'Not yet, Major. But give me a little time. Comrade Caviar here is never happier than when he's got his nose to the bone, so to speak – elbow-deep in pancreas, liver and kidneys.'

*

On the other side of the road, a small gathering of women huddled together, anonymous in the darkness of the early winter morning. They gazed up at the barred windows of The Crosses: hoping for a wave, a message, a sign of life from loved ones. Not far behind them, ice floes creaked and clattered their way along the Neva.

'Snipers are supposed to be our fucking heroes,' said Nikitin as he strode along the pavement, heading for the Finland Station where he had left his Pobeda.

'They would have to hide it,' said Rossel. 'The rifle, I mean. Wrap it up in something and pass it off as, I don't know, a shovel or a drill or some sort of construction tool. Something like that. A Mosin–Nagant is not a short weapon.'

Nikitin nodded.

'Lenfilm is a mix of wide open spaces and cramped rooms barely bigger than cupboards,' he said. 'A sniper could hide but not get a clear shot, or get a clear shot and be seen by everyone.'

So Akimov had been brought down somewhere else, thought Rossel. Then hidden so that he could be tortured, which he would not have endured in silence. And then moved to Lenfilm and dumped so that his body would be found.

All this in the middle of Leningrad.

No wonder there was talk of a malevolent, supernatural and above all invisible killer on the loose.

18

One of the streetlights in front of the Museum of Atheism and Religion was faulty, blinking on and off as if sending an urgent message in Morse code to some watchful deity. The huge curve of neoclassical pillars that stood in front of what had been Kazan Cathedral, before the Bolsheviks gave the building a new purpose, gaped before them like the jaws of some huge beast.

As they walked past the bronze statues of General Kutuzov and Field Marshal Barclay de Tolly – heroes of Russia's 1812 war with Napoleon – the streetlight buzzed, burned brighter and went out.

Nikitin tutted.

'Perhaps we should say a prayer, Rossel?'

'To whom?'

'Our Lady of Kazan, of course. They say General Kutuzov came here and did the same before he defeated Napoleon.'

'"The struggle against religion is the struggle for social-ism." When I was in the League of Militant Godless that was our mantra – the only prayer we knew.'

They stopped in front of the museum's huge bronze doors. A lamp above the door cast the major's scarred face with its missing eye into a thin, blue-tinged light.

'I got the call this morning to say he wanted to see us. Make sure you tell General Pletnev you were in the League, Rossel. Restoring their fortunes to the way things were before the war is his life's work.'

*

The League of Militant Godless had millions of members and thousands of offices all across the Soviet Union. Its aim was simple: to seek out and destroy religious belief in all its manifestations – Russian Orthodoxy, Islam, Judaism – and replace it with a zealous Marxist purity. Churches, mosques and synagogues had been closed; many, like the Kazan Cathedral in the centre of Leningrad, turned into anti-religious museums.

As Nikitin led Rossel into what was now the Museum of Atheism, the major glanced at his watch.

The old nave of the former cathedral was massive. More than fifty pillars lined its aisle and, high above, the dome was modelled on St Peter's in Rome. Rossel craned his neck to look even as Nikitin hurried him along. Presumably, it had been created to evoke the hope of Heaven among the faithful. Instead, he thought, its epic scale suggested a paradise that remained out of reach.

Three enormous portraits of Marx, Lenin and Stalin – a Holy Trinity of Bolshevism – now stood on the altar in place of the some of the main ikons and wall paintings. Under Marx was an inscription from his writings: 'Religion is the sigh of the oppressed creature, the heart of a heartless world, and the soul of soulless conditions.'

Like the altar, the interior of the building had been stripped of most of its religious artefacts. Only a few saints remained, painted high up on the walls; mute witnesses to the complete destruction of the ideology that had sanctified them. An empty space marked only by rusted brackets was the place where the ikon of Our Lady of Kazan, to which General Kutuzov had prayed before his ultimate victory over the French, had once looked down upon the faithful. The Holy Virgin had been unable to perform the same miracle for the Legions of the Lord in the face of the forces of Lenin.

It was a working day and most people were at an office, factory or school. Wandering among the pillars and exhibits were a few women with children in tow, two or three groups of respectful pensioners and a chattering line of about thirty children policed by two harassed teachers.

Although meant to detail the triumph of Marxism over the world's great religions, many of the exhibits seemed more suitable for a fairground peepshow. Chief among these was a waxwork displaying figures from the Spanish Inquisition – depraved nuns, sinister monks, swaggering conquistadores. Among them was the figure of Torquemada, the Grand Inquisitor, standing next to a rack upon which a hapless victim was being stretched. A hooded executioner was presenting Torquemada with a selection of torture instruments that included a two-pronged 'Heretics' Fork', which could impale the chin and breastbone simultaneously, prolonging the torment without ending the life of the blasphemer. In another glass case was a full-size effigy of Savonarola, the Florentine friar who had embarked on a campaign of religious zealotry to rid his home city of vice.

Nikitin led the way through a side door and down a dark staircase that was longer than it should have been. Overhead lighting revealed two small wooden chairs near the entrance to the sacristy: formerly the robing room for Orthodox priests, and now the headquarters of the Leningrad division of the League of Militant Godless.

'General Pletnev spends most of his time here,' said Nikitin. 'If not at the General Staff building in Palace Square, this is where you'll find him.'

*

After a few minutes' wait, a young GRU officer appeared out of nowhere, strutted towards them and pointed in the direction of the door to what had been the sacristy.

They entered a room covered in polished rosewood shelves – for storing priestly robes, or these days more likely the by-products of military bureaucracy. Among the heaped files were two pictures in simple wooden frames. One was Lenin. The other was of Marshal Zhukov, Pletnev's commanding officer during the war. It was Zhukov who had reassembled the various shattered components of the Red Army, just as the Motherland teetered on the brink of collapse, and hauled it to its feet; and it was Zhukov who had won the race to the ultimate prize: the capture of Berlin. Pletnev had been one of a select few to have accompanied Zhukov to the signing of the Instrument of Surrender at Karlshorst in May 1945. An honour beyond any medal the Kremlin could have bestowed on him.

But the Hero of the Heights had not become one of Stalin's favourite generals by dint of charm. Like Zhukov,

Pletnev had cleared minefields by sending *shtrafnye batal'ony* – punishment battalions – into them as human minesweepers. Like Zhukov, Pletnev had shelled areas of enemy territory that lay between his forces and his objectives, regardless of what stood on that territory. In the Great Patriotic War, life was the currency with which you bought victory. And only victory mattered.

The general watched as Rossel and Nikitin advanced to his desk. His head and face were shaved but not quite smooth, peppered with grey stubble. Pletnev was broadshouldered and tall but to Rossel he still seemed smaller than he had anticipated. The man's legend was such that you expected to have to look skywards to meet him in the eye.

Grey pupils peered out from thick lids. The general held out a hand.

'Sit, comrades.'

On the desk was a file with Rossel's name on it.

'Where I sit, the archimandrite once did,' General Pletnev began. 'Where you sit, his priestly acolytes used to. In this very room, they conspired to pour poison into the minds of the people. As Marx tells us, man makes religion, religion does not make man. This sacristy was the inner sanctum of the most despicable bourgeois superstition of them all. Their factories did not produce radios or dresses or other such beguiling bourgeois trinkets, but something far more sinister – hope. A fake vision of another world, which prevented the workers from transforming this one.'

Pletnev's voice was soft, even gentle – a beguiling and sonorous tenor – where Rossel had expected a commanding bass. But there was a military precision to his diction.

A practised ability to marshal an argument into something that could not be contested.

'Now, thankfully, the citizens of Leningrad understand, exactly as I do, that Heaven only exists at the end of the next Five-Year Plan.'

The general picked up Rossel's file.

'When I was told you were working with the major, I asked for your file. Are you a superstitious man, Comrade Rossel?'

Rossel's left hand moved towards his chest of its own accord. He let it drop again.

'Not especially, Comrade General,' he said.

Pletnev turned a page.

'And yet. During your time as a senior lieutenant in the militia at Station 17 on Vosstaniya Street, there was the image of a bird? A metal relief on the mantelpiece that you used to touch for luck.'

Rossel nodded, acknowledging Pletnev's eye for the kind of detail that could tell you more about a person's character than a hundred speeches, drunken or otherwise. He wondered who the informants in Station 17 had been. Not that it mattered any more.

'So far, it hasn't brought me much,' Rossel said.

Pletnev closed the file and tossed it back onto the table.

'You think not? Twice arrested by the secret services, twice interrogated in the cells of the Bolshoi Dom, yet still alive. A man who survived the sheer slaughter that was the Volkhov Front. A man who, when not at the front, lived through the Siege of Leningrad. A man to whose continued existence Comrade Beria himself objects, if only he could get hold of him. A man who until recently was an inmate in a corrective labour camp colony north of the Arctic Circle: one that might be considered remote even by the terns that breed there. Not lucky? On the contrary. Had I commanded you at Kursk, or the Seelow Heights, or at any point en route to Berlin, I would have kept you close by, comrade.'

Pletnev clasped his hands and regarded his visitors over the top of them.

'When Death unfurls a crooked finger,' he said, 'some men always find a way to give it the slip. In war, every soldier needs his fair share of that kind of luck. Religious superstition, however, I deplore. Those who long to arrive in a paradise above will never apply themselves to serious business of building one here on Earth.'

The general ran the palm of his right hand across his rough skull. Everything about him was grey – his eyes, his scalp and stubble. Almost as though, Rossel thought, all he needed to do was still himself and he could be set upon a plinth.

'Major Nikitin assures me you are just the man to find this Koshchei, our murderer. He is taking the lives of former Red Army heroes. I want that stopped, and fast. The militia are incompetent, and as for the MGB . . . they have their own agenda. The victims may not be serving soldiers but they are our heroic veterans. I am the Defence Minister and I cannot have people saying I am powerless to defend my men. So, find this Koshchei.'

The voice had changed. Now they were on the battle-field and the general was ordering his officers to attack, regardless of losses.

'I am honoured by Comrade Major Nikitin's faith in me,' said Rossel.

'You should be,' said General Pletnev. 'He has staked a great deal on your abilities.'

*

'Three corpses, all veterans. All in the same section of the army. All tortured in a similar way. All three left with a little Italian ditty stuffed into their mouths.' Nikitin smacked one hand into another as he summed up the similarities.

The major and Rossel had walked away from the Museum of Atheism and into the snowy gardens.

'Yes, but what about the differences?' said Rossel.

'Not many. Two are Jewish, one is not – at any rate, Akimov is not a Jewish name,' Nikitin replied. 'And Comrade Akimov also got a sniper bullet to the leg.'

Rossel nodded.

'Back to similarities. All the bodies were left for someone to find. In Akimov's case, however, anyone in Lenfilm would have heard him screaming. So, he was not killed there – or not tortured there, at any rate.'

'Tortured and then dragged in through a side entrance?' said Nikitin.

'He was a lump,' said Rossel. 'You'd need to be strong to carry him. In fact, a dead body that size? You'd have to be a weightlifter. And where would you hide him while you were stubbing your cigarettes out on his skin? He would likely make a little fuss.'

'In one of the buildings around Lenfilm?' Nikitin looked doubtful. 'It's a busy district.'

'Agreed. Even if you gagged him, you'd have to take the gag off if he was supposed to confess to something,' said Rossel. 'Same with Samosud, too. If he was tortured in his apartment, the whole of Sennaya Square would have known about it.'

The major swore, his curses puffing into the winter air.

'How did the killer do it?' he demanded. 'It's as if he had his own MGB basement interrogation cell. And could then make his victims walk in silence to where some idiot investigators would find them, sit down, and be slaughtered like animals.'

They reached the end of the gardens and the edge of Nevsky Prospect. No one paid them any attention. Leningrad was busy – trams trundled down the street; a troop of Young Pioneers marched by, heads held proudly in the air.

'There is one other thing,' said Nikitin. 'Common to the first two dead men, at least.'

He took a gold medallion out of his pocket and showed it to Rossel.

'I found this at Samosud's. Katz had one too. Maybe, it could all just be a squabble among Thieves?'

'They weren't Thieves,' Rossel said. 'No criminal records. No time in the camps. No tattoos.'

Rossel fell silent for a moment.

'You only tell me about this *now*?' he said.

Nikitin shrugged.

'Simple theft I can deal with. Dead men with messages in their mouths, that I need you for. I wanted you fully focused on the scrolls. Besides, I've got a lot on. As you've just seen, General Pletnev is a demanding master.'

Rossel held the major's gaze for a moment. Then took out a *papirosa* and lit it.

'Have you looked at Akimov's residence? Perhaps, he has one, too?' he said.

They had reached the major's car. Nikitin pulled open the driver's door.

'Got people doing that now, while the place is empty,' he said. 'While you and I go and talk to his girlfriend.'

19

A cowboy wearing spurs, leather chaps and a black ten-gallon hat was walking down the corridor. He was chatting to a man in buckskin, a headdress and full war paint.

As Rossel stood aside, he heard the headdress say: 'Get anywhere with little Sveta last night?'

The cowboy shook his head.

'The bitch says she is still in love with her husband. Remember him? The ice hockey goalkeeper who died in that plane crash. "I've got spurs and a ten-gallon hat, Sveta," I said, "I'm Leningrad's very own Billy the Kid!" Still nothing, fuck your mother . . . '

As Rossel and Nikitin turned a corner, a red light above a huge, soundproofed door blinked off. The major pulled at the handle.

Extras in the costumes of the Wild West mingled with the less glamorously dressed members of the Soviet movie industry. Everyone seemed to be shouting. On either side of a raised platform were two huge cameras, with a third in a gantry above and to the back. The set was elaborate and detailed and for the most part almost entirely taken up by the giant prow, paddle and black funnel of a Mississippi steamboat christened the *Red Star*.

It was a surreal sight. St Louis on the Neva.

They had come back to Lenfilm to talk to Akimov's girlfriend. Rossel looked around the room.

'See her?'

Nikitin shook his head.

The set was for a brand-new musical called *Red Dawn-Red Dusk*. Igor Volodin, a wily Lenfilm producer, had decided to combine Stalin's favourite film *Volga-Volga* – the story of a group of amateur actors travelling on a steamboat up the Volga – and the Great Leader's well-known love of Westerns. Looking around at the chaos, Rossel suspected that Volodin was either going to end up as a Hero of the Soviet Union or running a film society in a Siberian corrective labour camp. Depending on how the film turned out.

The frenzy intensified as crew and actors prepared for the next shot. Electricians adjusted cables, make-up girls powdered the noses of extras, the director and his camera-men gathered in a huddle.

Just then, a second stage door opened on the other side of the set and a group of six people came into the room. The new arrivals worked the miracle of sudden and total silence, punctuated by raucous laughter coming from a man at the centre of the group of interlopers. A short, stocky bald man in his mid-fifties was regaling his hangers-on with a story. They hung on his every word.

Rossel caught Nikitin's eye. 'Khrushchev,' the major mouthed at him from across the set.

But Rossel had already recognised him. It was an easy face to remember: like a gargoyle on the side of a medieval cathedral. A study in mischief and pugnacity. As if Khrushchev was so surprised by the power that a miner's son from Kalinovka, like him, had been able to acquire that he was incapable of hiding his glee.

Khrushchev finished his story, something about the terrible fate of a corrupt director of a collective farm in the southern Urals. The acolytes slapped each other on the back to demonstrate how amused they were. This soon became a competition. Khrushchev grinned. Then he spotted something – a broom resting against a wall. He grabbed it and made a couple of vigorous sweeping movements.

'Comrade Stalin calls me the Janitor – did you know that, Orlov?'

Orlov, a thin man with a grey moustache who was still wiping away tears of laughter, shook his head.

'Yes, the Janitor, that's me. Either because I am a dead ringer for Sergei Antimonov who plays Okhapkin, the janitor in *Volga-Volga*. Or . . .' He gave an exaggerated stage wink, 'because I'm the man he brings in to do the really shit jobs no one else wants to do . . .'

As one, the group collapsed in dutiful laughter. But Khrushchev's attention was already wandering. He stopped and surveyed the set, as if noticing it for the first time. Actors, extras and crew – all uncertain as to how to behave in the presence of such a Kremlin heavyweight – remained silent. Khrushchev pursed his lips. His cheeks coloured slightly.

'The Janitor,' he shouted, 'get it? The Janitor . . .'

After an awkward moment, the director, Boris Bamet, broke into a strained chuckle and everyone else except Rossel followed suit.

Khrushchev put a finger to his lips. The laughter stopped. Then he nodded at Bamet, who picked up a loudhailer and shouted for everyone to take their positions. Cast and crew shuffled into place, the overhead lights dimmed. Then Bamet raised his voice again.

'Action!'

Boris Tarkovsky stepped on to the prow of the *Red Star* and began to sing.

The actor was no longer the dashing, handsome 'Comrade Callimaco' who had won the hearts of Soviet womanhood in *The Mandrake*. The midriff was too flabby, the hairline in retreat. But he still had the firm jaw, strong mouth and smouldering eyes that had not only beguiled his audiences but brought comparisons to Yakov Dzhugashvili, Stalin's handsome eldest son.

Which had once been considered a highly useful characteristic for an actor planning his career. Before the war, at least. No one spoke of Yakov now.

Tarkovsky struck a pose that suggested stage lights and cameras had only been invented so that they might one day discover him.

But the microphones were less accommodating.

> 'Run, river, run, run to the sea, the People's cause runs with you, just as it runs through me . . . *Krasnaya Zvezda! Krasnaya Zvezda! Red Star! Red Star!*'

'"Tarkovsky sings!"' whispered Nikitin. 'I don't think they'll be putting that on the posters.'

*

Take four.

Tarkovsky was still managing to belt out his section of the musical number, but his singing had not improved.

'He's putting everything into it, though, eh?' said Nikitin.

Rossel nodded.

You couldn't fault the actor for effort. Just for tuning, rhythm and any semblance of control. With neither any training as a singer nor any musical talent, Tarkovsky kept missing his cues or losing his place or breaking down in mid-song, clutching at his throat and making frantic signals for more water.

Another break.

Rossel moved closer to the set. Tarkovsky was dressed in a blue uniform and wore a blue peaked cap with gold braid trimmings: a Soviet costume-designer's interpretation of a Mississippi steamboat pilot's uniform. A make-up girl dabbed at his brow, doing her best to stem the sweat dribbling down his cheeks, and fixed his stage-paint.

This close, under the harsh lights, Tarkovsky looked far older than when Rossel had last seen him on screen. He retained the Puckish grin and traces of the outrageous good looks of his youth but his jowls had moved in the opposite direction to his hairline, and some of the gold buttons on his blue pilot's waistcoat looked like they were about to pop.

These days, Rossel thought, he's got more of Stalin about him than the unfortunate Yakov.

'Positions, please,' shouted the director.

A spotty youth with a clapperboard gave the signal for take five.

'Action!'

'Run, river, run, run to the sea, the People's cause
runs with you, just as it runs through me . . .
*Krasnaya Zvezda! Krasnaya Zvezda! Red Star!
Red Star!*'

This time Tarkovsky was better. He kept close enough
to the rhythm for the sound editors to have something to
work with and even hit the top note on 'Red Star! Red
Star!' with some panache.

Bamet was windmilling his arms in the air to give his
star encouragement. But just as the second verse began,
Tarkovsky began to lose control, his voice wobbling and
wheezing like a broken locomotive.

Khrushchev, fingers in his ears and a fresh grin plastered
onto his face, grabbed his broom again and made another
series of exaggerated sweeping motions. His lackeys were
once again unable to contain themselves. Warming to his
role, Khrushchev began dancing beneath the prow of the
Red Star. Everyone was grinning.

'Cut!'

The actors and crew all looked at Tarkovsky. Even beneath
the stage paint it was easy to see the actor's face had reddened.

A puffing Khrushchev bowed to the director, the cameras and to no one in particular.

'I just couldn't stand it any more,' he said.

Tarkovsky recovered himself. He smoothed his uniform,
cleared his throat and took several deep breaths through
his angular nose.

'Your criticism is well justified, Comrade Khrushchev.
I am in your debt. Perhaps if we take a few moments break
I can prepare for an improved performance?'

Khrushchev waved the broom in Tarkovsky's direction as a gesture of mock thanks, took another bow and announced that time and political duties meant he would not be able to stay for it. The actor managed to look disappointed – a piece of acting that Rossel could only admire.

As Khrushchev's delegation departed, Tarkovsky placed a towel over his head and headed for his dressing room.

20

After twenty minutes of asking around, they found Akimov's girlfriend in the canteen.

She seemed to know little, and every time Rossel pressed her she began to sob. She had known about Akimov's military service – he was proud of it – but he had never given any indication that his war record nor any other aspect of his past might either bring surprise benefits or cause his unexpected demise.

She was upset, shocked and disbelieving, but said little to give the impression that Akimov had been the love of her life. 'He was not the sort to hit you, like others. Lived up at Udel'naya, you know, right up in the northern district. We met at a dance and he was lovely, treated me well. He fixed our apartment fusebox and said he knew about that stuff, so when I heard we needed an electrician I brought him in and he got the job. Am I in trouble?'

They had not lived together and had sometimes not seen each other for days. She lived in a communal apartment and therefore had a dozen people who could back up her claim to have been at home ever since leaving work for the day.

They let her go. Nikitin left, saying he had business to attend to. Rossel spent the morning pursuing other standard lines of inquiry. He talked to the film's director and the props man who had discovered Akimov's body but uncovered nothing new. Then he spoke to a lighting technician, who had told the militia he had heard something coming from the direction of the *Ivan the Terrible* set after the sound stage had been switched off for the night. But the man now insisted it had been nothing more than a rat that had found its way into a basket full of costume jewellery.

His head full of unanswered questions, Rossel retraced his steps towards the entrance to the studios.

*

Away from the main sound stage, Lenfilm was a maze of corridors filled with cramped offices – the homes of writers, script editors, make-up girls, minor producers and countless bureaucrats. No one paid Rossel any attention. A runner carrying a tray of herring and a bottle of vodka pushed past him and a few metres further on opened a door.

Beyond that door was darkness, a flickering light and an ill-tempered voice. On a leather chair, surrounded by a dozen empty seats and watching a black-and-white film, sat Boris Tarkovsky.

Without announcing himself, Rossel entered the screening room and closed the door behind him. He took his place four or five seats away; on the same row, roughly in the middle of the room. Engrossed in the film, Tarkovsky did not turn to look at the intruder, not even when Rossel lit up.

The film was one he had seen before. *The Mandrake.* It was Tarkovsky's breakthrough, a pre-war sensation. As far as Rossel could remember, the story was an elaborate farce in which Callimaco, Tarkovsky's role, sought to bed another man's wife.

On the screen was a scene in a convent garden between Callimaco and a corrupt priest, Friar Timoteo.

'But why would the Lord make women so delightful if he did not want man to sin? Why create such delicious pleasures and wish that only foul Beelzebub be allowed to partake of them?' said the friar.

As Callimaco replied, so – seemingly entranced – did Tarkovsky, mouthing the same words.

'But what if God and the Devil are conspirators, noble Friar? What if they both dance together to music no one has – as yet – understood?'

Rossel blew out a ring of smoke that drifted across the screen. He glanced down at the small zinc table that extended from one of the chairs. Tarkovsky, he could see, was onto his third plate of herring and his second bottle of vodka.

At last the actor turned towards him, his face registering no surprise, as if he had all along known he had company. His face was patterned with blotches. Traces of white make-up still adorned his eyes and his cheeks still bore the tracks of his recent humiliation.

'Tell that shit Bamet I'm not coming back,' he said. 'Tell him, Comrade Callimaco says he has quit. Tell him to get some other idiot to bellow barnyard tunes from the prow of that stupid fucking steamboat.'

Rossel offered a cigarette. Tarkovsky took it, saw it was a simple *papirosa*, grimaced and lit it anyway.

'I'm not from the studio, Comrade Tarkovsky,' said Rossel.

The actor appeared not to have heard him. He took another glass of vodka from the tray and downed it in one. Then he stabbed at a small piece of herring before hurling the glass against a picture of Sergei Lukyanov, star of *Cossacks of the Kuban*, which was hanging on the wall. Both the glass and the picture frame shattered.

'They're giving Lukyanov a People's Artist Award. Can you believe that? I only found out this morning. He's already got the Stalin Prize, second class. The planks of wood they used to build the *Red Star* have more emotional range than that prick. And yet here I am. Boris Tarkovsky! Singing "Red Star! Red Star!" off the back of a fucking paddle steamer. And that's supposed to be Soviet culture these days . . .'

Drunks, Rossel thought, required a little patience. But getting them to talk was never a problem.

Tarkovsky grabbed the vodka bottle by the neck and took a mouthful. He swallowed hard and shut his eyes.

'You're not from Bamet?'

Rossel shook his head.

'Then who?'

'I'm an investigator.'

It took several seconds for the words to register. The actor straightened in his seat. For a moment, Rossel expected him to try and make amends, to apologise in abject terms for his many indiscretions. But he was wrong.

'I have friends,' Tarkovsky said. His voice was slurred, his tone defiant rather than aggressive.

'Everybody does.'

'In the Party.'

The two men stared at each other. Before the war, the newsreels had covered the deeds of Yakov Dzhugashvili extensively. But, afterwards, the face of Stalin's elder son was one you were supposed to forget. Something impossible to do once you found yourself face to face with Boris Tarkovsky. Yakov had always worn the uniform of a courageous defender of the Motherland, but could never rid himself of a mournful gaze that hinted at something else lurking beneath his heroic façade.

But with middle-age had come shadows of Yakov's father – shadows that lengthened with Tarkovsky's suspicious look. As he stared at the actor, the hint of a shiver ran through Rossel.

'I would expect nothing else, comrade.' he said. 'You are aware of the recent murder that took place here at Lenfilm?'

'How could I not be?'

'Were you filming that day?'

Tarkovsky did not reply.

On the screen, Harlequins and Pierrots whirled around the dance floor at a masked ball. Callimaco threw passionate looks across the room at the object of his desire: the pure and beautiful Lucrezia.

'Let me assure you that I have no wish to threaten you and nothing to threaten you with,' Rossel said. On instinct, he added: 'Comrade Callimaco.'

Tarkovsky sat forward.

'No one calls me that any more. *Pravda* did. *Izvestia*, too. The name, I am told, was talked of with approval in the Kremlin. But . . .'

'But?'

'Then that idiot Yakov got himself killed in the war.'

It had been assumed that Tarkovsky's spectacular rise, the reason he had got the leading role in *The Mandrake* in the first place, was because of his resemblance to Yakov Dzhugashvili. Doors had been flung open, merely because directors and producers believed that by promoting Tarkovsky they would, by means of a miraculous political osmosis, gain favour with Stalin himself. A process that became even more pronounced once it became known that Stalin loved *The Mandrake* and had conferred on its star the title of 'Comrade Callimaco'.

Then Stalin's elder son had been captured by the Germans only days after the Nazi invasion. Captured, not killed, and thus disgraced.

Two years later, he died in Sachsenhausen concentration camp. His name was forgotten. His fate had tainted Tarkovsky's career.

Tarkovsky reached for the bottle again. Rossel stretched out his hand and, taking the actor by the wrist, stopped him.

'The murder, Comrade Tarkovsky, of your colleague Akimov. Were you here? Did you see anything?'

The actor glanced down at his wrist.

'I am on the Party committee here, comrade,' he said. 'I took my examinations in Dialectical and Historical Materialism two weeks ago. And passed them.'

You can't touch me.

Rossel let it go.

'The Party committee is lucky to have you, Comrade Tarkovsky. Your vigilance is an example to us all,' he said.

He stood, getting in the way of the projector and casting his silhouette over the screen.

The actor looked up.

'I wasn't on that day,' he said. 'There had been a problem with the set. They couldn't get that stupid funnel to stand up straight. They brought in carpenters to take a look. I spent the morning with an old friend before visiting the stage orphanage at Kirovsk. I used to be a pupil there. They ask me back from time to time, *pour*, with apologies to Voltaire, *encourager les orphelins*.'

Rossel stopped at the door.

'I went to a state orphanage, too,' he said. 'In Kostroma. Along with my sister. It had high walls and small windows. We didn't like it much.'

They had been sent there after the arrest of his mother and father. As children of 'enemies of the people', he and Galya were themselves suspect.

Tarkovsky had relocated the vodka.

'Then you will understand better than most how far I had to climb to become Comrade Callimaco.' He poured and raised his glass. 'Long live the world revolution.'

He turned back to the screen. Callimaco, who was on the point of bedding the innocent Lucrezia, was removing his black mask.

'Why, child, from our very selves we hide – even from his own mirror the wise man remains a mystery . . .'

As before, Tarkovsky repeated the words exactly as Callimaco said them.

21

Rossel had hoped to slip away, to take time to reacquaint himself with Leningrad. To get some of its grime under his fingernails, put some miles under his feet.

But Nikitin was waiting for him at the studio exit.

'We must report to the general,' he said.

'Why? We've only just seen him and we haven't got anything to tell him.'

Nikitin smiled.

'Yes we do. Take a look at this.'

*

General Pletnev adjusted the pictures of Lenin and Marshal Zhukov behind him so they were straight. He sat back down at his desk in Kazan's old sacristy and fixed Rossel and Nikitin with a stare.

'I have many things to occupy my mind. As a native of Leningrad I have been given the honour of organising the city's Party assembly in a few weeks' time.'

The assembly was the main preparatory meeting before the following year's All-Union Conference. A very important event.

'Stalin himself will attend,' said the general. 'So, be brief. What have you got?'

Something interesting, Comrade General. Let's see how you react.

'The third victim's name was Akimov,' said Rossel. 'He was also a veteran of the 8th Guards Corps during the war. I instructed the militia to go through the war records of all three of the deceased, since all three were in possession of one of these.'

He took a large gold medallion about ten centimetres in diameter from his pocket and dropped it onto the table.

The militia had found it in Akimov's room, under a floorboard. In normal circumstances they might not have taken such a thorough look, but Nikitin had told them what to search for, and they had found it.

General Pletnev stared at it. On the face of the medallion an eagle, its wings spread, carried a swastika in its talons. Around the rim in capital letters was engraved a single word: Neubrandenburg.

The general picked it up.

'That is the Luftwaffe insignia,' he said. 'Loot, perhaps? Something these soldiers stole while rifling through a bomber pilot's attic in Germany?'

Rossel watched him.

'Possibly.'

'And the others. You say they had medallions like this, too?'

'Correct,' said Rossel. 'The first man to die – the welder, Katz – tried to sell his to a Jew who has a stall out near Malaya Okhta, according to the militia. The next day Katz failed to turn up to work, and the day after. He was a serial absentee but his boss was annoyed enough to send round a comrade to drag him out of bed to the factory. That comrade instead found him dead – dead in an intriguing fashion. The militia arrived and found the gold medallion on the floor.'

'Comrade Katz miscalculated,' said Nikitin. 'The Jew may have had links to the Thieves but he was also an MGB informant. He knew a swastika spelled trouble. So, he told the MGB blue-hats.'

'Wait a moment,' said Pletnev. 'The killer and the MGB knew about the existence of a large gold medallion in the possession of this welder, and yet it was left for the militia to recover?'

'It is interesting,' said Rossel, who had been wrestling with the same problem without coming up with an explanation. A killer who left Italian verses inserted in the throats of his victims, but who ignored a lump of gold in each corpse's possession.

Pletnev ran a finger over the lettering around the rim of the medallion.

'And what, or where, is Neubrandenburg?' he asked.

'An eastern German city,' said Nikitin. 'Our boys took it at the end of the war. Pretty much burnt it to the ground.'

The general grunted. 'I do not remember it,' he said. 'And yet . . .'

He stood, placing his fingers on his brow as if trying hard to remember something. Rossel looked at Pletnev for every twitch of every facial muscle. The general exuded power, absolute confidence in his ability to handle every situation.

A moment later, Pletnev straightened his shoulders and nodded. He marched over to a row of filing cabinets and without hesitating pulled open a drawer and removed a file.

He tossed it on the desk.

'Open it,' he said.

Rossel did. Inside was a photograph of what looked like an enormous, low-ceilinged cellar. Two men in US army uniforms, clutching notebooks, were surveying row after row of crates and sacks.

'That is the bottom of a mineshaft in a village called Merkers in Germany. Summer of 1945,' said the general. 'In those crates and bags, and in many others, was more than one hundred tonnes of gold. Bars, rings, jewellery, gold fillings. And thick wads of Reichsmarks. Our intelligence concluded that there were other such caches. Places the Fascists had hidden their spoils of war with aim of returning to it one day.'

Rossel pointed to the medallion.

'You'd need a lot of these to add up to one hundred tonnes,' he said.

Pletnev nodded. 'You would. But there are stories.'

'Stories?' said Nikitin.

'Stories of buried treasure. Hidden under Himmler's *schloss*. Or was it Göring's? Or in the cellar of the mansion of a murdered Jewish banker? Or in a bunker near the hunting lodge of a high-ranking SS officer? And so on.'

Rossel looked at the only other sheet in the file. It was a typed inventory, in English, of the contents of the mineshaft at Merkers. The list continued over the page.

The general laced his fingers behind his back and set off pacing at the slow march.

'At the time Beria said it was all nonsense, but then it emerged he'd been questioning high-ranking Fascist prisoners about it. The MGB are rumoured to have interrogated a few suspects down the years. None of them confessed to anything – well, anything useful.'

Rossel closed the file. He was beginning to see what the general was driving at.

'But now this turns up,' he said.

'And now this turns up,' agreed Pletnev. 'And there was one other story I haven't mentioned. A rumour of a small band of Red Army soldiers who went astray for a few days at the end of the war. Who discovered the location of one of the troves and took the secret with them back to Russia. Hoping one day to return. A rumour, I might add, that has been remarkably slow to die.'

Pletnev resumed his seat and looked straight at Rossel.

'Hidden Nazi gold. Seven years of fruitless searching and then this. Imagine the reaction when the MGB found out.'

'They must have got themselves a little overexcited,' said Nikitin.

The general leaned back.

'If these murders are linked to this wartime treasure hunt, whatever the truth of the matter, I will need you to redouble your efforts,' he said. 'This hoard would be of considerable interest to the Soviet state. We need currency and gold. Every single day, the Americans outspend us.'

So it's not just Beria who has gold fever . . .

'You are aware of the ritual aspect of the three murders, Comrade General?' asked Rossel. 'The torture, the double shot to the head . . .'

'Yes.'

'And the scrolls in the throat?'

Pletnev raised his eyebrows.

'Scrolls?' he said.

'Pieces of paper on which someone has written lines from a play by Machiavelli, *The Mandrake*, and placed in the victims' throats.'

The general ran his hand over the downy stubble that pockmarked his pate. For a moment, he seemed lost in thought.

'"Confuse the enemy, disguise your true intentions, make them concentrate their forces in the wrong place",' he said eventually. 'This must be a diversionary tactic, a ruse. Military commanders use them constantly. I suggest that you do not fall for it.'

Pletnev nodded at them as if to say their time was up. Rossel got to his feet, picked up the medallion and pocketed it.

He and Nikitin headed for the door.

*

As Rossel and Nikitin walked back to the major's car, trams, buses and cars were fighting their way through the icy wind that blew down Nevsky Prospect.

'If you wanted to get the secret location of a hoard of gold out of someone, why do all that – the lyrics, the tongue, the mutilation?' Rossel said. 'Surely you would just put a gun to Katz's head and ask him in a very direct manner – "Where did you get this bar of gold from, Comrade Katz?" Or Comrade Samosud, Comrade whoever . . .

163

I mean it wouldn't be any more complicated than that, would it?'

Nikitin shrugged.

'Unless all that is just to throw us off the trail – make it seem as though we are looking for a Koshchei, a phantom, a maniac. When in fact it's just a treasure hunter.'

Rossel took a *papirosa* from his pocket and lit it.

A tram passed by on the other side of the street. A pretty girl dressed in the uniform of an Oktyabrina, the youth group for girls dedicated to Lenin, had her face pressed against a partially misted window. She half-smiled at Rossel just as the tram disappeared around a corner.

Rossel blew a stream of smoke after the tram.

'But is the gold the real treasure?'

22

The temperature was falling again; the kind of cold that made factory smoke and exhaust fumes hang in the evening air. The car stopped a street away from the Drugovs' former home.

Rossel made a move to get out. Then sat back down again.

'Has she joined the Party?' he said.

Nikitin looked straight ahead.

'Has who joined the Party?'

'Vassya.'

Just saying her name, the soft familiarity of his own intonation, made him realise how much he had missed her. In Igarka, the memory of their time together had been something to block out. Their brief happiness too painful to recall. A way to weaken his spirit.

But ever since Nikitin had brought her to the camp, he couldn't stop thinking about her.

The major still didn't look at him.

'Tatiana Vasilyeva is doing well,' said Nikitin. 'One of the senior engineers on the new metropolitan railway system. She has a new apartment in the centre of town. A telephone. A prosperous Soviet life in the proletarian paradise we are all building together. A would-be Party member.

A romantic dalliance with someone like you would only set her career back.'

Everyone who wanted to make progress in Soviet society had to join the Party. Rossel reflected on how little he really knew about Vassya's life. Had she been in the Komsomol? Had she done well in her Marxism–Leninism studies? Had she spent summers picking fruit on a collective farm?

All they had ever really spoken about was the war. They were both loners, both survivors.

That instinct, he thought – survival – was why she would try and join the Party. But she would have needed a helping hand.

'A boyfriend?'

'Why don't you ask her yourself, investigator?'

The major pulled out a piece of paper from the inside breast pocket of his coat and held it up. On the paper was written an address in a very respectable part of town, and a number.

'She didn't look too delighted to see me last time, Major.'

Nikitin sniffed.

'I don't understand my wife. But she understands me. As far as wisdom goes that's the only real gold-plated insight I have ever possessed, comrade. And yet, when I asked her out the first time and she said no, I was wise enough to ask her again.'

Rossel took the paper, got out of the car and breathed in a lungful of cold air.

Leningrad's air, Leningrad's lamplight, Leningrad's snow. Leningrad's stillness . . .

In that, for him at least, there had always been wisdom.

*

The manuscript for Vustin's prelude and fugue thirteen in E minor was complete. Rossel sat at Ivan Drugov's grand piano, on which he had placed a notepad and pencil and a brass ashtray that was now full. But he neither smoked nor wrote a word as he picked out the winding, interlocking themes of the fugue as best he could with his right hand and the two fingers of his left.

The fugue had a title, which was unusual. Neither Bach nor Shostakovich, in his most recent masterpiece, had given names to any of the component parts of their complete cycles of twenty-four preludes and fugues. But Vustin had. 'The Song of Lost Souls.'

The Steinway was a shade out of tune but its tone was warm and beguiling. An arpeggio, followed by ornamentation around the fifth note, teetering there like a gymnast at the top of her routine on the double bars before falling to the minor third . . . then the preparation for modulating to the dominant. The second statement of the theme, this time in the tenor register.

Without the requisite fingers, he had to hum the bass notes as best he could. The process took him back to the torturous score-reading exercises he had to do as student at the Leningrad Conservatoire. His first love had always been the violin. But he had been an enthusiastic if indifferent pianist. Nevertheless, he managed to get to the end of Vustin's fugue. It was slow, ingeniously constructed, exquisite. Six pages of eerie melancholy – Igarka and its desolate colonies at night, captured in sound.

The gulag's collective sigh . . .

He listened to the final notes fade away.

Then turned his attention back to the notepad.

The three bodies of Katz, Samosud and Akimov: each with a Machiavellian lyric placed in the throat their tongues cut out, the two executional shots to the right temple.

The killer seemed to be accusing Katz of gullibility. *'That ignorance is bliss is widely known . . .'*

Samosud, the opposite. *'How gentle is deception . . .'*

Nikitin had put his Italian translator to work on an accurate Russian rendition of the Akimov scroll.

'Oh gentle darkness, oh holy and sweet nocturnal hours / That soothe the burning pain of love's desires . . .'

Was it a love letter? Dispatching Akimov with such brutality was an odd way to show infatuation. Unless it was a revenge attack on an unfaithful lover.

Or a way of denying the victim to a rival?

But it still didn't make sense. The three sentiments – naivety, deception, love – were all in *The Mandrake,* but the film had been released before the war and hardly seemed relevant to three murders committed several years later.

The victims' shared past, their time in the 8th Guards, still seemed the most salient connection. And the one of which Nikitin was most convinced.

A killer who was invisible, yet eager to leave messages to those investigating the crimes. And who seemed indifferent to the possessions of his victims, even if they included a large, solid-gold medallion.

Rossel stood up and sighed. He stepped away from the piano and sat down in what, he assumed, had been Ivan Drugov's favourite armchair. It was squat, functional and covered in brown leather – a mass-produced item out of keeping with some of the luxury imported items that a member of the Party could get their hands on. But it had an antimacassar with a deep discolouration, which also gave off a whiff of hair oil, suggesting it been well used.

The stain was, he thought, now all that probably remained of the unfortunate Drugov.

He stared at the black telephone, on a small table, just out of reach.

In the silence, he could feel the eyes of the teenage Drugova on him, staring out from one of the picture frames with her fiddle on her shoulder.

He looked down at the paper Nikitin had given him and lifted the receiver. He half-expected the line to have been cut off, but the tone told him otherwise.

Rossel dialled Vassya's number. Waited. Nothing. As he let the receiver drop onto the cradle he thought he heard one of the tones cut short and the sound of someone's voice. But it was too late.

Silence.

His hand moved towards the phone again.

It rang.

For a split second, he had the surreal feeling one of the Drugovs might be on the other end of the line – the daughter ringing to ask for Vustin's number.

He picked up the phone.

It was Nikitin.

'He's killed someone else,' the major said.

23

Lieutenant Yelchin – a lifelong militiaman in his fifties, with mousy hair and a hacking cough – met Rossel and Nikitin on the street with a wave to slow them down. He followed it with a stiff salute, then led them into the building site covered with wooden scaffolding and tarpaulin, and guided them to the lift. They descended to the cavern that would, he said, one day be the main platform of Vladimirskaya Metro Station.

'It's so deep because everything here is built on a swamp, as you know, Comrade Major,' Yelchin said as they stood on a simple platform with a filthy floor. He was nervous, casting looks at Nikitin as if inviting his approval for the tip-off he'd given him. 'That makes the ground unstable.'

The lift stopped and he pulled back the gate. 'Also, it's being built to withstand one of those atomic bombs the capitalists have.' Aware he might have implied a techno-logical advantage on the part of the enemy, Yelchin quickly added: 'Imperialist criminals.'

Nikitin took no notice and strode forward, Yelchin half-running to catch up. Rossel looked around the vast, grey tunnel. The metro project had been started in the 1930s but the war had interrupted. Progress in recent years had been slow.

The air was dank and smelled of wet concrete and plaster. Pillar after pillar, thick and squat, ran along the concourse. Rossel looked over the edge of the platform, but there was only more concrete and a few sacks.

He caught up with Nikitin.

The major was in a foul mood. He had grumbled all the way to the scene of the crime – 'This stupid piece of shit gets his brains blown out just as I was sitting down to a decent bowl of *solyanka*' – but Rossel knew it was more than that.

He would have to report again to General Pletnev in the morning. And they had nothing. Instead of finding answers they had only found another dead body – and if this one was another veteran . . .

The militia officers who had been summoned to the scene at this late hour kept a wary distance, unsure of Nikitin's uniform. Not MGB, not standard military, not militia. Rossel scanned them for familiar faces but to his relief found none. They looked harder-nosed than the militia cops who had been at the film studios, though. This was a tougher area. The big employer in the neighbourhood was the Kirov Factory, which had kept going even during the blockade with a skeleton crew and any equipment that had not been stripped and reassembled in the Urals.

The body was tied to a plastic seat, next to a wheelbarrow and a couple of open bags of cement. It had been left in the middle of the platform. The officers had found two huge lights, meant for penetrating the darkest corners of the Leningrad Metropolitan's tunnels, to train on the latest victim. It was an inadvertent recreation of the Akimov murder scene at Lenfilm.

Nikitin looked at Rossel, who nodded. The two men approached the body.

'There it is,' said Nikitin.

A tiny piece of rolled-up paper. Rossel took a pen from his inside pocket, slipped the end of it under the fold, lifted it out and unravelled it.

> . . . *tu, col tuo gran valore,*
> *nel far beato altrui fai ricco, Amore;*
> *tu vinci, sol co' tuoi consigli santi,*
> *pietre, veneni e incanti.*

'Understand it?' said Nikitin.

'No. Something about courage, love, sanctity. We'll need your friend. One other thing.' Rossel pointed at the man's right temple. 'Two shots again. And everything else is the same – the chair, the bindings, the position of the body. How was this one found?'

Nikitin summoned Yelchin. Two security guards had heard screams and then a shot, then another shot. It took them another few seconds to reach the bottom and, being unarmed, they took only the briefest look around before taking the lift back up.

'As soon as they were at the surface they called us. And I called you, Comrade Major.'

'Good lad,' said Nikitin.

On the other side of the corpse, two tunnels led into the murk.

Rossel turned towards Lieutenant Yelchin, who eyed him back with wariness. Rossel knew the type from his own days as a militia lieutenant. If you didn't ask the wrong questions, you didn't get the wrong answers. And the best way to make that happen was not to ask many questions at all. Keep your nose clean by not sticking it into the wrong places. He wondered what Nikitin had on him.

'You said the guards heard the commotion at around 19.00, correct?' Rossel said.

Yelchin took out a handkerchief and coughed into it, making a noise like a pneumatic drill as the phlegm rattled around his throat. He nodded.

'Yes, and we got the call at around 19.15. I don't think they saw much more than I just described.'

'And do we know who he is?' Rossel said, gesturing with a thumb to the body.

Yelchin took a notepad from his pocket and read from it. 'Glaskov. A cook, from Repino. We are checking as you requested, Comrade Major, for his wartime . . .'

The militia lieutenant's voice trailed off. He stopped and put his notebook away. Then stood to attention. As one, his men did the same.

Rossel looked back along the platform, at the group who had just pulled back the safety bar of the lift and stepped out from it. Four men wearing the distinctive blue-rimmed caps of the Ministry for State Security service were walking towards them.

'MGB,' said Nikitin. 'This should be interesting.'

*

The MGB colonel introduced himself as Colonel Belsky of the Fifth Directorate. The Fifth was responsible for

173

monitoring and repressing dissent within the Party apparatus and the wider Soviet Union.

'GRU, you say?' Belsky looked from Rossel to Nikitin and back again. He was short and stocky, with a pasty complexion and large bags under his eyes. 'This isn't a military intelligence matter. Besides, I have orders from the highest authority that my men and I should take over this case.'

'I have orders too, Colonel. From General Pletnev, Defence Minister. Perhaps you have heard of . . .'

'A great war hero.' Belsky spoke over the jibe. 'I shall be sure to mention the general's name to Comrade Beria.'

Beria's name was Colonel Belsky's trump card. A single word that had the ability to unlock any door, cast aside any barrier, stifle any objection. But when you go to work every day as a blue-hat, Rossel thought, in every street you're a tsar riding in a procession. Everyone defers to you. Until, one day, you bump into a Nikitin. Running into someone like the major, who didn't back down, had unnerved Belsky's officers, who were looking at their boss for cues.

'I thought it was Comrade Ignatyev who led the MGB now,' said Nikitin.

'Oh, please, please,' laughed Colonel Belsky. 'I think we are all aware of the reality.'

Nikitin set his jaw and shoved his face close to the colonel.

'Of course,' he said, 'Ignatyev sits on Beria's knee, while Beria grabs him by the balls. And squeezes.'

The MGB colonel and his men moved their hands towards their pistols.

Nikitin did the same.

Rossel heard a dog bark. All eyes swivelled to the tunnel on the right. Two militia officers, one holding an excited Alsatian on a leash, had emerged, and were shouting to Yelchin to come quick.

'We have him! We have Koshchei cornered.'

As one, officers, MGB agents, Nikitin and Rossel headed for the mouth of the tunnel, dropping off the edge of the platform and running into the dark.

*

We're close now, we have to be . . .

Footsteps echoed around the tunnel walls, creating a mesmerising percussive effect – the sense of pursuers both behind and ahead. Beams from half a dozen flashlights made dancing patterns in the air and on the walls, while the stench of the new paint being used on the tunnel caught in the back of Rossel's throat.

The two officers with the growling Alsatian led the way, with Rossel close behind. Temporary lights dangled from the roof, not all of them lit. Both Rossel and the dog handler had already smacked their faces on a couple of them as they ran forward.

'Which way?'

Rossel didn't know who had spoken, but the reason was clear. They had covered about 500 metres and now the tunnel split into two.

'That's the main line,' said one of the officers. 'That's just a service tunnel – look, it stops there.'

The handler dropped to one knee, patted the dog, whispered in its ear.

'Which way, Annika? Which way, girl?'

Everyone took a moment, panting and gasping. Both Rossel's lungs and legs were giving out. Hands on his knees and his brow dripping with sweat, he glanced behind him, but half a dozen torches made it impossible to make anything out.

In front of him, the Alsatian growled. The militia officer unclipped the leash and the animal shot off, taking the left-hand fork; its handler running after it. Rossel, forcing his tired limbs to obey, followed.

He chased after the light up ahead as best he could but the distance between it and him widened. The heavy breathing behind faded.

He was alone.

How many paces?

No more than two hundred covered, he thought.

After that he'd lost count.

The tunnel curved. For a few seconds he was in total darkness. He followed the bend, one hand on the wall, and caught up with the dog handler.

The handler was crouched behind a wagon filled with spades, buckets and an enormous drill. Perhaps fifty metres ahead stood a rail carriage, its outline clearly visible thanks to a dim light swinging from the ceiling – a bulb slung over a hook.

Beyond it, a dead end.

Lieutenant Yelchin ran up behind them.

'I think we have him, Comrade Lieutenant,' the handler said as his superior tried to catch his breath. 'This looks like a siding or some sort of service tunnel. If I know anything about my Annika she'll already have that bastard by the—'

A loud bang. Everyone dived for the floor.

'Who was that?' shouted Yelchin. 'Kozlov, you fucking idiot.'

'Sorry, Comrade Lieutenant – I saw him, I swear,' said the underling.

Rossel's cheek was pressed to the cold metal of the rail track. He could see under the carriage. There was a shaft of light at or near the end of the service tunnel.

Annika was lying on her stomach beneath it. She was still.

Rossel clambered to his feet. So did the dog handler.

'Koshchei is not here,' said Rossel. 'The dog wouldn't just lie there like that if he was.'

Rossel stepped forward, squeezing down the right-hand side of the carriage towards the animal. He paused at the end, using it as cover, looking up to find the light source. Steel rungs embedded in the concrete showed him where the escape route was. A metallic scrape far above told him the rest. He darted past the dog, which snarled and jumped to its feet. A hunk of meat dangled from Annika's jaws.

Clambering up the same pile of boards the fugitive must have used, Rossel made sure his pistol was easy to reach, pushing it into a jacket pocket, and began to climb.

Heaving a manhole cover off, Rossel waited at the top, listening.

A few cars. A tram going past.

Three times he stuck his head up and down, before daring a longer look. Grunting with the effort, his arms screaming for him to stop, he hauled himself out into the silent road and the biting wind. A few flakes of snow were twirling round the chimneys of the Kirov Factory, which rose above a forbidding brick wall a couple of hundred metres away.

Koshchei had vanished.

*

Nikitin kicked at a workman's bucket. It somersaulted a couple of times and then splashed black paint across the wall.

'Shit. We lost him.'

Rossel sat on the steps of the rail carriage, recovering his breath, as a procession of militia and MGB officers went up and down the exit shaft.

'This explains it,' said one of the officers from inside the carriage. 'A mattress, blankets, some milk, a tin of *tushyonka,* and the rest of the nice chop he threw the dog.'

Rossel entered the compartment. A military-issue mat, a thick sleeping bag, rough blankets. Tea, sugar and a small stove.

On the floor, catching the torchlight, he saw something glinting amid the grey cement dust. He bent to pick it up. Holding it in his left hand, he held it to the light and stared at it – a small silver locket with a scratched glass cover, containing a lock of hair. On the back was inscribed a number: 1500.

He showed it to Nikitin.

'Odd,' said the major. 'What do you think it means?'

Rossel shook his head.

'I don't know. A factory batch number, perhaps?'

Nikitin took it.

'And some hair. How romantic.' He thrust it into a pocket. 'I'll add it to Dr Bondar's list. Though my feeling is he'll just give us more questions and no bloody answers.'

24

Rossel sat at the Drugovs' piano; a full ashtray in front of him, as well as a half-bottle of cognac he'd found in a kitchen cupboard. He took a pull on his *papirosa* and a drink from the bottle, and looked again at the little gold calling-card that had been left on his doormat.

Dear Comrade Detective,
I called, you were out. Feverishly detecting, no doubt. I am having a small gathering this evening. Orphans come free. Your presence would honour and delight me.
With respect,
Comrade Callimaco.

On the back was a celebrated address. The Yusupov Palace.

Rossel's first instinct had been to ignore it. But another evening surrounded by the shades of the Drugov family was becoming less inviting with each glass. He stubbed out his cigarette, stood up, walked into the hall and adjusted his coat in front of the mirror. As he pulled his gloves over his broken fingers, the last line from *The Mandrake* he'd heard Tarkovsky mouth along to at the film studios came back to him:

Why, child, from our very selves we hide – even from his own mirror the wise man remains a mystery . . .

Ivan Drugov's luxurious sable *ushanka* was hanging on a coat stand. Inwardly promising to return it, Rossel slipped it on. After all, he thought, it wasn't every day a man received an invitation to the Yusupov.

*

Tarkovsky's apartment was, indeed, palatial. The drapes, chandeliers and rug – a rich blue one with the Yusupov coat of arms: two oddly malnourished lions holding up an ornate shield – looked almost new, as if the room had only been recently decorated in anticipation of the arrival of the last Romanov tsar and his family. It was said the Romanovs had even been Russia's second-wealthiest aristocrats – after the Yusupovs.

Everything was polished, ornate, priceless. By day, most of the palace was a museum, including an exhibition of the notorious death with which it was forever associated: the murder of Rasputin. By night, Tarkovsky – whose private rooms were in the furthest recesses of the palace – sometimes walked the corridors alone.

A grand piano occupied the centre of the room. Beyond it, windows led onto a balcony overlooking the Moika. Scattered about were dozens of bottles of Soviet champagne: enough to suggest the party had taken up the entire evening and much of the afternoon as well. But the mood among the twenty or so guests – most in what looked like costumes borrowed from Lenfilm – was languid.

Everyone seemed to have eaten and drunk their fill. In his rough suit and cracked leather shoes, Rossel could only hope that the throng would assume he had come dressed as an archetypal apparatchik down on his luck.

Only Tarkovsky, who was in his element, and a gaggle of mostly female hangers-on fought off the ennui. The actor was playing the master of ceremonies, regaling the company with tales of rapacious aristocratic cavorting at the palace. He was ringed by a ballerina, a squaw, a couple of Marlene Dietrich lookalikes and a very pretty redhead called Dasha, who was barely out of her teens. A sailor and what could have been Ivan the Terrible completed the crowd around the piano.

Holding an almost empty glass, a tall, thin man with long grey hair and the demeanour of a hungry crow circling a battlefield stood a little apart from Rossel. He was listening to the chatter with his head inclined slightly away from the revellers; like a priest behind a confessional screen, mulling over the necessary level of a penance. On Rossel's arrival, Tarkovsky had introduced him as Alexander Fadeyev, the Head of the Writers' Union.

Next to Fadeyev, at the other end of a green and gold chaise longue, was a woman in her late twenties. She had dark hair tied in a bow, wore a simple red dress and was smoking a cigarette of black paper. Her pose was relaxed and carefree, but also disdainful. Her soft smile sometimes curled into something resembling a sneer as her face moved in and out of the light. Tarkovsky had presented her with mock awe. 'Beautiful Natalia. Natalia Ivaskova.'

Rossel took refuge behind a *papirosa* as the party went on around him.

At first, he'd wished he hadn't come. But the chatter and the laughter were both bewildering and invigorating. After life in Igarka, the carefree atmosphere was addictive.

Natalia tipped her head in his direction and spoke over Fadeyev's long grey hair.

'Is it true? Are you a real detective, like Boris says?' Her voice was soft, quite low. 'Or are you just playing one on screen in some cheap Lenfilm potboiler?'

'As it happens, I'm not a detective. Not any more. But I'm not an actor either. What about you?'

'I am an actress. Learning to be one, at any rate. A career change.' She pointed at her left ankle. 'I was a dancer at the Kirov. A good prospect, some said. But then I shattered the end of my fibula. In a rehearsal of *The Nutcracker*, of all things. Brittle bones, the doctors say. And now . . . I am not a dancer any more.'

'A detective who isn't a detective and dancer who can't dance,' he said. 'We have something in common. Where are you from? Not Leningrad, I think, with that accent.'

Her face darkened. She glanced at Fadeyev, but he was still scowling at the group around the piano. Rossel wondered if they were together.

'So you *are* a detective, of sorts,' she said, recovering her smile. 'Well, I'm from a city that no longer exists, near a lake that has no name.'

Rossel shook his head. 'There are many of those,' he said. The authorities were closing off more and more towns and cities to the outside world to keep their military secrets away from spies. Only residents with permits were allowed to come and go. And the MGB, of course . . . Many of the closed cities were in the Urals. Natalia's accent had that lilt – not quite Siberian, but heading in that direction.

'I'd say Sverdlovsk, or Chelyabinsk,' he said. 'I'd need another clue to be sure.'

She put her hands together in mock applause. 'Very good, comrade. Not quite a bullseye, but close enough.'

She held out her empty glass.

'Get me another?'

*

A raucous rendition of a song from a musical Rossel didn't know came to an end. A ripple of applause went around the room as the other guests came back to life.

Various toasts drifted across the smoky air – to friendship, to love, to happiness . . .

Tarkovsky, teetering slightly, took a long drink from the neck of a bottle of champagne and cried out, 'To success!' Instantly, it was agreed that this was the perfect salutation for such an evening. Shouts of 'To success!' echoed around the room.

The host grabbed one of the two girls dressed as Marlene Dietrich around the waist. He turned her towards him and then kissed her.

'And so, as I was saying,' he said, breaking off the kiss and breathing hard, 'before I was so rudely interrupted . . .' Now he did the same thing to the other Dietrich. Then he continued his speech. 'You may have heard, and who am I to persuade you otherwise, some say . . . and by some I mean those in the very *highest* echelons . . .' Boris paused here and looked around the room, which went quiet, '. . . that, in my youth, I bore more than a passing resemblance to a certain Comrade Yakov . . .'

Boris pointed to his own face so no one could possibly miss his point.

The actor picked up a box of cigars that he claimed were a gift from the Soviet ambassador to Havana. 'One of them, the ambassador assures me, contains a secret microfilm of President Truman doing unspeakable things to a two-dollar whore dressed as a hotdog,' he proclaimed. 'Let's see which of you gets the lucky cigar!'

Fadeyev snorted in disgust and moved off to another part of the room. Rossel looked at Natalia.

'Alexander is a big man in the world of Soviet culture,' she said with a shrug. 'A devotee of Socialist Realism: the only artistic principle with any validity, so he claims.'

'I can't imagine a Lenfilm production of a musical Western sits too well with that particular aesthetic,' said Rossel.

'He is not happy. And his mood has not been improved by this evening. It is not what he was expecting.'

'Just what was he expecting from Tarkovsky?' Rossel said.

She was about to answer but their host was demanding more attention, this time apparently in response to a challenge to his own Marxist–Leninist purity.

'I tell you I am becoming a leading authority on Marx and Lenin,' he said, 'as befits someone blessed with this face.' He adopted the classic pose of Lenin himself, arm in the air at the Finland Station. '"While the miser is merely a capitalist gone mad, the capitalist is a rational miser"!' he said, declaiming Marx.

The woman dressed in a tutu untangled herself from the arms of the sailor and drunkenly saluted Tarkovsky. Encouraged, Boris tried again. '"Capital is dead labour, which, vampire-like, lives only by sucking living labour . . ."'

Ivan the Terrible jumped to his feet, belched with vigour and joined in enthusiastically. 'These bourgeois vampires will not taste one single drop of my blood!' he said, laughing.

As the room burst into mock applause, Tarkovsky shouted out a passage Rossel remembered well: '"Perseus wore a magic cap that the monsters he hunted down might not see him . . ."'

At this, Dasha, the pretty redhead, ran to the pile of coats and hats stacked on a sofa near the door and grabbed an outsize *ushanka*. She returned and reached up to place it on Tarkovsky's head, pulling it down so it covered his eyes. 'Now you are Perseus, Borya,' she said, smiling.

Tarkovsky began to move around the room, going from person to person, embracing them blindly while shouting, 'I see no monsters!'

'Here,' the guests were shouting, 'Borya, this way – I am a monster!' Some he groped, others he kissed or licked or nibbled, all the while shouting out the mantras of Bolshevism, most of which were drowned out by howls of laughter.

Tarkovsky arrived at a sitting figure. The actor moved his hands across the man's hair and face, shouting out names at random. Then he slapped his victim a couple of times on the face. This time there were no matching shouts and cheers of 'I see no monsters!'

Natalia got off the sofa, walked forward, and removed Boris's hat.

The actor found himself staring into the face of the Head of the Writers' Union.

'Alexander Sergeyevich, I do beg your pardon,' said Tarkovsky.

Fadeyev smoothed his long hair back into place, taking his time about it.

'You didn't finish Marx's quotation,' he said.

'I didn't?'

'You said, "Perseus wore a magic cap that the monsters he hunted down might not see him." But do you know the other half?'

Tarkovsky gulped. 'Yes, Alexander Sergeyevich. *Wir ziehen die Nebelkappe tief über Aug' und Ohr, um die Existenz der Ungeheuer wegleugnen zu können,*' he said.

Rossel's impromptu German lessons in the labour camp had left him with only a basic grasp of the language. But he could tell Tarkovsky knew it well.

'Which means?' said Fadeyev.

'It means, "we draw the magic cap down over our eyes and ears as a make-believe that there are no monsters" . . .'

'Quite so,' said Fadeyev. 'It was Marx's condemnation of the wilful blindness of the bourgeoisie to the evils of their own capitalist system.' He looked around. 'All this frivolity. It suggests to me that you yourself are blind to your own Marxist duties. This spectacle compares poorly to the sobriety of the Soviet leadership and the iron will of our great leader, Comrade Stalin.'

Fadeyev walked to the end of the room, picked up his coat, flung open the door and slammed it behind him.

'Poor darling Boris,' whispered Natalia returning to Rossel. 'Leningrad is a minefield. And almost every day he finds a new way to step on something explosive. I hear that Khrushchev has invited him to declaim and sing for Stalin himself at the Anichkov Palace in a few weeks' time. A big Party gathering – a rarity for Leningrad, and an honour. Boris is petrified.'

She touched him on the arm.

'The snow has stopped. Will you walk me home?'

*

At this hour, they seemed to have Leningrad to themselves. But even if the streets and embankments had been filled with cheering hordes on a May Day celebration, Rossel wasn't sure he would have noticed.

Heaven knew how long they had been walking before they arrived at her building, or even where it was. She leaned forward to kiss him on the cheek and lingered close to him.

He breathed in her perfume.

The scent reminded him of Sofia; a girl he had been in love with when he was a student at the conservatoire.

A relationship that had not ended well.

Natalia looked at him and touched his face.

'Call again,' she said.

She turned and disappeared inside. Rossel listened to her shoes clicking on the stone steps all the way up.

25

In the unexpected winter sunshine, a woman and her two children, a girl and a boy, were throwing snowballs at each other in front of a newly built statue of Rimsky-Korsakov.

The great composer was absorbed in one of his own scores. His right arm was raised a couple of inches above the metallic manuscript, as if surprised to have found a mistake – a false note amid the harmonies of his own operatic rendition of the story of Koshchei the Immortal.

Rossel looked past the statue at the building of the Leningrad Conservatoire, where he had honed his talents as violinist. His mind was a whirl of bittersweet memories – of pieces he had played, concerts he had given, people he had known. People he had loved.

With his right hand, Rossel shielded his eyes from the sun. The thumb of his left tapped at the stubs of its missing little and ring fingers, an occasional nervous habit.

He had been nearing the end of his studies – winning prizes, getting top marks in his recital examinations – when it had all ended. First, an arrest – a denunciation and a midnight knock on the door – and an interrogation from which a violinist could not recover.

Then the Siege of Leningrad. He had been freed from the dungeons of the secret police to be thrown into the city's frantic defence. A reprieve that was meant to be brief.

But he had survived.

In a city of ghosts, this was where his own past was buried. But he seemed fated to return. Not for the first time, he was hoping that someone inside could shed some light on his current mysteries.

*

Professor Belova was a musicologist and an expert on the history of Italian opera. She was short, plump and on the wrong side of sixty. Her grey hair was tied up in a bun, as it always had been, and her wireframe glasses had not moved from the end of her nose in the twelve years since Rossel had last sat in one of her classes. They gave the professor the air of an intellectual purist; someone for whom the mechanics of music were all that mattered, while to actually play it was an indulgence.

Violin and piano teachers got the best rooms at the conservatoire. So Belova had led a nomadic existence as a professor, shunted around the building from lecture to lecture. Today she had led him to a sparse side room containing a few chairs, a small wooden table and a jumble of discarded instrument cases and music stands lining the walls.

'A detective? I am surprised,' she said.

'Me, too.'

'But then, the blockade changed many things.'

'Yes.'

The professor waited for further explanation.

'You said you have something to show me,' she said, giving up.

Rossel took copies of the verses taken from the mouths of the victims out of his pocket and laid them on the table.

The ode to Katz:

> *That ignorance is bliss is widely known;*
> *How bless'd the imbecile is with head of bone!*
> *He thirsts not after gold, nor aches for pow'r,*
> *Believes what he is told, hour after hour.*

To Samosud:

> *How gentle is deception*
> *When carried to fruition as intended.*
> *For it defies perception.*

To Akimov:

> *Oh gentle darkness, oh holy and sweet nocturnal hours*
> *That soothe the burning pain of love's desires . . .*

Finally, the GRU's translation of the scroll found in the mouth of Glaskov, the latest victim:

> *Our hearts are racked with hope and then with terror;*
> *For thou strik'st fear into the very marrow*
> *Of gods and mortals with thy bow and arrow.*

Belova straightened her glasses and stared down at them.

'Is there anything significant about these particular lyrics, professor?' Rossel said. 'Why would someone select these pieces and put them together? Why *The Mandrake* – what might its significance be?'

She reread the four verses, mouthing the words.

'They are very different, are they not?' Rossel added.

'Yes and no,' said Belova, looking up. 'Yes, in that they appear to express very different sentiments. But no, in that they have one thing very clearly in common.'

She read them once again.

'Every student who listens to me for the first time thinks how odd it is that I talk about Machiavelli, but he really was a pioneer,' Belova said, almost to herself. 'He wrote *The Mandrake* around 1518. By then he was in exile from the political life of Florence following a return to Medici rule. Indeed, some scholars read the play as an overt critique of the Medici.'

For a moment she fell silent.

'I occasionally lecture on the phenomenon of *canti carnivaleschi,* carnival songs.'

'Carnival songs?'

'Yes. They celebrated the carnival season in sixteenth-century Florence. They were usually satirical and often obscene. But Machiavelli did something completely new with them. He put them in his plays. Mostly because he was infatuated with a woman called Barbera Salutati – a singer, a courtesan, a muse . . . He wrote a series of them for her to perform between the acts of the play. This was decades before Monteverdi, who is popularly regarded as the inventor of opera, had so much as hummed a nursery rhyme.'

'And these verses,' Rossel said. 'They are all from those songs?'

'Yes. Not the play itself but from the songs between the acts. His gift to Salutati, in the hope that she would, shall we say, look favourably upon him.'

Belova turned up her palms in apology. 'That is about all I can tell you.'

'Thank you, Professor,' he replied. 'You have been most useful. I am sorry to drag you away from your duties, I hope they are not too onerous?'

'A lecture on the early work of that inimitable composer, Maestro Vronsky. I met him once. Charming man . . .'

Rossel glanced at his watch.

'Incidentally, what do you think of *The Mandrake*?' he asked.

Belova pushed her glasses a little further up the bridge of her nose.

'In academic circles, where rational argument is often taken to the level of a bloodsport, its meaning is of course disputed. But I, for one, have always sided with Voltaire's interpretation.'

'Voltaire's?'

She nodded.

'He held it was a play that "mocks the religion which Europe preaches". Especially the Pope.'

'*The Mandrake* is an anti-religious work?'

Belova shrugged.

'Well, Voltaire believed it was, and vehemently so. But then he would. And so, I suspect, does the Party and Comrade Stalin himself. Hence the commissioning of that film before the war starring that beautiful man. What was his name? The actor who played Callimaco . . .'

Belova picked up the piece of paper with lyrics on it.

'This one reminds me of a line from *The Prince,* for which Machiavelli is far more famous.'

She pointed at the lyrics that had been found in Samosud's mouth, which began: 'How gentle is deception . . .'

'Can you remember it?' he asked her.

'Yes. "Everyone sees what you appear to be, few experience what you really are."'

'A wise man, Comrade Machiavelli,' said Rossel.

'Other academics assert that *The Mandrake* holds a mirror to his politics. That it expresses, albeit in a frivolous manner, the deep cynicism of his more renowned and lasting political work.'

Belova waved the paper in front of Rossel before placing it back in his hand. She glanced at his missing fingers but made no comment.

Rossel was about to leave when Belova took a breath as if about to speak. She hesitated.

'What is it, professor?'

'You don't think . . . no, I'm being foolish.' She shook her head.

'Think what?'

'Machiavelli wrote those lyrics into the play to win over a woman. Perhaps they might mean the same thing to the murderer as they did to him. Could they, in fact, be a declaration of love?'

26

He was a small man. A big coat, yes – expensive material, well cut. But the wiry frame within it was decidedly small. Nikitin was certain he could reach across the table, put a hand around his scrawny white throat and – a sharp twist would be all it would take – break the man's neck.

And yet . . .

This forgettable Party bureaucrat – nothing more than a clerk – wearing his best coat so he could pretend to be at home in the luxurious surroundings of the Hotel Astoria; right now, this pompous idiot was his best chance.

His whole world.

The room in which they were meeting was of modest size but well appointed. Between them sat a low, polished table, upon which were laid three photographs.

'Kristina is your wife, yes?' said the man. 'Dima, your son. The girl, Svetlana, your daughter.'

Nikitin stared back at him.

'They are, as you correctly suspected, on a list,' the man added. 'I do not need to tell you what that means.'

'But?'

'My minister is still confident that he can intervene and . . .'

'Yes?'

The major heard the note of fear in his own voice. He reached up and touched the scar tissue on his cheek.

How can a man with a face like mine be so afraid?

The clerk sat back.

'They sell lapel pins in the lobby here with pictures of Lenin on them,' he said. 'I'm going to buy some and take them home to my own boy in Moscow. He is a great collector of *znachki*.'

He would have to play along.

'Dima, he collects things, too,' said Nikitin. 'He likes football. Zenit is all he talks about. He has a little book of players' autographs.'

The clerk took a sip of coffee from a gold-rimmed porcelain cup.

'Minister Beria has a little book,' he said. 'You have met him, you know some of his habits. You can imagine the kind of things that get jotted down in it.'

Nikitin leaned forward and picked up the picture of his son.

'I have brought Dima up in a very down-to-earth fashion,' he said. 'I have not encouraged him to think for himself. A simple man does not make life complicated, I tell him. Even though he is too young to understand what I mean. The child thinks only of Grandpa Lenin, of Comrade Stalin, of the Party. My wife and daughter are blameless, too. They do not deserve to be on any list.'

The clerk put down his cup.

'Names go on lists. Names come off them. As I have told you before, my minister assures me he is in a position . . .'

'Enough of the games,' said Nikitin. 'Ask me.'

'Ask you what?'

In the dark night, I know that you, my love, are sleeping . . .

'Whatever it is you need me to do to save my family.'

27

Oleg Novikov, Deputy Chief Engineer of the *Leningradsky Metropoliten*, had the sallow skin of a man who hadn't seen daylight in some time. Once winter was in full swing, he said, he went to work in the dark and went home in the dark, spending the hours in between either in this concrete block just south of the Fontanka or installing signalling in the tunnels.

Aged about sixty, his face was so pockmarked he looked like it had been rolled in gravel. His clothes were grey and functional, and the forefinger and middle finger of his right hand so yellow with nicotine it was as if he had dipped them in paint.

He was also very loud. Listening to him, Rossel felt like he was being hit over the head with a hammer. Novikov spread the large blueprints of the new metro out on the trestle table in his office.

'When my men have built this beauty, the workers of Leningrad will travel to their jobs like they were the fucking Romanovs. You too, Comrade Rossel,' he said. 'You'll feel like your balls have been dipped in caviar and your arse is being transported to Heaven on a feather bed. Eight stations connecting the Moscow railway station in the centre with Avtovo.'

The engineer tapped at the plans.

'We're here, at Tekhnologichesky Institut. And that will just be the start. There are already shaft and service tunnels running directly north, almost up to the top of Nevsky. Eventually, there are even plans to tunnel under the river. Can you imagine that? Peter the Great built this whole city on a swamp but even he didn't have the *khui* on him to tunnel under the Neva.'

Novikov took the cigarette that seemed permanently stuck to his bottom lip out of his mouth and began coughing, bringing up an industrial amount of phlegm. He spat out a dark brown gobbet into an empty metal wastepaper bin, which made a loud pinging sound. Then he slapped his chest twice in an attempt to regain control of himself and pointed at the blueprints again.

'These tunnels will be the death of me, comrade,' he said.

'I do hope not. But sadly, they have been exactly that to Comrade Glaskov.'

'That the name of the poor bastard they found last night?'

You'll never guess what, Nikitin had said. Glaskov was in the same platoon as Katz and his comrades. Isn't that a surprise?

'That is why I wanted to look at these plans,' said Rossel. 'The line from here to Uprising Square and the Moscow Station cannot be the only tunnel, correct? You need sidings, ventilation shafts, storage . . .'

'Yes,' agreed Novikov. 'And like I said, we have already started the excavation for more lines. This one, for example, from here running south to Park Pobedy, is well underway. The tunnels have been carved out as far as Moskovskiye Vorota in the south. Some of the stations, too – or at least where the stations will be once we get round to it. The signalling, though – it's always the bastard, signalling, especially in this damp.'

'But you said service tunnels were running north,' asked Rossel. 'Can a man fit in them?'

'Easily. But they are half-flooded in some areas, they need pumping out. There, look – up to Nevsky. And after Uprising Square, almost up to the river. It's the Neva that's the barrier. We've not cracked it. Yet.'

Rossel looked closer at the map. Up to the river in two directions there were shafts all over the place: for access, ventilation, pumping . . .

'Easy to get in and out?' he said.

'Not until recently. The covers are heavy; metal set in concrete, which sits on a lip inside the shaft. Then you can lock the cover into place, if you have the right key. And it's a long way up and down, fuck your mother. But now we have the lifts working. And enough open tunnels to connect to most of the city centre.'

'Lifts?'

'Service lifts, the builders use them to take down bricks, cement, scaffolding . . .'

'Big enough to transport a body?'

Novikov gave him a stare. 'If you wanted to.'

The wall of Novikov's office was half metal, half glass. On the other side three people – two men and one woman – were in a meeting, all jabbing fingers at a clipboard. The woman seemed to be having the final word. She stuck a pen back in her top pocket and strode off. Rossel watched her go.

'Our senior engineer, Tatiana Vasilyeva, can be ferocious in argument,' Novikov said, winking at him, 'but I am still happy to introduce you, Comrade Detective?'

Rossel shook his head. 'You mistake my—'

An office boy with a pudding-bowl haircut and carrying a Manila file under his arm knocked at the door. Novikov waved him in and took the file.

He pointed at the boy. 'Young Yura here, like all our city's youngsters, has had his head filled with tales of Koshchei the Immortal and other childish rubbish. Even so, it's dark and deserted down there, fuck your mother. Even the parts where we've made the most progress are a long way from being ready. You might not be looking for Koshchei – just a hairy-arsed builder with a map.'

*

After a day of clear skies and only a few flurries, heavy snow was falling from a bleak evening sky.

Ploughing your way along the wide main roads such as Zagorodny in this weather was energy sapping, but, on the quieter side streets like this one, the snow restored to Leningrad its faded beauty.

As he watched the flakes descend, his grandmother's words came to him.

The Lord is all around us, Revol. Even in the snow that falls from the sky . . .

Something she would not have said in front of his mother, a music teacher, and his father, a naval officer, who had been a zealous Marxists – volunteering for collective farms in the summer and teaching literacy and numeracy classes in far-flung regions in winter. Both had even been delegates to Party congresses in Moscow.

Though that had not saved them. They had been arrested as Stalin tightened his grip and eliminated the Old Bolsheviks: those who had been the first footsoldiers of the Revolution. Rossel and his sister, Galya, were branded 'family members of enemies of the people' and placed in an orphanage.

'Your mother, your father, they are traitors to the Soviet Union. So you will not have any difficulty in denouncing them.'

He could still feel the NKVD investigator's question hanging in the air.

Rossel's cheeks reddened.

I didn't have to answer it.

He turned his head skywards, stuck out the tip of his tongue, let a flake fall upon it.

Yes, all around us. Can't you see? Each tiny snowflake is a communion host . . .

'You must forget your mother now, boy,' the investigator had said. 'Just like you, she has a traitor's heart . . .'

*

A woman wrapped in a black fur pushed her way out of the metro offices. She was carrying a bunch of roses wrapped in newspaper, holding them close to her chest to protect them from the snow and wind.

Rossel crossed the street.

Vassya saw him move. She slowed and then turned towards him.

'No, Revol,' Vassya said.

'No?'

She gave a deep sigh.

'I thought I made my feelings clear on the plane back from . . .' She stopped and looked around. 'Back from Igarka.'

'I only want your professional assistance. Your engineering knowledge of the underground, your great achievement.'

He was not being completely honest.

The lies we tell, his grandmother's voice again, *God hears them . . .*

'I am a detective once more,' he added. 'In a sense, at least. My congratulations on your new role. I mean it.'

She did not reply.

Rossel pointed to the flowers.

'From a friend?'

Vassya shook her head. She began to walk away but stopped and turned.

'No, he's more than that,' she said.

As Vassya disappeared into the night, a single petal fell from her bouquet and blew towards him.

Rossel reached down to pick it up. But then thought better of it.

*

Why spend another night with the Drugovs?

A man could only spend so much time among the dead before he craved the attentions of the living. There would be laughter and dancing at the house of Boris Tarkovsky, Rossel thought.

But when he arrived, there was none.

Tarkovsky tried to push a plate of smoked fish and boiled potatoes into Rossel's hand but Rossel put it on the dining table. 'You are still a skeleton, Comrade Detective,' Tarkovsky said, 'you must eat, you must drink . . .'

Rossel picked up a small portion of potato salad and ate it.

The actor's own apartment was in a wing of the Yusupov Palace that had once, he said, been the servants' quarters. It consisted of three rooms, all in a line: two living rooms – with a kitchen at the end of the first – and a bedroom.

'Time was I had the run of most of the palace. But since the war – since poor Yakov came to such an unhappy end . . .' Tarkovsky said. He kept his voice low while the radio played.

This discreet version of the actor was unnerving.

Some audiences even Boris prefers to disappoint.

'These days my requests to entertain are more and more frequently denied,' continued Tarkovsky. 'The food and drink come out of my own pocket or from favours. My jolly evenings are not what they were. And Party bureaucrats have taken away my key to the ballroom. I was scolded. Never mind,' he whispered, leaning in. 'I have another key.'

Rossel looked around. Compared to the poky rooms and greasy kitchen of his old *kommunalka* it was luxurious, the type of accommodation ordinary citizens such as himself heard about but rarely had the chance to see from the inside. It had carpet and rugs instead of linoleum; comfortable chairs and a sofa; floor lamps; a round dining table . . .

Tarkovsky had heard the bell, descended the stairs, thrown open the door and beckoned Rossel to follow.

Threading his way in and out of the courtyard and through darkened rooms, he had led the way to his private quarters.

Inside, they passed a marble bust of Lenin that was turned to face the wall.

The actor tutted.

'Whatever I do, Vladimir Ilyich always looks so disapproving,' he said.

He turned the bust the right way around. 'But when I have guests, I always invite him, too.'

'You're a wise man, Comrade Tarkovsky,' said Rossel.

As soon as they sat down, Tarkovsky produced a bottle.

'Ah, Schumann,' he said, closing his eyes to a tenor voice on the radio. ' "*Dichterliebe*". "A Poet's Love". Do you know it?'

'I know it.'

> *Das Mädchen nimmt aus Ärger*
> *Den ersten besten Mann*
> *Der ihr in den Weg gelaufen . . .*

Tarkovsky leaned back and crooned along with the singer. At the end of the verse, he walked over to the radio and turned it up ever so slightly. Returning to his seat, he poured them both stiff measures of vodka and stared at Rossel.

'Have you heard of biomechanics, comrade detective?'

Rossel shook his head.

'I studied drama under Meyerhold's system. Please tell me that you have heard of Meyerhold.'

'The director,' said Rossel. Meyerhold had been shot after a show trial in 1940, but it seemed churlish to mention it.

Tarkovsky exhaled, threw his vodka down his gullet, and sniffed. He took a moment to gather himself.

'Biomechanics is an acting method that emphasises the replication of gesture,' he said. 'In essence, when I copy you, I become you.'

Tarkovsky drew his left arm close to the side of his body. His expression changed. Rossel recoiled. The characteristic positioning of the arm, the light, the tilt of the head, the soft smirk . . . whatever it was, there was the face of Stalin. It had not been there before, at least nothing like so clearly. Now it had appeared. That mix of the avuncular and the cruel, the thickness of the lips and the dark eyes set back in their sockets.

When Stalin was twelve he had been injured in an accident and sustained a lifelong disability to his left arm. As a result, he always held it close to his side.

With a broad smile, the ghost vanished.

'You intrigue me, detective,' said Tarkovsky, as if nothing had happened. 'You appear out of nowhere, a skeleton dressed in a suit. A senior army officer – they say he's in military intelligence? – ferries you around as if you were in the Politburo. Yet here you are, drowning your sorrows with me, an almost total stranger who you cannot possibly trust.'

Rossel took his own turn on the vodka. It was fiery on the gums but smelled clean enough. He picked up a morsel of herring with his fingers and dropped it into his mouth.

'You draw the eye of Natalia Ivaskova – and believe me very few men interest Natalia – yet you fail to pursue her.'

The actor finished his analysis. Then sat back in his chair, cradling his drink, expecting an answer.

'I find it puzzling myself, Comrade Callimaco,' said Rossel.

'Should I invite her over? You can be her Orpheus, she your Persephone. I bet she is a wonderful lover. I can tell just by looking.'

Rossel shook his head. 'I just need a good sleep.' He tapped his glass. 'And perhaps a last one of those.'

Tarkovsky regarded him with disappointment, as if Rossel had proven poor company and of dull intellect.

> *Und wem sie just passieret,*
> *Dem bricht das Herz entzwei.*

In flawless German, the actor sang the lines about the poet's broken heart.

Rossel held out his glass.

'Fair enough,' said Tarkovsky. He poured.

Rossel sat back in his seat and closed his eyes.

Two shots to the temple. A body sitting in a chair.

When I copy you, I become you . . .

Who, Rossel wondered, was Koshchei pretending to be?

28

The House of Books was on Nevsky Prospect, directly opposite Pletnev's lair in the Museum of Atheism. Like most of Leningrad's citizens, Rossel had always loved it. They crowded into its rooms and competed for browsing space in an intense, respectful silence. His mother would bring him here when he was young and buy him either children's books or scores from its music department. Something simple for his young fingers by Prokofiev or Rimsky-Korsakov.

Besides the allure of the music and literature, the building itself had a special charm. Before it became a bookshop it had been built for the Singer sewing machine company and the name was still stencilled on its windows: a last capitalist flag left fluttering on a battlefield they had long since fled.

'At the MGB they call this place the House of Bait,' Nikitin said as he and Rossel pulled up outside.

The heavy grey clouds suspended over the city, becoming visible in the morning half-light, hinted at the snowstorm that was coming.

'Why?' said Rossel.

Nikitin switched off the engine and put the keys in his pocket.

'If you're not reading Marx and Lenin, comrade, why are you reading at all? A suspect with the wrong book is already wriggling on your hook.'

*

Inside, the two men made for a door marked *Administratsiya*.

It was opened by a middle-aged woman wearing a green dress and an icy stare. But as soon as Nikitin brought out his GRU card and barked the name of the man they were here to see, she went pale.

'Fourth floor,' she said, pointing to the ornate stairs. 'Comrade Ivashin is checking our stock.'

*

Rossel pushed the stockroom door open and entered, followed by Nikitin.

Books were everywhere: scattered in untidy, teetering piles on tables, chairs and the floor, or crammed into the shelves.

'Can I help you, comrades?' asked a man on the bottom rung of a small stepladder.

Nikitin pushed a tall pile of books off a chair, tipping them all over the floor, and sat down. He removed his gloves, stretching out the fingers of his right hand. The knuckles cracked.

'I suggest you take a seat, too, Comrade Ivashin,' said the major.

Ivashin – a pale, thin man wearing spectacles – did as he was told.

Just out of Ivashin's sight, Rossel leant against a wall. There was dust in the air that irritated his nose and throat, and the beguiling smell of paper. Faint sounds drifted up from Nevsky Prospect. He noticed a patch of damp on the wallpaper.

Not good for books . . .

All around, Marxist historians and social analysts rubbed covers with economic theoreticians, classic nineteenth-century novelists, avant-garde iconoclasts of the Revolution, folk-tale tellers, mathematicians, collectors of Lenin's speeches, of Stalin's speeches, of butterflies and moths . . . Ethnographers, linguisticians, carefully selected foreign poets, chess grandmasters.

And, of course, Pushkin. The poet was the acknowledged master of Russia's soul. *Better the illusions that exalt us than ten thousand truths . . .* Rossel's mother had often recited that line to him when he was a boy. Back then, he had loved the romantic nature of the sentiment. These days, he preferred the truth. Hungered for it.

'We are here about some missing gold, comrade,' said Rossel.

'Gold? I know nothing of anything like that.'

The bookseller's tone was intellectual. And just a little condescending.

'And yet this room feels a little like a vault to me, Comrade Ivashin,' Rossel said.

'A vault?' Ivashin had to turn to look at him.

Rossel nodded.

'To a man of learning like yourself, these books are like gold bars, are they not? To a professional bibliophile, a miser's hoard?'

Ivashin's blue eyes flickered. He made a show of uncon-cern, scanning the shelves and nodding in return.

'A vault, yes, indeed. Whenever I come to work, step through the door of this building, I feel . . .'

'Rich?' said Nikitin.

Sensing a trap, Ivashin shook his head.

'Rich? No – a venal bourgeois notion. Unless one means that I have been blessed. Spending every day in the company of Tolstoy and Dostoevsky is the greatest of privileges.' Ivashin thought for a moment. 'And among Marxist–Leninist theory and the teachings of Lenin as well, of course.'

Nikitin looked around the room.

'Dostoevsky, you say?'

'Over there.' Ivashin pointed to a pile a couple of metres away. He got up and took two books from the pile, handed them to the major and then resumed his seat.

'*The Gambler* and *The Idiot*,' he said. '*The Idiot* is a particular favourite of mine. The story of Prince Myshkin, whose unworldly goodness is often mistaken for stupidity.'

Nikitin examined the book. Then dropped it onto the small table he and the bookseller were sitting around.

'Unworldly goodness,' he said. 'That's not a concept I'm particularly familiar with, Comrade Ivashin.'

He reached out and took off Ivashin's glasses. The bookseller blinked but did not move. Nikitin balanced the glasses on his own nose.

'These are good, comrade. Very good. With these on . . .'

He closed one eye – his good one. 'Even like this, I can see right inside you.'

The major took off the glasses and began to crumple the frame in his hand.

Ivashin reached out to snatch them back.

'No, I . . .'

The right lens popped and skidded across the floor. The major loosened his grip. Although now buckled, the frames resumed something of their normal shape.

Nikitin leaned forward. 'I have seen your sort a million times in the cells, Comrade Ivashin,' he said through his teeth. 'Read a thousand stories, so they think, "How much trouble can it be to invent a new one to fool this imbecile interrogator."' Nikitin picked up the Dostoevsky novel again. 'This shit-kicking idiot who never went to university, like I did.'

Rossel picked up Ivashin's glasses and placed them back on the bookseller's head. Something about the gesture, its unexpected kindness, touched Ivashin.

He began to sob.

'Coffee, I think, comrade – a warm reviving cup to keep out the winter chills? Then you can tell us everything you know about the gold?' said Rossel.

Nikitin stood up.

'I'll get that frosty bitch downstairs to make us some.'

*

Ivashin was holding on to his coffee cup with both hands as if it was the last lifejacket on a boat in stormy seas.

Rossel took out his notepad.

'We have been investigating the attempted sale of a gold medallion that a welder called Katz tried to sell on the black market. It has the name of a German city, Neubrandenburg, engraved on it. Katz came to our attention by virtue of being murdered and mutilated by the killer every citizen in Leningrad is afraid of. Koshchei the Invisible.'

Ivashin pulled a handkerchief from a trouser pocket and dabbed at his eyes.

'I know nothing of this man, this Katz . . .'

'Your file says you were a committed Communist, member of the Komsomol, that you joined the fight against Hitler in October 1941,' said Rossel. 'You appear to have been in units that followed the front line, which meant that you saw very little fighting until Berlin. Your experience in the capital of the Third Reich must have been a brutal introduction to warfare.'

'It was . . .' Ivashin began. But his memory of that time seemed to defy expression.

'You were in a Guards platoon along with a man called Pavel Grachev. Of course, if I am wrong in any of this, please correct me. And address your remarks to Comrade Major Nikitin, who will be happy to note them down for further investigation. Until we get to the truth, and to Soviet justice, the goal of every investigation.'

Ivashin's imagination regarding the path of Soviet justice would do the rest, Rossel thought.

The bookseller was breathing hard.

'All right, all right. There were six of us – Sergeant Grachev, and five men he trusted.'

'Why did he trust you?' said Rossel.

Ivashin reflected for a moment. 'Different reasons,' he said. 'Akimov was in his own mould: a killer, and none too choosy about who he killed.'

212

'Akimov?' said Nikitin. The major gave Rossel a look.

'Yes,' said Ivashin. 'He was a cruel man. Said he'd left his family behind in Minsk when the Germans came crashing through. Never bothered to find out what had happened to them, and didn't seem to care.'

He emitted a sound that was more a shudder than a sigh. 'You understand, we were bound together by war. Afterwards there was nothing to keep us together. But . . .'

'But?' said Nikitin.

'Grachev would hold reunions, and for some reason those of us who were still alive would always go. Even though I didn't have much in common with the others, the blood we'd seen together was a bond I could not break. And Grachev liked to talk when he was drunk. Mostly about women he had been with. I suppose he needed an audience.'

'The others, please, Comrade Ivashin,' Rossel pressed him.

The bookseller looked frightened. 'Katz and Samosud?'

'Yes.'

'Volodya Katz was a simple man,' said Ivashin. 'He believed every word in *Krasnaya Zvezda*, he lapped up the agitprop entertainment for the troops. Friendly enough, though. Brave. He trusted Grachev to keep him alive. The sergeant was fond of violence, but he was not entirely reckless with the lives of those under his command.'

'And Samosud?'

'Misha Samosud was another Jew. He'd been one of the first into the death camps. Majdanek, maybe? And had seen plenty of mass graves left by the Einsatzgruppen. It changed him, took something away that had been inside. Grachev replaced it, I think.'

'And you?'

Ivashin hesitated.

'I . . . Well, before you get to me, there was Zvirbulis. Viktor. The only luck poor Viktor ever had was bad luck. It made him wise. He was killed on the very last day of the war.'

'Not wise enough to dodge a Kraut bullet, eh?' said Nikitin.

The bookseller looked down at his hands.

'He was shot by an NKVD officer who mistook him for a deserter,' he said. He was quiet for several seconds. 'Viktor never took a backward step,' he added in a small voice.

Nikitin chuckled.

'I think I understand. You had a soft spot for this Viktor?'

Ivashin lowered his head but did not answer. Sexual relations between men brought a punishment under Article 154a of the Soviet Criminal Code of up to five years' deprivation of liberty. Not expanding on this part of his story would be prudent; silence would serve Ivashin best.

So that was the squad. Sergeant Grachev and his band of Red Army reprobates.

'So how did you get hold of that gold?' Rossel asked.

Ivashin wiped his brow. 'It was in the very last days of the battle for Berlin,' he said. 'Right at the end. It was still savage, mind – young boys and grandads would pop out of nowhere and hit one of us before we could mow them down. Booby traps in every house. But there was time to go looking for souvenirs.'

'Did everyone do that?' asked Nikitin.

'Yes, of course. Some of the military postal depots couldn't keep up. Rugs, clocks, fancy tables and chairs, clothes . . . anything that you couldn't get back home, we'd strip it. It was our due – right, comrades?'

Nikitin nodded and slapped his thigh. 'Yes, comrade. After what those bastards did to us, to our Motherland, the property of the Hitlerites became *our* property.'

Ivashin started to tell his tale with greater enthusiasm.

'So one night we are out on the hunt and we see two or three men next to a blown-up Tiger tank on a bridge crossing a railway line. It was near a station, I remember that. So we opened fire with everything we had. Two minutes later we're going through the uniforms of two dead Nazis. One must've got away. And next to these corpses is a knapsack. Well, we couldn't believe our luck.'

Ivashin rubbed his nose.

'Days of rummaging through the pants of dead Germans for a few cigarettes or photos of darling little Claudia or Heidi and suddenly it's gold medallions all round. One each. And some other stuff. We grabbed it and got the hell out of there.'

'What other stuff?' interrupted Rossel.

Ivashin thought about it.

'*Juno* cigarettes – there was some squabbling over them, I can tell you. A water canteen of some sort, an expensive one. A book. And a picture of a saint, a Russian one; a proper ikon, about the size of a big book, covered in gold leaf – Akimov saw it as a sign. And a dirty postcard from some French tart on the front. That's all.'

Rossel closed his eyes to help him think, then opened them again.

'So who, Comrade Ivashin, got the gold?'

'Like I said, we all did. One each, and an extra for Grachev. By themselves they were useless. You can't just go out and sell Nazi gold in the Soviet Union. You have to smelt it, mix it with other metals. You have to know someone who can do that without snitching on you or blackmailing you. We agreed to wait a few years until all the fuss over hunting for Nazi gold, art, antiques, weapons, rare books, all that had died down.'

'Looks like Comrade Katz got impatient,' said Nikitin.

'So where is yours?' asked Rossel.

Ivashin didn't answer.

Nikitin cleared his throat and stood.

The bookseller put his hands up. 'All right,' he said.

He went over to the shelves and pulled down a large book. On the front and spine were embossed the words: *Observations on the Use of Mechanised Agriculture on Collective Farms in the Ukrainian SSR, Vol III.*

Ivashin opened it. Inside a circular hole cut out of the pages, which appeared to be largely blank, was a medallion.

Rossel got up to take a closer look. There was the eagle and swastika emblazoned on one side. And the same word round the edge. Neubrandenburg.

'Anything else in that knapsack?' asked Rossel.

'The dirty postcard, like I said,' answered Ivashin. 'And a book.'

'A book?

Ivashin nodded.

'Yes,' he said. 'But I never had the sergeant down as much of a bibliophile. He probably used the pages to wipe his backside with.'

216

Rossel took a step forward. 'You're to come with us, Comrade Ivashin.'

The colour drained from the bookseller's cheeks.

'To prison?'

Rossel shook his head.

'I need you to take us to Grachev's old apartment.'

29

The light was closing in as Rossel, Nikitin and Ivashin stood before what remained of Grachev's former lodgings.

Thanks to the Luftwaffe's nightly bombing raids during the city's 900-day siege, Rossel had seen many buildings like this one. With only the facade still in one piece, it was an enigmatic stone mask concealing a past that had been eviscerated. Its window frames, with peeling paint, containing only shattered glass. Out of one billowed a single white curtain, as if a belated flag of surrender. A table and chairs were visible in a room that now had no walls or ceiling. A huge and twisted steel beam dangled at an unlikely angle: a surreal sword of Damocles hanging over a child's crib.

The street was near the railway lines, which probably explained why it had taken such a pounding from all those Dorniers and Heinkels. It looked as though there had been ten apartment blocks like this one before the war. Now, only three were left standing on one side of the street.

The rest were just holes in the ground, rapidly filling with snow.

'This is it,' said Ivashin. 'We had a reunion here, not long after the war had ended – that time it was just me, the sergeant, Katz and Samosud. We drank a lot and swapped tales of valour, the way old soldiers do. They were rebuilding everything round here. And then one day a couple of years ago – spring of 1950, I think – a labourer working on the site next door to this building took his drill and drilled right into an unexploded bomb. No more labourer, no more building and not much left of the two on either side. That's what Grachev told Katz, anyway. Those two were close. Thick as thieves.'

'Where was his apartment, can you remember?' said Nikitin.

Ivashin shrugged. 'Not the exact position, but it was on the fifth floor, I remember that much.'

'Let's go around the back,' said Rossel. 'There's too much rubble blocking the front door.'

The rear of the block was in better condition. A fire escape had buckled and at its base had peeled away from the brick, but, after a couple of failed attempts, Nikitin managed to hoist himself up, followed by the others. After a storey and a half the floors were in a better condition and they clambered into the apartment block via an empty door frame.

The building was in complete darkness. Using light from Nikitin's torch to pick their way through the debris, they made their way along the fourth floor. From there, an interior stairwell led to the fifth. They turned left and found themselves at the end of a long, wide corridor with doors on either side. The torchlight picked out a mural of workers harvesting sunflowers on the wall, still perfect. At the far end, a glass vase containing dried stalks stood on a small wooden sideboard. Rossel had the strange sense that, at any moment, one of the doors might open and a laughing family, buttoned up to keep out the winter chill, would emerge, heading for a day in one of the city's museums or galleries.

'It's this one, I think,' said Ivashin, stopping in front of the first of two doors on the right.

Nikitin tried the handle.

It was locked.

The major stepped back and kicked at the lock three times. The door buckled in the frame. Rossel pushed it open.

Unlike the corridor, the large communal apartment was badly damaged. There were holes in the floor and the three men had to balance on a steel beam to cross one of them. The layout was similar to Rossel's old *kommunalka* – a big main kitchen, a couple of bathrooms and, off a central corridor, various small rooms. The ones on the right-hand side had all been damaged in the explosion. The ones on the left were in better condition.

Ivashin stopped at the last left-side door and pushed it.

They went in.

Nikitin ran his torch around the walls. Grachev's former bedroom was about three metres by two, reasonably large by *kommunalka* standards. But it had not escaped the explosion – the window had been blown in and glass was scattered across the floor. Next to the window was a gaping hole through which a bitter wind blew. There was a small table and couple of chairs, and a metal-framed single bed with a rotting mattress. At one end was a small stove in the middle of a high bench built into the wall.

Rossel, shivering, looked through the window and clapped his hands together to warm them up. He took a *papirosa* from his pocket and lit it.

'Can I have one?' Ivashin pointed at the cigarette.

'It's my last, but . . .' He handed the cigarette to Ivashin, 'I'm sensing, Comrade Ivashin, that today hasn't been one of your better days.'

Ivashin took the cigarette and sat down in one of the chairs. His hands were trembling. He shut his eyes for a moment, steadying himself with the smoke.

'Here, Rossel, have you seen this? I found Grachev's girlfriend.'

Nikitin shone his torch on the wall just above Grachev's bed, picking out a black-and-white postcard of a naked woman. Rossel reached out and took it. A name was printed on the front. Odette. On the back was something written in French and an address in Germany.

'Odette. That's the name Grachev mentioned to the boy he escaped with,' said Nikitin. 'He swore he was going to find her.'

'Unless he simply meant he was coming back here,' said Rossel. 'Comrade Ivashin,' he called out. 'Does the name Odette mean anything to you?'

Ivashin did not reply.

'Comrade Ivashin, does the name . . .'

As he spoke, Rossel turned to face the veteran.

Ivashin was sitting still in the chair; his head lolling backwards, the *papirosa* sticking to his lip, its tip glowing.

'Hit the floor!' Rossel shouted to Nikitin.

Nikitin did. Then he fumbled for his torch and killed the light.

'Sniper?' he whispered.

'Yes.'

Ivashin's body shook briefly, as though attempting to quell a fit. A second bullet hole appeared in his forehead, only millimetres from the first. He slumped forward and the chair crashed over.

Nikitin rolled his body three times and then, scrambling on all fours, hurled himself out of the room.

Making sure he could not be seen above the bottom of the window frame, Rossel inched towards the door.

An empty vodka bottle next to Grachev's bed exploded.

From the corridor, Nikitin reached in with one hand and, grabbing Rossel by his coat lapels, dragged him out of the door.

Both men got to their feet and started running.

*

Avoiding the last few broken stairs, Rossel leapt from the fire escape, landing almost knee-deep in a drift.

Nikitin jumped after him.

'Fuck your mother!'

'Are you all right?'

Nikitin stood up, grimacing.

'Ankle.' He swore again, putting his hands on his knees.

'I can't run but if I can get to the car, I can use it for cover.'

'Your car is on the sniper's side of the building.'

'Then you'd better kill the bastard, hadn't you, Rossel?'

Rossel pulled out his pistol and started to make his way towards the front of the building.

In the war, the rules to avoid getting shot by a sniper had been simple. Stay in your trench or shell hole, 'keep your fucking head down, comrade,' and, at night, 'don't show your stupid fucking face while having a smoke.'

Pulling out your pistol and charging towards the opposite trench was something only the rawest of recruits might do. Some country bumpkin who had watched *Moscow Strikes Back* far too many times and could hear its soundtrack – Tchaikovsky's Fifth – booming in his ears. A siren voice of heroism.

But what choice did he have?

Rossel patted the seabird on his chest once.

He had survived the bloodiest moments of the war at the Volkhov Front.

Stranded. Pinned down. Refused permission to retreat.

It had been a slaughterhouse.

And yet, he thought, I survived.

He patted the bird again and began to move forward at pace.

After a moment, he reached the edge of the building.

To fire into Grachev's room the sniper had to have been in one of the opposite blocks at about the same height.

Nearly all the windows were dark.

They would have moved. Unless they had an exit planned and could for the time being sit tight, scanning the white street below for slow-moving dark figures.

Luck. In the labour camp, he had made a god of her . . .

Rossel began to run.

He dived behind a van that was missing a wheel, its axle propped up on paint cans.

Hitting the ground, he rolled from the back doors towards the front, hoping the rusting engine would stop a bullet.

On cue, a dull thump.

A hole appearing in the rear wheel arch.

He scanned the ground ahead.

That burnt-out tree – thick enough?

'Hey, you – bastard!'

Nikitin's voice carrying from the other side of Grachev's building. Followed by more curses and taunts.

Enough time?

Rossel got up and ran for the tree, feeling as if time had slowed. He tripped and fell, rolled again, thought he heard something smack into the ground.

Ten paces later he reached the rough walls.

Safe. For now.

He rattled a side door to the building. Only partly on its hinges, it swung open. Pistol in hand, he ran to the stairs, peering ahead into dim light.

Step by step he moved steadily upwards: weapon held high, back pressed into the walls, his breath coming in short, sharp bursts.

Every corridor had half a dozen doors, plus three more on the landing.

At last, he reached the fifth.

He crept along the corridor, pushing at doors to see if any of them gave, but none did.

Then, just as he was about to return to the stairwell, he saw a door to his left, slightly ajar.

He kicked it open. Ran through.

'Fuck your mother . . .'

Nothing. An empty space.

Engine noise. Then a shot.

Rossel thrust his head through an open window.

Nikitin was in the middle of the road, legs apart, blazing away at a retreating motorcycle. The bike teetered as it hit a patch of ice but then, its engine misfiring, turned a corner and disappeared.

*

Ivashin's *papirosa* had gone out but was still hanging from the lips of the dead man. Rossel took it.

'Flying cap, plus a black leather coat. Long. Face covered by a scarf, nice and tight,' said Nikitin.

'That's all you saw of him?'

The major nodded.

'You didn't notice anything else?'

Nikitin shook his head.

'A small man, that's all, like I said.'

Rossel lit the remnants of the cigarette.

'Habits of the camps, eh?' said Nikitin.

'The army,' said Rossel. 'A smoke was never a gift, always a loan.'

Rossel sat down on Grachev's mattress.

'I don't know how I'm going to explain this total *bardak* to the general,' sighed Nikitin. 'He can be an unforgiving man. There are stories.'

'Stories?'

'In Ukraine, in the thirties, when they were closing all the churches: they say he built a bonfire of Bibles and vestments,' said the major, 'and then put the Archimandrite of Poltava on top of it . . .'

Rossel blew out some smoke.

'"Fire goes before Him. And burns up His adversaries round about . . ."' he said.

'I'm not with you.'

'Something my grandmother used to say. And an old Armenian priest I once met. They had things in common.'

Nikitin shrugged.

'Either way, they say the archimandrite sang the Litany like an angel while Pletnev's men roasted him to death.'

The major stood up and rubbed his hands together. He pointed to the little gas stove. 'Fuck, it's cold. I wish we had some tea to boil up on that.'

'Yes, I would . . .'

Rossel's voice trailed away. He stood up and walked towards the stove.

'Give me that torch,' he said.

'Why? What is it?'

Rossel knelt down. Something was propping up one of the legs of the bench that stretched along the wall. A piece of cardboard.

And under that . . . a book.

'Heave this up a notch,' he said.

Nikitin did and Rossel pulled the book free. He held it up and blew the dust from its front cover.

'Something?' said Nikitin.

Rossel showed the major what he had found. It was a slim volume with thick leather covers, with the title embossed in gold.

'*Der Fürst*. Niccolò Machiavelli. *The Prince*, but in German. Grachev hardly read a paper. This must be the book from the knapsack. It has to be.'

'The book Ivashin was talking about is by Machiavelli, too? Koshchei's favourite author? A big coincidence, don't you think?'

Rossel looked at the cover again, his mind racing.

'Or, much more likely, not a coincidence at all.'

He opened *The Prince*. On the first page was an ornate bookplate. At the top were the words EX LIBRIS in white letters on a black scroll. Below that, an eagle with wings unfurled perched on top of a swastika, the latter encased in a laurel wreath.

And underneath, in Gothic type, a name.

Adolf Hitler.

ACT 3
HERO

30

Just before sunrise, with the surrounding pines, firs and birches draped in snow, they waited, slumped on opposite ends of a wooden bench.

'She's late,' muttered Nikitin, sunk deep into his greatcoat.

His words were barely audible but Rossel could see them – puffs of breath marked each syllable.

Captain Morozova, a code and cipher specialist within the GRU, had insisted on somewhere out of the way. Association with Major Nikitin – the Directorate's newest recruit and still tainted by his previous career with the rival MGB – was not much sought-after by his colleagues.

The spot was well chosen. In this far corner of Pavlovsk Park all approach lines were visible. The tracks leading this way were just that – tracks, not paths, nothing a mother pushing a pram would tackle, not in two feet of snow. Most people kept close to the palace and the other imperial monuments nearby.

'She'll come,' said Rossel.

Nikitin grunted, then resumed grumbling. 'I don't trust the GRU and they don't trust me. We shouldn't have told them about the book.'

'We have to show General Pletnev we are making progress,' said Rossel. 'How else could we decipher any messages that might be in it? Like you, I understand barely any German. And even less about codes.'

They sat in silence. Instead of the sun coming up, the dark-grey sky merely grew paler, shade by shade, revealing a light mist hanging at head height.

It was Nikitin who spotted the figure first – an androgynous black stroke against a white canvas.

'There she is,' said Nikitin.

The codebreaker strode towards them. However cautious she had been in their choice of rendezvous, she was making little attempt to make it look like a chance encounter.

Within his coat pocket, Rossel toyed with the safety catch of his pistol.

When the new arrival was twenty paces away, Nikitin stood, shoulders square, glowering.

'Comrade Captain Morozova,' he said.

The woman nodded. She was very short, red-cheeked and hard-eyed.

'Here,' she said.

She took out the leather-bound book and tossed it at Nikitin, who caught it at boot height. She thrust her hands back into her pockets.

'You wasted your time and mine, Comrade Major,' the captain said. 'Nothing in invisible ink, none of the pages can be split into other pages. Too many passages are underlined for anything to stand out, either as marked or unmarked.'

Rossel tugged his coat tight around his shoulders in annoyance.

She hasn't even tried . . .

'What about the numbers at the back?' he said.

The codebreaker looked at him for the first time, apparently not liking what she saw.

'The series of numbers at the back of the book *might* be some sort of code,' she said, 'but unless we have the key – the one-time pad, as it is known – which could be in another book entirely, they are meaningless.'

'What kind of analysis did you run?' he asked.

'The usual – frequency analysis of the most common German letters, patterns of repetition. I gave up after half an hour. It was obvious that further efforts would be pointless.'

Nikitin looked disbelieving. 'Perhaps you missed something? Some little bit of the language, some unusual Fritz phrasing . . .'

'Missed something?' Her voice hardened. 'Comrade Major, I speak extremely good German – but I don't need to,' she said. 'The chances are that this is not even a Hitlerite artefact. A fake of some sort. In the West, there is already a market for memorabilia of this kind, where items are commonly counterfeited. Twenty million Soviet citizens killed by that man and the capitalists just see that as good advertising. The toilet brush Hitler used would set a bourgeois back a month's wages. This is most likely the property of an ordinary officer who plastered in a stolen book plate. Perhaps in the hope of selling it on the black market at a later date. Did you read the inscription on the page opposite the plate?'

Nikitin opened the book at the front and read aloud.

'This bit? *Jetzt . . . bin . . . ich . . .*'

He gave up – 'Rossel, you read . . .'

'*Jetzt bin ich Soldat und Ihr treuer Diener,*' snapped Morozova before Rossel could do so. 'It means "now I am a soldier and your loyal servant". Oberst Halder, 115th SS Panzer Division, 22nd Brigade, March 12 1945. In every detail, nonsense.'

They waited for her to explain.

'Humour us, comrade,' said Rossel.

She turned her back on them.

'The SS didn't even have 115 Panzer divisions,' she said as she began to walk away. 'Thank you for wasting my time, comrades. As I said, your precious artefact is a fake.'

'We need more time,' said Rossel as they watched her walk away.

'We haven't got any,' Nikitin replied. 'The general is a man who wants results, and fast.'

He got up and kicked at the snow.

'She may not have brought us the goods we wanted but that snotty bitch has got me thinking,' he said.

Rossel turned to him.

'Not normally your style.'

'About Koshchei. A small man, you said, from what you saw.'

'Quite small, yes.'

Nikitin reached down into the snow and packed some of it into a ball. Then he half-heartedly tossed it in the direction of the diminutive figure of Captain Morozova.

'Or . . .'

Rossel stood up and, to his own surprise, slapped Nikitin on the back.

'A woman,' he said. 'Of course.'

*

A one-legged man of Rossel's age in a smart blue uniform was bellowing to all passengers that the heavy snowfall of the past two days had caused disruption to the timetable.

The next train to Leningrad took forty minutes to arrive and was three-quarters full. But Nikitin had the kind of face people didn't want to sit next to. So, he had little trouble locating a quiet corner. The major stared out of the window, brooding, as Rossel studied the book.

There were indeed numerous passages underlined. Scribbles in the margin, the work of an agitated hand. Phrases in German that were apparently taken from a different text entirely. Some of those had now been annotated in turn in Russian, presumably by Morozova. From *Mein Kampf*? Or from his last testament?

Occasionally there was nothing but an exclamatory *Ja!* of critical approval and an arrow towards a particular paragraph. As though Hitler – if it was him – was saying, *My thoughts exactly, Herr Machiavelli.*

Flicking through, Rossel saw a dark red line along one section of the text that he had not noticed previously:

Jeder sieht, was du scheinst. Nur wenige fühlen, wie du bist.

The codebreaker had taken the trouble to translate it:

Everyone sees what you appear to be. Few experience what you really are.

As the train moved through a thickening blizzard back towards Leningrad, he began to doubt Captain Morozova's dismissal of *The Prince*. He turned it over and over with his broken hands. Rationally, it was just another war trophy. A Nazi bookplate made it neither more or less than a collection of paper. But its link to Grachev, to the murdered men . . . the inscription, the numbers in the back.

It had an aura, like a sacred object. Or a satanic one. In his hands, it felt like a mythical chest that he could not open. But he was certain that within it lay the answer to his quest.

Rossel stared down at the underlined quotation. His thoughts travelled to the besieged bunker near the Reich Chancellery in April 1945, and the mind of the man who most likely had drawn the line. Hitler, too, must at some point have gazed down at this exact page. Perhaps when all around him Berlin was in flames and Marshal Zhukov's soldiers were only days away from dragging him out into the light and . . .

Everyone sees what you appear to be. Few experience what you really are.

Rossel glanced around at his fellow train passengers. Sombre, mute and inscrutable. At the very end, he wondered, did the little Austrian corporal who had set the world on fire understand the impossibility of ever truly knowing another human being? And see it as the ultimate means of escape?

The train halted at a signal. Rossel stretched out his limbs as far as he was able in the confined space.

Something else was bothering him. The sniper. *How did I not realise she was a woman?*

'In the Great Patriotic War, the People's Commissariat of Defence set up special Sniper Training Schools,' he said. 'I remember *Pravda* crowing about it. "Brave Soviet women cradle their rifles as they would their children." That kind of thing. Heard of them?'

Nikitin nodded. 'That girl, what was she called? Comrade Shanina. I think she was one.'

Roza Shanina had more than fifty kills to her name and had received the Medal for Courage before she was killed in action. For a while, all the snipers, men and women, were lauded and lionised throughout the Soviet Union.

'The main school was in Moscow but they trained a few of them up here during the blockade,' said Rossel. 'They closed everything down for the women even before the end of the war.'

Still feeling pleased with his own detective powers, Nikitin smiled.

'Of course they did,' he said. 'But a sniper would never forget her training.'

31

Back in his apartment, Rossel stared out at Koshchei's mist-covered realm, where more than half a million souls lay in Piskaryovskoye Cemetery. He remembered his grandmother and her friends sharing the tale of 'the Deathless, the Immortal'. How their eyes would gleam when they talked of the diabolical spell that protected him, relishing the terror they inspired in a small child.

How Koshchei would hide his soul in nested objects to preserve his immortality. In one version, in a needle that was hidden inside an egg, which is carried by a bird who flew away so no one could catch it.

The snipers he had been thinking of were all men. Vasily Zaitsev, Ivan Sidorenko, Semyon Nomokonov. Heroes of the Soviet Union, their tales often repeated in newsreels and the papers.

But what would Koshchei do differently if she was a woman?

His own prejudice had blinded him. The locket should have opened his eyes. What stung his pride most of all was that Nikitin had seen it before he had.

The sniper must have been tracking Ivashin and had followed them to Grachev's old apartment. Did she know about the book?

A murderer who puts the words of Machiavelli into the mouths of her victims, following them to a place where they discover a unique copy of *The Prince*. The two cases seemed to fit together.

Perhaps, Rossel thought as he took a step back from the window, one is nested inside the other? Hidden away like Koshchei's soul.

*

Rossel walked back to the piano, lowered its music stand and shut the lid. The watching Drugov family had haunted him long enough. Now he needed their help. He had been plonking out one of Medtner's piano sonatas to help him think.

It hadn't worked.

He slapped his damaged left hand down on the lid. He needed a composer who could make a virtue of simplicity – Prokofiev, perhaps. Maybe he could prevail upon the composer to create a piece specially tailored to his own unique needs – 'Concerto for a Man with Missing Fingers' – and to make it a stumbling, jazz-like reverie filled with lost hopes and bleak, discordant frustration. Although, in composing such a piece, Prokofiev would need to take care to avoid the Soviet crime of 'formalism'; not produce the 'muddled, nerve-racking' sounds for which that brutal arbiter of taste Andrei Zhdanov had condemned him and so many other composers.

Since Zhdanov's decree, the soul of a Soviet artist could only soar upward in a pre-agreed direction. The rubber stamps of Party bureaucrats had smudged black ink on their hearts.

Photographs of each member of the missing Drugov family stared at Rossel from the top of the piano. Like a detective in an English country house murder mystery, he had assembled his audience.

Captain Morozova's observation was still troubling him – *'The SS didn't even have 115 Panzer divisions . . .'*

Nikitin had confirmed this as they had parted company near the Admiralty. 'Just under forty, depending on how you count them,' he'd said. 'Most of the later ones were cannon fodder, made up of Hitler Youth or pensioners or desperate foreign collaborators who preferred to be slaughtered in battle than face Soviet justice. I was one of those who had to root them out, get them to confess, bang heads together, and sometimes . . . Well, you get the picture. So that's how I know. At the end, entire German armies existed only inside Hitler's head. I should have realised, but she's right. There was no 115th SS Panzer Division.'

Rossel walked over to a little stove he had set up. He warmed his hands on a teapot and his insides with the tea. The apartment was still very cold. Bureaucrats decided when the district's heating was turned on and off and had finally relented a few days ago, but it took time for the entire block to warm through, even with, as now, every radiator throbbing.

He lit a *papirosa* and started pacing up and down.

'Let us assume that it is not a fake,' he addressed the Drugov family members in turn, showing them each the book. 'Who props up something with Hitler's copy of Machiavelli's *The Prince*? Most people would use a piece of cardboard, or half a brick, or a piece of wood. But Sergeant Grachev *would* prop up a table with a Nazi copy of *The Prince*, because he took it from a dead German in Berlin and brought it back to Leningrad without having the first idea of its value.'

He took a sip from his cup.

'In sum, is it plausible that this book came back from Berlin with Sergeant Pavel Grachev, but that he was indifferent to it because it wasn't a gold medallion with a swastika on it? Yes, it is plausible. The sergeant's kitchen stove was unsteady and he used what was to hand to solve the problem.'

The museum director stared back at Rossel, hostile and disdainful. Had he, Drugov, been afforded this level of reasoned inquiry at his own trial – if he'd even had a trial? Of course not.

Rossel appealed next to Madame Drugova, stout and matronly with a kind face.

'At the end of the war, members of the SS took off their uniforms and tried to pretend they were regular army or civilians,' he told her. 'But Oberst Halder, Commander, purportedly of the 115th SS Panzer Division, 22nd Brigade, which did not exist, was happy to inscribe his name in a gift to the Führer himself a matter of days before the Third Reich ended.'

Now Rossel looked into the bright, hopeful eyes of the young teenage violinist, Anna, his favourite of the family. A handwritten note near the bottom of the picture frame read: 'Alas, our little Anna loves only Borodin, Schubert and Arensky!' The note was adorned with three kisses.

'The key point, dear Anna, is this. If the book is significant and if Oberst Halder is real, then consider the fact that when inscribing a gift to the Führer, a German officer does not get his own Panzer division wrong.'

Rossel sat down and stubbed out his cigarette.

'Unless, of course, he did it on purpose.'

32

'I need a German speaker.'

'At this time?'

Tarkovsky was still half asleep and bewildered to be roused at five a.m. He was also, Rossel could tell, a little relieved to see that it was him, and not the people who usually came knocking shortly before dawn.

It had taken hours of staring at words he didn't understand before inspiration struck. Hours of examining *The Prince* in German, from cover to cover, looking for something that the GRU codebreaker had missed in her impatience.

The clue, when he saw it, was so simple that he'd spent several minutes berating himself before throwing on his coat and setting out for the actor's apartment in the Yusupov.

'It's to do with your old friend Machiavelli, if that piques your interest, Comrade Callimaco,' said Rossel. 'A quick translation and then I will be gone.'

Tarkovsky thought for a moment.

'I'll need my glasses,' he said, opening the door a little wider. 'Whatever it is, it's got to be better than the horse-shit they have been writing for me at Lenfilm recently And I'm not back on set until eleven.'

*

'I want you to read from this page for me.' Rossel tapped a finger on the book, which lay open on a small coffee table between them. They were sitting in Tarkovsky's living room, next to his piano.

Tarkovsky picked up the book.

'Page 115?'

Rossel nodded.

Captain Morozova had found the cipher, or part of it. She just hadn't realised it.

A German officer does not get his own Panzer division wrong.

Back at the apartment, the insight had finally led him from 115th Panzer to page 115. 22nd Brigade? That had stumped him for a while. Then he had counted down 22 lines from the top, to find nothing of significance.

But 22 lines up from the bottom . . .

'See that heading,' he pointed it out for Tarkovsky.

Von der Grausamkeit und Milde, und ob es besser ist, geliebt oder gefürchtet zu werden.

'Can you translate it and the text beneath it for me?'

Under it was a lone unmarked passage. An island of virgin text in a sea of scrawlings, underlinings and margin notes:

Denn man kann von den Menschen insgemein sagen, daß sie, undankbar, wankelmütig, falsch, feig in Gefahren und gewinnsüchtig sind; solange du ihnen wohltust, sind sie dir ergeben und bieten dir, wie oben gesagt, Gut und Blut, ihr Leben und das ihrer Kinder an, solange die Gefahr fern ist; kommt sie aber näher, so empören sie sich.

'Let's have some music?' said Tarkovsky, pushing his glasses further up the bridge of his nose.

He turned the radio on.

'*Swan Lake*. Of course. The epitome of banality, perfect for pacifying the masses. When is it not *Swan Lake*?'

Yet it would do nicely to mask their voices from any eavesdroppers.

The actor beckoned Rossel closer and cleared his throat.

'*Von der Grausamkeit und Milde*. "On Cruelty and Kindness. Or whether it is better to be loved than feared."'

Tarkovsky paused, straightened his back, and assumed what he presumably imagined to be the bearing of a fifteenth-century Italian diplomat. He picked up the book with his left hand and turned the palm of his right out, as if delivering a lecture. Then, translating as he read, he began to declaim in the manner of a sorcerer intoning a spell.

'"Because one can say this in general of men,"' he continued. '"That they are ungrateful" . . . not sure about that next one, something about stumbling – faltering? "False, cowardly in the face of dangers, and mercenary. As long as you benefit them," so, er, as long as you are good towards them, "they are to you beholden," or maybe devoted, "and will offer you," as I said above, "goods and blood, their lives and that of their children, as long as the peril is far away. But should it come closer, so do they turn on you."'

Tarkovsky removed his glasses with a flourish. 'That's it,' he said.

Rossel looked around for a pencil and some paper.

'Can I write on this?' he asked, holding up a copy of *Literaturnaya Gazeta*.

Tarkovsky shrugged. 'It is dangerous, even illegal, for an ordinary Soviet citizen to possess *The Prince*, is it not? So I might as well allow you to deface the principal cultural organ of the Soviet establishment as well. Anyway, over the years they've never been particularly kind to me.'

'Say it all again, please.'

As Tarkovsky translated the paragraph for the second time, this time with more precision, Rossel scrawled on the newspaper.

He read it back to himself. It was something, he was certain of it.

A step forward.

But he didn't feel that much closer to Pletnev's mysterious hoard of gold.

'Turn off the lights when you leave,' said Tarkovsky.

The actor stood up, put the book down, switched off the radio and walked towards his bedroom. 'I don't understand the attraction of *Swan Lake,* do you?' he said. 'The message of it, I mean. A swan that wants to be human? A life spent climbing the greasy pole as opposed to one floating regally across a lake. I mean . . . why would you?'

Rossel pointed at the book.

'Men are ungrateful, false and mercenary. I think Comrade Machiavelli agrees with you.'

*

Just over an hour later, the streets were starting to fill with the early shift workers, their headgear rammed tight down against the cold. A few were hopping up into Rossel's tram, adding more bodies to the press. Chunks of snow fell off their boots, turning the metal floor wet and muddy. One half of the carriage emptied at Nevsky while the other half filled up with new passengers. The tram rattled on under the blazing streetlights, up to the Field of Mars, where he got off. Over the Fontanka at the intersection of canals, down Mokhovaya, which was deserted, and to the corner of Liteiny and Nekrasova.

Back to his former life in the militia and Station 17.

He knew she would be early. She was the most conscientious officer in the station. That was why they always had got on.

Lidia Gerashvili was small and half-Georgian, with dark hair and darker eyes. She used to dye her shoulder-length hair blonde but had let it return to its natural colour. Her pupils were more guarded and introspective than when he'd first known her; the side-effect of a previous temporary incarceration and subsequent release by the agents of state security.

'Lidia. Comrade Senior Sergeant now, I see,' he said, glancing at her insignia.

For the briefest moment, Gerashvili paled. She stared at Rossel as though she had been walking through a cemetery and encountered an old friend climbing out of one of the pits. But she had the presence of mind not to yell or take flight when he placed a hand on her elbow.

Recovering, she led him straight inside, where she demanded the night officer bring them tea from the samovar.

As they walked down the corridor, doors closed. He saw a couple of familiar faces but they immediately turned away. He might as well have been marked by the plague and ringing a bell.

Fair enough, he thought. What could Comrade Albatross – a former senior member of Station 17, who had crossed swords with Beria and ended up in a labour camp – bring them but trouble? If he was in their place, he'd be thinking the same thing.

Treachery can be catching.

*

They proceeded to the archive room. Gerashvili's domain. They sat without speaking until the tea arrived, after which they sipped and blew and sipped again.

Rossel glanced around the boxes of files that lined the shelves, and at the metal cabinets that were also full of them. When he had been senior lieutenant here, he had made nightly pilgrimages to spend time with the files of the missing: those kindred spirits of his lost twin sister who he felt – in some way he was unable to explain – kept Galya company.

She had left him, he knew, because of what she believed he had done to their mother and father. Informed on them. Whether he had meant to or not was immaterial. In the Soviet Union, it was the most unoriginal of sins. Babayan's words about Vustin came back to him: 'That's why the boy liked you, Rossel. He was jealous of your soul's burden.'

The image of Galya's face on the night he had last seen her came to him again. He had watched her from a window: curious, uncomprehending. His sister had stepped out from beneath a light and disappeared. Been enveloped by the dancing flurries.

At that moment, he thought, she became a shade to me.

An ever-accusing finger. One of the old priest's shadows in the snow.

'Are you all right, Revol?' Gerashvili asked. 'You've gone missing.'

'Yes, sorry. I'm fine.'

He wasn't. But he gave the briefest of smiles anyway.

The last time he had seen Gerashvili, almost exactly a year ago, she had been a rank lower. She had also been mentally broken as the result of a prolonged spell of interrogation at the hands of Nikitin's MGB colleagues – former colleagues, he corrected himself. Not many who were that far gone managed to find their way back again.

That was something else they had in common.

'Would you be able to check all the files available on the two sniper schools for women in Moscow and Leningrad that operated during the war? Particularly the Leningrad school.'

He watched her reaction as she turned over the request in her mind, looking for danger. 'It is not official work,' he added. 'You should feel free to refuse.'

'What would I be looking for?' she asked.

'Anyone who had a particular way of killing. A kind of signature.'

Gerashvili nodded. 'We are allowed to request access to Red Army files in certain circumstances. I will do so. But it might take a little time.'

'Thank you,' he said.

'Is that it?'

Rossel shook his head.

'No, sorry. Lidia, I need something else, too. You have a reasonable grasp of German,' he said.

She inclined her head.

'I was right to suspect you hadn't come to ask me to go dancing at the Hotel Astoria,' she said.

'Next time, I promise. And during the blockade, you carried out radio and signals duty for a while?'

She nodded again. 'Well, they gave me the radio to look after. I was only a teenager when I was sent to the front for the first time. I learned and listened out for words such as *Angriffsziel, Unternehmen Nordlicht* and *feindliche Truppen*. A notch or two above the standard words like *Hände hoch* and *Scheisse*.'

'How about for codes and ciphers?'

She hesitated. 'I did my best. At least, I tried to spot words that might signify that a code was being used. Or any apparently innocent message that might have another meaning.'

'I see,' said Rossel. 'And a signals unit had to send coded messages as well as intercept them. Correct?'

'Yes.'

Rossel took out the copy of *The Prince* and outlined his reasoning so far.

Gerashvili listened. Then picked up the mugs from the table.

'For this,' she said, 'I'm going to need more tea.'

33

The book lay between the two mugs. It was open at page 115.

'As I told you, the numbers 115 and twenty-two led me to this section of the book,' Rossel said, showing her the relevant passage. 'So, the numbers are significant. Next comes the date – 12 March 1945. I feel that must be important, too, but that's where I am stuck. I can't see why.'

Gerashvili frowned.

'Everything they have used so far is about numbers. So maybe this is, too?' she said.

'Not March, not the month itself?'

She shook her head. Distracted, she straightened some files on her desk. Tapped a finger on the side of her cup. Once, twice, three times . . .

She grabbed a pencil, scribbled something down on a notepad and pushed it across the desk towards him.

'1, 2, 3, and 45. March is the third month. So perhaps the correct way to read this is the very simplest one – numerically.'

'A sequence,' said Rossel. 'You're a genius, Lidia.'

Suddenly he felt weary. He stretched out his arms and yawned. But helping to fight his fatigue was the thought that another obstacle was crumbling.

'Now I see it. The man who wrote this wants us to look at a sequence of some sort. Every word in turn.' He looked up at her. 'But how?'

Gerashvili shrugged.

'I don't know. What else do you have to show me?'

Rossel turned to the back of the book and the jumble of numbers on the inside back cover.

Someone had already taken a look and dismissed this part, he explained. 'I was told by the GRU that these numbers were so random they could not be deciphered. That you would need a particular text, a separate text, that would give you the key. But that you could only use such a text once without compromising its security. And there is no chance of us ever getting that text.'

'Then we are at a dead end,' Gerashvili said. 'And not even a third cup of sweet tea will help us.'

Rossel leaned back and looked at the stacks of files all over the room. He had spent hours here, leafing through missing person's records, of which there were still so many. Immersed in stories, tragedies and mysteries.

'Unless.'

She tapped the side of her head.

'It would be perverse on the part of whoever wrote all this in the book to set out a clue on the opening pages, indicate the significance of a passage in the middle, and leave a row of random numbers at the end,' Gerashvili said.

'Lidia, I am no longer your superior officer,' he said. 'Please speak freely.'

'It looks to me like the cipher and its key are meant to be all in one place.'

'Please explain it to me.'

'You have reminded me of my wartime radio duties,' she said. 'The most basic military cipher was to assign numbers to letters. The simplest would be to take the first letter of a sentence and replace it with the number one, the second letter and replace it with the number two, and so on.'

'The Germans used that?'

She shook her head.

'No, they had sophisticated machines. Our job was to pick up phrases indicating that they were sending messages using those machines. You know – *Hans, there's an important message coming, wake up*. That fact alone might suggest an attack was coming. We used this method all the time, though. When we needed to get a simple message from one place to another – something to act on quickly, a secret that would be useless an hour later – we would sing the first lines of a revolutionary song or a nursery rhyme over the radio. Something every Russian would know but the Germans would not. And we'd say the number three, which was an instruction to note down the third letter of every word and write them out in a row. Then the recipient would substitute those letters for numbers and wait for us to send a numerical message by runner.'

Rossel tried to imagine this. But failed.

'Then why send a runner? Why not just read out the numbers on the radio?'

'The Germans took prisoners,' she said. 'Prisoners can be persuaded to sing revolutionary songs or nursery rhymes when their fingernails are being torn out.'

'Runners get shot by snipers or tread on mines,' Rossel said.

'There was always another runner.'

Rossel stared at the book. An act of desperation. Perhaps the sender was in a hurry. Perhaps the gold medallions were a calling card – a sign of the sender's seniority? And the book contained instructions on how to find something more important. Use keys the other side won't know, like the numbers of SS Panzer divisions. And then indicate that it's a simple sequence. Put in a dirty postcard and some *Juno* cigarettes to distract attention from the main prize.

But what if you had only one book and one courier, and the message never got through?

'Let's try it,' he said.

Gerashvili pulled open a drawer, took out a notebook and got to work.

Denn man kann von den Menschen insgemein sagen, daß sie, undankbar, wankelmütig, falsch, feig . . .

'If it's just a sequence and the sender is keeping things very simple, then the letter d will be 1, e2, n3, n4, m5, a6, n7 . . .'

Rossel pulled a lamp closer to her.

She frowned. 'Wait.'

'What is it?'

She pointed to the jumble of numbers at the back of *The Prince*. 'The highest number here is twenty-six. And it occurs repeatedly. That is a big clue that this is an alphabetical cipher in German. But in such a case, one would be more likely to use only the first occurrence of each letter in order. So we give the letter n only one number.'

Gerashvili kept up her rapid scribble before stopping. She stabbed the pad and cursed.

'Nonsense,' she said. 'Let's try the numbers in reverse order.'

Rossel closed his eyes, listening to the scratch of pencil on paper.

'So,' she said, just as he was dropping off. 'Are you ready? This might not work – we may have missed a clue. Or it might be an instruction to take the first letter, then skip two, then three, four five, and then back to one.'

'We should know within a few numbers,' he said. 'Though my German is not good, I warn you, so we may need a few sentences for me to be able to distinguish actual words from gibberish.'

'Then take this. I'll turn the numbers into letters and read them out. You write them down – do rows of ten at first.'

She began.

'D. E. N. N. D. E. R. G. O . . .'

There were seventy numbers in all and it took only a few minutes for Gerashvili and Rossel to work their way through them.

They scanned the results:

D E N N D E R G O T
T E R E N D E D A M
M E R T N U N A U F
S O W E R F I C H D
E N B R A N D I N W
A L H A L L S P R A
N G E N D E B U R G

'Does it mean anything to you, Revol?'

Rossel looked at the letters. At first, they just swam in a sea of gibberish.

But then . . .

WALHALL . . . GOTTER, or rather GÖTTER . . .

'Yes,' he said. 'It's from an opera. By Wagner.'

She suppressed a laugh.

'Opera? Was this opera about war? Are there tanks on stage?'

Rossel stared at them again. He was no expert on Wagner but students of orchestral instruments at the Leningrad Conservatoire were given a gruelling education in the symphonic and operatic repertoire, and he had done long stints rehearsing a couple of Wagner's major works, including *Götterdämmerung*. It had not been a hardship: the music was divine, shattering, intoxicating. He'd even taken the score out from the library, spending a couple of evenings revelling in its brilliance.

But *here*?

'This bit doesn't fit,' said Gerashvili.

She pointed at a line of letters and numbers at the bottom of the page. They might have been written in the same hand as all the other numbers, but it was hard to be sure.

15OSRD18B

'Not with number substitution anyway,' she said. 'You get ZPOSRZLGB. Or possibly IOSRDSB, if 1 and 5 are 15, and 1 and 8 are 18. Either way, it isn't German, or any other language.'

Gerashvili tore out the pages of her notebook on which she had done her workings and handed them to Rossel. Then she replaced everything in her desk drawer.

They both stood.

'Thank you, Lidia,' Rossel said.

'It might take me a week to get the records for the sniper school. Can you wait that long, Revol?'

'No,' Rossel said. 'But I suppose I will have to.'

As they walked back down the corridor, Rossel tried not to look through the door to his old office, but it was slightly ajar and he could not resist. The only thing he glimpsed was the dark fireplace with the engraved metal decoration, including the outline of the seabird that he used to touch for luck.

So far, he thought, it hasn't really brought me much.

*

Major Nikitin was waiting in the Drugovs' apartment, seated at the dining table like a suspicious spouse.

'General Pletnev is getting very impatient, Rossel. I hope you have made progress.'

Rossel needed to sleep. He yawned to see if Nikitin would take the hint but the major just stared back at him. With a sigh, Rossel pulled up a chair and took out the scrap of paper on which he had written the letters. He smoothed the paper on the table so Nikitin could see it:

> *Denn der Götter Ende dämmert nun auf.*
> *So werf' ich den Brand*
> *in Walhalls prangende Burg*

'Which means?' said Niktin.

Rossel wrote out the translation in Russian:

> For the end of the Gods draws near,
> So I throw this torch
> onto the shining walls of Valhalla.

'Wagner,' Rossel said. 'It's from Wagner.'

Nikitin grimaced.

'That's . . . that's *everything*?'

'So far. That, and a small but impenetrable jumble of words and numbers, which I still have no idea about.'

The major gnawed at his upper lip.

'Tell me about bastard Wagner, then,' he said.

'The text is from his opera *Götterdämmerung*,' said Rossel. '*The Twilight of the Gods*. The final scene. The very last bars of *The Ring*, his epic operatic masterpiece in four parts.'

'More,' said Nikitin.

'Brünnhilde, a Valkyrie who became a mortal, sets fire to the funeral pyre of her lover Siegfried. She rides her horse into the flames. At the same time Valhalla, the home of the Norse gods, disappears for ever. A new era begins. A celebrated scene, one of the most famous pieces of music ever written. The Nazis adored it.'

Before the Great Patriotic War, the authorities had tolerated performances of Wagner in the Soviet Union. After it, even whistling the 'Ride of the Valkyries' on the tram was risky.

'But is it enough?' muttered Nikitin.

'Enough?'

The major scowled. 'For Pletnev.'

'I don't know. It's all I have got.'

Nikitin jabbed a gloved finger into Rossel's chest.

'Get some sleep, comrade. An hour only. Then we report to the general.'

34

A dull headache tapped like a Morse code signal at his temples.

Rossel rubbed a porthole into the misted passenger window of Nikitin's Pobeda and stared out at morose afternoon pedestrians with heads lowered into the whipping breeze. Daylight was one of many winter scarcities in Leningrad. The weather was often fickle, with blizzards and bright sunshine alternating without warning.

As they arrived at his office in the museum, General Pletnev was in conclave with two officers. He looked up from their deliberations, his face pale.

'News?' he said.

Several paces from the desk, Nikitin saluted and stopped, placing a hand on Rossel's arm. Shaking it off, Rossel walked straight up to the officers, took out *The Prince* from one coat pocket and the gold medallion from the other, and threw both on the desk.

'Yes,' he said.

The general looked down at the book and back up at Rossel.

'Comrades,' he said to his officers. 'A moment, if you will.'

The officers left the room.

'You should know your place, comrade,' said Pletnev.

Behind him, Nikitin stifled a cough.

But the general opened *The Prince* and inspected the bookplate.

'Who was Oberst Halder, Comrade General?' asked Rossel. 'And why is someone ready to kill, and keep on killing, for this book?'

Pletnev's eyes moved between the two objects but he did not answer.

'Like all the other dead men, the war veteran Ivashin had kept his gold medallion,' said Rossel. 'He had no clue that it was in any way significant. I wager that none of the victims did. Under torture, the first one screams out the name of the second one, who does the same for the third one, and so on. But none of them gives the killer the information they seek. Because they do not understand what they have.'

With the crooked forefinger of his left hand, Rossel tapped the desk.

'But I think you do.'

Pletnev leant over, resting on his elbows, collecting his thoughts. Then he straightened up. He marched over to a table in the corner to retrieve his coat and cap, which he put on with care.

'And have you reached any other conclusions, Comrade Detective?' he said.

'I have,' said Rossel. 'Using a code he wrote into the book, Oberst Franz Halder, whoever he was or is, was issuing an instruction,' answered Rossel. 'A command to set fire to Valhalla. A coded message to bring about the end of the world. The next question is: a message to whom?'

Pletnev finished doing up his buttons.

'Comrades,' he said, 'follow me.'

*

Just ahead of them, in the dying light, a platoon of down-trodden conscripts was shambling its way towards the vast Palace Square, oblivious to the presence of one of the Soviet Union's most senior commanders. Underneath the triumphal arch that led into the square, the general slowed and watched them.

'Just look at them,' he said, pointing to the young soldiers. 'Already we are weak. The Motherland is losing her resolve and discipline. I foresaw as much when we reopened some of the churches. The Americans and British at our borders, always probing, preparing for invasion . . .'

He resumed his walk. The conscripts, orders yelled at them by a fat captain in the middle of the group, veered right.

Pletnev strode forward several more paces, glanced around the square and stopped. He looked up for a moment at the Alexander Column, the monument to Russia's victory over Napoleon. On the far side of the square was the Winter Palace. Away to the left, the gilded spire of the Admiralty, once headquarters of the Imperial Russian Navy. This place had once been the centre of tsarist power. Now it all belonged to the Soviets. In theory, to the workers.

'Franz Halder is a man we have sought since the final weeks of the war,' the general said. 'A German aristocrat. A fighter ace. The commanding officer of the elite Jagdgeschwader 26: a group of more than one hundred fighter pilots flying Me-109s. He was an officer who inspired complete trust and loyalty.'

He turned back to watch the conscripts performing a slovenly drill and cursed under his breath.

'But then Halder was reassigned to work on the Luftwaffe weapons research facility at Peenemünde, on an island in the Baltic Sea,' resumed the general. 'Rockets and missiles. Some of which were devastating, most of which were expensive failures. When military intelligence agents conducted their interrogations of leading Nazis after the fall of Berlin, they established that Halder was in effect number two to Albert Speer, the Third Reich's armaments minister. An uneasy relationship, by all accounts, but they put up with each other.'

Pletnev took off his hat and ran his right hand over his scalp.

'Indeed, Halder's position was such, and he was so highly thought of, that he became an adjutant to Hitler himself. We believe he was in the Führer's bunker until the very last hours of the war.'

Nikitin whistled. 'Hitler's adjutant,' he said.

'And a way for Speer to keep an eye on what the Führer was up to,' said Pletnev. 'Speer spent the last weeks of the war countermanding Hitler's orders to raze Germany to the ground. Blow up bridges, destroy factories, set fire to crops. Speer stopped that. Well, most of it. He wanted to be the leader of a new Reich, not of a wasteland.'

The conscripts trundled off Palace Square behind the Winter Palace, their captain administering kicks to the backsides of the stragglers.

'You were once a musician were you not, Comrade Rossel?' said Pletnev.

'A student, yes,' said Rossel. 'Of violin, at the Leningrad Conservatoire.'

'One with a future? A career in music?'

'People said so.'

After one of Rossel's examination recitals, the head of the strings faculty had stopped him in the corridor and told him he had never heard a finer performance of Beethoven's Kreutzer Sonata.

'But I never got to finish my studies,' he added, to forestall the next question. 'The defence of Leningrad came first.'

'As a musician, even a former one, this detail will interest you then,' Pletnev said. 'The last time we saw anything of Halder was in April 1945, at the final wartime concert of the Berlin Philharmonic. The Reichstag had not yet fallen but we already had spies all over Berlin. One of mine was looking after the coats of important fat Krauts who were about to become a lot less fat and significantly less important.'

He gave the ground a kick. 'We were already in a race with the Americans to find Hitler's scientists, rocket designers, chemical and biological weapons manufacturers . . . But many threw themselves into the arms of the capitalist West.'

Pletnev pulled out his watch, checked it and replaced it in his jacket.

'At the concert,' he said, 'our agent observed Halder deep in conversation with Speer, though he could not overhear what they said. Speer, of course, was captured, but Halder disappeared. For years we assumed he had been killed, or had committed suicide, or fled to Argentina or Brazil. We sent out agents but they heard not so much as a rumour.'

The general began walking again. Rossel and Nikitin kept pace.

'Speer was a defendant at the Nuremberg trials, was he not, Comrade General?' said Rossel.

'Yes, but the man is a charmer. Someone who could not only talk the birds down from the trees, as they say, but then persuade the trees to lie down next to them. A gifted story-teller who managed to convince the judges he was not a Nazi but a saint. Through his penitence, he escaped the noose. Which, to be fair to him, was indeed some kind of miracle.'

After the war, the papers and radio broadcasts had been full of the Nuremberg trials – the denunciations by Soviet prosecutors, who had demanded justice for the heinous crimes of the German leaders and their people. They con-demned the Western judges as Fascist collaborators for jail-ing some of the leading Germans rather than hanging them. *Nazis who garrotted Soviet heroes and hung them from hooks in their torture chambers for the spectacle of it. Yet the capitalists show mercy to these animals.*

'What happened to him then?' said Nikitin.

'Albert Speer is one of seven senior Hitlerites residing in Spandau prison in Berlin. They are guarded by us, the British, the French and the Americans, on rotation. But Soviet wardens are always present. The other three pow-ers cannot be trusted with the prisoners. They will bar-gain with them, offer them freedom for any last scraps of intelligence.'

Pletnev tugged his coat tight and checked his epaulettes. 'If Herr Speer has one last secret to impart, then I would wager that he knows the fate of Oberst Franz Halder.'

As they arrived at the entrance to the General Staff building, two huge guards standing outside came to atten-tion and saluted as Pletnev approached.

'I want you to go to Spandau, comrades,' said Pletnev. 'Find out from Speer whatever he knows about Halder, whatever he knows about the message in that book.'

The general took it out from his greatcoat and pressed it back into Rossel's hands.

Rossel was struggling to take this in. For most people, a trip to the West was unheard of. Only the most trusted citizens were permitted foreign travel.

'Why would he talk to us, Comrade General?' he asked.

'Because you will be conveying a personal offer from me,' replied Pletnev. 'In exchange for intelligence that leads us to Halder, I will make representations at the highest levels of the Kremlin that will help reduce his sentence.'

Rossel looked straight back at the general. This was an unexpected commitment. Even more surprising was that the general was entrusting the message to him and Nikitin.

'Forgive me, Comrade General,' he said. 'I am still thinking this through. Halder's message in *The Prince* includes an instruction to set fire to Valhalla.'

'Yes.'

'One interpretation of that instruction is to order an attack of some sort?'

A guard opened the door to the General Staff building, revealing more soldiers lining the corridor. On sight of the general they saluted in unison.

'That would not be an entirely foolish interpretation,' said the general. 'As well as being Hitler's adjutant, in the last months of the war Oberst Halder was also a senior official in the Fascists' programme to develop an atomic weapon.'

From somewhere within the building Rossel heard raised voices and an unexpected burst of laughter. Pletnev checked a button and adjusted his cap.

'That, comrades, is the real gold I seek,' he said.

The general swivelled on his heel and marched inside.

35

In the dusk, under the yellow streetlights, snow whipped over the roads and round the corners of buildings.

At last, a tram came. Rossel and Nikitin got on board and found seats away from the handful of other passengers.

Nikitin slumped down in his.

'This could put you back in the camps, Rossel, and me alongside you. Or worse,' he said. 'Failure will condemn us.'

Rossel kept silent.

It makes no sense.

Within the confines of the Soviet Union, the GRU, as a military entity, was nothing like as powerful as the MGB. On foreign territory, however, it had carte blanche. It would be quicker and easier for General Pletnev to order GRU agents already located in Berlin to convey his offer to Speer, especially when it was the turn of Soviet forces to take responsibility for guarding Spandau.

On the other hand . . .

The only possible explanation was deniability. A former MGB officer of uncertain loyalty, acting with a former militia officer and camp inmate of complete political unreliability. With a record of challenging Soviet authority. If they failed, they could be quickly removed. If they were caught, they could be disowned with ease.

The tram clanked to a halt.

Rossel stood up but Nikitin pulled at his arm.

He could see something in the major's eyes. Something he'd never seen before. Fear.

'It's my wife and son, and my daughter, Svetlana,' Nikitin said. 'They'll come for them, too. Little Sveta has already been through enough. She couldn't cope with the camps as well . . .'

Rossel looked down at Nikitin, disgust welling up in his stomach. He thought of the terrified pleas of the hundreds of people the major had dispatched to the care of the GULAG. Or beaten senseless in the cells of the Bolshoi Dom.

He shook off the major's hand.

'My stop,' he said.

Then he exited the tram in a hurry.

*

Dr Maxim Bondar emerged from the morgue at The Crosses prison to greet Rossel in his office.

He opened a desk drawer and pulled out the locket.

'I am a pathologist, not a jeweller, but I can tell you that this was mass produced,' said Dr Bondar. 'No fingerprints. A little residue from some oil, probably gun oil.'

He dropped the locket. The chain uncoiled from his palm and cascaded onto the desk.

'The hair inside was a little more interesting,' Dr Bondar said.

'A family memento, perhaps?'

The pathologist shook his head.

'I highly doubt it. When a person dies, the pallor of the skin, the temperature of the body, the stiffness of the muscles, the breakdown of the cells, all these things happen rapidly and tell their own story. But the hair, apart from the root in the follicle, is already dead. You cut your hair and it doesn't hurt, yes? It can last for years, centuries, longer, provided it is relatively dry and free from fungal attack. Mummies have been unearthed with their hair intact . . .'

'Hair lasts a long time. I get it,' said Rossel.

Dr Bondar smiled.

'But,' he said, 'hair can still tell a story. The follicle is linked to the blood supply, so any toxins in the blood can show up in the hair. It is an excretory tissue, as we say.'

'Have you found poisons?'

'No. Something else.'

The pathologist paused for effect.

'Max, please.'

Dr Bondar grinned.

'Gunpowder, traces of zinc and copper, and one or two other substances that point to the owner of this hair having been shot in the head at close range.'

The kill shot. A sniper's work? But a sniper operated from range. More likely an executioner's shot, thought Rossel. As for the hair – a trophy taken from a victim? Or a keepsake from a friend or lover. Or a talisman. A reminder that vengeance was demanded.

'On the subject of the hair itself, I can tell you that it was human hair, from the head, probably European. This lock was hacked off rather crudely – jagged edges, no follicles – so it wasn't ripped out. It was also slightly redder than yours or mine, though that's because the red pigment pheomelanin hangs around after death more than the darker pigment. Our victim was no redhead, more a coppery brown. Very fine hair – only thirty-five or forty micrometres. I'd say it belonged to a relatively young person.'

'Can you tell when that person was killed?' asked Rossel.

Dr Bondar shook his head. 'No. Not recently, but it's not ancient either. I would be guessing if I tried to be more precise.'

Rossel thanked him.

'Not at all,' said the pathologist. 'You're looking a little fuller than the last time I saw you, though just as pale.'

'An occupational hazard,' Rossel said, 'for men like us who spend too much time in the shadows.'

*

Nikitin gave him no respite. As soon as Rossel was back at his apartment, the phone rang and the major declared he was on his way to pick him up.

'Where are we going?'

'Tarkovsky,' said Nikitin. 'I'll explain as we go.' The line went dead.

They did not exchange a word for the first few minutes of the journey. Not far from the river, a lorry swerved into their path. They both aimed a barrage of invective at its driver – a moment of release that thawed the ice.

As the two of them entered Tarkovsky's apartment, they found the actor cradling a bottle of cognac, recumbent on a chaise longue. He opened an eye, gave a soft moan at the sight of Nikitin and, closing it again, began to mumble.

'I can't sing,' he said. 'I have to sing at the Anichkov Palace and I can't hit a single note.'

'I don't know about the Stalin prize for acting,' said Rossel, 'but they should definitely give Boris's liver the Order of Lenin. From what I've seen since I moved in here, its daily labours are more heroic than anything Pletnev ever undertook.'

'So, the words you decoded are definitely from Wagner?' said Nikitin.

'Yes, and definitely from *Götterdämmerung*.'

'A flying bomb?' said Nikitin. 'Like the ones at the end of the war?'

Rossel shrugged. 'How else do you set fire to Valhalla?'

'Wagner, at his best, I always found sublime,' Tarkovsky said in a loud voice. He had sat up on the chaise longue and looked at the two of them with pleasure – as if his guests would take his mind off his troubles. 'Before the war there was talk of a Soviet film of the Ring Cycle with Lev Kuleshov directing. I was offered the part of Siegfried. Was going to take it, too. But then I saw a lecture Kuleshov gave all about how the only important element of filmmaking was editing and knew that little shit would cut all my best scenes out. It was filled with endless close-ups of plant pots.'

He snorted. 'After the war started, of course, Wagner was *kaput*. I'm glad I didn't take that part now. Otherwise, the MGB might have come to visit me one night and done a little editing of their own.'

'The major and I are going on a little trip to Berlin, Boris,' said Rossel.

'Berlin?'

Rossel nodded.

'Yes, and we need a guide.'

'A guide?'

'A translator. I don't speak German and neither does the major.'

Rossel took out a *papirosa*, lit it, took a hard drag and looked over at the still-befuddled figure on the sofa – a terrible singer who nevertheless had a talent for singing Schubert and Schumann in German.

'But I know someone who does.'

Nikitin followed his gaze.

It took a moment for Tarkovsky to understand.

'What? No. No, no, no. Berlin, me? No thank you, comrades. I turned down Kuleshov so I have no difficulty in turning you down. Kuleshov was a real big shot back then, I can tell you. It took a bit of nerve . . .'

Nikitin took off his jacket and hung it on the back of a chair.

Rossel walked across the room and sat down next to the actor.

'You should have taken that role, Boris. You would have made a wonderful Siegfried. So brave, so handsome. Slayer of dragons, seducer of Valkyries . . .'

Nikitin began to roll up his right sleeve.

'Though I suspect,' Rossel added, 'that the noble knight may have fared less well if he had ever sallied forth to meet Major Nikitin . . .'

36

By the time their flight landed in the late afternoon, Berlin's Schönefeld Airport was shrouded in drizzle and darkness. As they were towed to the aircraft's berth, the long lines of runway and perimeter lights were gradually extinguished. Only the main terminal building remained illuminated as they disembarked, soon separating themselves from the other twenty or so passengers – mostly military or diplomatic staff returning from home visits, along with a party of grim-faced low-ranking politicians from First Secretary Ulbricht's East German government who had boarded from a connecting Moscow flight.

East German guards, a couple of them holding back Alsatians on leashes, patrolled the arrivals area.

'Documents, please,' said the German officer seated at a large desk in front of the only door out of the hall for arrivals.

'Smirnov, Senior Lieutenant,' said Tarkovsky in a firm voice as he came to a halt in front of the desk. 'Camera operator, Special Information Films Unit, Soviet Army.'

'I've never heard of it,' said the German officer, meeting Tarkovsky's glare without flinching. His Russian was excellent.

'Of course not,' replied the actor. 'We are here on what is known as active measures. If you had heard of us, something would have gone wrong.'

The officer leafed through every page of Tarkovsky's passport, travel permit and military identification. Then he started again. Rossel stared straight ahead; Nikitin looked bored and impatient. Other passengers had caught up and joined them but besides the panting of the dogs the hall remained silent.

Finally, Tarkovsky and Nikitin were waved through.

The German officer leant back in his chair and looked Rossel up and down.

'Where are you based?'

'In the Leningrad Region,' answered Rossel. '19th Guards Rifle Division.'

'I thought that was a fighting division,' said the officer, fixing him straight in the eye.

'Your knowledge of the Soviet military is impressive, comrade. It *is* a fighting division.'

'Your documents say Special Films Unit? That does not sound very warlike to me.'

'The Special Films Unit was formed by the Defence Ministry in 1948 and consists of politically reliable and technically accomplished officers with excellent war records,' said Rossel. 'There is more than one way of waging war, comrade. Control of information is vital.'

Even to himself, his voice sounded too rehearsed.

The officer thought for a moment. Then he turned to a statuesque uniformed woman who was sitting behind him sorting through a pile of documents.

'Hey, Irina.'

She looked up from her paperwork.

'I always said you should be in the movies. There is a Special Films Unit here. Now's your chance to audition.'

Irina gave him a frosty stare in return. She slammed a rubber stamp down onto a travel permit, but said nothing.

The officer turned to Rossel and shrugged.

'The film business, eh?' he said.

With a little more force than was necessary, he took hold of his own stamp, applied it to Rossel's passport and handed it over.

'You lucky bastards must get plenty.'

*

The driver was fat, middle-aged, and smelled like he'd been fried on a griddle with some bratwurst. But the smell of onions was not his least appealing feature. He would not stop talking in a coarse pidgin Russian.

'Over there, comrades,' he said, pointing to a pile of bricks, 'that was a cinema. Der silberne Stern. I went out with an usherette from there before the war. Tits like zeppelins. And in bed . . . *Es war unglaublich . . .*'

'It was crazy what she did,' said Boris, translating.

The driver pointed at another heap of rubble, tidied into a pyramid. 'St Hedwig's Church, bombed in forty-three.' And again. 'The Lessing Theatre. Bombed in forty-five . . .'

Rossel looked out at a city that was half-missing: wide open spaces of flattened gravel and concrete punctuated by damaged buildings, of which only one or two sides might remain, or neat piles of bricks placed here and there by optimistic construction workers. Their driver had appointed himself tour guide to a Berlin that no longer existed.

What the Germans did to Leningrad, he thought, came back to haunt them.

Actual buildings had become more numerous as they drove further into the city, but so had the evidence of the war – once-grand blocks that were occupied in one half yet charred, twisted ruins in another; others that were little more than husks. Almost anything that was still standing had been left alone, for the time being at least, while the rubble around it was cleared away. Here and there – scaffolding, cranes, wire fences – signs of some reconstruction were in evidence.

After a few more minutes, Nikitin tried to shut the driver up.

'Who needs a travel guide, eh, comrade, when all that's left of Berlin is fresh fucking air?'

The man started laughing. 'Not much of that either, Ivan, when you live next to a sewer plant in Hellersdorf like me.'

He began to whistle a jaunty tune.

'Where are we staying?' asked Tarkovsky to no one in particular. He sounded as weary as Rossel felt. 'The Kaiserhof? The Kaiserhof used to be quite the thing . . .'

The driver chuckled. 'Only if you want birdshit on your head while you sleep,' he said. 'Also hit by bombs. Lots.'

'What about the Adlon? That was the best of the best, wasn't it? Sergei Eisenstein told me he stayed there before the war.'

'Survived,' replied the driver. 'Then some Red Army boys got pissed in the wine cellar and torched it. Nothing left now.'

Tarkovsky turned to Rossel. 'Then where?'

Rossel didn't answer. He looked back out of the window and stared at every face that went past, whether on a bicycle or peering out from a crowded tram. Berliners looked much like Leningraders, he thought. Gaunt. Tough. Tired.

'Welcome to Hotel Beatrice,' said the driver as the cab pulled up.

Nikitin wiped away the moisture on the window. The three men stared out at its grubby façade.

'Perhaps it's nice inside,' said Tarkovsky.

*

Like the Kaiserhof and the Adlon, the Beatrice had once been frequented by Berlin high society. Unlike them, it had the virtue of still having walls and a roof. It was now a dark and creaking edifice, a long way from its luxurious past but with pretensions of grandeur nonetheless, including a portly major-domo. He was short, with an oil slick of black hair brushed from the back of his neck over his balding pate. There was also a suspicion that he was topping up his bonhomie with the odd shot of schnapps. He introduced himself as Herr Bernard.

He had once, he said, worked at the Kaiserhof. 'I met all the big stars back then,' he told them via Tarkovsky, who was the only one showing any interest in his tales. 'Chaplin and Clark Gable at the Kaiserhof. Marlene Dietrich stayed when she was filming *The Blue Angel*.'

The three of them had convened in the Beatrice's gloomy restaurant, which was deserted save for themselves and a table of Red Army colonels making their way through several bottles of Beaujolais.

Bernard leaned towards Tarkovsky and lowered his voice. 'A local Schöneberg girl and occasional sister of Sappho. I brought some flowers to her room in the morning and . . . well, let's just say even the roses started blushing.'

He bowed and left. Rossel watched him go, being bullied all the way to the kitchen by the Russian officers still determined to put any Germans in their place – 'Hey, Fritz, fetch us another bottle of the Moulin-à-Vent – and be quick about it.'

The major-domo was, he thought, a bit like the Beatrice's tangled crystal chandeliers or dented oak panelling: a relic of the heady days of the Weimar Republic, a piece of bourgeois driftwood washed up on the most unexpected of shores.

Bernard was not long in bringing their food. Chicken was the only meat on the menu, accompanied by ersatz puréed potato and some lacklustre beans.

'Berlin seems quiet,' said Rossel, elbowing Tarkovsky for the translation.

'Yes and no. Tensions are rising,' said Bernard, doling out the beans. 'Since the blockade and the airlift – when was it, two, three years ago? – people are crossing over to the West all the time. The roads are being blocked. Guards are demanding papers and passes. But there is still the railway, and the S-Bahn.'

'We know all about blockades, Comrade Bernard, we're from Leningrad,' said Nikitin. 'A million dead, remember? Did you even know? If you ask me, it's good to see you Fritzes getting a taste of your own medicine.'

Tarkovsky kept silent and Nikitin did not insist on a translation.

'But you are still here, Herr Bernard,' said Rossel, risking a few words of German.

Bernard smiled, pleased at the effort.

'This is my place,' he said. Then he bowed to them, each in turn. 'But perhaps your friend the major is right and we Fritzes must . . .'

He delivered a stage wink.

'. . . learn to enjoy our punishment. As, I'm told, they used to in a special upstairs room at the Eldorado nightclub in the twenties. Great days. Back then, it was known as a workers' city – the reddest city after Moscow. Now the eastern half is red once more. *Plus ça change*, as the French say.'

Bernard began to sing. '*Politicians are magicians who make swindles disappear, the bribes they are taking, the deals they are making . . .* That tune is by a Russian composer, *kameraden*,' he said. 'Mischa Spoliansky. "It's All a Swindle". Spoliansky was in Berlin before the Nazis. He was a friend of Dietrich's. I think of that song often these days.'

He glanced at the table of colonels just as one of them threw an empty bottle against the fireplace.

'In Berlin, regimes come and go. But the music remains the same.'

37

Two turrets stood on either side of the gatehouse to Spandau prison, a small block that was dwarfed by the keep looming over it. To the right of the gates stood a gaggle of Soviet officers in caps and coats – relaxed and cracking jokes until, at an unseen signal, they all turned to look up at one of the watchtowers.

A Soviet soldier ascended the stairs, walked past the French sentry without a word and took up position, AK-47 strapped tight to his body. The Frenchman disappeared from sight – the cue, it seemed, for a Soviet column of about twenty men in three lines to tramp its way towards them along the wire perimeter fence that ran parallel to the heavy red stone walls of the prison.

This was where the opposing sides of the Cold War came to dance.

All eyes watched the column come to a halt outside the gates. It waited.

Almost immediately, the French detachment emerged, though with less frantic energy. They marched through the gate and took up station directly opposite the Soviet force. Their commander, an avuncular man in his sixties, handed over a file, shook hands with the Soviet commanding officer and saluted. Then the French were on the move once more, wheeling smoothly right along the perimeter and towards two buses that would ferry them to their own zone of the city.

For the next month, the Soviet Union would be in control of the seven most notorious prisoners in the world.

Among the less formal group of officers, Major Nikitin leaned towards Rossel so that their heads were almost touching. He leant out again, chuckling, and patted Rossel on the shoulder. Trying his best to look at ease.

By contrast, Tarkovsky looked stern, hefting his bag of camera equipment and ignoring the furtive glances of men who had been through the war and who had a good recollection of what Stalin's disgraced son Yakov Dzhugashvili had looked like. Here's 'spoilt Yakov' again, some of them must have been thinking; a little fatter, a little less hair, a few more wrinkles, but large as life. Even though they all knew the Nazis had imprisoned him in a concentration camp and then shot him.

Or perhaps, they were wondering, that's just what we have been told?

*

'Comrades, I do not believe I have been notified of your arrival,' said the warden.

Nikitin saluted.

'I am Major Nikitin, this is Captain Ivanov and Senior Lieutenant Smirnov, all normally of the 147th Guards Rifles, ultimately of the 8th Army, now on secondment to the Special Information Films Unit. We are here to interview

Albert Speer for a propaganda film on senior surviving Nazis, on the order of the Defence Ministry . . .'

The warden looked shocked. 'I have received no advance warning of this.'

'It was all requested at short notice,' said Nikitin. 'We will be in and out before you know it.'

'Absolutely out of the question,' said the warden. 'Access to the prisoners is limited and only granted by permission of the governorate, which means obtaining the agreement of all four powers that run the—'

'Call Defence Minister General Pletnev,' said Nikitin, pulling out a piece of paper from the file tucked under his arm. 'This propaganda mission is of the utmost importance. Part of a broader plan to discredit the Western occupying powers, expose the German denazification process for the charade that it is, and reveal American and British complicity in permitting Adolf Hitler's most loyal henchman to escape . . .'

He paused for breath. 'Of course, if you think this is a bad idea you are most welcome to address the general himself,' Nikitin added.

The warden swallowed.

Rossel took a piece of paper from his own pocket. 'Or Lieutenant Colonel Timofeyev, the head of active measures in the Foreign Ministry in Moscow. Or his deputy, Colonel Kirillov. I have their numbers here,' he said.

Nikitin took it from him and waved the paper in the warden's face. The man tried to swat it away but Nikitin pressed it upon him.

'It would be extremely irregular,' the warden said. 'Under the regulations, only the governorate can determine who can visit a prisoner and—'

'For private visits, yes,' said Nikitin, slipping into a smoother gear. 'We are here as representatives of the Soviet Union at a time when the Soviet Union has control of Spandau. I would, of course, be more than happy to consult with the Soviet governor of the entire sector here, Major Viktor Alabyev, who is aware of our mission . . .'

The warden's eyes darted about. To say 'no' was to risk incurring the wrath of General Pletnev. To say 'yes' would be to go against procedure. The punishment for an incorrect choice would be severe.

But Nikitin had given him an escape route.

'Major Alabyev knows?' he said. He pulled at his lower lip, considered his options and nodded. 'In that case, comrades, you are most welcome. Major Alabyev is very angry at the Americans over recent anti-Soviet lies in the Western press about Spandau.'

And Major Alabyev could therefore take the blame. The warden turned and led the way into the prison.

38

Boots clanged on the metal stairs as the warden and two Soviet guards led the way up to the third level of the prison.

'Prisoner Four is in there,' the warden said, gesturing to a cell door as they passed by.

'Which one is he?' asked Rossel.

'He is Prisoner Four. That is all they are now. A number.'

'And before, who was he?'

'Grand Admiral Erich Raeder. He speaks excellent Russian, incidentally.'

'Which number is Speer?'

'You mean Prisoner Five. You are not permitted to address him by name,' said the warden.

'He doesn't even deserve a number,' said Tarkovsky. 'These Fascist scum were fortunate not to be executed.'

The actor was warming to his role and the guards looked like they approved of this sentiment.

'This is a big place for seven people,' said Rossel. 'How many cells are there?'

'There are 132 cells,' said the warden. 'At all times, there are seven wardens by day, five by night. Guarding the prison are forty-four sentries, plus sergeants and officers.'

Soviet newspapers had printed tens of thousands of words about the Nuremberg trials. *Now, when as a result of the heroic struggle of the Red Army and of the Allied forces, Hitlerite Germany is broken and overwhelmed, we have no right to forget the victims who have suffered. We have no right to leave unpunished those who organised and were guilty of monstrous crimes . . .* The Soviet prosecutor had demanded a Soviet response, his every word transcribed for the grim approval of Russian readers.

And in summing up: *I appeal to the tribunal to sentence the defendants without exception to the supreme penalty. Death.*

There were other trials – of captured Nazi party officials, German military leaders, members of the SS, German and non-German. And thousands of collaborators, Russian, Ukrainian, Belarussian, Polish, Latvian, Estonian, Lithuanian, Romanian, Bulgarian . . . In courts throughout the Soviet Union, they had been tried, sentenced and executed with neither mercy nor delay. Some had followed Göring's example, cheating their captors and accusers by killing themselves before retribution could be taken.

And then there were the seven who had been spared the noose. The seven prisoners in Spandau.

The party marched down a corridor and came to a halt outside another metal door studded with locks.

'It is now 08.35,' said the warden. 'The prisoners normally have work until 11.45 before they have their midday meal but in the winter this rule is relaxed, depending on the weather and the health of the prisoner. All except Prisoner Seven, of course, who refuses to do any work.'

'Prisoner Seven?' said Rossel.

'Rudolf Hess.'

Tarkovsky flexed his right fist, a gesture he had copied from Nikitin. 'Give me a minute with him,' the actor growled.

Careful, Boris. Don't overact . . .

'Physical punishment is forbidden unless a warden or guard needs to protect themselves, which is unlikely. These are old men with bladder problems. Once they ruled the world. Now they don't even get to choose the times in the night they get up to take a piss.'

'Does Number Five speak any Russian?' said Rossel.

'A few words only. In any case, according to the regulations you are only permitted to speak to the prisoners in German.'

The warden moved aside to allow one of the guards to open the door. Behind it lay Hitler's favourite architect and the Reich Minister of Armaments and War Production. A man who had once seen himself as successor to the Führer.

Speer had escaped one bunker only to end up in another.

39

Prisoner Five had a receding hairline and prominent ears, accentuating a broad forehead. Below his thick eyebrows, the face still had traces of youth – strong, even features and the ghost of a conspiratorial smile. He took another puff of the pipe that rested on his lower lip and crossed his legs, appraising the unexpected visitors at leisure. But as he analysed the possible implications of a Soviet delegation led by a figure who looked like Nikitin, his shoulders hunched a little.

The warden snarled at him in German.

'He is telling him to stand up and put his pipe out,' Tarkovsky translated. 'Prisoners must be respectful at all times.'

Albert Speer got to his feet and tapped out his pipe on a metal ashtray.

'My National Socialist German Workers' Party number was 474481,' he said with a curt bow. 'Now I am Prisoner Number Five. If only from a purely numerical perspective, gentlemen, I have of late risen in the world.'

This elicited another volley from the warden. Speer responded by holding up the book he had been reading.

'Dostoevsky,' said the Third Reich's former Minister of Armaments with a wry smile. '*Schuld und Sühne. Crime and Punishment*. Ich hoffe, das findet Ihre Zustimmung.'

'He says he hopes we approve,' said Tarkovsky.

'The *svoloch* is all yours,' said the warden, as he left. The bolts clanked shut behind him.

Speer smiled at them, but his eyes flickered from one visitor to the other. Then he held out his hands as if to express uninhibited cooperation.

'Tell him that we are making a documentary about the final days of the war,' Rossel said to Tarkovsky. 'Specifically, we are interested in the movements of the leading Nazis in the very last days. Not just Hitler, but his closest aides also.'

Tarkovsky relayed the question in a voice that echoed around the cell. He looked Speer in the eye as he was talking, playing a dual role – part ardent Bolshevik and, with his excellent German, part interrogator for the Gestapo. Or perhaps the Stasi, the recently formed East German secret police, thought Rossel. The methods of both organisations were likely to be very similar.

Boris was convincing.

Most people would have been intimidated. Especially with Nikitin sitting next to him and glowering across the table.

Speer did not seem cowed. Perhaps he was unsure of the situation – if a trap was being set, if a punishment was being prepared. Or if they were telling the truth. His expression was . . . not blank, exactly. Expectant. A confidence perhaps born of having tiptoed through the minefield of the Nuremberg trials and having avoided detonations.

'A documentary crew, eh?' said Speer, through Tarkovsky. He looked at each of them in turn. 'Which one of you is Sergei Eisenstein? I would have hoped that the great Soviet cinematic maestro was the least I deserve.'

Tarkovsky, unable to resist, leaned forward and assumed an air of eager friendship.

'What was he really like?'

'He?'

'Hitler. Who else?'

Speer thought for a moment.

'On reflection – and as you can imagine, I have had much time for that – only a man, like you or me. Who for some reason known only to itself, History had decided to listen to.'

Speer picked up his empty pipe and tapped it on the table.

'By the end, however, he was a different man to the one I had once known. If the Führer – if Hitler had had his way, Germany would have burned. Everything gone – industry, infrastructure, transport networks, the German people themselves, everything. Had I not disobeyed him, thwarted his desires, it would have been . . .'

'A *Götterdämmerung*?' said Rossel.

Speer gave him a sharp look.

'That is one description.'

He waited for Tarkovsky to catch up before adding: 'A musical reference. Does that mean you are a musician?'

'A violinist,' said Rossel.

'Do you still play?'

Rossel held up his left hand and removed the glove, showing the missing fingers.

'Regrettably not,' he said.

'A war injury?'

'Something like that.'

Rossel replaced the glove. 'You are still an architect at heart, I see,' he added, pointing to the large piece of paper that took up practically all of the only table in the cell. It was a detailed scheme of what appeared to be an enormous building, embellished with Gothic lettering.

'A fanciful castle,' said Speer. 'Rather in the style of Ludwig II of Bavaria. Given your reference to Wagner's music, one should remember that Ludwig was Wagner's greatest and richest admirer. My own work here is a homage, if you like, to the mad king. When you have fourteen years left to serve behind bars, a man needs to kill time. So I design buildings that will never be built, worlds that cannot be, empires that exist only in the mind.'

Rossel stared down at the plans. The dutiful servant of a mad king. That was how Speer had portrayed himself at his trial.

'Prisoner Five, a story that I have heard concerns the music of Wagner,' he said. 'A concert that took place on April 12 1945. Less than a month before the Third Reich's capitulation. Can you remember what was on the programme that night, Comrade Speer?'

Speer's expression did not change as Tarkovsky relayed the question, but a tiny note of recognition crept into his eyes.

'What makes you think I was even there?'

'You were there,' said Nikitin.

Speer cut short the translation with an irritated wave.

'The Beethoven violin concerto,' he said. 'Performed by the orchestra's leader, a young and gifted man. He was the only member of the orchestra who accepted my offer of help to leave Berlin. Half an hour after his performance he was in a car on his way to Bavaria. The others stayed. Too proud to leave their city.'

'Was that it?' asked Rossel.

Speer tilted his head – *do not treat me as an idiot.*

'A short section from *Götterdämmerung.* Brünnhilde's Immolation Scene, from there to the end. But it is evident that you already knew that. And Bruckner's Symphony Number Four. That piece was my signal to a select few. If they heard the Bruckner on the radio, it was time to leave the city. Via certain checkpoints manned by guards who also knew to listen out for the musical code.'

Speer stood and leant backwards, pressing a hand into the small of his back.

'Bruckner was a wonderful writer for strings,' he continued. 'The Führer adored him – even more, I believe, than he admired Wagner. And no one knew better than Hitler that admiration and adoration are two very different things. One gets a man a little respect, the other allows him to conquer worlds.'

Rossel gave what he hoped was an encouraging smile.

'Messages within music,' he said. 'Always fascinating. But I was thinking more about the Wagner. The symbolism. Valhalla in flames.'

Speer did not reply.

'Was the ending of *Götterdämmerung* a message of some sort, too?'

'From whom?' asked Speer, toying with his pipe. 'To whom?'

'A message from Oberst Franz Halder, Hitler's Luftwaffe adjutant, to the Nazi resistance,' Rossel said.

Speer picked up his tobacco and began to fill the bowl.

'A documentary crew, eh?' he said, tamping down the tobacco. 'I don't recall Leni Riefenstahl asking so many pointed questions before she made *Triumph of the Will*.'

Picking up a heavy steel lighter, he put the pipe to his mouth and tested the draw. For half a minute, he did nothing but regard his visitors, lips pursed. His calculations made, he spoke.

'The Russian cooks here are worse than my mother, and bless her, she couldn't bake a Zwiebelkuchen tart without cremating the onions.'

Speer smiled at Rossel.

'A Sachertorte,' he said. 'Do you know what that is?'

Rossel waited for Tarkosvky to translate. Then shook his head.

'A Viennese chocolate cake. That's my price for talking to you a little more, comrade.'

Speer looked up at the cell's little window.

'As memory serves, just one morsel will feel almost as good as climbing over Spandau's walls.'

*

'No,' said the warden as he leapt up from his office chair. 'Absolutely out of the question. The seven Spandau prisoners get the same calories as ordinary German citizens, as stipulated on their ration cards. But you want to give Speer a Viennese chocolate cake. Fuck your mother.'

Rossel held up a hand to silence him.

'It is a test,' he said. 'We need to demonstrate to Speer that we have some influence here.'

The warden didn't look convinced. Rossel went in for the kill.

'We will, of course, be sure to mention your cooperation and invaluable assistance in our report to the defence minister,' he said.

The warden sat back down again.

'All right,' he said. 'Spoil him if you need to. But next thing you know, that stuck-up bastard will be asking for some cream.'

*

'Your cake is on its way,' said Rossel. 'Though the warden insists that you eat it out here. It took a little persuasion for him to allow your request.'

Raised beds full of black soil and neat lines of plants ran in rows of thirty or forty metres, some pruned almost back to the root, others allowed more leeway to lie dormant and sagging. Trellises ran up the bricks of the prison walls. In one distant corner a greenhouse stood at a slight angle, misted up. Large areas were dug over and covered with matting, old carpet or mulch. Transported to a collective of Russian dachas, Rossel thought, the ensemble might have earned a coveted *ideal'nyi uchastok*, or 'model plot' award, a plaque that inveterate dacha dwellers displayed with pride on the side of their huts or houses.

But this little garden was tended by men who had dreamed of ruling the world.

Speer nodded.

'Thank you.'

For a winter's day it was bright and sunny, but Speer still slapped his hands together to ward off the cold before wandering over to a garden bench. Then he sat and surveyed the movements of the other middle-aged or elderly men scowling amid the shrubbery.

'That's Dönitz,' he said, flicking a finger in the direction of the white-haired former admiral, who sported a sneer above his jowls. 'The man he is pretending to ignore is Admiral Raeder. They are inseparable, really, though they pretend on occasions not to get along. The one sitting on his own is von Neurath, the former Protector of Bohemia and Moravia. Very ill. Heart, he says. Unlikely, since I've always suspected he doesn't have one. Another aristocrat who cannot abide a hint of dirt beneath his fingernails.'

He pointed again. 'There you have Prisoner One. Von Schirach. Head of the Hitler Youth and Gauleiter of Vienna. Who else? That's Funk. Odious man. But very musical. Sometimes he plays the organ at our Sunday services. Yes, we have those, comrades. The battle to save our souls never ends. Perhaps, when I die, the Good Lord will make me his Minister for Munitions. I have little doubt I would be able to rapidly increase production of both hymn books and holy water.'

Speer sat back.

'Hess?' said Rossel. 'Where is he?'

'He refuses to do any work and is wary of setting foot outdoors in case you Russians force him to do any. No one likes him, anyway.'

Speer nodded at von Schirach.

'Unrepentant Nazis like von Schirach say that Hess betrayed the Party by fleeing to Scotland. The rest of the world simply sees him as a horrible unrepentant Nazi. Rudolf doesn't get many invitations to parties these days.'

'But you are repentant? Battling to save your soul. Is that what *you* are doing here at Spandau, Comrade Speer,' said Rossel, taking out some cigarettes and offering one. 'A penance?'

Tarkovsky translated. Speer gazed into the middle distance for a moment.

'When I married Margarete, my mother felt I'd married beneath me and would not allow us to visit her for seven years. That was a penance, I think. Its sting never fades. This is merely a purgatory, of sorts. I can survive it. Besides, *tout comprendre, c'est tout pardoner, n'est-ce pas?* A sin explained is a sin forgiven. I intend to write a book. My side of events. Every man's story can, after all, only ever really be that.'

Rossel was already on alert. The familiar prickle on his neck, under his jaw where his fading fiddler's mark lingered; the skin, once dark red from constant playing, now a tinge of pink. A mark that mocked him every time he looked in the mirror. And he could hear the change in Speer's voice – the same subtle difference he had heard as a prelude to so many confessions. His skill was in listening, in letting others fill the silence.

'Atonement, then,' he said. 'Have you something to offer the world by way of that? That might be of interest to people who watch our film?'

Speer seemed about to reply. But then something caught his eye.

A Soviet corporal was walking towards them holding a porcelain plate on which rested a silver fork and a large piece of cake.

'Look at them.' Speer gestured to the other prisoners in the garden. Each man had straightened his back, turned his head towards this astonishing gastronomic spectacle. 'The last time they eyed up something as hungrily as that was, I'll warrant, an empty seat next to Hitler at the Führer's dining table.'

*

Speer dropped the fork onto the plate with a clatter. He wet the tip of his little finger and then used it to pick up a last crumb of Sachertorte.

'*Wunderbar*,' he said. 'Not only was it delicious, but it has also allowed me a few much-needed moments of reflection.'

He looked up at the other prisoners going about their gardening and noticed von Neurath frowning at him. Speer smiled.

'In our little realm of Spandau, gentlemen, the most a man can hope for is to be king for a day. For when he wakes each morning, he once again discovers he no longer possesses even his own name.'

He leaned back and turned down a finger.

'Now, to business. Here you are, a mysterious Russian delegation who haven't so much as touched their cameras or microphones or lighting gear, but have heard something about Oberst Franz Halder, *nicht wahr?*'

For a moment Rossel held his tongue. Then he nodded.

'They cut out many references from the papers they let us prisoners read,' Speer said. 'But they miss some things. Mentions of the leading lights of the Kremlin, for instance. Beria, Malenkov, Khrushchev, Kaganovich, Pletnev. Molotov less so, thus I assume he has fallen from grace.'

Speer picked up the fork and inspected it for traces of icing as Tarkovsky translated.

'I know better than most that leaders do not last for ever,' he continued. 'Stalin is an old man. His inner circle will be making calculations and dreaming of taking his place. I assume that you represent one of them. Whoever sent you, I want a deal. I have another fourteen years in this prison and Stalin won't last that long. When he's gone, I simply ask whoever you represent to remember that I helped him.'

A sparrow flew close by. Speer watched it skimming low through the air before soaring round the building and out of sight. He dropped the fork back onto the plate.

'I will request that your assistance is recognised, Herr Speer,' said Rossel.

Speer sat back and nodded.

'In my current circumstances, that's the best I can hope for,' he said. 'The wisest beggar is the one who understands he still has a tin cup to shake. You know about the concert, and the Bruckner and the Wagner, and that both myself and Halder were present. I take it that Franz Halder has never been found?'

'No, he has not,' said Rossel.

'Yet he has apparently not made use of the information he was charged with concealing and delivering to the underground resistance.' He looked up at the Russians. 'I also take it our glorious German resistance never actually resisted?'

Rossel and Tarkovsky shook their heads. Nikitin curled his lip.

'It was a ridiculous idea, anyway,' said Speer. He examined his nails. 'But, even at the very end, the Führer was convinced.'

'What was the information in Halder's possession?' said Rossel.

Speer waved across the garden at Funk, who ignored him. The others were also turning their backs.

'While we were all awaiting trial,' he said, 'the Americans dropped their bombs on Japan. The world changed in that moment.' He sat up straight, pressing the small of his back, wincing. 'But the American bombs were as nothing compared to what our scientists had designed,' he said. 'It was a design only, of course. Had it been tested and built, Moscow and London and New York would have been eradicated. Yet the Yankee bombs proved, too late, what our scientists had been saying. The big bang was possible, and if it was possible then a bigger one was also possible. Calamity would breed ever greater calamity.'

Two of the guard towers had sight of the gardens. At least one of the Soviet guards had his eyes on the prisoners at all times. The other might turn away to scan the world outside but only for a few moments.

Over by the heavy doors that led from the main prison block to the garden, the Soviet warden emerged. He kept his distance but Rossel could sense they were running out of time.

Opening one of the cases containing camera equipment he had no idea how to use, he pulled out *The Prince*.

'Herr Speer,' he said. 'Halder encrypted a message to the German resistance. This was the key text.' He read the lines from *Götterdämmerung*. 'Was that his meaning? To create this new weapon?'

Speer took a moment.

'The guards here talk. I'm told that in Moscow General Pletnev is highly thought of,' he said. 'The coming man.'

Rossel nodded.

'He is. And I'm sure if we bring him good news back from Spandau, the general will also think highly of you, Herr Speer.'

Speer sniffed the air. Considered. Then smiled.

'Yes,' he said. 'To destroy the old order and build a new one. That was the instruction. To create a bomb of unimaginable power.'

Rossel opened the book at the back and showed Speer the last numbers.

1 5 O S R D 1 8 B

Speer took the book and squinted at it.

'Aha. I was wondering when we would get to this,' he said.

Rossel waited for Speer to elucidate but he did not.

'I think this is the code for a location,' Rossel said. 'A place with nine letters, perhaps. Scrambled through one of the Nazi code machines . . .'

'*Nein, nein,*' answered Speer. 'A location, yes. You are right about that. But the answer is simpler than you think.'

He looked into Rossel's eyes, his expression almost tender.

'It is a map reference,' he said. 'The Luftwaffe system. Oberst Halder was in the Luftwaffe.'

'How does it work?'

'It is a grid. A series of grids, in fact, each one fitting inside the other. Rather like your Russian dolls. Look at this.'

He pointed to the first few characters.

'You start with 15 OS, or Ost Sud. East South. A pilot would know instantly, but my guess is that it is a large piece of Europe.'

Rossel waited for Tarkovsky to translate.

'And the rest?'

'Then the grids get ever smaller. So 15 Ost Sud is divided into a twenty-by-twenty grid, and the letters RD identify a particular square. The north-west corner is AA, then AB, AC and so on as you move across to the east on the map. You get to letter number twenty and then start again for row two – BA, BB, BC and so on.'

'So RD would be . . .' Rossel had to think for a moment. 'Bottom left – south-west?'

'Yes, I suppose so. It has been a long time since I stared at maps with the Führer, or anybody else,' said Speer.

'And then what?'

'Then the square RD is itself divided into nine – three by three. Then nine again, and then the smallest square.' He looked at the paper once more. 'So, the one means the top left square within the grid RD. The eight means the middle bottom square within *that*, and the last reference is B. I suppose B would be top middle, after A.'

'How accurate was it?'

'If I remember, the smallest unit of the grid system was about one square kilometre.'

Nikitin threw up his arms. 'That's not exactly pinpointing our destination, is it? Not exactly X marking the spot, comrade . . .'

Rossel reached out a hand and placed it on Nikitin's left arm.

'Where is this location, Herr Speer?' he said.

Speer bared his teeth. Picked at a small morsel of food stuck between the front two. Then he shrugged.

'Without a map I can't help you,' he said. 'I have told you all I know. But I can offer your general one more name that might be of interest to him. That of a scientist, a physicist. *Ein Kernphysiker*. Baron von Möllendorf. Hitler sometimes called him "the man who knows too much".'

Then all his humour left him, as if it were dust he had brushed from his sleeve. Albert Speer got to his feet.

'Two places in Vienna claim to have invented the Sachertorte,' he said. 'The Hotel Sacher and the Café Demel. In the thirties they went to court. As far as I know, they still haven't settled it. In my humble opinion, gentlemen, the Führer understood human nature all too well. We human beings were not placed on this earth to peacefully coexist.'

Speer's finger located a last crumb on the plate.

'Why, just think of the Sachertorte,' he said. 'Two men in Vienna bake a cake and then, a short time later, go to war over it.'

He turned and walked away.

40

Back at the Hotel Beatrice, Rossel wandered about in search of the major-domo, Herr Bernard. Tarkovsky took a nap. Nikitin fumed, muttering curses at Speer.

The hotel was silent, save for some rhythmic and angry grunting behind one door on the second floor and the strumming of a guitar behind another on the third. The crimson carpet might once have been a fixture to be proud of. Now it was threadbare and stained.

He ran Bernard to ground on the fourth floor, polishing the brass buttons of the lift.

'Comrade Bernard,' Rossel began. 'I recall you saying you could get your hands on anything a guest needed.'

The major-domo gave his instinctive bow.

'Anything, comrade.' He gave Rossel a wink. 'Or anyone?'

'Perhaps another time,' Rossel said. 'For now, however, I am hoping that you know where to find some old Luftwaffe *Kameraden*. For once, the Soviet Union has need of them.'

Bernard looked pensive.

'I imagine they might be reluctant to talk to you,' he said.

'There is no need for them to meet us,' replied Rossel. He explained what he needed.

Herr Bernard beamed.

'By tonight, comrade.'

*

After a small plate of chicken, which Rossel devoured but the others barely touched, the three men drank some schnapps.

Nikitin had gone from angry to morose. Tarkovsky was subdued. Rossel waited until the restaurant was empty of the same group of noisy Soviet officers, knowing that Bernard would not deliver his package before then.

On cue, the major-domo materialised with what looked like a rough, oil-stained tablecloth. Rossel thanked him.

Nikitin's cheeks were flushed. 'More schnapps, Bernard,' he shouted after the retreating German.

Rossel pushed their glasses aside and unfolded the map. Across the top, on either side of an eagle gripping a swastika in its claws, were the words *Luft-Navigationskarte in Merkatorprojektion*.

Rossel dropped his notepad next to it.

'We are looking for 15 Ost Sud, RD, and then 1, 8 and B,' he said.

Sure enough, *15 Ost S* encompassed a chunk of territory on the right of the map – a section of the Baltic Sea and, below that, northern and central Germany. The place names were faint under the grid lettering, but in the south-east corner of this section Rossel could make out Kattowitz, which he assumed was Katowice, and below that Oswiecim, which he didn't know.

On the south-west side were Fürth and Nuremberg.

The map section yet further east, *25 Ost S*, ran from Warsaw almost to Kiev. The westernmost edge of the map, at that latitude, was Kursk. At one time, all of this – every number, letter and place name – had been within range of the Luftwaffe's Dorniers and Heinkels and every other plane at Hitler's disposal. And everything within the confines of *15 Ost S* had been fought over.

For a moment, Rossel lost himself in the towns and cities of the immense battlefield that had been the main theatre of the Great Patriotic War.

'So where is RD, then?' said Nikitin, his voice slurred.

They searched, Rossel running his finger down from AA to RA. Names of towns swam before his eyes.

'Gerolzhofen. Ebrach.'

'Never heard of them,' said the major.

RB. 'Bamberg.'

RC. 'Strullendorf. There's RD. What's next?' said Nikitin.

Even Tarkovsky was showing an interest.

'The top left,' said Rossel. 'Imagine a grid of nine and choose the first square – number one. And if the next number is eight, it should be at the bottom of *that* square in the middle.'

Nikitin sighed. 'You're making as much sense to me as one of the *mudaki* who work in the GRU archives.'

Rossel tapped a finger at a place on the map. He stared down at it. The lettering was on a crease and had faded, but he could make out the first letter and the last half of the word.

'Oberst Halder, I have you,' he murmured.

'You do?' said Tarkosvky.

Rossel looked up.

'This Halder is a warrior, a Wagnerian, and a man unable to resist the power of symbols.'

He tapped the map.

'Tomorrow, we go to the West. We go to Bayreuth.'

41

'Gutenfürst! Gutenfürst! Have your papers ready!'

The conductor's warning to passengers was drowned out by the steam engine's shriek but he lost no opportunity in repeating it as he progressed along the passenger wagons. He was Rossel's idea of a German conductor: burly but jovial, with a moustache that must demand considerable attention every morning.

A few kilometres back they had slowed for the *Sperrzone* – the restricted zone that gave advance warning of the inner German border. Before that, East Germans without passes to the West had got off the train in droves. Locked out of half of their own country.

Since then the locomotive had trundled along, steam and smoke whipping past the windows. Reaching the edge of the Soviet Zone, the barriers became increasingly formidable – a fence, then a trench. A control strip for vehicles. A watchtower.

Tarkovsky shrank into his greatcoat.

'More trouble?' he said.

'No trouble,' said Nikitin. 'Until six months ago this crossing was under our control. Officially, we have handed it over. But Fritz knows who is really in charge.'

Two dozen branch lines between East and West Germany had been closed in the past year, the woman in the Berlin station ticket booth had informed them, cursing all Communists as the enemies of freedom. That meant that crossings like this one, even sleepy Gutenfürst, were well stocked with East German soldiers and plainclothes spies. But none was brave enough to challenge a GRU major. The young officer from the *Grenztruppen* who had inspected Nikitin's ID had even saluted.

A few hundred metres beyond the border, the Americans didn't even come out of their guardhouse, merely waving at the Class 52 locomotive as it crawled past. Through the guardhouse's little window, Rossel could see them playing cards.

A minute later they picked up speed.

The rhythm of the train and the enveloping trail of steam was comforting. But nothing was more comforting than the thought that no one in the Soviet Union had any idea where he was. Nikitin seemed on edge, never taking his eyes off him and Tarkovsky. Eventually, Rossel understood why. The major feared that one or both of them might make a run for it, might follow the millions of East Germans who had tasted Communism and didn't like it.

The German countryside meandered by. Yes, Rossel admitted to himself, the thought had crept up on him. He looked through the window and wondered if he would be happy here. No Siberian camps, no MGB, no Stalin. None of the cruelty of Bolshevism.

But they had gone mad here too, hadn't they? One world war had ended and the promises of eternal peace had been made, only for insanity and slaughter to resume two decades later, but worse.

More than that – he was Russian.

If he defected, he would be setting himself against his own country. He was a Leningrader, and his fight to save Leningrad would be meaningless if he could never see her again.

Would any of that matter?

If he jumped from the train, Nikitin would be finished, of course. But so would the major's family. Tarkovsky wouldn't stand a chance, either.

And Galya? His missing sister would be gone for good.

If he quit the city, the country, the Union of Soviet Socialist Republics, his chances of ever tracking her down would be over.

At Hof they switched trains, swapping the Deutsche Reichsbahn of the East for the Bundesbahn of the West.

'For Bayreuth you'll need to change at Neuenmarkt-Wirsberg,' another ticket seller had told Tarkovsky, amused by his over-the-top gallantry and formality. 'No need for the airs and graces, your highness, you're in Bavaria now . . .'

Another hour went by. Tarkovsky was asleep in his seat opposite Rossel and Nikitin. As the train came to an unexpected halt it juddered and woke him. He stretched and sat up.

'Explain it to me again, Rossel,' he said.

'What exactly?'

'The bit about the grid reference.'

'All right.'

Rossel shifted in his seat to stop one leg from going to sleep. 'The Luftwaffe grid is accurate enough for an aerial attack, a bombardment, perhaps a landing zone. But not for a particular building, let alone what we are looking for. A square kilometre is a lot of ground to search.'

He thought back to Gerashvili's reminiscences as a radio operator. If you were a Red Army soldier humming Russian revolutionary ditties, a Wehrmacht radio operator would be left clueless. Conversely, if you were a Nazi Wagner fanatic quoting a few lines from *Götterdämmerung*, what were the chances any Slavic savage would be any the wiser?

'But let's say you were in the know. Let's say you knew something about Wagner. Then you would understand that he persuaded a mad German king to build him a huge opera theatre in the town of Bayreuth, which became the place of pilgrimage for his acolytes and the venue for an annual festival of his works.'

'That takes us to Bayreuth,' said Nikitin, raising his chin. 'But what are we looking for when we're there?'

'I'm not certain,' said Rossel, 'but Speer gave us another name, remember? Von Möllendorf. A baron. A man who knew too much. My guess is that there is something in Bayreuth connected to this von Möllendorf. It's a place to start.'

42

The three Russians tramped southwards towards the Hofgarten, just as Halder had instructed. A thick directory at the train station had given them their destination. There were only two von Möllendorfs, and only one of them was listed with a title.

Bayreuth was quiet. Also beautiful, Rossel thought. A town built like a stage set, waiting for an audience to arrive, a conductor to pick up a baton, singers to respond to their cues.

They entered a long boulevard, gazing at the tall, stocky Franconian buildings, their sloping roofs flecked with snow. At ground level, a cluster of stalls wrapped in multi-coloured lights offered steaming drinks and what looked like outsized twisted biscuits.

'It's like stepping back in time,' said Tarkovsky. 'You know, I have always wanted to play Peter the Great. Riding boots, gold epaulettes and, perhaps, a powdered wig. This place would make a perfect location for that movie. I can see the poster now – "He conquered an empire but not himself!"'

'Yes,' said Nikitin wearily. 'You're an actor. I get it.'

Once or twice as they looked down a side street, they glimpsed a still-ruined church or a historical building propped up with beams and boards. But for the most part, under the yellow gas lights and a blanket of snow, the Bavarian fairy-tale town had come back to life. Bayreuth may not have been made whole again since the bombing raids but American money had already wrought some miracles.

'Quiet,' said Rossel. He pointed. 'Over there.'

In the midst of the stalls, a quartet of Amercan GIs were drinking from large steins of beer. One, a large black man, broke into song. His words had an irresistible sway and swagger to them, even though they could not understand their meaning.

They took the nearest exit into a warren of side streets. As they walked on, the man's voice – something about *boogie woogie boogle* – began to fade.

The dark was drawing in. Soon they were lost.

Tarkovsky spotted an elderly man about to enter a narrow pink building. He stopped and asked him for directions to the address they had found in the directory.

'Down that street, which is Friedrichstrasse,' he said, reporting back. 'Go left when we see Ludwigstrasse, then we'll see the park.'

They set off in the direction the actor was pointing.

'The boogie woogie bugle boy,' said Tarkovsky, laughing. 'I think I might like America . . .'

*

'Ludwigstrasse.' The actor read out the sign.

They took the turn and almost immediately followed a path towards the park.

Nikitin pointed through the trees and across a small lake. 'On the north side, the man said – we need to go that way.'

They followed the line of a long, palatial building that in style was like one the Romanovs might have built. Then they went right again.

'There,' said Rossel.

It was an L-shaped mansion with a circular summer house in the courtyard. The smaller of the two wings had suffered extensive bomb damage. At the main entrance to the grander structure, a coat of arms was carved above the door. A knight's shield containing an eagle. The bird held a sword in one claw and a book in the other.

Beneath it, the family name. Von Möllendorf.

Rossel looked up at it.

'Let's hope he knows as much as Hitler thought he did,' he said.

*

'Locked,' said Nikitin.

He banged on the door but there was no response. If any lights were on, they were not visible. Shutters shielded the interior from prying eyes.

'Let's split up. There must be a hole in the wall some-where near the bombed section,' said Rossel.

Most of the courtyard was gravel, which had been raked even. The grass and hedging that bordered the mansion was neat and well cared for. Someone was looking after the place.

Nikitin and Rossel went in opposite directions, each surveying the length of the mansion in the hope that an entrance would present itself. As he reached the end Rossel looked back but he had lost sight of both the others. He was about to walk down the side of the building and along the back when Tarkovsky's voice reached him.

'Here!'

Rossel could see a dark figure waving an arm. He walked back at a brisk pace to see the double doors at the front were open.

'Welcome to the palace of Peter the Great,' Tarkovsky said, bowing low. 'The back door is hanging off its hinges.'

Nikitin marched straight past him.

Rossel shook his head.

'You just can't resist making an entrance, Boris,' he said.

*

Inside the mansion of von Möllendorf, whoever he was, an entrance hall led straight to a wide marble staircase, one banister of which was missing. They struck out to the left, finding themselves in a grand ballroom that was almost empty. In one corner, a huge crystal chandelier lay like a collapsed constellation of stars on the parquet floor.

'This place is huge,' said Tarkovsky. 'But it already looks like it's been stripped of anything of value.'

'I can't see a thing,' Nikitin complained.

Guided by a thin moonlight that had been let into the room when one of them had pulled back the curtains, Rossel reached the far end and stood before a beautifully carved door.

'We will have to do this the old-fashioned way,' he said. 'By splitting up and . . .'

He pulled the door open and then sprang back, fists raised at the spectre staring back from the other side of the threshold.

The figure had its fists raised in return but they were shaking – with frailty, Rossel realised, rather than fear.

Behind him, Rossel heard a sigh from Tarkovsky and an oath from Nikitin, who strode towards him.

'Who the fuck are you, Grandad?' said the major.

Hands still raised, the figure took a small step forward. In a soft, low voice, it spoke German.

'He says only the stupidest thieves break into an empty home,' said Tarkovsky.

The man shuffled forward, moving into the moonlight.

Tarkovsky took a step back.

Nikitin swore. '*Kakoi-to prizrak*,' he hissed.

But it was not a ghost.

*

Rossel fetched a chair from the corner of the room and offered it to the man who, after a moment's pause, sat.

He was cadaverous, his shirt and trousers hanging off him. He was deathly pale save for a livid pink that covered half of his face – all of the brow, most of the left cheek, sweeping under the chin and across the neck. Malnourished. Neglected. Much of his hair was gone but some was left in clumps.

Rossel stared at him. To his own surprise, he reached out with two fingers to touch the affected skin on the man's face and neck, which was everywhere peeling. The man did not flinch. He did not move at all.

'Scar tissue,' said Rossel. 'He's been burned.'

'Are you the baron?' Nikitin said to him. "Are you von Möllendorf?'

Before he could answer, Rossel shook his head and pointed to the walls. They were covered in black scrawl from an obsessive hand. Pen, charcoal, paint. One word, repeated over and over.

Neubrandenburg.

He called for Tarkovsky to translate.

'I would like to say I do not believe that the past can return to haunt us, but events have proven to me that they can,' said Rossel. 'And you, Oberst Franz Halder, of the town of Neubrandenburg, have just discovered the same thing.'

At the sound of the name, the man closed his eyes. In the silence, Rossel could hear Nikitin's breathing.

Then the German straightened his back and drew his heels together.

'Yes. I am Oberst Halder,' he said. 'Are you here to kill me?'

Halder peered at them through pink, watery eyes. He spoke as though each syllable shocked him, as though every word was a feat he no longer expected to be able to perform.

A click of the fingers. 'No, I am being foolish,' he added. 'Goethe said that one is inspired only in solitude. And yet it seems that I am still found lacking, even after so much time alone.'

Halder scratched at a patch of dry skin on his cheek.

'You have discovered who I was and want to know what I know.' He sighed. 'The British imprisoned me for two years without knowing who I was. They kept me in solitary, hoping to break me. Question after question. In some ways, they succeeded. But I never told them anything. Why would I tell you?'

This much speech appeared to tire Halder. He went quiet again.

'At last, I've found a part I would not wish to play,' whispered Tarkovsky to Rossel as he stared at the German.

Life flickered once again in Halder and he bowed to the actor with military precision. 'In that British prison I at least learned something. Each man rules his own realm, however small,' he said. 'No man who realises that is in need of pity.'

Rossel took a step forward.

'In Leningrad, we found a copy of *The Prince*. Hitler's copy,' he said. 'It was in the possession of an ordinary Red Army soldier, a man who would only have taken it as a trophy. It has your name in it. You were using it to send a message to someone. We would like to know what is here in Bayreuth, and how we may find it.'

Halder shook his head.

'You deciphered it?' he said. 'Well, I was merely a Luft-waffe pilot, not a spy. I was with the Führer in his bunker. The telephone lines were down, the radio was not safe. I had to improvise a cipher . . . something a German would know.'

He began humming. Rossel tried to listen, but the sound was without tune or tonality.

'Then with Bormann and his friends – Axmann and some others – we all tried to get out of Berlin,' Halder continued. 'We ran into some Russians. Marauders, trophy hunters. Bormann was killed. I escaped. But I lost my knapsack. I assumed the Russians took it. A day or two later I was captured further west, by the Americans.'

'We haven't got all night, Rossel,' said Nikitin. 'Let me talk some sense into this Hitlerite bastard . . .'

Rossel shook his head.

'It was taken, Oberst Halder. They found the book, your postcard from Odette. Your gold medallions. But I need to know about the book. The lines from *Götterdämmerung*, and the grid reference, leading here. What is in Bayreuth?'

Halder prodded at his face again, dislodging some flakes of skin that fluttered to the ground.

'Odette,' he said.

His face crinkled.

'A very beautiful woman.'

'Rossel . . .' said Nikitin.

'Your friend is impatient,' said Halder. 'So why don't I show you?'

'Show us what?'

Halder stood up.

'This way,' he said.

*

Halder led the way through the mansion. Almost at the end of one wing, he ascended a narrow flight of stairs with surprising ease and disappeared at the top. Rossel, Nikitin and Tarkovsky chased after him. At first, they thought he had made a run for it.

But then a door opened at the opposite end of the room, which turned out to be only a few metres across. Halder had returned with a lantern.

'My home,' he said, holding up the light.

Rossel looked around.

More scrawl on the walls. The same word on every surface.

Neubrandenburg.

Halder traced a finger over one of them.

'It was my battle cry,' he said. 'But, these days,' he touched his face, 'my nerves aren't what they were. Neubrandenburg is known as the City of the Four Gates,'. 'When I was young my dead father would sometimes appear to me in my dreams and say, "The gates are open, Little Franz, walk through the gates with me."' He traced a finger over one of the words on the wall. 'At the end of the war, I was offered a cyanide pill by a girl from the Band of German Maidens. Almost every night since then I have wished that I had swallowed it. So that I could be with him.'

'Oberst Halder . . .' Rossel began.

'What you seek is a secret hidden within a secret. At one and the same time gigantic, of a size beyond comprehension, and yet it derives from something so small that you could look for eternity and never find it,' he said. 'Atoms within atoms, worlds within worlds. A cosmos of dots. The three of us – Speer, myself and the physicist, von Möllendorf – managed to hide a universe within a single room.'

As Tarkovsky translated, Halder smiled.

'Or, to put it more prosaically, hide it inside a score hidden inside a piano,' he added.

'A piano?' said Rossel.

They all looked around the room. There was no piano.

Halder began to chuckle.

'It has not been here for years,' he said. 'In the summer after the end of the war, the Red Army trucks arrived.

Bayreuth was in the American Zone but they had been allowed in to take some German art and artefacts. Cultural looting. The locals are still angry about it. They still talk. That is how I know.'

'So they took it? Russians?' said Rossel.

Halder nodded.

'They were emissaries of a high-ranking Soviet. They went to the Hermitage Castle and the Opera House. Then they came here. Instruments, music, even the velvet curtains from the opera house. And before the war the von Möllendorf family had taken ownership of one of Wagner's pianos. The maestro's own instrument. It was their pride and joy. A piece of musical history. The Red Army carried it away and every score in this mansion.'

'But who?' said Nikitin. 'Who was this Russian?'

'Oberst Halder,' said Rossel, stepping in front of the major. 'Please. The name.'

Halder glanced up at the words written on the wall.

'"The gates are open, Little Franz,"' he whispered. 'Perhaps, if I tell you, I can, at last, make myself walk through them and be with my father.'

Seized by a coughing fit, he fought to regain control of his breathing.

'The man we duped,' he said, wiping his mouth. 'The man to whom we Germans promised friendship. And then invaded his country. A man who, I suppose, sought a petty recompense. Your former foreign minister, Comrade Molotov.'

43

Leningrad's temperature had risen, turning everything to slush and ooze, and then abruptly fallen again. Dirty, shrunken snow that had been piled at random along pavement edges had turned into rock, while icicles the length of a Cossack *shashka* dangled from the eaves of buildings, forming lines of frozen sabres posed to impale the unwary or unlucky. The city's roads were cracking up under the pressures of expansion and contraction.

At the late hour of their aircraft's arrival, most taxis had given up for the day. Though several other smartly uniformed individuals were picked up by limousines as they arrived at the airport, no such greeting awaited the three of them.

Rossel, Nikitin and Tarkovsky had to walk more than a mile to the nearest bus stop and endure a long journey into the city centre, where they had parted company under a broken streetlight. Tarkovsky had grumbled all the way. He looked shattered, and announced his intention to go to bed. Nikitin stomped off without a word. Rossel was reluctant to return to the Drugov residence, but he'd spent enough time with the actor.

Without the score, they had nothing.

All they had was an ageing Nazi's word that Molotov had it.

And if Molotov had it, Pletnev did not.

As soon as Rossel got back, fighting his tiredness, he picked up the phone and called his old militia station, asking for Gerashvili.

'Anything, Lidia?'

'Something, I think,' she said. 'I only got the files yesterday. I can't . . .'

She stopped herself.

'Can you meet me tomorrow?' Rossel said.

'Of course. About eleven. Where?'

Rossel looked out of the window.

'I know the perfect place.'

*

Even in the grip of winter, survivors of the Siege of Leningrad came to lay bouquets on the mounds of frozen earth that marked the mass graves of Piskaryovskoye Cemetery. They brought pictures of the victims of the Siege, too, on white ceramic disks. They pinned them to trees or tied them to small wooden staves and, where possible, stuck these into the icy ground – as if Piskaryovskoye had in places become a field of mournful flowers, seeded from the half-million or more corpses in its ground.

Elsewhere, blocks of granite and bags of sand lay strewn around, proof of plans to turn the cemetery into a memorial worthy of the great sacrifice of the Hero City.

Gerashvili, wearing her militia uniform under a trenchcoat, was waiting for him near the cemetery's main entrance.

'I see what you mean about the perfect place,' she said as he approached. 'For you, anyway, Revol. A man who

320

used to spend nights at the station browsing the files of the missing. It makes sense you would come here to make friends with the dead.'

He shrugged, but was pleased to see that the old spirit she had once had in abundance was returning.

He reached out with both hands and tapped her twice on both shoulders.

'For a little while, you went missing yourself, Lidia,' he said.

Her cheeks coloured. Then she took out her notepad, tore a sheet from it and gave it to him.

There were three names written on it:

Irina Bok

Mila Kitsenko

Lada Vinogradova.

'That's all I've got,' she said. 'Army files are a mess. When the women's sniper academy closed, individual records got lost or were sent to a hundred different places. Most of what I have managed to acquire are records of exceptional valour. Also some misdemeanours – not reporting back on time, minor insubordination, that kind of thing. At first, I thought they would be of no use to you. But I stayed up the last few nights to go through them anyway.'

Rossel folded the paper and put it in his pocket.

'And the three names?' he said.

'I found a report of a reprimand. All three were mentioned in it.'

'What had they done?'

'The three of them must have been close. They trained together and went to the front together. Apparently, they even referred to themselves as the *troika*. A sisterhood of three. Perhaps it's not surprising they got into trouble together.'

'How and when?' he asked, trying to contain his impatience.

'Towards the end of the Battle of Stalingrad,' Gerashvili said. 'They were reported for a breach of discipline.'

She pulled her coat tighter.

'After the Soviet counteroffensive in November 1942, pockets of German soldiers became isolated. For the snipers, it was the easiest kills they ever made. On December 3 1942, the *troika* set up three positions from which they could cover as wide an area as possible, according to their training. They shot an entire platoon dead. But then they climbed down from their hiding places and shot them all again in the head.'

Pulling one hand out of his pocket, Rossel gestured at the burial grounds around them.

'Considering the scale of suffering in the Great Patriotic War, not the worst of crimes.'

Gerashvili nodded.

'I agree. But it was ill-disciplined. They gave their positions away. They wasted ammunition. And their commanding officer reprimanded them formally.'

Like bullets, rifles and battleplans, discipline was something that had sometimes existed only on paper in the defence of Stalingrad. Yet it had also existed in reality, and in large enough doses to bring victory.

322

'And your killer has a habit of a double shot to the head. And like a sniper, Koshchei is invisible. And, so you tell me, possibly a woman. So I thought—'

'It is excellent work, Lidia,' he interrupted.

Her face lit up. He thanked her and prepared to leave, eager to pass on the news to Nikitin.

'Aren't you going to ask me who their commanding officer was?' she called after him.

He stopped.

'You have found that out as well?'

'Major Anastasia Firsova,' she said. 'She trained them and then joined them in Stalingrad.'

Gerashvili handed him another piece of paper.

*

Major Firsova lived in a communal apartment near the Vitebsky railway station. A note on the wall outside gave the doorbell codes for each of the five households that lived there. He rang three times for Firsova.

She was in her fifties. Despite her civilian clothes, everything about her was military – her formality, her posture, her short-cropped red hair.

'Ah, the school,' she said. 'The happiest time of my life. I have found it hard to adjust to life since the war. But I am not alone in that.'

'Where was it?' he asked her.

'Partly in a large hut in the grounds of the Peter and Paul Fortress,' she said. 'That was for theory, learning to strip and reassemble the rifles, movement, how to work in teams. Timing your shots to mask them. Making a hide.

Many of our principles were formulated by the great Vasily Zaitsev. We sometimes had the honour of his personal instruction. We learned from him how to understand the minds of our opponents. That the hunter must become the prey.'

She smiled at the recollection. 'But we would go out into the countryside for practical experience. Until the Germans imposed the siege. And then we were learning on the job, if you like.'

Rossel took out the list of names Gerashvili had handed him.

'Do you remember these women?' he asked.

The major took some wire-framed spectacles from her pocket and held them up to him.

'I scored 307 kills before I became an instructor. If you gave me a rifle now, I couldn't hit the tram that brought you here.'

She put the glasses on and read the names on the paper. Then she looked up.

'Yes. I taught all of them.'

'What were they like?' Rossel asked.

'Young and foolish, naturally. Especially Irina and Lada. Barely adults. But dedicated. And excellent shots – after they had done their training, excellent. They notched up sixty-seven and thirty-two kills respectively before . . .'

Major Firsova sighed.

'Before?'

'They were both killed in Germany, in hand-to-hand fighting near the end of the war. Not far from Berlin. I believe it was the 5th SS Panzer Division, the *Wiking*. The girls were forced into one of our trenches, which was overrun. The SS cut their throats. A good sniper always knows the way out, knows where the exit is.'

The major sighed. 'They forgot what I taught them.'

'When was this?'

She thought for a moment. 'Right at the end. March 1945, I'd say.'

As Rossel pointed to the third name on the paper, he felt his mouth go dry.

Both killed, he thought. *It has to be . . .*

'What about Kitsenko? Is she still alive?'

'Mila? I don't know. We lost touch after the war. I never heard of her being killed. I heard of her killing a lot of other people, though. She came from the Urals and was as a patient and as still as the mountains themselves. I've met corpses that blinked more. And what a shot. Her father had been a hunter and took her out with him when she still a child. In terms of shooting, there was not too much we needed to teach her – I mean, 277 kills and she made it through to the end. Only Lyudmila Pavlichenko and one or two others managed more, and that includes the men.'

'But there was a disciplinary matter,' Rossel said. 'A formal reprimand?'

Firsova picked up her cup and pressed it to her lips, looking at him over the rim, taking a little longer than she needed to. She wasn't sure. The encounter might now have taken on a different character. Matters of discipline, or perhaps of insufficient discipline, could come back to old soldiers and create problems.

'There was,' she conceded, setting the cup down again. It rattled a little in its saucer.

'Which organisation did you say you . . .'

'I am from the Defence Ministry,' Rossel said.

'I understand, but which . . .'

'Can you explain the circumstances, please, Major Firsova?'

She picked up her teacup again.

'Elite snipers aim for one shot, one kill,' she said, sitting upright. 'The closer you are, the easier it is, but it is also more necessary. When you are close, your shot will be heard, your position will be easier to pinpoint. They broke this rule. It seems there was a . . . competition.'

'An extra bullet to the head,' said Rossel.

'You have heard about it? Yes.'

'And you were the officer who reprimanded them?'

She hitched her shoulders back. 'I had to,' she said. 'For a sniper to lose discipline like that can be fatal. The irony was that Mila was the one to survive.'

'Irony?'

'Yes. She was the one to instigate the game. If one can call it that. And yet it was the others who were killed.'

Rossel leant forward.

'How can you be certain, Major?'

'Oh, I knew my girls very well,' said Firsova. 'She was the ringleader. And something inside her was never the same as the others, comrade. She became obsessed with death. Infatuated with it.'

In the sudden silence came a distant boom – the traditional midday artillery shot from the Naryshkin Bastion of the Peter and Paul Fortress.

'Perhaps she thinks death is something that only happens to other people,' said Rossel. 'If you are Koshchei the Immortal, after all, you might well come to believe that.'

326

44

Fighting to keep his balance on the iron pavement, Rossel slipped and skated along the banks of the Moika towards the Yusupov Palace. He was already anticipating what Tarkovsky called his 'Ottoman gold', the rich Turkish coffee he served in a copper pot. As well as telling Nikitin the news about Mila Kitsenko.

A subdued party of schoolchildren was filing into the main entrance of a school. Further down the road, a militia officer was plodding along towards them, head bowed against the cold. Probably one of the *uchastkovyi*, the local militia officers whose job it was to know their neighbourhood as well as anyone could know it.

As his gaze turned to the little side door that led to Tarkovsky's apartment, he stopped in his tracks. A figure in a fur coat with a violin case by her side was standing at the door, hesitant, not pressing the bell.

Rossel crossed the road.

'Vassya,' he said.

She turned and recognised him with a small smile. She lifted up the violin case.

'I kept her safe for you, Revol.'

Seeing his old instrument was like seeing a long-lost family member.

'Thank you,' he said. 'How did you know I was staying here?'

'I asked Ilya to enquire . . .' She coloured a little. 'He has some influence in the Party.'

'Ilya?'

'The man who buys me flowers.'

'Ah, yes.' For a moment he was at a loss. He fumbled for the key Tarkovsky had given him. She looked like she was feeling the cold, so he added: 'Do you want to come in?'

She shook her head and held out the case.

'No, I just wanted to give you . . . sorry.' The apology was not to him but to the militia officer, who had doubled back on his beat and was now trying to pass by on their side of the pavement.

The officer stepped behind them and stopped. He turned and pointed something in Rossel's direction. The gleaming muzzle of a Makarov pistol.

'That's what I always hated the most about you, Rossel,' said Pavel Grachev, sergeant in the Red Army; sergeant in the militia; survivor of war, purges, labour camps and the long, long walk to freedom across Siberia. 'Always chasing pussy like the rest of us pricks . . .' He shoved them inside. 'While all the time pretending to be some kind of fucking saint.'

*

'Who is she?' said Grachev, waving the Makarov at Vassya.

He had shoved them down the corridor into Tarkovsky's private quarters.

'She is just a violinist from the conservatoire,' said Rossel. 'I'm giving her lessons. You and me, she has nothing to do with that. Let her go.'

Grachev's pistol hovered between them. He moved his bony hips in and out a couple of times and leered.

'Lessons, yes. I bet.'

Grachev's features were twitching and contorted. He was already anticipating the blood to come – could hardly wait for it. In the war, Rossel had seen men get like that. Licking their lips. Flaring their nostrils as if Death wore an alluring scent.

But before the kill, he needed to preen, needed to rub Rossel's nose in it.

'Not many make it back from Vorkuta,' Grachev said. 'Brain two guards with an axe, shoot a third, take their weapons and go. That was the easy part. You'll know that. As a former zek.'

Of Tarkovsky there was no sign. Rossel hoped that the actor had gone to Lenfilm and was well out of the way. Unless Major Nikitin turned up soon – and they had not set any specific time to meet – Grachev would kill both of them. He knew how to control two people, and how to finish them off. He would kill one. Make the other one watch. Then finish it.

'You went north instead of south,' Rossel said. 'That was what I would have done. You persuaded that boy to go with you. If you made it far without anyone picking up your trail, he could be the *myaso*. Provide you with a meal or two in the middle of the taiga. But they were after you faster than you'd bargained for. So you sent the boy into the forest as a decoy while you hid out for a while. In one of the mines, was it? You could burn a fire there without being seen.'

The sneer on Grachev's face curdled into a look of cold contempt. Rossel knew he had got it roughly right.

'Then you doubled back. Made it back to Vorkuta and bluffed your way onto an aircraft.'

'Always the great detective, you smug bastard,' said Grachev. 'But you didn't see me coming today, eh?'

'Pavel, it wasn't me who—'

'It's amazing what you can do if you wander around in a militia uniform,' said Grachev. 'All this shit about Koshchei. I hear chatter about a corpse at Lenfilm, of all places. So, I stand guard there – literally stand guard, like a statue. A few days later you walk straight past. I follow, and you are staying at the Yusupov Palace. Living in a fucking palace. You always did think you were a cut above . . .'

The journey back from Siberia, Rossel noticed, had taken its toll on the sergeant. The dry skin on his face was rough and reddened, the lobe of his left ear was gone. It was a reasonable assumption he'd lost a toe or three. He looked tired, too. Exhausted.

Maybe I can jump him.

Grachev's lips sank backwards to reveal dark brown teeth. He tried to imitate Rossel's voice.

'*Pavel, it wasn't me who* . . . You think you can lick my arse like you did with Captain Lipukhin or one of those idiot superior officers in Station 17?'

'No,' said Rossel. 'And I had nothing to do with—'

'You informed on me!' Grachev yelled, leaping forward, a heartbeat away from putting a round in Rossel's face. 'I know it was you. That's why they sent me to the fucking *camps*.'

Vassya was sitting and had not moved a muscle. Her hands rested on the table. She looked straight at Grachev.

'It's impressive what you did, escaping like that,' she said. 'Not many men could do it.'

'No,' Grachev said, settling a little. 'Not many men could. But if you think you'll save your neck just by making me think you want to suck my *khui* . . . Every whore we booked in the cells in the station used to try that trick.'

He tapped the Makarov.

'Four bullets for you and one for the bitch,' he said to Rossel. 'But before I kill her, I'm going to fuck her.'

Grachev's right forearm was in range.

Now make a—

An object came hurtling out of the shadows. Rossel threw up an arm to parry it. As it smashed into his shoulder and deflected into the middle of Grachev's face, Rossel still had time to recognise it – the bust of Lenin that Tarkovsky hated, the one he would turn to the wall.

There was a deafening retort – Grachev's pistol firing as it dropped from his hand. Tarkovsky stood pale and motionless in the corner of the rooms, unable to believe what he had done.

The Makarov slid across the floor.

Rossel dived for it.

Vassya hurled herself at Grachev.

The sergeant threw her off him and kicked her twice in the face. Rossel's hand was under a sideboard, groping for the weapon. Grachev leapt on top of Rossel, dirty fingernails clawing at his face.

Rossel's own fingers closed on the Makarov. He pressed the pistol against Grachev's temple.

Fired.

At the last moment, Grachev pulled his head back and rolled. The bullet missed and removed a chunk of brick and plaster from the wall. Then Grachev scrambled to his feet and started running.

A moment later, the apartment door slammed shut.

*

Up ahead, Rossel heard the main door to the street smack against the wall. He raced down the corridor and out into the light, which was blinding against the ice and snow.

The detective scanned the street.

Left. Right. Nothing.

There.

Grachev, a way off to the right, heading along the Moika towards Isaac's Square. A group of children and adults spilled out onto the street from the school. A little girl screamed when she spotted Rossel with his pistol levelled.

He lowered the weapon and set off in pursuit, pushing through the frightened crowd. Grachev was limping. He must have hurt his leg in the fight.

Rossel was closing but the embankment curved at this point and his target was always just out of sight.

Twenty metres.

Ten.

Five.

Where is he?

Grachev exploded from a doorway, going for Rossel's throat rather than the pistol. His body pinned Rossel's right arm to his side and knocked the weapon from his fingers.

They twisted and turned together. In a slow, ungainly *pas de deux*, they toppled over the embankment rail.

Picking up speed, they plunged through the ice.

*

Blackness.

He blinked twice.

Still black.

Above him nothing but a roof of white. Below and around him, only freezing murk.

Follow the bubbles. Upwards, towards the light.

Rossel clawed at the ice, his palms and knuckles sliding without effect on the white crust that had become his coffin lid.

But the Moika was narrow. If he got lucky, he'd find the granite bank.

If I get unlucky?

On hitting the freezing water he'd gasped – the reflex that killed so many ice fishermen who trod in the wrong spot and went through, sucking in water.

He already had no air in his lungs but plenty of foul liquid in his mouth and stomach.

A distant, muffled pounding.

A few last apologetic notes. A disappointing final aria . . .

Black spots multiplied on his vision like ink spreading on paper.

He had become a score. Or some strange being that hid inside it.

The pounding grew louder, like the crashing of the percussion. A last dazzling whiteness before the fade to black.

Hands pulling at his clothes.

Angels will take us, Revol. His grandmother's voice. *Angels will carry us up to heaven . . .*

Rossel lay on his back on the bank and vomited black, grainy liquid all over his own face.

His ears drained themselves of water, only to fill up again with the sound of someone screaming. His arms were being pulled out of their sockets as he was rolled over onto his front. A knee to the ribcage made him vomit even more.

Vassya was kneeling next to him. Beside her was a twisted chunk of broken metal rail that she'd used to smash a hole in the ice.

Angels will take us, Revol. Angels will carry us up to heaven.

45

Vassya tugged hard at his coat, tearing it free. A shove in his shoulder blades to propel him further along the corridor and into Tarkovsky's ornate bathroom, with its plush carpet on the floor.

Helpless, teeth chattering, he let Vassya remove his jacket and shirt. She sent the actor to fetch more towels and steered Rossel into the bathroom. Turning on the shower, she started to pull at the buttons of his trousers but he fended her off and clambered into the bath, straight into the scalding stream.

After a couple of minutes, the bathroom door opened again and more towels were thrown in. Ignoring them, Rossel sat on the bath floor, arms across his knees, and let the hot water cascade over him.

Still shivering, he closed his eyes.

Black spots again. Ink on paper.

Another image came to him.

A cosmos of dots. Worlds within worlds. The gigantic hidden within the shell of the infinitesimal.

A sound, too.

Sung by a madman to the dark Siberian skies.

A single leitmotif.

*

Rossel and Ilya Koshkin were about the same height, though Koshkin's waist was a little larger. As befitted a Party man.

'Thank you, comrade,' said Rossel.

Koshkin grunted. He was handsome, with piercing blue eyes and straight black hair that was turning grey. He wore a permanent half-smile that seemed to flit between friendship, aggression and deference. He was, Vassya had said before his arrival at Tarkovsky's apartment, a senior manager in the Ministry of Machine Tool Building.

It must be the engineer in her, Rossel thought. When they're in bed, they get to exchange pithy anecdotes about quotas and five-year plans.

Koshkin eyed the clothes Rossel was wearing.

'I bought that suit last summer.'

'It fits well,' said Rossel. He was hoping it was Koshkin's best.

'I bought boots, too, and a coat, just as Vassya asked.'

'Thank you again.'

Vassya reappeared with a teapot in one hand and the coat in the other, which she tossed at Rossel. Koshkin did not protest. A well-connected Party man could always get another coat.

'I must go. Work,' said Koshkin. 'They're building a new tractor-part factory out near Chudtsy. I have to attend the opening ceremony.'

Vassya nodded at him.

She turned to Rossel. 'Are you still in trouble?'

He blew on his tea. Then nodded. 'Unless I can find a way to see Comrade Molotov.'

'Don't ask him questions, Vassya,' said Koshkin. 'Not ones we don't need to know the answer to. When you have opened one tractor-part factory I can assure you, Comrade Rossel, you have opened them all. But, as I believe you already know, there are worse ways of spending a day in our glorious Soviet state. Your past is well known to me. For many, Igarka is a one-way ticket . . .'

'You have no need to worry,' said Rossel. 'Our investigation appears to have reached a dead end. Access to Comrade Molotov is unlikely to be granted to me.'

Koshkin drew himself to his full height and pulled on his gloves.

'Molotov, you say? Pah. Yesterday's man,' he said. 'I hear he has fallen so far out of favour that his wife has been arrested and sent into exile. Molotov himself is merely counting the days until his own fate is sealed.'

With an effort, Rossel sat upright.

'How do you know?'

Koshkin turned to face him.

'If you want rise in the Ministry of Machine Tool Building, comrade, you need to develop a keen ear for more than just the sound of the carburettors on the new MTZ2s they are producing in Minsk. And a keen eye, too. An eye for the tallest stalks of corn. Especially the ones that have been marked out for the harvest.'

Koshkin put on his *ushanka* and centred it.

'I gather Comrade Molotov has fallen so far they have even taken his Party dacha away. They say he has been forced to retreat to his own country residence, where he now awaits Soviet justice.'

'But where is it?' asked Vassya. 'His own dacha, I mean.'

Koshkin walked across to her and kissed her.

'An ugly little smear on the map called Valdai. He's there now, apparently. Brooding. He has no power in Moscow and no friends in Leningrad, so it is appropriate for him to languish halfway between the two, welcome in neither. Nothing to do there but fish. And wait.'

46

'You know what, in my opinion, is better than having friends in high places?' the minister said.

Nikitin shrugged. 'No.'

'Loyal comrades in low ones.'

The minister seemed pleased with his joke.

It was the same room in the Astoria hotel as last time. He wore a big coat, just like his underling. Unlike him, he filled it.

'And we are still friends you and I? I'm right about that, am I not, Major?'

'Of course, Comrade Minister.'

But he hasn't come all the way to Leningrad just to see me, thought Nikitin.

Something else must be about to happen.

'Excellent. I gather that you, like me, are from peasant stock. I myself am from a village so poor the peasants there couldn't even afford a sign. Herded cows and sheep as a boy.'

He lifted the sleeve of his coat and gave it an exaggerated sniff.

'Sometimes I think I can still smell the cowshit.'

Nikitin leaned forward.

'My wife, Comrade Minister. My son. My daughter. You will still intervene on their behalf? As your representative has promised me?'

The minister sat back.

'Later on, I worked down a mine, and then in a chemical factory. I can see from the scars on your face, your accent, the way you lump about the place, that you are hoping the next *apparatchik* who walks past will spit in your face just so you can give them a good kicking.'

He sniffed his sleeve again. 'And I can tell that you can smell the cowshit too. You're a man like me, who's not ashamed of having done peasant work, of having dirty hands. Or a dirty conscience. Am I right?'

'My wife, Comrade Minister. My son, Dima.'

The minister did not reply.

Sometimes, a man breaks easier when he is still allowed a little hope.

The minister understood that, too.

Finally, he nodded.

'Yes, I'll keep them safe. Providing . . .'

'Providing?'

'You continue to keep me informed.'

His eyes creased at the corners.

'So, tell me a little more about this man Halder . . .'

47

Grey-white sky above, dirt-white road below.

Small, three-hut villages raced past the car's misted windows and became dots in Rossel's rear-view mirror.

Valdai. *An ugly little smear on the map.* But also a place of recreation for second-tier members of the Party, according to Koshkin. Lakes, spas, a smattering of summer dachas for middle managers and bureaucrats. Very few people there at this time of year. Easy to find, and nowhere to run. A perfect place to hunt down Molotov, cocooned in bourgeois luxury, waiting for Stalin's axe to fall.

Nikitin had barely raised his voice to question Rossel's request to take the car. He seemed distracted, on edge – on the verge of another meeting with General Pletnev.

After four hours, Rossel was skirting Lake Ilmen and the town of Novgorod, once a rival power centre to Moscow. Until Ivan the Terrible had sacked it and slaughtered or deported its inhabitants with Stalinist thoroughness.

The light was fading. He pulled in for petrol, receiving assurances that he was on the right road but that it would take him another three hours.

For a while he sang to keep himself awake – an old peasant song about fortune tellers. A little hymn offered up to Fate.

Without a map and by now in the dark, Rossel had to guess the turning and guessed wrong, necessitating several stops for assistance from tiny settlements amid the thickening forest. A tractor driver returning to his *kolkhoz*, respectful but sullen, set him straight for a while. Soon lost again, he saw in his headlights a peasant woman gathering wood.

'Valdai? Comrade Molotov?' he asked her through the window. She was bent almost double by years of physical toil. She pointed down the road and then, with a jerk of her whole arm, towards the left. He followed the road until, sure enough, there was a left turn.

The road grew rougher and the wheels of the car began to spin against the deepening snow.

There it is.

A fine, two-storey wooden dacha, a mere couple of hundred metres from the lake, with a bright moon flashing on the water.

Between the house and the lake, silhouetted by light from a long wooden veranda, a man sat lost in contemplation on a small wooden bench. He turned to face the car. If he was alarmed he did not show it.

Rossel stopped the car and got out.

Head to one side, the First Deputy Chairman of the Council of Ministers waited for him to approach. Wearing a dark fur coat, Molotov was flat-faced, with a moustache that had starred in a thousand newsreels and newspaper photographs.

'I have been waiting for you,' Molotov called out, his tenor voice quavering. 'But you don't look like Mercader.'

Rossel kept walking towards the bench, hands out of his pockets and by his sides.

'Mercader?'

'Ramón Mercader. The man who put an ice axe in Trotsky's head.'

Rossel stopped.

'I'm not here for that. And I'm not here from them – the MGB. Besides . . .'

Rossel glanced around. Pine and birch encircled the lake, which was ice until the last few centimetres before the water lapped against a beach.

'As far as I can see, this isn't Mexico.'

Molotov stared out at the lights that dotted the distant shore.

'No,' he said. 'It's a lot closer to Moscow than that.'

The two men faced out to the water, taking a moment to revel in the silence and stillness, both grateful for a moment of peace.

'In Stalin's court, every prince sleeps with his head on the block. If not Beria, who sent you?' said Molotov.

'General Pletnev. I came for some information, comrade. Information vital to the security of the Soviet Union.'

Molotov stood.

'Pletnev. I see. You have had a long journey, comrade, I can tell,' he said. 'Let's eat.'

48

Inside the dacha, three walls of the main room were covered with paintings in the Russian folk style. For the most part they were winter scenes. One was particularly impressive: a downed stag impaled by arrows. Alongside happy peasants in the fields, there were more scenes from fairy tales and landscapes of forests and lakes. The curtains and furniture coverings were a riot of red berries and gold leaves. A subdued fire crackled in a simple brick fireplace.

The fourth wall was covered in books from floor to ceiling – hundreds of them. At least three and a half rows were taken up by musical anthologies and biographies of great composers.

Molotov walked over to an ancient gramophone and began to wind it up.

'No staff?' Rossel asked.

Molotov snorted.

'In the Kremlin, every day you learn to take the temperature,' he said. 'How blows the wind today from Gori, we ask ourselves.'

Gori was Stalin's birthplace.

'For some time now an unexpectedly cold breeze from the Georgian mountains has required me to take particular care when buttoning up my coat.'

The needle dropped onto the record.

'I sent my staff away last week,' Molotov continued. 'Just because I have caught a cold, doesn't mean they have to.'

The music began to play.

'Glazunov,' said Rossel. He caught Molotov's eye. 'I studied violin at the Leningrad Conservatoire.'

'The conservatoire? So we have the appreciation of music in common.'

For the first time, Molotov smiled.

'Have you ever seen the portrait of Glazunov by Ilya Repin? He looks so severe. A priest confessor who has ceased to believe in the concept of mercy.'

Rossel shook his head.

'No,' he said. 'But from your description, I think I'd quite like it.'

They listened to a few more bars.

'I myself dabble. I have attempted this concerto,' said Molotov, 'but it demands more attention and talent than I can give it.'

To play the Glazunov concerto required an advanced technique. Molotov was a man possessing some unexpected gifts.

Through a door off to the right, Rossel could see a long dining table, large enough for a dozen people. But set for only two.

'You were already awaiting a guest?'

Melancholy passed over Molotov's face.

'My wife, Polina,' he said. 'She was exiled to Siberia over the matter of Jewish settlement of the Crimea. I was forced to denounce her. Yet I set the table each night so we might one day dine as we used to.' He took off his glasses and then replaced them. 'There's a little hope in ritual, I find.'

'Exile is not death, at least,' said Rossel.

Molotov laughed. 'Mostly, it is death,' he said. 'But let us eat while we can.'

*

For several minutes the two men had chewed away in determined silence, grunting or jabbing a fork into the air to indicate their approval.

After a second helping of the *pelmeni* Molotov had brought from the kitchen and another enormous dollop of sour cream, the old Bolshevik poured out two glasses of vodka.

'To the artists, musicians, directors and writers of the Soviet Union,' Molotov said, raising his glass.

He took a sip, and then a longer, greedier gulp, setting the glass back down on the table and rubbing his cheeks.

Rossel drank his vodka down. The warmth of the alcohol cheered him.

Molotov pointed at Rossel's left hand. 'There's a story in your hands, I think. A violinist with missing fingers. Someday I'd like to hear it. But not tonight. Let's get down to business.'

In the next room, the Glazunov was halfway through the finale: a joyous, rumbustious dance. And a challenge, Rossel remembered. Left-hand pizzicato, harmonics at considerable speed, and you needed a free, supple bowing arm.

'You are in possession of a piano,' he said. 'Brought back to the USSR from Bayreuth. One that used to belong to Richard Wagner. And with it, a musical score that must have accompanied the instrument. The latter is of interest to Defence Minister General Pletnev.'

Molotov swept a hand several times across the table. The old Bolshevik thought for a moment. In the centre of the table was a white plate on which were the last of the dumplings. Three of them were round and perfectly formed. The fourth was small and stunted, a runt the chef had made from the last scraps of dough.

Molotov picked it up.

'So why doesn't the general simply place a call to me? Or send a platoon. Why send you?'

Rossel shrugged.

'I am a person of no importance. The general does not confide in me. I am simply here to do his bidding.'

Molotov frowned.

'"I am a person of no importance." I might print that phrase on a card and hand it out to the next people who come calling at my dacha. That way, I might live a little longer.'

He tossed the dumpling in the air and caught it again.

'Permit me to pass on some news that may not have been in the newspapers,' he said. 'A few weeks ago, the Americans carried out the first successful test of a hydrogen bomb, somewhere in the South Pacific. Do you know what a hydrogen bomb is?'

'No.'

Molotov held the palm of his right hand flat so that Rossel could see the dumpling.

'The bomb they dropped on Hiroshima was 16 kilotons. That is equivalent to 16,000 tons of TNT,' said Molotov. 'In that explosion, about 140,000 people died.'

He picked up one of the bigger dumplings with his left hand and held it out.

'Our people estimate this recently detonated hydrogen bomb was 10 megatons. That is equivalent to 10 million tons of TNT.'

Molotov raised up the larger dumpling in his left hand.

'That's Moscow, gone. Leningrad, gone. Sverdlovsk, Chelyabinsk, Omsk, Gorky, Stalingrad, Kuibyshev, Vladivostok, Kazan. Not a brick left, not one child's cry, not a single mournful bird singing in a tree.'

His eyes were round and set well back in his face. He spoke with long pauses to complete the calculations taking place in his mind. Rossel began to see why he had survived for so long when so many of Lenin's comrades had slid beneath the quicksand of the revolution.

The record crackled to a stop and Molotov rose again to replace it.

He took a while with his choice. Then the mournful opening bars of Mozart's 'Requiem' drifted into the room. Still a Russian favourite, even in the atheist's paradise.

'Immediately after this new American bomb, Stalin held a meeting of the Politburo,' Molotov said, resuming his seat. 'Myself, Kaganovich, Khrushchev, Beria, Mikoyan, Pletnev, Malenkov, a few others. The Great Leader screamed at us. Called us useless fools. He worked himself up into such a rage I thought his heart would give out. When he was finished, he sat back and was silent. He looked very old in the way people do when they have seen too much and become a little tired of living.'

Requiem, the basses rumbled.

The tenors agreed. *Requiem aeternam.*

'Without our own hydrogen bomb there will soon be no Union of Soviet Socialist Republics, was the main point he was making. As we sat at the table and looked across at Stalin's grey skin and glassy eyes, every man there suddenly understood – Stalin won't be around forever. And the man who builds that bomb will most likely take his place.'

Et lux perpetua luceat eis . . .

Molotov got to his feet and gestured towards the door of the next room.

'And now here you are, comrade. Sent by General Pletnev. In pursuit of a piano that was shipped to me, along with many other items of musical interest, from the Bayreuth house of the German nuclear physicist, Herr von Möllendorf.'

*

Molotov led the way into a large, homely living space with more books on all sides. And a Bechstein piano resting on a green-topped table in one corner.

'There,' he said.

Rossel stared at it. It was a rich walnut brown, sleek and polished, its only fault being that it looked like someone had cut the legs off.

'I had expected something more imposing.'

'The composer had more than one piano, of course,' said Molotov. 'After all, he was Richard Wagner. But this was the instrument on which he composed *Götterdämmer-ung*. So they tell me, at least. A table piano. Simple to move from place to place. Practical. And yet an artefact.'

From the gramophone, the choir sang of judgment and resurrection.

'And talking of the Twilight of the Gods . . .'

Molotov gripped Rossel's elbow and led him to a central section of the bookshelves.

It was an extensive collection of musical scores. Rossel could see long rows of symphonies and concertos; music for solo piano; a vast collection of violin works . . . and about two metres of operatic scores, mostly Russian. There was Rimsky-Korsakov, Glinka, Tchaikovsky – even the out-of-favour Prokofiev. And the banned Rachmaninov.

There it is – the Ring Cycle.

The four music dramas, *Das Rheingold. Die Walküre. Siegfried. Götterdämmerung.*

Molotov reached out and picked it up.

'Sometimes the wind from Gori will chill a man's bones no matter how many buttons he has done up. Do you understand, comrade? Tonight, you were not who I thought you might be. But tomorrow . . .'

'There maybe somebody else,' said Rossel.

'Precisely.'

Molotov handed the score to Rossel, who opened it.

It was monumental.

'Tell General Pletnev that this comes not from me but my wife, Polina. Do you understand? That with this gift he is in her debt.'

Rossel nodded.

'I will impress that fact upon him, Comrade Molotov. That whatever happens, he must set her a place at his table.'

*

A gentle snowfall had resumed. 'Be careful on the road,' said Molotov, leaning into the window of Rossel's car, his face half in light, half in darkness. 'This snow will only get heavier.'

The minister stepped back and looked out towards the bench on which Rossel had found him sitting. 'Your name, comrade? It sounds foolish but I was born in Kukarka, where peasant superstitions once reigned before Soviet modernity swept them away. I did not want to ask you when you arrived, in case you were indeed a shade and the sound of the words alone might have stopped my breath.'

'Rossel, Comrade Minister Molotov. Revol Rossel.'

'Revol. A good name. *Revolyutsionnaya Volya*. The Will of the Revolution. Your family must have been greatly committed to the cause.'

Rossel nodded.

'When they gave me the name, yes. Later, circumstances may have convinced them something else may have suited me better. They were both sent to the camps.'

Molotov sighed.

'As Marx said, "There is only one way in which the murderous death agonies of the old society and the bloody birth throes of the new society can be shortened, simplified and concentrated, and that way is revolutionary terror." It is regrettable but we Russians have had to make many sacrifices for the great peace to come. I must soon make mine.'

Rossel started up the motor. It took a couple of tries to get it going.

'One last thing, since you work for General Pletnev,' said Molotov, leaning into the window again. 'A word of

351

caution. In April 1945, at the Seelow Heights, the First Belorussian Front was taking a beating.'

'I know,' said Rossel. 'Everyone knows that General Pletnev saved the day.'

'But listen,' said Molotov, pressing a finger to his lips. 'Zhukov was throwing more men into the fray but the Germans had burst a dam to flood the ground. A brilliant defensive move. Everything was sinking into the mud. It's true what people say. Pletnev reorganised the assault, the artillery tactics, the tank formations. Broke through, raced forward to the outskirts of Berlin. And halted.'

'To let Zhukov through,' said Rossel. 'To let him have the honour of capturing the Reich's capital city.'

Molotov drew a rough circle in the snow with his foot, and then dragged his heel to make a line next to it.

'No, Comrade Rossel. General Pletnev halted there because that was the approximate range of the *katyusha* rockets he had available. Nine kilometres. He lined up every mortar regiment in the First Belorussian Army – every *katyusha*, every howitzer – and opened up. His intention was to obliterate everything between him and the Reichstag.'

Molotov stepped onto the circle.

'He maintained fire for approximately twenty minutes before Zhukov could get through on the telephone and ask him what the hell he thought he was doing. Apparently, the answer was, "What Hitler wished to do to Leningrad I will now do to them."'

A breeze was getting up, skating off the lake and shaking the smaller branches of the trees. Molotov's jacket whipped open but he was content to let it flap as he took a step back out of the car's way.

'Beria is the poison that runs through Stalin's veins,' the Old Bolshevik said. 'But Pletnev is the knife at his throat.'

He shoved his spectacles up the bridge of his nose and peered through them at Rossel.

'Polina, comrade. Be sure to tell the general about her.'

*

After half a kilometre, Rossel pulled over and grabbed the score.

> *Denn der Götter Ende dämmert nun auf.*
> *So werf' ich den Brand*
> *in Walhalls prangende Burg.*

Brünnhilde's great soprano aria came right at the end of *Götterdämmerung.*

In the thin light provided by the overhead bulb, Rossel could barely see the music or the words. He clambered out of the car and used the headlights instead, half-blinding himself until he got the angle right.

A fusion of instruments and voice, music and drama, gods and men – dozens of leitmotifs converging for the climax.

And amid the notes, a line of Brünnhilde's aria. *Denn der Götter Ende dämmert nun auf. He* followed it to the climax. A massive fanfare on the word *Burg* in the woodwind and brass, dominated by the trumpets.

Protons. Electrons. Neutrons . . . Even smaller particles, and smaller still.

A cluster of notes that looked darker than the rest.

Perhaps a dozen.

Black spots again. Ink on paper.

He removed the glove from his withered left hand and traced them with his forefinger. The nerve endings were long dulled but the sensation was evident and undeniable. Lost in the cosmos of ink, a short fanfare of notes, which, like Braille, were raised from the paper. Almost imperceptible bumps that gave off tiny shards of reflected light.

The gigantic hidden within the shell of the infinitesimal. Worlds hiding within worlds.

And within each of them, the power to destroy this one.

ACT 4
GODS

49

Nikitin drove his reclaimed GAZ through a dilapidated arch into a courtyard somewhere in the middle of Vasilievsky Ostrov – the island district of the city, out west, where every building looked like every other building.

That was the point. When on Soviet territory, GRU agents had every army base in the Leningrad Oblast to hide in, so that was where they were expected to be. But on occasions, a hideout in the city that Beria's Ministry for State Security did not know about was safer.

As they got out and headed for the elegant, pre-revolutionary apartment block, both men had to step from side to side to avoid the puddles of slush that pockmarked the courtyard. For all that, they moved with purpose and pace.

Outside, up four flights of the stone staircase, a man in blue overalls stood to attention.

'My balls have shrunk to one kopek pieces,' muttered Nikitin as he rapped on the door. 'Hurry up, *ublyudki*, it's fucking freezing out here.'

From inside came the sound of a complicated lock being turned.

Now that he was back in Leningrad, Rossel could not shake off the fear, real or imagined, that a sniper's sights were trained on the back of his head. He remembered a moment of quiet while jammed into a crater with another soldier during the Sinyavino Offensive, right in the depths of the war – a moment when both sides were reloading and the sun came out. They had shared half a damp cigarette and memories of childhood before a sniper had picked the man off. It was not for several minutes – as Rossel lay face up, pressing his shoulder blades as far as he could back into the mud and slime – that he discovered a small grey piece of the man's brain stuck to his right lapel. As if it was a badge.

Snipers, he thought, usually preferred the distance kill. But Koshchei was different . . .

'Something on your mind?' said Nikitin.

Rossel tried to stop feeling as if he was being hunted.

'Something Molotov told me,' he said.

'Which was?'

Beria is the poison that runs through Stalin's veins. But Pletnev is the knife at his throat.

Rossel shrugged and took a step forward. The door swung open.

'Nothing important,' he said.

50

The room was large but still filled with the fug of smoke from imported Bulgarian cigarettes – better quality tobacco, for those who could get access to it.

In a corner was a pink-tasselled standing lamp. On one wall was a black-and-white photograph of a man standing next to an ageing elephant: a once-beloved beast named Betty that was killed by German bombs at the very beginning of the city's wartime bombardment. This room, Nikitin had told him, used to be the elephant keeper's apartment. The GRU had long ago appropriated the building, though for some reason had maintained the animal theme for the décor. On another wall was a tapestry of deer grazing in a forest, similar to the one Rossel had seen at Molotov's dacha but not as well executed.

At a large, polished table in the centre of the room sat a small, thin woman with neat black hair and horn-rimmed spectacles. Rossel recognised her – Captain Morozova, the GRU codebreaker who had been so dismissive of the markings and clues within *The Prince*. She had the score of *Götterdämmerung* open before her – at its final pages. Next to her was a microscope with some cumbersome attachments.

'A pleasure to meet you again, Captain Morozova,' said Rossel.

She acknowledged him without enthusiasm.

'Likewise, comrade,' she said.

At the far end of the table sat two more people, a man and a woman, going over outsize sheets of photographic paper on which were printed images of documents. Three men, dressed in suits and ties, were peering over their shoulders. All five were whispering to each other. They looked excited. Rossel did not have the spy's facility for reading upside down but the images looked like pages of typed paper, in Roman script, interspersed with handwritten equations and rough diagrams.

Sitting behind them on a stool against the wall was a bald man in his late thirties with a small red goatee and doleful eyes. No one introduced him.

'Captain Morozova,' said Nikitin to the codebreaker. He was as agitated as ever. 'How long before everything is ready?'

A door that Rossel hadn't noticed opened. Beyond it was a dark red gleam. He caught the whiff of chemicals – a strangely pleasant scent.

'Microdots, when all is said and done, are photographs,' said Morozova, who looked displeased at having her name said aloud. 'You take a standard photographic image of your chosen document on a high-contrast film. Then you take that negative, which is already smaller by approximately ten times, and you reduce it again – shining a bright light on it from where the eye would be, through a lens to shrink it another thirty times or so, and focus the positive image onto a glass plate coated with a special emulsion . . .'

Nikitin sighed. 'It doesn't sound very simple.'

Morozova picked up her cigarette from a metal ashtray and took a thoughtful drag – a gesture that seemed to suggest that simplicity was a relative concept, dependant on the intellect of the beholder – before continuing:

'Then you cut out the emulsion from the backing – a slightly enlarged hypodermic needle is favourite for doing that, to stamp it out. *Pozhaluista* – you have a *mikrat*.'

'A *mikrat*?' said Rossel.

'A microdot. The Hitlerites were masters at it.'

Nikitin was losing patience.

'I don't need a detailed lesson in how microdots work, comrade. All we need to know is, have you found anything significant yet?'

Morozova coloured a little. 'To preserve their clarity, we have a two-step enlargement and development process.' She jabbed a thumb in the direction of the room with the aroma of chemicals, and Rossel realised it was where her colleagues were developing and printing the film. 'There are more than 250 pages here. We are up to page . . . page twenty-three. Please allow us to do our work, Comrade Major Nikitin. Once developed they must be fixed into slides – we'd blow them up bigger but there isn't that amount of quality photographic paper in the city. Only a sample are being turned into larger images.'

She looked at Rossel.

'You can hide a microdot anywhere,' she said. 'On the hem of a doll's dress. In the full stop at the end of a love letter. In a packet of tobacco. Under a stamp is a favourite.'

She leafed through the many pages of *Götterdämmerung*.

'In an opera the size of this one there are hundreds, thousands, maybe tens of thousands of places you could put one. How did you know to look on this particular page?'

Rossel lent forward and tapped a finger on the score.

'I started studying the violin at the age of four,' he said. 'Over two decades of training I learned a few things about what composers wrote, and what they meant. And I had some further direction from the ghost of a man we found in a haunted house. How long until everything is ready, Comrade Morozova?'

'Four hours should do it.'

Nikitin checked his watch.

'It is 11.30. You have until 15.00. I must report to General Pletnev by 16.00 and not a moment later,' he said.

Morozova reattached her eye to the microscope.

'I will go as fast as I can, comrade. But no faster . . .'

*

'Where are we going?' asked Rossel, yawning.

'Tarkovsky's place,' answered Nikitin. 'You need rest. And you won't get any in that room. In a couple of hours, it is going to have half a dozen GRU officers in it, all the general's men, plus all those scientists we saw and a few more besides.'

Red and gold banners streamed from buildings and lampposts, bearing rousing slogans and images of Stalin.

Rossel and Nikitin passed a *Produkty* with a long queue outside, citizens pulling up their collars and clutching their string bags in anticipation of some *kolbasa,* or tinned fish, or some other delicacy for the evening meal. Many of them would be queuing because there was a queue to join, happy to find out what was on offer once they were inside. A car coming the other way lost its hold on the road and slid diagonally towards them. Rossel could see the eyes of the driver as he whirled the steering wheel in his effort to regain control. They missed each other by inches.

'You saw the man with the red beard?' said Nikitin. 'That's Dmitri Fironov. Two years ago he was expelled from the main nuclear research team that reported directly to Beria.'

'Not so smart,' said Rossel.

'Wrong. He is now the lead scientist on this project. He got the boot because he fell out with the project's leader, Igor Tamm, and its star physicist, Andrei Sakharov. They set up the entire thing from scratch, on the site of an old munition factory. Place called Sarov, officially known as KB-11. Fironov told them their design was flawed and that they were on the wrong track. He got reported for defeatism.'

'Then he was lucky not to be shot,' said Rossel.

'In forty-two, he was in the air force when he noticed that American academics had suddenly stopped publishing anything public in the field of nuclear physics. Now why would they do that, he asked himself. More importantly, he asked the question in a letter to Stalin. It turned out to be a very good one. He had correctly deduced the capitalists were building a bomb. When you do something right in Stalin's eyes, even Beria sometimes has to wait before he puts a noose around your throat.'

'And Pletnev took him in?'

'Yes,' said Nikitin. 'He did. He likes to take in the occasional stray mongrel. In case we prove useful.'

*

Nikitin turned right, onto the embankment, heading for Lieutenant Schmidt Bridge.

'The snowploughs have been out at last,' the major said.

Rossel stared at some of the saltwater-stained hulks moored on the river, but began to close his eyes. He was exhausted, and the cough that had plagued him in Igarka had returned.

After a few minutes, he felt the car begin to slow down. Then roll to a stop. His eyes blinked open.

'Visitors,' said Nikitin in a low voice.

Rossel sat up.

About fifty metres away, he could see two black vans parked outside the entrance to Tarkovsky's apartment. Six men in the blue-banded caps of the MGB were bringing the actor out of the front door. They bundled him into the back of the van that was furthest from Rossel and Nikitin.

Rossel pointed at the van that was closer to them. Sitting in the passenger seat was a thin, grey-haired man.

'Fadeyev,' he said.

The Head of the Writers' Union looked rather pleased with himself. Like someone who had been putting off tidying a messy bookcase for some time and had finally got around to doing it.

'Poor Boris,' said Rossel. 'Tonight was going to be his big night at the Anichkov – Tarkovsky sings for Stalin!'

Nikitin shrugged. 'Be honest,' he said. 'He was never going to get close to any of those high notes.'

The major revved the car and they set off again.

'We'd better make for the Drugovs' place instead,' he said. 'Let's hope it's safer than here.'

51

Four hours later, after a restless sleep that had made Rossel feel worse, he and Nikitin returned to the GRU safe house. This time, it was crammed full of gleaming belt buckles and cap badges.

Good news, Rossel thought. In the GRU, like the militia, senior officers always make an appearance when it turns up.

A large piece of plywood, recently painted white, had been nailed to a wall. Morozova was feeding slides into a holder, marking the edge of each with red pencil and cataloguing them in an exercise book.

Professor Fironov was rubbing his hands together in excitement, telling a tall, middle-aged man with red cheeks and a weathered face whom he addressed as Colonel Zotov that even he had no idea what to expect from the images that had just been developed. A young man smelling of chemicals was fiddling with the slide projector. A German brand, labelled *Liesegang*. Sleek, minimal, efficient.

Rossel barely noticed the short opening speeches of congratulations, though at one point Nikitin dug an elbow into his ribs and he realised that everyone was looking at him. The lights snapped off and soon Fironov was waving his hands through clouds of smoke, the light from the projector dancing through them like flashes of sunlight on an overcast day.

To Rossel, all the slides looked the same. Technical drawings, impossibly long equations, pages and pages of theoretical physics. His tired brain could barely follow Fironov's simplified explanations to the GRU senior officers, let alone the technical details.

A GRU officer soon lost patience and demanded assurances that this was important information. His epaulettes denoted a colonel.

The room seemed to be full of them. 'What I want to know is, how is this different from Sakharov's work for Beria? Sakharov claims he is close to the hydrogen bomb.'

Fironov removed his tiny spectacles and dabbed at his brow.

'For years, it has been our thinking that it would be the neutrons from the first atomic explosion that would compress the fuel sufficiently for the secondary thermonuclear explosion. But this Hitlerite document tells us it is the radiation. The radiation all along . . . This, and the more complex design, will send the necessary shock wave towards the centre.'

'How can you be certain, Comrade Fironov?' asked yet another officer. A thin man with dark eyes.

'Certain? That is not a word I would use. You have different types of physics in play, all interrelated; multiple reactions and effects happening in impossibly short timescales. Flow of fluids, heat transfer, pressure inwards, pressure outwards.'

Fironov thought for a moment. 'Every reaction has to happen in precisely the right order for the next one to occur. Put crudely, the pressure that will force the particles together for the second reaction must take place at sufficient scale before the whole contraption is vaporised by the first explosion. Sakhorov's "layer cake" design has never solved that. But I believe this one will do so.'

The projector clicked through more slides – more equations. Fironov was encouraging the projectionist to get to one slide in particular.

'Here it is,' the scientist said.

The slide was entirely taken up by a drawing of a large cylinder on its side. At the top were three concentric circles. Below them was an open-topped container with sloping sides, inside of which was another cylinder.

Fironov rubbed his hands together.

'This is the missing part. *This* is what Minister Pletnev will want to see and understand. The principle is similar to that pursued by Sakharov's team. Fission to create fusion, to create fission again. But Sakharov's layer cake doesn't work – not because the physics is wrong but because of the order in which the reactions take place.' He tugged at his goatee. 'Get those reactions in the right order and . . .'

'How big?' demanded Colonel Zotov. 'The explosion, I mean.'

Fironov looked around the room. 'The bombs the Americans dropped on Hiroshima and Nagasaki were small compared to the hydrogen bomb the American imperialists tested on November 1. It reached more than 10 megatons . . .'

Rossel sat up. What did he mean, the hydrogen bomb the Americans had tested?

'Some of us have seen the film,' said the GRU colonel who had not been identified. 'I did not believe it at first. Is this the same design?'

'Hard to be sure,' said Fironov, 'but I believe so. And as to Colonel Zotov's questions, the explosive power of a hydrogen bomb is theoretically limited only by the availability of the fuel. We could make a king of bombs, with the right materials and design. One to strike fear into the hearts of the capitalists.'

'What film is he talking about?' Rossel said to Nikitin in an undertone. His question was masked by the chatter around the room.

'I have not seen it,' said the major. 'But a Soviet spy ship took some film of the American test. I am told it looks like the fury of the gods.'

'Silence!'

Colonel Zotov had lost patience. 'Comrade Fironov, you are confident that Sakharov's design, this layer cake, cannot achieve such explosive yield?'

'It cannot,' said Fironov. He took off his jacket. His shirt was soaked through. 'It might destroy Manhattan. This' – he gestured at the screen – 'could annihilate the whole of New York city and flatten most of New York state in the process.'

The room fell silent. Only the whirring of the projector could be heard.

'A two-stage weapon,' said Fironov. 'With a core of fissionable material inside the fusion fuel to provide a third reaction: an added dimension to a blast of already extraordinary power. We still need several things, though. The material for the core. The composition of the inner casing and the calculations for the reaction between that substance and the radiation. And how they have countered the instability. Next slide, please.'

'Comrade Fironov,' said Morozova. She was examining her notebook and looking at the projectionist, who nodded back at her. 'There is only one more slide.'

'What?'

The projectionist pressed the button and the cartridge of the Liesegang clunked, throwing the last image upon the wall.

A small photograph of a man. In his army uniform, with hair swept back from his forehead, he looked every inch the Teutonic Knight. He had hooded eyes and a sad expression.

And a short, white scar above one eye, such as might have been made by a sword in a duel. Printed beneath the photograph was a small coat of arms. An eagle holding a sword in one claw and a book in the other.

'There's nothing else?' said the professor. 'That cannot be . . .'

Morozova shook her head.

'Go back three slides, one at a time,' said the scientist, a note of panic in his voice.

The projectionist did as he was asked. Fironov counted the slides back, squinting hard at each one as he did so.

'There is information missing,' he said, swallowing.

'Something important?' said Rossel.

Fironov's shoulders slumped. He took out a handkerchief and mopped his brow.

'Vital,' he said.

The last slide of the man with the thin white line above his eye came back round.

'Does anyone recognise him?' asked Colonel Zotov.

Everyone shook their heads.

But Rossel was lying.

As he looked up at the screen, he noticed Fironov and Nikitin were staring at him.

A phone rang. Colonel Zotov picked it up. A raised voice at the other end of the line gave an order. The colonel's back straightened as soon as he heard it.

'Yes, Comrade General,' he said. 'At the headquarters of the League. We will come at once.'

52

Lines of workers swaddled in thick coats battled the snow and wind as they trudged homeward up and down Nevsky Prospect. The two ZIS-50s that had rolled into the courtyard outside the safe house, complete with armed guards, drew to a halt on the road near the former cathedral. Nikitin parked his car directly behind them.

Rossel got out of the car and stood on the pavement next to the major. He took out some matches and cupped his hands to shield the thin flame from the wind.

As a dozen soldiers clambered down from the back of the trucks, Colonel Zotov and Fironov got out of the front of the first one. They waited for Rossel and Nikitin to join them.

'Birds of good omen,' said Colonel Zotov. Everyone followed the colonel's gaze. A flock of black dots was flying over the dome of the museum. At this distance, it was impossible to tell what species they were.

'We still have a modicum of good news for the general,' said Fironov. 'But . . .'

He left the rest unsaid. His meaning was understood.

'Men, stay here,' Colonel Zotov told his troops. 'We will be back shortly. Comrade Fironov, you have the photographs?'

'Yes, Comrade Colonel.'

'Very well. The four of us will go to see the general now. He will want the full story.'

Zotov led the way towards General Pletnev's personal headquarters in the Museum of Atheism. As they passed one of the two bronze statues that stood at the end of each encircling arm of the former cathedral, the GRU colonel pointed upwards.

'Marshal Kutuzov. A lucky fool. Claimed to have prayed to Our Lady of Kazan before defeating Napoleon.' Zotov snorted. 'Imagine telling Stalin you were depending on an ikon to beat the Fascists at Stalingrad or Seelow?'

They were still thirty metres away from the huge bronze doors when Colonel Zotov stopped to straighten his cap and check his uniform. Rossel almost walked straight into him and had to sidestep to the left to avoid the collision.

'Bad news is best delivered in sharp creases,' said the GRU officer. 'That way it always looks like it's somebody else's faul—'

His hands went to his throat. A thin red geyser bubbled up through his fingers. He took a hand away and examined the bloody palm of his right glove.

Rossel grabbed Zotov under the arms as he slumped to the ground. The statue of Kutuzov – the best cover they had – was only a few metres behind them. For a few seconds, Rossel dragged the colonel towards it. But then, realising he was dead, he left him and ducked behind it.

Pistol drawn, Nikitin appeared on the other side, crouching down and pushing Fironov to the ground. On Nevsky Prospect, the contingent of soldiers by the trucks were sharing cigarettes and talking among themselves, unaware their commanding officer had been hit. Nikitin began to yell at them, but they were busy laughing and stamping their feet. One of them dropped to his knees, stayed there for a moment, and toppled over. The others gazed incuriously for two or three seconds at the body of their comrade.

Then they leapt for cover.

A bullet zinged off the granite plinth on which Kutuzov stood. Another pinged off the statue itself. Rossel pressed himself into the stone while Nikitin yelled at Fironov to keep still. The scientist was shaking with fear. By now a passer-by – a middle-aged man – was shouting in panic, and people on Nevsky Prospect were beginning to notice, and to scatter. The soldiers were using their vehicles as cover and were scanning the cathedral for the shooter, rifles raised in futile defence. Nikitin yelled at them, too – 'Fan out, you idiots, get behind the museum, get under the field of fire, stay low!'

Fironov was pale and gasping for air. 'I can't stay here, I can't stay here . . .'

Rossel slapped the scientist hard across the cheek. His eyes widened in shock.

'Don't move, not a step. Stay here and keep your head down. Understand?' he said.

Fironov nodded.

'Good lad,' said Nikitin.

He turned to Rossel.

'Is it her?' he said.

'Who else is it going to be?' said Rossel.

The major rubbed his nose with his sleeve.

'Left and right?'

'No,' Rossel replied. 'If the sniper is on the roof, she can move fast to change the angle of fire. For both of us, the best chance is get to the colonnade; moving between each column; varying our pauses, no pattern. As soon as you hear the next shot, move.'

Nikitin nodded.

Seconds later a bullet zipped past. A soldier screamed.

'Now,' said Rossel.

As they leapt from the cover provided by the base of the statue, Rossel fixed his eyes on the huge circular portico to the left of the museum and began racing towards it. In his peripheral vison, he could see Nikitin just to his right, slightly behind him. To their left was the Griboyedova Canal.

A lucky bullet for him, he realised, was any that hit the major.

A lucky bullet for Nikitin is any that hits me.

He covered the final few metres and flung himself behind the steps leading up to the entrance on the canal's side. A curse told him Nikitin had also made it. Round the corner came one of the army trucks; three soldiers running alongside, using it as a shield.

The doors on this side were locked, possibly barricaded if the sniper had had enough time. But there were windows leading straight into the main hall. It was a way in, but, if they were slow in climbing through, it would be an easy place to get picked off, assuming the sniper had seen them and retreated inside to deal with the threat. Nikitin was too bulky to be quick, and Rossel was still nowhere near up to full strength. Both men were breathing hard. But it was the quickest route.

Rossel scanned the ground for something to smash the glass. There – a hubcap, battered out of shape. Something that had fallen off a bus or a tourist coach. He ran to pick it up and advanced back towards the window, carrying it as if it were the rusting shield of a down-at-heel knight. The thought reminded him that he had lied to Fironov, lied to them all, about the final slide. He had recognised the face on it. It had taken him another few minutes to place it in his memory. But then, with shock, Rossel realised he knew exactly who the Nazi with the duelling scar was.

Gripping the hubcap on both sides, he made two sharp stabbing motions. Two panes of glass, each about a third of a metre square, popped out of the frame and smashed against the stone floor within.

They peered into a storage room complete with a sink and an overflowing bin.

Two more thrusts, and two more panes dropped out.

A couple more blows took out the crossed wooden stanchions of the frame.

Nikitin began to haul himself inside. Rossel followed.

*

They pulled the main door of the storage room ajar and looked out into the shadowy hall of the museum. On the far wall, the grave face of a partisan – armed to the teeth and vowing destruction to the enemies of the Soviet Union – looked back. The partisan's eyes gave nothing away, but his palm was raised.

A warning. One they didn't have time for.

'I'll go first,' said Rossel. 'You wait half a minute and follow.'

'Follow where?'

'Pletnev's office. I think we can assume the sniper is not here to admire the exhibition.'

He pushed open the door and stepped out into the Museum of Atheism.

Cover was not the problem. There was plenty of it, thanks to the long double lines of columns that ran to the centre.

But the sniper had her choice of cover, too.

He weaved his way through the columns, trying to remember where the door that led to Pletnev's subterranean office was. The former sacristy.

Near the centre of the nave was the display of waxwork figures from the Spanish Inquisition – monks, conquistadores, Torquemada, the figure of a man being stretched on a rack and the hooded executioner – all looking just as he remembered them.

The layout came back to him. The staircase that led to Pletnev's office was off to the left. Not at the far end of the nave, but close by. He tapped the bird on his chest.

At last, a lucky break . . .

He pushed the door open. The stairs descended into darkness.

Surely, she could not have made it this far, this fast? Unless there is another way?

He went through and pulled the door behind him to blot out his silhouette.

No sound. No movement that he could discern.

There was a dim light at the bottom, and as he reached the end of the stairs he swept the space in front of him with his pistol. The door to the general's office was ajar. He pushed it a little wider with the barrel of his pistol.

Back turned, a cowled and hunched figure was sitting at Pletnev's desk.

Rossel stepped into the room.

'Comrade General?' he said.

Pletnev did not move.

Rossel crossed the room. He stepped behind the desk and reached out with his left hand to tap the seated figure on the shoulder.

Lifeless, the body in the chair slumped forward.

As it did so, the hood slipped off the side of its face, revealing a forlorn, brutal countenance with two neat holes in the side of its head.

Sergeant Grachev might have escaped the icy waters of the Moika.

But he had not, it seemed, got very much further.

'The gloom of the world is but a shadow, yet within our reach is joy,' said a voice behind him.

Rossel placed his pistol on the general's desk with care. He put his hands up and turned around.

Mila Kitsenko's skin was so pale it was almost translucent. Her eyes were green, wide and unblinking, filled with the certainty of faith. Like Grachev she was hooded, in a dark green cloak that looked well suited to her work. It gave her the appearance of a melancholic nun.

'The words of Savonarola,' said Kitsenko. She pointed at Grachev. 'I have read them on his display case so often that the sentence has become like a psalm to me. I have been here many times.'

She had the barrel of her Mosin–Nagant rifle pointed at Rossel's stomach. She was small, yet handled the weapon without apparent effort.

'You've been using the new metro system to move the bodies. One of them, I know, runs very near here. Slipping up silently behind your victims, pressing a pistol to their backs, walking them into the tunnels. But, once there, Akimov ran, I assume. So, with him, you had to use your rifle.'

She nodded.

The hunter must become the prey.

That, according to Major Firsova at the sniper school, is what Mila's father had taught her. To understand how a quarry moves, thinks, hides . . .

He raised his hands a little higher. 'The struggle against religion is the struggle for socialism,' he said. 'When I was young, I used to believe that.'

Kitsenko lifted the muzzle of her rifle.

'I still do.'

53

Rossel, hands still high, was walking in front.

Kitsenko ordered him back up the stairs and told him to halt next to a huge banner declaring the liberation of the proletariat from the shackles of religion.

On another wall, a piece of plywood proclaimed the words of Lenin in crimson paint: *Religion is one of the forms of spiritual oppression that weigh on the masses no matter where they are, crushed by eternal toil for others.*

They passed more display cases of objects Rossel had not yet seen. Medieval masks, more torture instruments, paintings of drunken monks and debauched nuns, caricatures of Jesus and the disciples in the style of Socialist Realism.

On the edge of the great central hall, in an alcove from where the famous ikon of Our Lady of Kazan had once looked down on her adoring worshippers, General Pletnev sat bound and gagged.

His eyes were closed, his head bowed. But he was alive.

Pletnev inhaled sharply through his nose and raised his head.

On the wall above him, in the space vacated by the ikon of Our Lady, was a photograph of someone else.

Another face Rossel recognised.

One of Babayan's shadows in the snow – the child the old priest had talked of at the very end of the railway line as they hauled their human steamroller through the wastelands. Alexei: the heir to the last tsar, the hope of the Romanov dynasty; murdered, along with his entire family, in the damp basement of the Ipatiev House in Yekaterinburg. Some of Babayan's words came back to him: 'God has raised these martyrs to his kingdom.'

Mila Kitsenko had raised Alexei, too. Inside Pletnev's museum. Inside his Kingdom of the Godless.

Pletnev's hands were tied behind his back and his waist was lashed to the back of the chair with some rough hemp. Kitsenko ordered Rossel to remove the gag. The general took several deep breaths, growing less pale with each one.

'Ah,' said the general. 'That is disappointing, I had my hopes pinned on you, Comrade Rossel. You have a quality I could have used at Seelow. Let's call it panache. But Mila always was a model of Soviet efficiency.'

There was no fear in the general's voice. He talked as if observing distant field movements through binoculars and then passing on orders to a subordinate.

'She has murdered six men, general,' said Rossel.

'At least. Mila believes in her cause. So did you, once. My enquires led me to understand you were, as a youth, a fervent member of the League. Someone who, given time and the right training, could have been one of our most zealous foot soldiers.'

'You have something of mine,' Kitsenko said to Rossel.

Rossel nodded and unbuttoned the top of his shirt, feeling for the locket.

He handed it to her. She took it and hung it on a hook just above the picture of Alexei.

She handed him a pair of handcuffs. With the barrel of her rifle she motioned him a few paces to the right, to a big water pipe that ran all the way from the floor to the distant ceiling. Without being asked, Rossel cuffed his right wrist to the pipe.

Kitsenko checked it.

'Sit,' she said, kicking a chair towards him. Rossel did so.

Then she turned and began to run, at pace, towards the back of the main hall – behind what once would have been the altar. She moved, Rossel noticed, with grace and economy, creating a sense of being ephemeral. As if, when slipping from one position to another on a battlefield, she might disappear.

*

Rossel and the general listened to the echo of Kitsenko's footsteps.

Rossel spoke first.

'I presume she's taking a position on the dome?' he said.

Pletnev nodded.

'There are stairs that lead to the roof,' he said. 'From up there she has a clear firing line to any point on Nevsky, plus points all around. For several hundred metres, at least.'

Rossel yanked his handcuffed arm a couple of times to test the heating pipe.

'Protocol 478 deals with counter-revolutionary insurrection,' said Pletnev. 'I'm assuming it has been authorised and that the museum is now surrounded. But if she gets a couple more shots away from up there it will keep the militia and MGB at bay for a while.'

'Time for what?'

Pletnev craned his neck towards the photograph of the tsarevich Alexei above his head.

'Isn't it obvious? We are to be martyred.'

'But she could have killed you at any time with just one shot from that rifle. Me too, for that matter.'

'Not close, not eye to eye, with each bullet a benediction. She started her little habit in the war, after her friends were killed. Now, I presume, it's the ritual to which she is addicted.'

Rossel gave another couple of half-hearted pulls at the water pipe.

Pletnev tutted.

'In the field, when nothing can be done, the best thing to do is often to do just that.'

'Major Firsova at the sniper school told me about them,' said Rossel. 'About her and her closest comrades. They called themselves the *troika*. She said they were the terror of the Germans at Stalingrad.'Pletnev nodded.

'All our snipers were. But Mila had her own unique calling card, if she got close enough to her victims. She would cut out their tongues. At first it was just a few Fascists. No one was really very bothered about that. But afterwards some of the men kept their distance, uncertain if she was a devil or a saint. Then she overheard a Red Army captain praying to Christ under his breath just before his platoon crossed a river for an assault. Later, he was found with his tongue missing and a quote from Lenin – "Paradise on Earth is more important than paradise in Heaven" – inside his throat. That was when I had to reassign her to another unit.'

Shots – one, then two more – heard; in the distance, but clear.

Answering fire. From more than one direction, and louder. The soldiers must have spread out, readying for an attack on the museum.

How can she hope to escape?

'Cut out their tongues? Words in their mouths?' Rossel said, meeting the general's gaze. 'So, you knew it was her all along? As soon as Nikitin told you about the scrolls?'

'Yes, Comrade Lieutenant Rossel. And I was meant to. Corpses left in places where I could not miss them, murdered in a particular way that I well understood. Mila was sending me a message.'

Lieutenant . . .

It was long time since anyone had called him that.

'A message about what?'

'About treachery. "How gentle is deception . . . for it defies perception." About the purity of faith our Marxist cause demands, and the price that must be paid by those who betray it.'

Rossel sniffed the air.

Smoke . . .

He looked up just as Kitsenko stepped out from behind the nearest column. Her rifle was slung over her back. She went over to Pletnev and examined his bonds. Then she stood and stroked the general's head.

'Stalingrad,' she whispered to him. 'Watching *The Mandrake* in your bunker as the shells rained down, seemingly unable to touch us. I have often thought of it.'

Rossel sniffed the air again. This time the smell of smoke was stronger.

'One hundred and seventy kills,' said Pletnev to Kitsenko. 'Not counting those you have assassinated since then for Comrade Beria, Mila. For the MGB. Am I right? Then, as now, you lived as a Valkyrie, as a chooser of the slain.'

The smoke was visible now, and it wasn't from a few candles.

Where the hell was Nikitin?

Kitsenko nodded.

'"When the last believer dies, so then does God himself." That's what we used to say to conclude every League meeting. That has always been my purpose.'

Pletnev smiled.

'Mine too. But if you think you've made some deal with Beria, Mila? That he'll help you restore the fortunes of the League? Then despite all you have done, you are still a child.'

Rossel could not see flames, but now he could hear them.

Kitsenko took a step back. Her face darkened. From somewhere in her jacket, she pulled out a large hunting knife and stepped towards the general. Rossel glanced up at the locket hanging above the picture of Alexei on the wall.

The hair in the locket, he remembered Bondar saying, was old.

Could it belong to the tsarevich?

'You worship the boy Alexei – is it that, Comrade Kitsenko?' Rossel said. 'You believe he directs your actions in some way.'

She stepped a little closer to Pletnev.

'It is his hair, yes.'

'A decent effort, Comrade Detective,' said Pletnev. 'But your bourgeois romanticism has blinded you to the truth. As a child in Yekaterinburg, Mila went on secret pilgrimages to the Ipatiev House, to visit the killing grounds of the Romanov family. But it was not Alexei she venerated.'

'Who, then?' said Rossel.

'The number inscribed on the locket, 1500, is the Party number of man called Yakov Yurovsky. The worker of a Bolshevik miracle. And a friend of her father. He cut off Alexei's hair as a souvenir. Later, he gave Mila some of it.'

'I've never heard of him.'

'Most have not. But when they executed Alexei, the boy sat bolt upright in a chair, a mute witness to the slaughter of his family. They stabbed and shot him but he wouldn't die. So Yurovsky finished him off with two bullets in the head. Mila has canonised Yurovsky as a Marxist saint.'

Mila now stood between the two men. With her left hand, she reached into her pocket and took out a scroll.

'On cloudless nights,' she said to Pletnev, 'through the sights of my rifle, playing across the faces of men who did not know they were about to die. Colonels poring over maps, captains peeping over trenches, sentries at their posts. In the small hours of the night, men let their minds turn to their deepest secrets. As I took aim, I felt I could read their thoughts. After we had been together for a little while, I could read yours, too, General.'

She placed the knife on a small table in front of Pletnev and unholstered the pistol at her hip.

'But at first, as we lay together in your bunker at Stalingrad, I believed you when you claimed to burn with Marxist purity. When you vowed to make the League of the Militant

Godless the true Soviet government once the war was over. The promises you made to me. All lies.'

The smoke was beginning to pour down the walls. Rossel felt the first heat of the fire. He could hear shouts from outside – an assault was imminent.

'Everything you claimed to be, you are not. You played the part of the atheist warrior monk to become leader of the League. You became leader of the League to gain political power. You play at being a man of the people, but think only of your own glory. Of becoming leader – you think this German bomb will give you that.'

Pletnev shook his head.

'Even now I think of the League,' he protested. 'Of the need to destroy every remaining church, synagogue and mosque. Do you think Beria will give you that? Not even Stalin himself will. Or why would he have reopened so many of them?'

At last . . .

Nikitin, his pistol drawn, was moving from column to column.

Rossel turned his head towards Kitsenko.

'Before you execute him, doesn't the general at least deserve to know what's written on his scroll?' he said.

She paused for a moment. But then marched – four quick steps – behind the general and, grabbing his brow with her free hand, pulled his head back. Pletnev grimaced, but did not cry out. She rammed the pistol into the general's temple and stared hard at Rossel.

'*Nikolai Alexandrovich, in view of your relatives' continuing attack on Soviet Russia, the Ural Executive Committee has decided to execute you,*' she said. 'That is what's written on the paper. Those were the last words Yurovsky read out before he executed the tsar and his family. Once those words were said, there could be no turning back. He was the man who ensured our glorious Revolution was unstoppable.'

Nikitin was moving through a cloud of grey smoke and black ashes.

Kitsenko coughed. She glanced up at the dome, smiling at the sight of the flames. She bent down, placed the pistol at a specific point on Pletnev's temple and craned her neck a little to stare into the general's face.

Pletnev's face remained a mask.

'Death holds no fear for me,' said Kitsenko. 'I know all her secrets.'

Nikitin fired. The retort boomed around the museum. In the same instant, the main door, only metres away, was smashed open. Firefighters, armed militia and soldiers began to stream into the building, shooting everywhere.

Rossel flinched as something hit his face. He raised his free hand and felt blood. A ricochet had grazed his cheek.

He looked around.

Kitsenko had vanished.

54

Nikitin raced towards Pletnev and started to undo his bindings. The general was coughing uncontrollably. Rossel's own chest was burning with the smoke. A soldier smashed at his handcuffs with a hammer, another used the butt of his rifle. More men tugged and twisted at the pipe, until somehow his hands were free and he was being pulled towards the main door, fresh air and the squeal of sirens.

Two soldiers hovered over the general and shouted for water.

It arrived in chipped tin bottles. Both the general and Rossel drank deep.

'Stay here and keep your head down,' said Pletnev as he doused and cleaned his face. 'My men will search the building and capture her.'

But Rossel was already on his feet and heading back inside. Straight for the stone staircase that led to the roof.

*

Even though he was breathing hard, he took the stairs two at a time. The higher he climbed, the denser the smoke. He reached the top and bent over, wheezing, sweating from his exertions but also the increasing heat. A dark vestibule had doors leading out to the eastern and western quarter-circles. Soldiers were ducking through both in ones and twos.

Left or right?

He chose right.

'She's there!'

A soldier was pointing towards the dome. 'We have her cornered.'

The man turned to wave on his comrades.

A bullet whistled past his face, removing most of one ear.

*

A good sniper always knows the way out, knows where her exit is.

Kitsenko would have selected her position with care. To get to that part of the roof, around the dome and above the main building, you had to clamber over a wall. Which gave a sniper an excellent view of the head of anyone coming over. Staying in a crouch, he edged his way around, looking for somewhere to place a boot and attempt the climb. The wounded soldier clutched at his head and screamed a vow of vengeance.

He had to get there first before Pletnev's men silenced Kitsenko. For weeks she and Rossel had fought for the same prize, for different masters. He wanted to know the truth, even if the knowledge was fatal.

What did Beria want? *We could make a king of bombs, with the right materials and design.*

How had Kitsenko tracked down her victims? What had they known?

Rossel hoisted himself up, legs scrabbling for purchase, and landed in a heap on the other side, relieved to see a row of small parapets just big enough to shield his head and torso.

Risking a look, he saw orange flames tinged with green licking all around the windows of the cylindrical structure that supported the dome. On the other wall, soldiers were trying to join him but one fell back – *she must be on the far side of it*. Rifles were appearing above the wall, their owners firing wildly. The heat was growing. Keeping as close to the flames as he dared, he went halfway round the dome, anti-clockwise. There had been enough snow recently to cover the surface; Kitsenko's footprints were clear as she had moved from one shooting point to the next. Below, militia cars, fire engines and military trucks were jumbled all over the ground in front of the cathedral.

Heart pounding, he took two sharp breaths. For the first time, he missed the pistol Nikitin had given him.

She must be close, unless she had retreated to the farthest edge of the roof.

He tried to listen, to focus his mind above the sound of the shots. Kazan's dome towered above him.

Still no Kitsenko.

There . . .

The tip of a rifle barrel. On the far side of what looked like a large metal box, probably a water tank.

The barrel disappeared. Then the box was covered by drifting black smoke – the fire was spreading across the roof. He started crawling towards it but the roof felt hot.

What better way for her to make her point as an atheist than by burning down the house of God?

He reached the metal box.

She was on the other side, about two metres away – had to be; the only other way was down.

Water was trickling out of the bullet holes. He'd been right, it was a tank: the ice was falling off it in chunks and hissing as it hit the roof. The smoke was constant now, and the heat becoming unbearable.

He reached up.

Snow on the surface but the ice is melting.

Rossel took off his coat, reached up once more and dunked it into the freezing water. He dragged it back on again, buried his head inside it and took a lungful of air. Then, having counted to three, waiting for a moment when the shooting would subside, he launched himself through the flames and around the back of the tank, pulling up his greatcoat around his ears.

As Rossel emerged from the inferno, Kitsenko half-turned, her rifle still facing the soldiers.

Right hand reaching out for her weapon, left aiming to pull her over, Rossel hurled himself at her.

At the last moment she stepped backward. She was quick and Rossel caught her only a glancing blow. But he still managed to tear the rifle from her hands. He landed and looked up, his stomach turning as he saw she had a pistol in her hand.

How did I miss that?

As he rolled her shot went wide.

He kicked out, hit her knee hard. A second kick smashed into her thigh.

Kitsenko – left ankle hitting the balustrade, one hand seemingly groping for the setting sun – toppled over the side.

Rossel yelled her name and raced to the edge. But she had not fallen far. There was a thin sloping roof above the biggest doors to the cathedral and she was gripping its edge.

Kitsenko stared back up at him.

Twenty, maybe twenty-five metres below her feet were solid stone steps or the icy road. The fall would kill her.

Rossel dropped down and onto his stomach. They reached out to each other. Kitsenko let go with one hand, swung herself a fraction higher and grabbed Rossel by his left wrist.

A serene look drifted into her eyes. For her, death was a decision.

'Don't,' Rossel said. 'You don't have to . . .'

As if about to speak, Kitsenko opened her mouth. But she said nothing, only taking a breath as if to steady her nerves. As if her next kill was coming into view and she needed to be ready.

She blinked once. Twice. Then her right hand locked into his and he began to pull her up.

From the street below, a single shot rang out. He felt her fingers loosen.

Then, eyes still open and staring up at the fiery dome of the cathedral, Koshchei the Immortal slipped away.

55

The taste of the smoke was in his mouth, in his chest and stomach. His eyes were red and stinging. As the ZIS hit yet another pothole, Rossel clutched his stomach and thought about being sick. He had lost his soaking coat, but water had seeped through to his jacket and shirt. With the tarpaulin over the truck failing to keep out the wind, he was starting to shiver.

Next to him in the back of the truck sat the scientist Fironov and Nikitin. Opposite them were four GRU soldiers, two on each side. A fifth – a thin Central Asian with the sedate expression of Buddhist monk at prayer; the man who had fulfilled Pletnev's order to silence Mila Kitsenko – was cradling an automatic rifle.

Death solves all problems. Another saying of Stalin's the general seemed to have taken to heart.

Almost hysterical with relief that he had not been killed, Fironov had made straight for the general and informed him of the key details of the hydrogen bomb programme that had so recently come into his possession. Pletnev had insisted on seeing the evidence for himself, without delay.

After only ten minutes, the truck came to a halt opposite the GRU safe house. The Mongolian leapt out and pulled back the tarpaulin. Before getting out, Pletnev leaned forward and tapped Rossel's shoulder.

'Thank you, Lieutenant Rossel. I must say that.' He turned to Nikitin. 'And you, Comrade Major.'

Nikitin nodded. 'Happy to do my socialist duty, Comrade General.'

*

Upstairs, the professor fumbled over the slides and projector. With no need to argue over equations and diagrams with his fellow physicists, it took him not much more than fifteen minutes to talk the general through the Nazi design, and his conviction that they had hit upon the solution to building a hydrogen bomb.

Pletnev sat in silence throughout, registering no emotion at the final slide and the sudden mystery of the man with the scar.

Then he sat up.

'Commendable work, Professor. And now I must prepare for this evening's screening at the Young Pioneers' Palace,' he said. 'It is very important that I attend. I believe it is going to be something of a spectacle.'

Everyone in the room tensed. The general looked at each one of them in turn.

'Our Soviet Union grows weak. And corrupt. Comrade Stalin grows old while his courtiers squabble and fight and intrigue. It is, in short, like the last, decaying days of the Romanov era. The death throes of the *ancien regime*.'

He stood. 'But with this weapon, with this power, the Soviet Union need fear no one. So it is time.'

Rossel's mind tried to process what he was hearing.

No one would dare . . .

'And I will complete what I started in 1945,' said Pletnev, setting his cap straight. 'I shall teach a lesson that the German people will not forget and send a message that the world will be forced to hear.'

As Pletnev reached the door, he turned.

'Oh, one last thing. Is your additional hypothesis still true, Comrade Professor?'

'I'm sorry, Comrade General?' said Fironov.

'The theory you put to me on the steps of the museum. Your belief that Comrade Rossel knows a little more than he is letting on about the identity of this mysterious scarred man.'

Fironov reddened.

'Well, it was probably nothing. I simply observed . . .'

Nikitin took a pace forward.

'He does, Comrade General,' he said.

Rossel turned to stare at the major. Nikitin looked straight ahead.

'As I said to you earlier: Comrade Rossel, like everyone else, saw the photograph and the coat of arms on that final slide. He and I have seen the coat of arms before – above the doors to a mansion in the German town of Bayreuth. The house belonged to the Nazi physicist von Möllendorf – Baron Karl Friedrich von Möllendorf. I believe Rossel knows where to find him.'

Pletnev inspected his nails.

'How so, Comrade Major?'

'I was watching him when von Möllendorf's face was projected onto the screen,' said Nikitin. 'He stared at the image for longer than the rest of us, as if trying to remember something. I noticed a look of unexpected recognition. As an experienced interrogator, I've seen plenty of faces of people who are trying to conceal knowledge that might drop them in the shi . . . endanger them.'

Bastard.

Rossel jumped from his seat and threw himself at Nikitin. But the major parried his outstretched hands and smashed a fist into the side of his head.

Rossel hit the floor and stayed there.

'Congratulations, Comrade Major,' said Pletnev as he peered down at the prone figure. 'I knew I could depend on your loyalty.'

'Once again, I am honoured, Comrade General,' said Nikitin.

'Get up.' Pletnev stared down at Rossel as he issued the order.

Rossel rose, feeling his head.

'Have you indeed recognised this Fascist scientist?' said Pletnev. 'And do you know where he is?'

'Whether I decide to tell you very much depends on who you are, Comrade General,' answered Rossel.

Pletnev glowered at him.

'And who I am?'

'Either the fabled Hero of the Seelow Heights. Or the man Mila Kitsenko said she was hunting.'

'Ah.'

'And I think I already know the answer to that question.'

Pletnev jabbed a thumb over his shoulder and addressed one of his GRU agents.

'Arrest that man for counter-revolutionary activity – the burning of the Museum of Atheism at Kazan will begin the charges. Others will come later when I return from the Young Pioneers' Palace.'

The general glanced over his shoulder at Rossel. 'And Lieutenant? Major Nikitin will supervise your interrogation. I gather he has done so once before. And I have great faith in his abilities to make you cooperate.'

He turned and left with the major. Nikitin did not look back as he left the room.

56

Do, re, mi.

How long had it been?

A decade, perhaps even more? A decade since he and Nikitin had first set eyes on one another.

Do – the left little finger.

You can stop this, Nikitin had said. *All it takes is your confession.*

Re. The ring finger. Broken.

Mi. Then taken.

A diabolic scale that stopped only when he passed out, was revived, and lost consciousness again.

As Rossel held his hands up to his face, the general's voice rang in his ears.

Major Nikitin will supervise your interrogation.

How many fingers would he lose this time?

He kicked another chair across the room and cursed Nikitin, the general and his own stupidity again.

But mainly Nikitin.

How could he ever have trusted him?

Then he rested his hands on the table to regain his breath. Finally, his rage had blown itself out.

Having regained control of himself, he glanced all around the room.

There was no hope of escape. The windows were not merely covered, but the thick wooden boards were nailed into place. He had some matches in his pocket. But if he set fire to the furniture he was likely to burn himself to death.

Wandering into the small darkroom, with its enticing smell of chemicals, he dropped a match into a tray of red liquid. Nothing happened.

The door to the main room was locked from the outside and the GRU captain who had been left to guard him was armed with a PPSh submachine gun and a fierce loyalty to General Pletnev.

Rossel slumped down at the table in the middle of the room. The score was long gone, taken by the general's staff. Pletnev himself would be preparing for a congenial evening at the premiere of *Red Dawn-Red Dusk*.

All the Politburo would be there. Stalin was walking into Pletnev's trap.

But who cared which tyrant ruled the Soviet empire? Could Pletnev be any more brutal than the men who came before him?

At first a whisper, finally a never-ending scream.

He remembered the line about Mayakovsky's longing for suicide. The same, he knew, was true of murder.

And, most certainly, of revenge.

He and Nikitin, torturer and victim, reunited after years of redemption in war and in peace, had found a mutual enemy and formed an alliance. They had papered over the past, pushed it to the back of their minds.

Not any more.

He held up his broken fingers again. If only he could get out of here. Seize a gun or a knife. All he needed was one chance.

Anger took hold of him again, anger born of his own impotence. The Liesegang projector was within easy reach. He grabbed it and hurled it across the room and it crashed into the wall, its casing splitting open and shedding its metal guts all over the room. The sound was tremendous, shocking – out of all proportion to the size of the machine.

The door rattled open. The GRU captain who had been left to guard him surveyed the damage, one hand on his PPSh.

Rossel shrugged an insincere apology at the man, whose large frame filled the doorway, before resuming his inspection of the debris on the floor.

The soldier stood his ground.

Mostly the innards of the projector seemed to consist of lenses and bits of metal that held the lenses, plus screws and nuts. One disc of glass had bounced off the floor, rebounded off the wall and was still spinning on its circumference. Rossel and the guard tracked it as it reached the end of its journey and clattered to the floor.

It landed next to something dark.

Rossel took three quick paces and picked this other object up. It was the size of a large thick button and made of tarnished steel.

Just like the object Nikitin had unscrewed from the light-fitting in the Georgian restaurant Shemomechama.

A microphone.

Idle chit-chat. Coarse military humour. Coughs and belches.

And the basic facts, along with a great many details, of the Nazi nuclear weapons programme.

'See what this is, comrade?' Rossel said, holding it flat in the palm of his hand.

The GRU man did not move. But yes, he had seen it.

'A bug. They've been listening to every conversation in this room, probably for weeks. Months. Someone knows what General Pletnev has. Someone knows what he is going to do.'

He paused. Giving the man the time to fill the silence with his own panicked thoughts.

'So, it looks like you have a choice, comrade. Either you keep an eye on me and let your commanding officer walk into a trap. Or . . .'

With his PPSh raised, the captain stepped towards Rossel, left hand extended.

Before his fingers could close around the bug, Rossel flipped it skyward with his thumb.

The GRU agent's eyes followed it upward.

Rossel swung his right fist and hit him on the underside of his jaw.

The man's head jerked backwards. There was deafening roar as the magazine of his PPSh emptied into the ceiling, the finger of the already unconscious soldier locked around the trigger. Wood chips and plaster showered down on them both.

The firing stopped when the man's head hit the floor. His eyes blinked open and shut again.

Rossel bent down and began to unbutton the captain's coat.

57

In the evening gloom the streets seemed to fuse with Leningrad's canals, as if they too were flowing out to merge with the waters of the Gulf of Finland.

Rossel pushed the ZIS truck fast along the icy roads, heading for the Lieutenant Schmidt Bridge. He took the left turn onto Angliskaya Naberezhnaya at speed.

The fire at the Museum of Atheism was almost out, but Nevsky Prospect, he presumed, would be cordoned off up to there, so he needed to go around the edge of it.

The ZIS careered through Isaac's Square and down Voznesensky. Rossel looked into the sky away to his left. He thought he could see a thinning spiral of dark smoke drifting above and along the lights on Nevsky Prospect, but he could not be certain. He looked back at the road and got his bearings.

Left here.

But the cordoning off of Nevsky was having its effect on the flow of trams, buses, cars and pedestrians elsewhere. A sea of black and brown hats, heads, scarves, gloves and coats blocked their way. The traffic had slowed to less than walking pace. Rossel checked his watch.

Already 18.30.

He'd have to go on foot.

Leaving the ZIS in the middle of the road, he got out and started pushing his way through the mass of bodies along the Fontanka, towards the Anichkov Bridge. The GRU coat, with its epaulettes, both kept him warm and covered up his creased and still-damp suit. The captain's cap kept the cold wind off his head, while the agent's stiff identification card dug into his ribs.

In the evening cold, the people were whispering a refrain. Rossel heard them in ones and twos, then in larger groups, until it was taken up as a chant all along the canal. As if, in hushed tones, the crowd was heralding the arrival of a comet, or an imminent eclipse.

Stalin is coming.

*

In the distance, Rossel could see a large black horse rearing up above the masses as if startled by a gunshot – one of the four famous equine statues positioned at each end of the Anichkov Bridge.

Rossel pushed past a grey-faced military veteran wearing his medals above a drinker's nose.

'Fuck you, comrade,' shouted the man, then stopping himself when he saw Rossel's uniform. His wife began to scold him for his bad language.

Rossel gave them a shrug and then wriggled past a plump woman in a huge fur coat. A large huddle of excited Young Pioneers now blocked his path.

The gate to a road leading off the Fontanka was shut and guarded by a couple of corporals. Rossel walked towards it and flashed his GRU captain's pass. The men saluted and opened the gate.

Free from the crowd, he picked up pace, until the Young Pioneers' Palace – formerly the Anichkov Palace – rose into view. It was a magnificent building covered with neoclassical pilasters and columns: one of Leningrad's many monolithic reminders of the three-hundred-year-old Romanov dynasty. Once the royal family's favourite home, the palace was the last place they had stayed before their fateful journey to the Ural Mountains.

Militia officers and soldiers were everywhere: holding back the crowds, cuffing anyone who showed too much enthusiasm for a glimpse of Comrade Stalin.

A shrill, impatient sound cut through the night air – the peeping of a horn.

All heads turned and more army and militia officers poured in, roughly separating the crowd and widening the road.

A black Packard limousine edged forward. In the passenger seat, Rossel could just make out a grey-haired man with a thin moustache and half-lens spectacles.

'In Stalin's court, every prince sleeps with his head on the block . . .'

Molotov, a stiff figure in the back, was looking thoughtful. A man unsure if he is returning to sainthood or the scaffold. Rossel was almost close enough to knock on the window. Instead, he turned his head away.

Something had changed.

Molotov was in disgrace. In near exile. Now he had returned.

Rossel pulled his shoulders back and, as if rehearsing for the May Day Parade, began marching towards the palace entrance.

Walk slow and with purpose, he thought, like everyone's waiting for me, not Comrade Stalin.

*

A line of black polished metal snaked from the palace as far as Nevsky Prospect – the cars of Party officials arriving late because of the disruption caused by the fire. Next to the outer gates were two large, whitewashed guardhouses. Always fresh paint for Stalin, Rossel thought.

Two soldiers stood to attention in each guardhouse, while four more were inspecting the credentials of the vehicles going in. They looked young. Brash. But also, he suspected, a little nervous.

Three giant red flags, each almost twenty metres tall, had been draped across the palace's façade. On each was printed the image of a man at the centre – Stalin; flanked by Beria and Pletnev. Stalin stared straight ahead while the other two regarded the Great Leader with open admiration. A perfect Soviet triptych.

The second part of the Young Pioneers motto – *Always prepared!* – was written in yellow letters on each flag. Rossel looked up at the huge image of Pletnev. His expression was firm-jawed and imperious – that of a man who believed he had just as much right to flutter on a flag as a hammer, sickle, swastika, crescent moon or cross.

Everywhere, senior officers from the Soviet armed forces stood around in small clusters, chatting before they went into the palace. High-ranking militia officers were here, too, but were firmly in the second tier of dignitaries. They kept themselves to themselves.

But something's wrong.

The entire Politburo – including Stalin himself – was converging in one place and the Ministry for State Security did not seem to be present.

Where were the blue-peaked caps of the MGB? They should have infested the place, projecting their own power in a setting where the projection of power was everything.

A phalanx of twenty men, dressed in black coats and grasping submachine guns, made a guard of honour as the cars of the Party officials rolled past them.

A woman with greying hair, wearing the uniform of a Young Pioneers teacher, was apologising for being delayed. 'They have blocked off half of Nevsky because of the fire. I have had to walk all the way from Palace Square.'

The guard she was talking to was tall, sleek and full of the self-importance a uniform often confers on those too immature to wear it. He scrutinised her pass while a second guard glared at her as she pleaded with them to hurry. Her Young Pioneers were waiting for her and would not know where to stand or when to shout hurrah for Comrade Stalin when he arrived.

She was let through.

'Documents, please.'

The middle-aged man in front of Rossel was also dressed in civilian clothes – some sort of *apparatchik* from one of the bureaus. He seemed nervous, stuttering his introduction and fumbling his papers. The brown hair oil he had plastered on his head was running down from under his *ushanka* and rolling down his left cheek. But, again, the guards said not a word, looking from ID document to face and back again. After a minute, he nodded. The man went in.

Rossel was next. Under his gloves, his palms sweated.

'Your documents, please.' The soldier glanced at the epaulettes and added. 'Comrade Captain.'

Rossel took out the GRU identity card. He handed it over but kept a grip on it as the soldier tried to take it.

He looked the youngster straight in the eye.

'You'd didn't see that?'

'See what?'

Rossel handed over his ID. As the soldier began to scrutinise it, Rossel pointed behind him.

'That last citizen,' he said. 'Nervous. Very. Why? And you missed something. You should have patted him down.'

'Missed something, Comrade Captain?'

'A shape under his coat. Could be nothing. But?'

The soldier went pale.

'I . . . I cannot leave my post, Comrade Captain,' he said.

Rossel took back his stolen pass before the guard could take another, closer look at the photograph.

'I'll let this go, comrade. On this occasion. Let me get after him. I will ensure that he is not about to cause any trouble.'

The youngster saluted.

'Thank you, Comrade Captain.'

Slipping the pass back into his pocket, Rossel walked through the gate.

'Not at all,' he said.

58

Inside the courtyard, a few final limousines were dropping off their passengers – more military dignitaries, weighed down with plump bellies and chestfuls of medals.

Rossel walked up a short gravel drive, interspersed with bleak winter flower beds blanketed in snow, to the main entrance.

On the steps of the building, in front of three symmetrical arched doorways, were more guards – GRU agents among them – standing to attention in greeting.

Trying a little too hard to look like these were the rarefied circles in which he belonged, Rossel strolled through the left-hand arch. He was in.

And somewhere, so were Nikitin and Defence Minister General Pletnev.

That was why there were no MGB officers, he realised. Pletnev had stationed his own men all over the Anichkov Palace. By tomorrow morning, Pletnev aimed to be in power. At that point, Nikitin would be untouchable.

It's now or never.

*

Everywhere there was the chinking of glasses, the salty aroma of caviar and smoked fish, and the murmur of overly polite, restrained conversation.

There was Molotov: not exactly surrounded by Party flunkies but not quite shunned, either. Then someone called his name in a loud voice – 'Vyacheslav Mikhailovich! What an honour!' – and General Pletnev was advancing with his arms outstretched, as if he was the host and this palace was his domain.

Rossel craned his neck to seek out Nikitin.

There he was, within touching distance of the general: sweating, shoulders hunched. As always, ready for a fight.

A grand marble staircase dominated the entrance hall. Chandeliers flecked with gold leaf hung from the stuccoed ceiling. Young Pioneers in their bright red-and-white uniforms and crisp scarves moved to and fro, serving plates of *blini* and glasses of champagne – French, not Soviet – on silver plates. All traces of the everyday activities of the Pioneers – sports classes, reading groups, lessons in Marxism – had been swept away. It was as though there had been no revolution, only a changing of the guard. The sense of history was palpable. If, at that moment, the dead tsar and his family could have materialised at the top of the stairs, all heads would bow down and Leningrad, cradle of Bolshevism, would become St Petersburg once more.

Khrushchev arrived, cracking jokes the second he walked through the doors, greeted by a fawning group of admirers. Trailing his habitual obscenities, he and his followers edged along the marble floor, a polished design of black-and-white squares. Molotov walked towards Khrushchev and the two fell into conversation in the midst of a group of generals, both men looking like chess pieces waiting to be moved. Molotov would be a worldly bishop. Khrushchev, Rossel thought, bald and bullet-headed, could never be anything other than a belligerent pawn.

They stepped onto the deep red carpet that ran up the stairs, towards the even grander room that hosted dramatic performances, propaganda concerts and film screenings to improve the young minds of the Pioneer movement. Arranged on either side of the staircase, like assembly lines of *matryoshka* dolls, were officers and minor Party members in a guard of honour.

On one side of the room was a table laid with a white linen cloth and silver salvers containing roast beef and pork. Rossel made his way towards it and slid one of the shorter knives into a pocket. The weapon of a labour camp prisoner.

Looking up, he could still see Nikitin standing at Pletnev's shoulder. He pushed past two militia officers and moved a little closer to them.

In Igarka, he had not found it within himself to kill.

This time, it would be different.

*

As he moved through the crowd, Rossel's eyes were fixed on the back of Nikitin's head. The major was still shadowing Pletnev but deep in conversation with a group of soldiers.

Rossel was close now. Only a few metres away.

He felt a firm tap on his shoulder. Without thinking, he turned around.

'Haven't we met, comrade?'

The man was dressed in a black suit, black tie and white shirt. His skin was the same deathly pale hue as when Rossel had encountered him before. Once in Moscow, and again on a moonlit night on the shores of Lake Ladoga. Through his pince-nez spectacles, Lavrentiy Beria was staring at him with bulging eyes in the manner of a royalist servant eyeing an unwelcome speck of dirt on an otherwise pristine linen table-cloth. Behind the lenses, his dark pupils were penetrating and predatory. Black ice on the surface of a fathomless pool.

'You look familiar,' said Beria, flashing an encouraging smile.

Rossel straightened and saluted.

'I don't think so, Comrade Minister.'

Beria was the most ruthless veteran of Stalin's eternal war on treason, counter-revolution, ideological deviancy and anti-Bolshevik thought. The man who had created the GULAG. Who ran his own operation to further develop the Soviet nuclear capability. And a merciless eliminator of anyone who placed obstacles in the way of his ambition.

As Rossel once had.

It was just over a year since he had uncovered Beria's twin vices of racketeering and rape, his victims a parade of young women and teenage girls. No matter that Senior Lieutenant Revol Rossel of the People's Militia had been looking for something else entirely.

Beria had enemies, too. And such indiscretions, however they came to light, were ammunition for them.

The minister took off his glasses, polished them with a handkerchief, and then replaced them. Under his coat, Rossel's hand closed around the knife.

'You're sure?' Beria said.

'Yes.'

'Name?'

'Captain Ivanov, Comrade Minister,' said Rossel, using the name on the identity card he had taken.

'Were my instructions not clear enough, Comrade Captain Ivanov?'

'Instructions?'

'You heard me. I issued instructions about the standards of dress for this evening to all Soviet officers, including GRU. Comrade Stalin is about to arrive and you look like you have been in a fight . . .'

Beria sniffed the air.

'. . . and you stink. Like an engine stoker.'

Beria clicked his fingers at an aide who was standing close by.

'Prokhorov. Get out your notepad and take this down.'

The man did as he was told.

'Ivanov. Captain. GRU. In disorderly dress and smelling like burnt toast . . .'

Beria reached up and tweaked Rossel's lapel. The minister's voice became soft, almost flirtatious.

'. . . is a cunt.'

'*Tak tochno,* Comrade Minister,' agreed the officer as he made the note with a flourish.

'Good.' Beria stared again Rossel's eyes. 'Now underline that last word.'

'Yes, Comrade Minister.' The man drew the line. 'Underlined.'

Beria turned to the aide.

'I wish to particularly impress upon you the necessity of placing that note in the centre of my desk tomorrow morning,' he said.

Then the minister gave a mocking salute and strolled away.

Rossel exhaled. Under the cap, with the epaulettes . . . the stolen uniform must have saved him. He began to walk across the lobby in an effort to lose himself in the crowd. But, unable to help himself, he looked over his shoulder, to see Beria staring at him once again.

This time in recognition. The look alone was enough to condemn him.

Beria turned to his aide Prokhorov, mouth open, ready to give an order.

But before he could do so, the crowd in the hall burst into applause. General Pletnev appeared halfway up the stairs. His dress uniform and medals gleamed. This was a different man to the one Rossel had first encountered in the museum. Someone who no longer felt the need to ride at the back of the parade. He radiated confidence and an unworldly sense of calm. Just as he must have done at Seelow, the general had the look of man who believed he could pluck bullets from the air.

Pletnev raised a hand for silence and the room obeyed. He gazed over the heads of the crowd to a cluster of musicians and a Young Pioneers choir, who had appeared to the left of the main doors. There was the woman who had preceded Rossel into the palace, her arms raised in preparation. She gave them a quick heave and the band started up – the Armenian composer Khachaturian's 'Poem about Stalin.'

The choir was in good voice:

Far and wide they sing
Songs of joy and labour;
Your name is always with us,
Like a banner, Comrade Stalin!

Behind them were another few rows of men and women, crammed into the grand hall to lend their vocal firepower to the later verses and fill out the faux-Oriental harmonies. After a few minutes, the cantata crashed to its end, rattling the chandeliers and bringing the conductor to convulsions.

A hush descended.

Men straightened their caps, women smoothed their skirts; every face adopted a fixed look of subservience. Even Beria, Khrushchev and Molotov straightened their backs.

But Pletnev didn't move a muscle.

The trap was set.

From outside came the roar of a motorcycle, then another drawing up next to it. From his vantage point, now half-hidden behind a fat column, Rossel could watch through the glass panes of the arched doors as four more outriders arrived, dismounted their bikes – low-slung Dnepr M-72s – and stood to attention. Next came two armoured cars, three ZIS trucks covered with tarpaulin, and finally a black America Packard limousine.

He heard everyone draw breath. A woman standing next to Khrushchev wobbled at the knees. The minister reached out a hand.

Standing just behind Pletnev, Nikitin was working his jaw underneath his scarred face.

Rossel took two steps forward. Then froze.

The snub end of a pistol was pressing into the small of his back.

'Don't move, comrade. Not so much as an eyelash.'

As the doors of the limousine were opened, a group of workers on the other side of the drive began to cheer, clap and shout – *Tovarishch Stalin zdyes', Tovarishch Stalin s nami . . .*

He is here, He is with us.

'Comrade Beria would like to see you again,' said the voice. Rossel realised who his captor was. Beria's aide, Prokhorov, who must have understood his boss's order, even though it had remained unheard.

A beautiful dark-haired woman, swathed in sable, began to sing a verse from *Zdravitsa*, the cantata Prokofiev had written for Stalin's sixtieth birthday.

> *'Your vision is our vision, O leader of the people!*
> *Your thoughts are our thoughts, indivisible!*
> *You are the banner flying from our mighty fortress!*
> *You are the flame that warms our spirit and our blood,*
> *O Stalin, Stalin!'*

It was only a short excerpt for soprano and harp, but no one had told the workers outside of this final performance and they drowned out the singing with their cheers until ordered to stop. Khrushchev was nodding along and grinning to someone in the crowd.

As they finished, a strange silence – the kind Rossel remembered from a battlefield just before a first shot was fired – settled upon the room.

One of the outriders took hold of the passenger door-handle and opened it. All heads in the room craned forward, in an impromptu competition to be the first to catch sight of the Great Leader.

After an agonising moment, a familiar figure – dressed in a white tunic, black boots and a military cap; left arm held close to his side in the familiar way – stepped out and onto the red carpet. Stalin turned to the distant crowd, and, standing with his back turned to the lobby, waved. Bulbs popped, photographers from *Pravda* and *Izvestia* fell to their knees to get a better angle.

Finally, Stalin turned and walked into the entrance hall of the Young Pioneers' Palace. Those nearest him were pushed back by armed bodyguards to make way for a little girl, about twelve years old, dressed in the uniform of the Pioneers and carrying a basket of flowers. She handed him a red rose and he patted her on the head.

Stalin took a moment to fasten it into his buttonhole.

As he did so, General Pletnev – vodka glass in hand, Nikitin by his side – descended the stairs. The crowd at the bottom parted, leaving them a path to the Soviet leader. Pletnev stopped a short distance away. When he spoke, his voice was soft and filled with reverence.

'Comrade Joseph Vissarionovich,' he began. 'As our father and mentor Lenin told us, there are decades when nothing happens and then there are weeks when decades do. On a battlefield, the same thing is true of minutes, of seconds, of moments. In them, history hangs low on the bough for those with the courage to take it. You have always been such a man.'

All around, Rossel could hear the metallic sound of submachine guns being cocked. More soldiers appeared, forcing their way towards Pletnev and Stalin. The crowd broke out in gasps and stifled screams as the weapons were levelled straight at the head and body of the Great Leader.

But Stalin still seemed focused on the flower in his buttonhole.

'A toast,' said Pletnev, his voice now loud and firm. He raised his glass. 'To history!'

At that, Stalin looked up and smiled. General Pletnev looked into his eyes and took a sharp backward step. The glass shattered on the floor.

With a click of his fingers, Nikitin signalled to the soldiers standing closest to the leader. As one, they swung their weapons round and aimed at them directly at Pletnev's head.

Khrushchev stepped forward and pointed at the general.

'Arrest that man,' he said.

From nowhere – from out of the armoured cars, from the courtyard; but also from the crowd, from behind pillars and through doors – MGB officers swarmed into the building.

Pletnev watched them enter. Then he glanced around with an air of what seemed to be amusement. As if he were attending some Red Army training event for junior officers that had not quite gone to plan.

He nodded at Khrushchev. A battlefield general acknowledging the prowess of a respected opponent.

Moments later, with his arms held tight behind his back, a group of soldiers led him away.

Beria and Khrushchev were shaking hands: the former without much enthusiasm, the latter with gusto and a volley of what appeared to be instructions to his men.

Then Khrushchev turned to Major Nikitin, slapping him on the back. As shouts and scattered applause broke out, Rossel thought he could hear Khrushchev yelling congratulations. With a wink, the minister – just as he had at Lenfilm – made a series of exaggerated sweeping motions.

'Yes, as always, I'm the janitor, comrade,' he shouted to Nikitin. 'You, too, I think, no? It's just as I told you, comrade. Our glorious socialist revolution will always need peasants like us to clean up the shit . . .'

Rossel felt the pressure in the small of his back ease.

'What is going . . .' began Prokhorov.

Elbows slamming into the ribs of anyone close, Khrushchev pretended to sweep some more, his curses and laughter rising above the din – one of puzzled cries, demands for explanation, the yells of children, a choir being shouted at to give an encore, calls for more champagne – a din that did not quite mask the adjacent sound of gunfire that everyone pretended not to hear.

Just another basement execution in the name of Bolshevik rule, Rossel thought.

Left all alone, the Soviet leader had slumped into a gilded chair against a wall close to where Rossel was standing. His left arm, hanging stiff by his side, relaxed and straightened. He took a silk handkerchief from his pocket and began to mop at the sweat that was streaming down his brow.

As he did so, rouge and powder began to stain it.

Then, taking a deep breath to steady himself and standing to acknowledge the crowd, Boris Tarkovsky got to his feet and gave them all his deepest bow.

CODA

PRAVDA

Obituary

General Sviatoslav Pletnev – The Hero of the Heights

Dear Comrades,

Stalin's brother-in-arms and the most fervent of believers in Marx's cause, the great Hero of the Seelow Heights, a giant of the Communist Party and of the Soviet people, General Sviatoslav PLETNEV, no longer walks among us.

The Central Committee of the Communist Party of the Soviet Union, the USSR Council of Ministers and the Presidium of the USSR Supreme Soviet announce with profound sorrow to the Party and all working people of the Soviet Union that at 21.50 on 25 November, Sviatoslav Ivanovich Pletnev, Defence Minister, Soviet General and leader of the GRU, President of the League of Militant Godless, member of the Central Committee of the Communist Party of the Soviet Union, died after a short illness.

His name is dear beyond measure to our great Party, and to the working people of the world. Comrade General Pletnev helped to create the mighty League of Militant Godless. He was a leader of those who led our country to victory over fascism in the Great Patriotic War. His victory at the Seelow Heights means he will live forever in the glorious pantheon of socialist heroes. We echo here the sacred words of Comrade Stalin, the words which General Pletnev also used to turn the tide: 'Not one step back!'

The news of Comrade General Pletnev's death will bring profound pain to the hearts of the workers, collective farmers, intelligentsia and all the working people of our Motherland, to the hearts of the warriors of our glorious armed forces, to the hearts of millions of working people in all countries of the world. But let those counter-revolutionaries who lived in fear of his wrath feel no solace, for we will follow his example and root them out without mercy. Fear not, comrades, for the Central Committee has decreed in his honour to double our efforts, and hunt down with unceasing vigilance all those who hide within their breast a traitor's heart.

Long live the great and all-conquering teachings of Marx, Engels, Lenin and Stalin!

Long live our mighty Socialist Motherland!

Long live our heroic Soviet people!

Long live the great Communist Party of the Soviet Union!

Long live Comrade Stalin!

Central Committee of the Communist Party of the Soviet Union USSR Council of Ministers Presidium of the Supreme Soviet

59

It had been a tense few hours as they embarked on the return leg of their journey from Igarka. Not even three weeks since they had left.

Rossel and Nikitin did not exchange a word. The third member of their party, the scientist Fironov, was trembling with anticipation of what they might find. He did not talk to them, instead scrawling calculations into a notebook.

Two hours into the flight north, Rossel finally spoke.

'Whose microphone was that? The one hidden in the projector, I mean,' he said.

Nikitin scratched his chin for a few seconds as he considered his reply.

'In the end,' he replied, 'it belonged to everyone who wanted Pletnev eliminated. MGB agents put it there, acting on Khrushchev's orders. But nothing happens in the MGB without Beria finding out sooner or later.'

'And Khrushchev did that because you told him to?'

Nikitin nodded, still not meeting Rossel's eye. 'After Pletnev gave me a job, I found out almost straightaway what his intentions were. I went to Khrushchev with a deal: my family's safety in return for everything I could find out about the general's plans.'

The plane lurched hard in a pocket of turbulence, making them both grab the seats in front of them.

'It turned out the general was already suspected of plotting to seize power by other members of the Politburo. Only Stalin refused to believe it.'

Out of the windows there was nothing to see but total darkness.

'So, a plan was hatched to trap Pletnev at the screening of *Red Dawn-Red Dusk,* right before the Party assembly,' Nikitin continued, 'to prove to Stalin that his favourite general was a traitor. They couldn't use Stalin himself, of course. But they quickly got hold of the next best thing. A convincing double.'

So Boris Tarkovsky had not been arrested by the MGB, thought Rossel. He had simply been recruited. Fadeyev, he presumed, had been in on the plan. His presence a ploy to convince any doubters that the arrest was real.

The plane's juddering appeared to have passed. Nikitin relaxed into his seat, relieved to be telling his story.

'And the general and his senior officers were taken to the basement of the Anichkov Palace and executed,' he said. 'Now there is talk of Tarkovsky playing our Great Leader in a Lenfilm production. Even whispers of the Order of Lenin.'

At Vorkuta, the three of them headed for the helicopter without delay. Just before they climbed in, Nikitin handed Rossel a couple of packs of cigarettes. Bulgarian, the good stuff.

Rossel opened a pack, lit two cigarettes and handed one over. By the time the bitter smoke had settled in the back of their throats and both had exhaled into the freezing northern air, a truce of sorts had been declared.

'Did Comrade Khrushchev live up to his end of your bargain?' Rossel asked as the blades began to turn.

But Nikitin had pulled his *ushanka* over his eyes and did not answer.

60

As the Mi-4's rotors stopped turning, Rossel and Nikitin clambered out of the helicopter and ducked down to shelter themselves from the driving wind and snow. The commandant of 105th Kilometre had ordered a large area cleared to make sure they could land, even in the bad weather.

Navigation had been simple. In places, the camp at 105th Kilometre was still burning, the flames visible from the air for miles. The prisoners had rioted, Nikitin had said. The guards had barred the gates and shot anyone who tried to get out. Inside the fence, the Thieves had gone on the rampage. The GULAG administrators in Vorkuta were in uproar.

Through the swirling snow, they could see that reports of the uprising had been accurate.

'Glad to be back?' said the major.

Rossel stared at the forlorn collection of huts set into the vast, barren snowscape, dwarfed by the endless blackness of the Siberian sky. Smoke trailed up like gnarled fingers from the walls and roofs of some of them. Others had been burnt to the ground.

'Not really,' he said.

The knifing wind fanned the fires, keeping them burning despite the blizzard. Under a guard tower to their left was a frozen pile of dead zeks: ten bodies or so deep, ten wide.

Up to a hundred corpses, thought Rossel, and counting.

Nikitin nodded towards the pile.

'Pletnev's new command?' he shouted.

Rossel nodded.

'Yes, a regiment of the damned.'

Dotted around them were the dark, heavy coats of the camp guards. Several had their rifles levelled at the perimeter fence.

Rossel walked across to the pile of bodies. Sticking out from the pile, half buried by his fellow inmates, was a face he recognised.

Babayan's eyes were open and staring skyward. As if the old priest was still searching for, and silently praying to, his God.

Rossel reached down and closed them.

'The rest, who knows?' he said. 'But not this man.'

*

Fifty metres away from the helicopter, the commandant was waiting to meet them. He was accompanied by a portly army colonel and a small group of soldiers.

Everyone except Rossel exchanged salutes.

'I think we have the men you're looking for, Comrade Professor Fironov,' the commandant said. 'Well, at least we have them cornered. The prisoners have been rioting for days. A dispute over rations. The malign influence of the criminal class. However, we now have the dogs cornered.'

'Good,' said Fironov in a clipped, bureaucratic tone.

429

Since his recent promotion – as recent as the previous day – the scientist was full of himself. After examining the information hidden in the microdots, Beria had transferred Fironov to the MGB and made him project leader of KB-11, the All-Russian Scientific Research Institute of Experimental Physics. All he had to do now was to find von Möllendorf and get him to reveal the last, vital details. That, Fironov had boasted, would enable the Soviet Union to build a bomb 'of unrivalled power'.

The commandant coughed as he pulled his coat tight around him.

'I regret to say a few of the German POWs have made a last stand with some of the Thieves,' he said.

'What?' shouted Fironov.

The Red Army colonel had tired of waiting and cut the debrief short. 'This way,' he said, striding off in the direction of the camp, bowing his head against the wind.

The rest of them followed, weaving a path through the guards.

'It took us nearly three days,' the colonel shouted over his shoulder, 'but we have almost quelled the insurrection.'

'Almost?' asked Rossel.

'A small group is holding out in the forge.'

The commandant picked up his pace, trying to keep up. 'About twenty Thieves and a few of the Germans,' he said. 'Led by two incorrigible criminals called Kuba and Medvedev. They have refused all offers to surrender peacefully.'

Rossel remembered the chant at morning roll call after Sobol had been murdered.

North, south, east and west, between the rising and the setting of the sun. Bitches, this will be your fate.

Even at the last, Kuba was refusing to be a Bitch.

The soldiers had driven trucks into the compound and arranged them in a defensive circle around the forge. In between the vehicles, they had built wooden barricades and wrapped them in barbed wire. The roof of the forge was on fire and the bodies of three men – one soldier, two zeks – were lying on the snow in between the building and the barricades. Too close to the Thieves for anyone to risk retrieving them.

A captain with a loudhailer was shouting out demands to the remaining prisoners.

'Today is your last day on earth, comrades. Unless you come out now – that's the choice you have to make . . .'

Rossel, Nikitin and the others stood close to a truck in the centre of the encirclement, about fifty metres away from the door to the forge.

'If it was up to me, I'd bake those *mudaki* like they were loaves of bread,' said the colonel.

'No,' said Fironov. 'We have orders from Comrade Beria. "Do what you like with the Russians, but the Fascists must be saved." The minister's order to me was very clear.'

As he spoke, the door of the forge was kicked open. A huge figure carrying a child-sized bundle in his arms walked out through the smoke and began to cross the snow. Behind them were two other Thieves with their arms raised. After that, a German with his hands in the air, followed by three more POWs.

Every single rifle was trained on the group.

The captain lowered his loudhailer. No one spoke. The wind was easing but the snow still fell.

Medvedev, the giant Thief, was now only a few metres away from where they were standing. He knelt and lay Kuba's body on the ground at Fironov's feet. A gift, it seemed, from the Thieves of Igarka to great Comrade Stalin, Tsar of all the East.

Kuba's head lolled at an angle. On his index finger, he was still wearing the brass washer he had slipped on the last time Rossel had seen him.

A line from the song of Kolka the Pickpocket rose in his head.

Tell them, Masha, that he don't thieve no longer . . .

A fitting elegy, Rossel thought, for the dead king of 105th Kilometre.

Medvedev stood up and stared at Rossel, recognising him.

'Greetings, Comrade Albatross. Being so short made Kuba too stubborn. And being too stubborn meant . . .'

Medvedev ran a finger across his own neck.

Fironov was growing impatient. He pointed at the German who had led his comrades out of the forge.

'This is him, I presume? Von Möllendorf. Are you sure, Rossel? He doesn't look much like the photograph . . .'

Rossel shook his head.

'No, that's not him,' he said. 'That's Walter.'

Walter, hands still raised, managed a thin smile that did not reach his eyes. In mangled Russian, he tried to tell Rossel that it was good to see him again.

'I'm here for Baron Karl Friedrich von Möllendorf,' said Fironov. 'The nuclear physicist. Where is he? He's not dead, is he?'

Walter thought for a moment.

'I could do with a cigarette,' he said.

Rossel handed him one. Nikitin took out a lighter and lit it.

432

Walter turned round and pointed to the forge.

'He's in there,' he said.

Fironov grabbed the loudhailer from the captain. 'Von Möllendorf,' he yelled. 'Baron Karl Friedrich von Möllendorf. Please show yourself, please come out, you will not be harmed.'

All eyes fixed on the door to the building. After a minute, a figure began to emerge through the smoke. Turning and twisting as if dancing a solitary reel, it moved towards them.

The moment Tsar Suka saw Rossel, he smiled.

'*Der Musikmann*,' he said. '*Der Musikmann*.'

Behind him, the roof of the forge collapsed, throwing sparks high into the night sky.

Fironov's hand fell to his side, the loudhailer slipped into the snow.

Then the Third Reich's most dangerous physicist, the man who had once known too much, began to sing a Wagnerian leitmotif. The same leitmotif that appeared in *Götterdämmerung*, at the exact point the microdots had been positioned.

It was the closest his shattered mind would ever get to comprehending the Nazi plans for the H-bomb. Let alone completing them.

Rossel stepped forward and shook von Möllendorf's hand.

'Yes,' he said. 'That's me.'

61

On the opposite side of Nevsky Prospect, the House of Books had disappeared.

All six storeys were covered by a huge red and yellow banner, on which was written the slogan of the League of Militant Godless: "The struggle against religion is the struggle for socialism." As if the Party had reduced all human knowledge to those few words.

Leningrad was a city in mourning. Rossel stood with Natalia Ivaskova not far from the scorched stones of Kazan Cathedral. The museum was wrapped in its own covering, a dowdy tarpaulin, as workers tried to save the dome.

A vast procession of black was moving in eerie silence down Nevsky Prospect. It would travel all the way to the Alexander Nevsky Monastery – a passing homage to another great Russian military figure – before transport by military vehicle to the Piskaryovskoye Cemetery. In death, it seemed, General Pletnev did indeed command an even greater army than he had in life.

Rossel looked over at his other companion. Anna Drugova had been freed from the camps along with the rest of her family, who had taken up residence once more in their old apartment. Nikitin, now with renewed influence, had been persuaded to intercede with Minister Khrushchev.

But the girl had not come to pay her respects to General Pletnev.

The three of them had been standing there for forty minutes and still the tanks, armoured cars, soldiers, Young Pioneers and lines of MGB and GRU crawled past. In the distance, they could just make out the ranks of members of the League of Militant Godless – a hundred deep, each carrying huge garlands of red and white flowers and greenery – as if even the forests of Karelia had come to pay their respects.

Rossel felt the city's collective sigh – soft, low and sorrowful. The mourners had caught their first glimpse of the general's coffin: drawn by six white horses and placed on a simple cart made, according to *Pravda*, from the shattered pieces of a giant Ukrainian cross.

A woman to Rossel's right broke into sobs. A big Cossack in front him took out a handkerchief and dabbed at his cheek.

As Pletnev's coffin drew parallel with them, the crowd cried out, moaned, exhorted – '*Narodny geroi sredi nas;* The people's hero is among us!'

And then – at first one lone voice, then another, and another – 'Not one step back, not one step back!' . . . Until the noise was so loud it scared into the air a flock of crows from the dome of the cathedral. Some old women, Rossel noticed, crossed themselves. One, near him, was even whispering an Orthodox prayer . . . Just as Marshal Kutuzov had once done to the Blessed Virgin of Kazan before his victory against Napoleon.

Rossel, Natalia and Anna were too far back to see, but the Soviet press had revealed that on top of the coffin rested

435

Pletnev's military cap, a copy of *Das Kapital* and – a great honour bestowed at the last moment to the military man and scholar – Stalin's own copy of *The Prince* by Niccolò Machiavelli, said to contain personal annotations, under-linings and jottings in the margins. 'The old bastard's lost none of his sense of humour,' Khrushchev had apparently remarked, grinning.

On a simple podium a hundred metres further down Nevsky, the leading members of the Politburo – Beria, Malenkov, Molotov and Khrushchev – had assembled. Rossel looked out for Nikitin. There he was, as promised; at the bottom of the platform, but close to Khrushchev.

And standing behind the major were his wife, his son Dima and his daughter Svetlana. As Rossel watched, Nikitin gave his wife a discreet kiss and patted his children on their heads.

According to *Pravda*, Stalin himself would meet his 'much-loved comrade-in-arms' at the cemetery. Where he would watch them inter the general in a temporary glass sar-cophagus and then lay the first brick in what was intended to be a mausoleum and place of communist pilgrimage, with Pletnev's body on permanent display.

As Pletnev's coffin reached the members of the Politburo, it slowed. A volley of shots was fired into the air by specially selected members of the Red Army who had fought at the Seelow Heights. As the sound died away, the coffin began to move on.

'It is time,' Rossel said to Natalia. They retreated a few paces to the gardens in front of the cathedral, away from the lingering mourners.

The former dancer stopped and bent down to open the violin case she had been carrying. Then she offered Rossel his old instrument, along with the bow. But instead of taking it, he pointed with his crooked fingers towards Anna, who took both violin and bow from Natalia.

'Thank you for coming today,' said Rossel to Natalia, as Anna tucked the violin under her neck, getting used to the feel of it.

'I had hoped you would call,' she said. Then she leaned in and kissed him on the cheek.

Anna began to play.

The girl was brutally thin. Under her fur hat, her once lustrous hair was brittle and even flecked with grey. Her eyes were tinged with the regret of those who had seen too much.

Rossel held up Vustin's manuscript to 'Fugue No 13', written in the composer's own neat hand on the back of a prisoner's death warrant.

'Pianissimo,' he said. 'And slow, so slow . . . That's how I'd play it.'

The girl began to move the bow across the strings. She was no Oistrakh. Uncertain. Unpolished. But, for this recital, Anna possessed something much more important than talent – understanding.

For to do justice to Alexander Vustin's *Song of Lost Souls* you had to have first been one of them.

Rossel took Natalia's hand in his left and tapped his chest twice with his right. His own prayer to a god of sorts that he knew would most likely go unanswered.

As they watched on, the end of the procession went by: two huge trucks with rockets on them and a last troop of Young Pioneers.

As he listened, Rossel could see another army marching behind them – the day's labour gangs setting off in the direction of the railway lines. The ghosts of the gulag, trudging through Igarka. An endless line of forlorn pilgrims marching out to meet saints they no longer worshipped.

All of Babayan's shadows in the snow.

Acknowledgements

Of the many books we have read to understand more about the machinations of Stalin's regime, perhaps our most important resources were Simon Sebag Montefiore's *The Court of the Red Tsar* and Robert Conquest's *Stalin: A Biography*. For detail of the labour camp system we turned repeatedly to Anna Applebaum's *Gulag*, as well as the website of the human rights organisation Memorial and (especially for maps and images) the Czech website Gulag.cz. But the most valuable insights into the brutality and lawlessness of the Soviet labour camps came from Varlam Shalamov's extraordinary *Kolyma Tales* – harrowing but mesmerising.

If Danzig Baldaev's series of books entitled *Russian Criminal Tattoo Encyclopaedia* was inspirational for Revol Rossel's first outing in *City of Ghosts*, his *Drawings From The Gulag* was handy for this novel, even if one has to look at much of its contents with one eye closed. Mark Galeotti's *The Vory* is another excellent guide to the world of the Thieves.

On the German side, *Tales From Spandau: Nazi Criminals and the Cold War*, by Norman J.W. Goda, was invaluable, and not only for the prison regulations in the appendix. Joachim Fest's *Speer: The Final Verdict*, was also instructive. We found a very large *Luft-Navigationskarte in Merkatorprojektion* – and many similar maps – in the British Library in London, which enabled us to pinpoint Bayreuth after some playing around with reference systems. Misha Aster's *The Reich's Orchestra* was also useful.

We are extremely grateful to Tony Comer, the former departmental historian at GCHQ, the UK government's communications and cyber intelligence service, who reviewed Halder's cipher and the thinking behind it, and suggested certain modifications and improvements.

We must also express our gratitude to Dr Eugene Shwageraus of the Cambridge Nuclear Energy Centre for patiently talking us through the basic elements of nuclear fission (pun intended) and the development of the hydrogen bomb. He also pointed us in the direction of *Dark Sun: The Making of the Hydrogen Bomb* by Richard Rhodes – as did Tom Plant of the Royal United Services Institute, who further suggested a look at the *Los Alamos Primer* by Robert Serber, the introductory lectures for scientists working on the Manhattan Project.

Despite the above research, and much more in other books and on the internet, this is a work of fiction. We have been wilfully inconsistent in sticking to the facts or applying what we have learned. In all cases, the mistakes, deliberate or otherwise, are ours alone.

On the transliteration of Russian: sometimes we have relied on the system used by most English-speaking students of the language; at other times we have followed generally accepted spellings as found in the guidebooks or on the internet in order not to confuse our readers. Where we have been sure of our ground, we have used the names of streets and places that were in use during the Soviet era (many have been changed since 1991).

Finally, huge thanks to Giles Milburn, Liane-Louise Smith and the team at Madeleine Milburn, and Jon Elek and Rosa Schierenberg at Welbeck, for their unwavering support, patience and encouragement. We could not have wished for finer counsellors and representatives.

About the Author

Ben Creed is the pseudonym for Chris Rickaby and Barney Thompson, two writers who met on the Curtis Brown creative writing course.

Chris, from Newcastle upon Tyne, found his way into advertising as a copywriter and, after working for different agencies, started his own. He has written and produced various TV programmes for ITV and Five, and some award-winning experimental fiction.

Before deciding to pursue a career as a journalist, Barney spent two years studying under the legendary conducting professor Ilya Musin at the St Petersburg Conservatory. He has worked at The Times and the Financial Times, where he was legal correspondent, and is now an editor, writer and speechwriter at UNHCR, the UN Refugee Agency.

Their first book, *City of Ghosts*, was nominated for the Crime Writers' Association Gold Dagger for best crime novel of the year.